Dean Bakopoulos is the author of the *New York Times* Notable Book *Please Don't Come Back from the Moon* and *My American Unhappiness*. He holds an MFA from the University of Wisconsin–Madison and is the winner of a Guggenheim fellowship and a National Endowment for the Arts fellowship. He is the writer-in-residence at Grinnell College, and lives in Iowa.

BY DEAN BAKOPOULOS

Please Don't Come Back from the Moon
My American Unhappiness
Summerlong

SUMMERLONG

Dean Bakopoulos

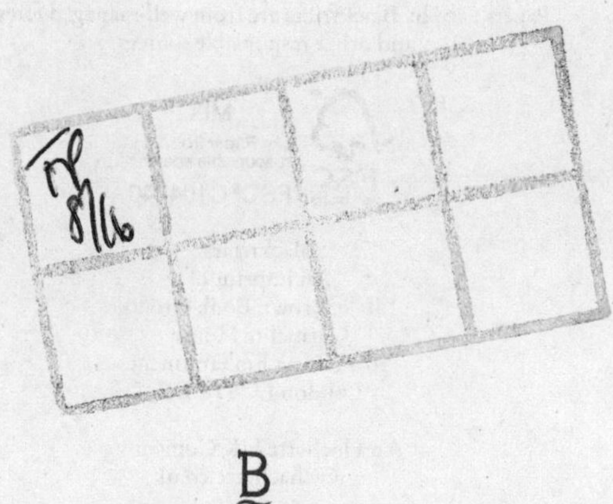

BLACKFRIARS

BLACKFRIARS

First published in the United States in 2015 by Ecco
First published in Great Britain in 2015 by Blackfriars
This paperback edition published in 2016 by Blackfriars

1 3 5 7 9 10 8 6 4 2

A CIP catalogue record for this book is available from the British Library.

ISBN 978-0-349-13438-3

Typeset in Garamond by M Rules
Printed and bound in Great Britain by
Clays Ltd, St Ives plc

Papers used by Blackfriars are from well-managed forests and other responsible sources.

MIX
Paper from
responsible sources
FSC® C104740

Blackfriars
An imprint of
Little, Brown Book Group
Carmelite House
50 Victoria Embankment
London EC4Y 0DZ

An Hachette UK Company
www.hachette.co.uk

www.blackfriarsbooks.com

In memory of my student and friend
Armando "Mando" Montaño,
Whom we lost much too soon

PART I

There was another life that I might have had,
but I am having this one.

—*Kazuo Ishiguro,* Never Let Me Go

1

In the hay gold dusk of late spring, Don Lowry takes his usual walk through town and out to the fields beyond it. In the newly turned black earth, he smells energy and promise, which buoys him in a way he has not felt buoyed in some time, and he feels, along with the whole twitching prairie, as if he is on the verge of something either beautiful or terrible. It is always hard for him to know which. And this is why, while walking home, when he sees a woman, her body sprawled beneath a thick, scabbed-up sycamore at the darkening edge of Merrill Park, he believes that she's fallen from a high bough.

Don stops at the edge of the park, reaching for his phone to call 911. But he does not bring his phone on these walks; his wife has urged him not to—he works too much, he has chest pains at night, and his face is often lit by a screen—and so he cannot call anyone. From this downhill angle, it's unknowable: has the woman in fact fallen from the tree or has she been injured or beaten in some way? But as he approaches her, it seems as if she is simply sprawled there for the pleasure of it, for the soft grass and a few stars salting the darkening sky and the moon, an icy coin.

For a moment, he wants to lie down next to her and whisper her name.

It surprises him that he knows her name: Amelia Benitez-Coors, or ABC, as she's called. He knows her name, and her nickname, in the strange, osmotic way people in a small town know things about perfect strangers; he knows some of her story: she had left the college a year before, and had gone off for a few months, and then, last fall when the leaves turned, she arrived in town again on a red bus from Omaha, to live with and care for the widow Ruth Manetti, whose lawn Don had cut as a teenager, twenty-five years before.

He looks at her form—peaceful, not bleeding or twisted in any way. She wears old jeans and a tight, gray WHERE THE HELL IS GRINNELL T-shirt, and she is barefoot, a hint of her midriff showing, her earth black hair thick and wavy and her skin an olive tone, deepened by sun.

Suddenly, she coughs, the wet hack of a summer cold, and opens her eyes.

Don steps back, as if she has caught fire.

"Were you watching me?" she asks.

"I was just making sure you were okay," he says, but he's been caught. He's lingered too long on the midriff and the diamond stud in the navel, the bare feet with painted toes and a silver ring on the third right one.

She props up on her elbows and says, "Don Lowry!"

He steps back a foot or two.

"Are you okay?" Don asks.

"I am!"

"Do you need anything?" he says. "I'm sorry, I thought you were—"

"You're Don Lowry!" she says.

This is something that happens. Don's picture is on business cards and FOR SALE signs and flyers all over town. He's recognized.

"It's your business!" she says, this woman, ABC, and sits up now and reaches a hand up toward him. He takes it, helps her to her feet. He is taller than she is, but not by as much as he expects. She is uphill from him, on a small slope, which gives her an extra inch or two. It's easy to look right into her eyes.

"It's your business!" she says again, and her dark eyes lock on to his, which is exactly what he wants.

Don has a slogan: "It's your home, but it's my business!" Now he is embarrassed by it. Also embarrassing: the sweat stains on his light blue golf shirt, the ill-fitting Walmart khakis, his newly formed gut, his hairline, the pen in his pocket, the permanent name tag, his thirty-eight years on earth. He lets himself look at her again. He looks at her legs, then at the soft fullness of the flesh under her thin T-shirt and begins to feel the first sin of middle age, which is self-pity.

"Yes, that's me," he says.

"Get high with me, Don Lowry."

"Pardon?"

A full-tailed orange cat struts his way across the park and the crows of some distant tree go crazy.

"I need someone to get high with me," she says. "Someone I don't know."

"How so?"

"Do you know anything about me?" she says.

"You're not special," he says, without meaning to, but that's the thrumming phrase in his inner ear and it comes out, the involuntary catharsis of a phrase he's been thinking all week, all afternoon, his whole walk.

"Ha!" she blurts out.

"I mean, I'm sorry. I don't know why I said that. I meant me. *I'm* not special."

"Perhaps you've been sent here for this very purpose?" she says.

"To get high?" Don asks.

"Isn't this a magical night?" she says. "Is it too early for fireflies? Because I just saw some! I think."

"Or did you mean," Don says, "that my purpose here is to tell you that you're not special?"

"I live over on Broad," she says as if no questions have been presented, and begins to walk away from him. The back of her T-shirt reads: WHO THE HELL CARES?

"I know," he says, catching up to her. "The Manetti place."

"Will you be funny?" she says.

"I don't know," he says. "Why?"

"Just be funny when you're stoned, Don Lowry," she says. "Okay?"

Among his friends at the chamber of commerce, Don Lowry is known as a funny man, a teller of jokes. He always has three new jokes memorized—he does this every Sunday night. But now, those jokes leave him. It's as if he's never told a joke in his life. Jokeless, he walks alongside her anyway.

Later, after six or seven beers, and two joints, and a feeling as if he is being lifted out of his life into some other separate plane where nothing familiar exists, Don Lowry—that's how she refers to him the whole night: first name, last name—is drifting off into sleep, slung into a hammock on the second-floor sleeping porch, and he hears a voice, her voice, of course it must be, but he is not sure if he is dreaming or not dreaming when he hears a whispered moan in his ear: *Don Lowry, by the end of this summer, I'm going to be dead.*

2

Claire is not a regular runner, but she is an occasional one, and when she wakes up from a dream that same Friday night in late May, she feels like running, wants to run until she loses her breath and sweat slicks her limbs. Perhaps she too can blame the pulsing muscles and buzzing bones on the prairie spring, that sudden flux and flow of energy that comes when the body finally understands that winter is actually gone.

She is sleeping in her daughter's bed. Wendy, who is ten and has already inherited her father's insomnia and her mother's capacity for worry, sleeps next to Claire. Wendy lies in bed each night and worries aloud—bedbugs, bullies, shark attacks in city pools— and Claire lies down and tries to remain calm beside her, listening to her daughter's dark rambles, an emotional sponge. Sometimes, Claire sings to Wendy, the classic rock B sides that her half-drunk father used to sing to her three decades before. Eventually, Wendy falls asleep; often Claire does too. Wendy cannot fall asleep any other way. For over eight years, Claire has lain next to her daughter until sleep has come.

At Christmas last year, they bought Wendy a double bed because of this, and before that, a white noise machine since every noise beyond the bedroom caused Wendy to bolt upright and say, "What was that?" The double bed, the noise machine, lying beside her singing "Simple Man" and "Shelter from the Storm"—was all this indulgence or necessity? Claire didn't know. It just was. Once your kids are older than five, you stop wondering, you stop reading the stack of contradictory parenting books, enjoy what you have as you have it, seeing the maw of the teenage years just a few steps away, realizing all of your new strategies and revised plans will simply evaporate with time anyway. A new obstacle will emerge and your routines will be useless.

On this night, the night in question, Claire has a dream that she is back in New York, seventeen again, smoking on the rooftop of a friend's apartment; "The Love Cats" plays on a boom box. Her life is before her, still shapeable and unknown, and the thrill she has from looking out at the skyline is palpable even when she wakes up, as is the craving for a cigarette, though she has not smoked in three years.

The dream is not just a dream, really, but a dreaming of a memory, a flashback to something that happened in real life, as vivid and clear as reality. Her brain becomes a time machine. In this memory, it is cold, and Claire is wearing a massive parka, and she hears herself saying, "I will never leave this city," before she takes a long drag on a cigarette and watches her friends raise their beer cans in agreement. "Never fucking ever," they say. They drink. "Besides," says Anna Holowka, who'd been, since birth, her best friend, "where the fuck would you go? Iowa?"

How do you ever know what you will do? How easy it seems, at seventeen, to shape a life with clarity, ridiculing all the possibilities that seem impossible.

Claire gets out of bed and a thought stays with her: *I was a different person then.*

And then: *where did I go?*

For mothers, there is a daily, or nightly, choice: sleep or solitude. You can rarely have both, and for most of her parental life, Claire has chosen solitude. She's woken early to write, has done yoga while babies napped, has stayed up until three or four binge-watching a television series all her friends on Facebook have already seen. The dark circles under her eyes will confirm this, though she is still pretty enough, she knows, and for a woman almost forty, happily, she is still fit. Lately, she likes to have that confirmed. She dresses with less modesty than she did even in college (though in 1995, admittedly, billowing sacks of cloth were the rage); this summer's swimsuit, just ordered online with the help of a virtual mannequin whose expandable curves fascinated Wendy to no end, will be a two-piece. Claire does not fear the gaze of men the way she did when she was younger. She does not welcome it, not exactly, but she also doesn't mind the flirtation or the second looks she sometimes gets. It is, she knows, part maturity, part fearlessness, and part vanity—but how happy she is to lose the constant chatter of insecurity she heard her first two decades of adulthood.

This is the best part of middle age, she thinks. Or maybe she doesn't think this. Maybe she has just read it in *O* magazine, while soaking in a bath a few nights ago. It is a bad habit of hers—possibly the curse of a blocked writer—to believe that she's come up with ideas she's read elsewhere only a few weeks before.

Claire goes to her bedroom and undresses, then slides on running shorts, a sports bra, and a white tank top. She finds her running shoes in the back of the chaotic closet. Stuffed inside them, a pair of athletic socks. Shod for a run, she checks in on Wendy, who is in deep sleep, and then listens at Bryan's door; she hears a soft snore. Bryan is her oldest, now twelve, grown sullen and moody in the last six months. He sleeps with the bedroom door locked. He does everything behind a locked door. If he can look at a screen, he will. This makes her sad—all of the parenting books she's read about raising free-range kids have been rendered impotent by the iPad his father bought him a year ago, on an unaffordable whim.

On the first floor, she shuts her laptop, closing first the eleven open tabs of distractive drivel that occupy her browser, then closing a document called NovelNewStartMay12_2012v39, and logging off to password-protect her computer. After this, in the kitchen, she looks down the basement stairs, sees the blue light of the TV and faintly hears the sound of a cable drama, the sound of televised gunfire. Her husband is watching his favorite show, a series about a sheriff in Kentucky; he has been trying to get her to watch it.

"I don't like to watch miserable things," she always reminds him, to which he always says, "But life is miserable."

He means it as a joke; she does not like his jokes anymore.

She does not go down the stairs to check in with him, to let him know she is leaving. He will look at her, puzzled. He might take it personally, somehow, that she won't slip in next to him, cuddle against him, graze his thigh with her hand. But the last thing she wants right now is to cuddle someone reassuringly. This, she has begun to believe, is the curse of her life: everyone around her demanding reassurance, as if there is a bottomless well of it, as if there is nothing that scares or overwhelms her, as if she is a source of endless cuddles, back rubs, and soothing tones.

She slips out the door.

She walks a block, then runs a block, then walks again toward campus, finally making a long diagonal dash across the abandoned lamp-lit green. The students are gone now, and most of the professors too. The campus feels abandoned, which is when she likes it best. She is almost never on campus in daylight.

Downtown, she jogs through the wide, empty streets. There is no traffic; the businesses—the café, the movie theater, the Mexican restaurant, and the sports bar—are all closed.

The only illuminated sign is ahead of her as she turns right on

Fifth Street and sees a brilliant red, moth-flocked sign that reads KUM & GO. Years ago, when she came to Iowa from New York for school and saw this sign, she thought she was passing by a porn shop, one of those interstate smut dens for truck drivers and closeted suburban dads. But no, it was a convenience store, earnest and well lit (which, she thinks, describes most of the Midwest).

She had taken a picture of the sign back then, and had the picture made into postcards that she sent to her friends back in New York. *Wish you were here*, she hand-lettered across each one with a Sharpie. On the back, she wrote only: *Where the @#$% am I again? XO Claire.*

She stops running in the parking lot, puts her hand on her hips to catch her breath, almost tasting the cigarettes she's about to buy, and from the sidewalk, she looks at the store and realizes that she has no cash or credit card with her.

This is why she begins kicking the ice machine.

3

Charlie Gulliver has been driving through the verdant yet desolate fields of I-80, through deadbeat postindustrial corridors oxidizing in the hazy spring light.

In Casper, and again in Denver, and again in Omaha, he stops to call old college friends, offering surprise visits, a fine time, beers and burgers on an outdoor patio somewhere—the winter is over, he texts, and I'm passing through town—but he can reach no one. Calls go unanswered, texts unreturned. It is so easy to feel ignored when you are carrying a cell phone on a road trip, sending out missives to friends who are pretending not to receive them until you have rolled safely past.

But how can he take this personally? The world is busy, just as he used to be busy. Now Charlie seems to be the only person in America who has time to kill.

These meandering and endless thoughts suddenly redeem themselves with a wild, spilling sunset in his rearview mirror, a melting of the sun into the horizon, blasts of purple and orange that make him forget all of this and focus on a sun pillar pointing up to the heavens just over his left shoulder, and so when Charlie pulls into the Grinnell Kum & Go not long after witnessing this, he feels happy as he parks his old minivan, given to him ten years ago by his mother, by the ice coolers.

The Check Engine light had come on near Des Moines and he's glad the vehicle has made it to Grinnell, glad too that his debit card still works, the modest balance of his account having been decimated by the high cost of gas on the three-day trip. He buys a twelve-pack of Moosehead. He buys bread. He buys bologna, sour cream and onion chips, and a small bottle of yellow mustard. Suddenly, feeling hunger swelling his tongue, he buys a box of day-old doughnuts and a can of coffee and some cream. He is back in the Midwest and he intends to eat like it, a thought he says aloud, as if he has an audience, and then he feels a soliloquy emerging, like he's back onstage doing a show.

But he is done with shows.

In the coastal cities where he's lived these past ten years, New York, L.A., Seattle, Portland, Boston, as he's drifted from one sublet to another, every so often sleeping, for a few days, in his van or on a filthy couch, every fellow actor he's met pretends to like junk food, claims at Monday rehearsals that they *binged* on pizza and cupcakes all weekend, but binges in the Midwest are not followed by three-hour workouts the way they are on the coasts. You can't call something a binge if you try to undo its effects the next morning with a juice fast or herbal cleanse or three hours of hot yoga. Bingeing had to involve a deliberate decision to live with the consequences of the binge.

He takes his loot to the counter, tossing in some cheese dip and a bottle of Coke before he gets to the register, as if he means to cement shut the end of his acting career through the consumption of empty calories.

He recognizes Ashlyn Harms behind the counter. Ashy, whom he's known since kindergarten, works the register as she did a decade ago, when Charlie was still in high school. She's heavier now, her hair shorter, but her smile is the same.

He pretends not to recognize her, because he is a dick.

Still, she begins to scan the groceries and, without looking up, starts a conversation.

"How you doing, Charlie?"

"Good. You?"

"All right."

"Rough week?"

"I guess."

"You look rough."

"Do I?"

"Mooseheads, are they dark?"

"No. They're light. See, green glass?"

"Do you ever hang out? You go to Rabbit's?"

"I've been away," Charlie says.

"Oh yeah? How long?"

"Six years. No, even more."

"We should hang out."

"My dad's in a nursing home. My folks got divorced last year and he got this thing right after that. So there're some things I need to do."

"I think I heard all that. He has Alzheimer's?"

"It's like that, but different. Lewy body dementia, it's like, I don't know. It's unpredictable."

"Weren't you an actor or something? I remember hearing that. Were you in anything I've heard of?"

"*Hamlet*?" he says. "Seattle Shakespeare."

"Didn't see it," she says.

"That's okay."

"Dude, it was a joke. What's next for you?"

"I'm between things," he says.

"Between what?"

Then her smile drops away and she looks beyond him to the windows and says, "Ugh, do you know this woman?"

Charlie shakes his head no as he takes in the vaguely familiar woman—short blond hair, lean, wearing running clothes and holding her hands on her head as if she's sucking wind, short on breath.

"She's a total bitch," Ashy says. "I think she's a professor."

And, almost as if she hears Ashy say this, that running woman, who had been pacing outside, kicks the ice machine as hard as she can, and keeps on kicking it.

"Oh, FML," Ashy says.

"I got this," Charlie says, and he goes out after her.

4

For ABC, the simple fact that Don Lowry actually follows her is somewhat thrilling, because though she talks to Philly every day, nothing worth telling Philly about has happened to her in months. ABC can sense Don Lowry behind her, so she pauses and waits for him to catch up. Standing still, without turning around, she waits for him and then when he doesn't appear at her side, she turns and sees that he is almost a whole block behind her. He has also stopped.

Looking at the still-dimming sky, the draining of its last light, she says, "Philly, you're so fucked up!"

She turns and waves him along. He looks up and down the block, then walks toward her. She's surprised by the strength of his posture, the fine slope of his shoulders—handsome, and, like a lot of men his age, maybe even more handsome than he used to be, in that brief sweet spot in the ascent toward middle age when one can appear suddenly sexy with gravitas and some gray at the temples, a salt-and-pepper stubble. But despite his attractiveness, he seems less arrogant and sure than the man she's seen on real estate signs all over town.

"You talk to yourself," he says.

"You walk slowly," she says, when he finally gets to her. "It's hard not to walk fast in Iowa. It's so flat. You have to decide to go slow."

He laughs, a nervous breath forced out through his nose and teeth.

"I guess," he says. Another of those hard breaths. "Does it bother you?"

"Does what?"

"The flatness?" he says.

She's considered the virtues of flatness before; eventually, with nothing at all on the horizon but corn and clouds—no mountains, no sky, no smell of sea salt—you forget that there is any place left to go. Your desire to wander leaves you. You settle down and accept whatever there is to be accepted. You assume something will come to you instead. This is why ABC had returned to the prairie last fall. It was wide open and free of ambition. She'd come from Los Angeles and its sprawl of human struggle smack between the majesty of mountain and sea.

"I like this landscape, Don Lowry," she says.

"You do?" he says.

"Yes. It doesn't try to alleviate your pain with splendor, some constant reassurance that the world is bigger than your grief."

"Are you grieving?" Don Lowry says.

"Don't you love that word? *Grief*?" she says. "It almost stops too soon, fading out before its time, almost like it's losing energy, that deflating after the long *e*—it feels like a sigh of defeat."

He shrugs. "I . . . ," he says, then nothing else.

"Fff," she says, "eiffff."

"Like the wind that comes off the prairie," Don Lowry says.

"Yeah!" she says. "That constant wind. Does it ever stop? Come the fuck on, wind."

She runs on ahead. What she's just said is something Philly once said during a storm, in the middle of campus, drunk and stoned and beaming with something ABC knows exists nowhere else.

At the house, they walk into the foyer and she notices Don looks over his shoulder before shutting the front door.

"Are you worried people will see you?"

"I'll just tell people Mrs. Manetti wanted an appraisal. If they see me."

"I suppose if you're a realtor, you can have an excuse to be in anyone's house," ABC says. "Not that you need an excuse."

"I'm married."

"No shit. I just want to get high. But if you want to leave . . . "

"No," he says. "No."

They walk by the den where Ruth is dozing in front of the television, an episode of *Law & Order*. As they walk up the stairs, ABC wonders what Philly would say right now. She'd be delighted and horrified. She'd say, "Oh my God! Don Lowry! The realtor? You smoked pot with Don Lowry? 'It's your home, but it's my business!' That guy?"

Sometimes ABC and Philly would joke about the parts of rural Iowa that they found funny—the way the clerks at the grocery store might say, "Well, that's different," when they came in with blue hair or a vintage disco dress to buy beer before a party; the way you could get stuck behind a tractor on Highway 6, ambling along at twenty-five miles per hour, and nobody would be in road-rage mode, laying on horns. Everyone would just be calm, as if it was perfectly okay to obstruct the productivity of the world in order to grow corn. And they laughed about the strangeness of the dive bars—meth heads and farmers and blown-apart high school football failures all drinking together, an invented family held together by bad decisions and muted rage and the occasionally intense night of karaoke with undergraduates.

And once, when they were lying in bed, after sex, stoned and sweaty, ABC had said (for no reason she could recall, maybe to get the morbid reassurance new lovers sometimes need), "What will I do if you die?"

Why had she thought to say this? What had she known? Had she felt it coming? No, of course she had not: it had only been that strange kind of postcoital conversation, those moments of intimate vulnerability unimaginable in the public light of day.

Tears down her face, a real crack in her voice. She had started shaking. Philly had wrapped her arms around ABC and had whispered: "If I die? Well, I'll come back for you. I'll come get you and take you to the spirit world."

"How will I know? How will I find you?" ABC had said.

There was a long pause and Philly's face grew grave and serious and all you could hear were the crows gathering in the locusts and a distant storm rolling up from Missouri, and Philly looked ABC dead in the eye.

"I'll send Don Lowry," she said.

"Who?" ABC asked.

"Don Lowry! 'It's your home, but it's my business!' I'll send that guy."

A fit of laughter came next, the kind of laughter they always shared when stoned and the kind of uncontrollable fits of it ABC so missed now. She had never had a friend so funny; she feels she never will again. Shaking with that laughter, they howled with pleasure until they cried and then smoked another joint and made love again then fell into the easy winds of sleep. Just before that sleep came, Philly had turned to ABC: "I just thought of something! Why, if I die now, you will have been the love of my life!"

But how had she said it? And had she really said it?

Was it possible that she was forgetting more than the exact words Philly had said? Was she forgetting Philly's voice? Was she remembering the voice she heard in videos, in the desperately saved voice mails? What was her real voice like, the voice she used when her mouth was up close against ABC's neck? That voice. Was she forgetting it?

What do you do with grief like that? When you can still hear her laughter, still taste her tongue? What do you do? Why do anything? Why work? Why read books? Why cough or refrain from coughing? Why fix a sandwich? When you have had and lost the love of your life before the age of twenty-five, well, fuck! Why wake up, ever, at all?

"Do you live upstairs?" Don whispers.

"Pretty much. Ruth moved to the first floor. Actually, she can still do the stairs. I guess we're planning ahead."

"Of course," Don says.

"There's a sleeping porch out back where we can smoke," ABC says as she points Don through the master bedroom. "Give me a minute. I gotta pee."

"I know the way. I've been here before."

"Have you?" ABC says.

"I used to do odd jobs for the Manettis. I used to cut their grass, hang their storm windows, all of that stuff. In high school and even in college; I've done odd jobs around Grinnell most of my life. I think I was probably the last person to paint some of the walls of that sleeping porch."

"You grew up in town?"

"I did."

"And you went to college here?"

Don nodded. "They give two local kids scholarships every year. Those two kids, when I graduated from high school, went off to the Ivy Leagues, so I got lucky. I sailed in off the wait list."

The long, rectangular sleeping porch is furnished with a free-standing hammock on a stand by the west windows. In the middle are two large armchairs; one of them looks as if it has been shredded by cats. Don sits in the sturdier of the two, a big maroon chair with a slanted back, though he still feels uncomfortably large. He pulls the fabric of his shirt, to lessen the obvious curve of his newly rounded gut.

ABC pulls a small baggie of weed and a metal pipe from a cigar box stashed in a hollowed-out flowerpot that holds an artificial plant.

"Pretty sneaky, sis," Don says.

"What?"

"Nothing," Don says. "Just a line from an old commercial. From when I was a kid. It wasn't funny."

"A commercial for what?"

"A game called Connect Four," Don says. "Have you played it?"

ABC lights the pipe and smiles at him while taking a hit, sly and sideways, as if he has just asked the silliest question in the world. She hands him the pipe. They pass it back and forth a few times, in silence.

"Where do you get it?" he asks.

"The librarian in Newton. There are books you can request. Anything by Updike will get you weed. Nobody reads Updike anymore. She knows what you mean if you request him."

"Nobody reads Updike anymore?" Don says. "That's hard to believe."

"Have you read Updike?"

"No," Don says.

He giggles into his hand, softly and in a sort of hushed chuckle, and finally ABC says, "What's Connect Four?"

"Pretty sneaky, sis," Don says and they both snort with laughter.

"That's really a game?"

Don stands and walks to the hammock. He slips off his shoes, sporty brown leather slip-ons that make his feet look too small, and he sets his shoes neatly against the wall, then flops in the hammock, rocking it turbulently until the whole works calm down, and ABC is watching this realtor she's just met swinging slowly in the hammock, barely moving, reminding her of a tiny child who's fallen asleep in a baby swing on the park set.

This is when ABC climbs in beside him, curling up in a kind of fetal position against him, which, from the way he stiffens his body, she can tell shocks him. He doesn't expect it but there's no protest. The hammock sways gently with the weight of them and outside the breeze of evening begins.

"When I saw you under the sycamore, you looked like you maybe were dead."

"Did I?" ABC asks.

They lie there in the darkness, silent. For a long time, it seems there is the sound only of cicadas and breath and the distant roll of passing cars on Highway 6.

"Are you gonna be funny now?" ABC asks.

She hears his breathing, labored, slowing. She turns her face toward his, her mouth an inch or two from his cheek. His eyes are closed.

"You were supposed to be funny, Don Lowry," she whispers. "What happened?"

Don Lowry doesn't answer. Don Lowry is asleep. And soon ABC falls into sleep too, so deeply that she begins dreaming and in her dreams, there is Philly, who has not been in her dreams before, though she has longed to dream about Philly, has prayed to see Philly in a dream. But Philly is there now, standing at the edge of a rocky beach, white-foamed blue waves, chunked with white stones of ice, crashing behind her. She waves to ABC and in the dream ABC waves back, so happy.

"Philly!" she says, turning over, moaning near Don Lowry's ear. "Philly! Is that you?"

But Philly is gone, and Don Lowry remains motionless, almost as if he is dead, as if he has died instead of her, and she knows now that she has dreamed of Philly because of this man, this Don Lowry, who had once been a joke to her, and to Philly, but was not a joke at all anymore.

5

Her hair is back in a tiny tight ponytail and her blue eyes and cheekbones are even more pronounced because of it. Charlie always felt as if he had a murky face, shadowed and dull in most light, unreadable. The women he dated would always ask him, "What are you thinking?" as if his own countenance was one failure of expression after another. Perhaps this is why he always felt a bit inadequate as an actor. He was inscrutable. He squinted when smiling, grew puffy when tired. You could not read his eyes.

This woman has the clearest eyes he has ever seen.

He knows this because she is staring at him, as if trying to place him, and he knows too that he has seen her before. But he would probably have been in high school then, maybe twelve years ago, or more. He's not been back here much.

At least she has stopped kicking the ice machine.

"You don't by chance have a cigarette?" she asks. His hands are full. He has a twelve-pack of Moosehead in his hands; a plastic sack of groceries hangs from each hand as well.

"Sure," he says. "Follow me. I'll set this down."

She scans him, looks to the minivan parked in a dark corner of the lot.

"I grew up here," he says, when she seems to notice his Washington plates. "I just got in from a long, long drive."

She follows him and he sets his groceries on the slanted hood of the van. He opens the box of Moosehead then, pulls out two bottles, cracks them open with his key ring, and offers her one. She steps into the shadows, out of the light, takes the beer, and drinks it.

"Are you twenty-one?" she says.

"Twenty-nine."

"Just making sure. If the cops come, I'd like to keep this to a misdemeanor."

"I don't think Ashlyn will call the cops. What's your brand?"

She looks at him, puzzled.

"Of cigarettes."

"Right. Whatever you've got. Marlboro used to be my brand. Lights."

He sets down his beer, goes into the convenience store, and faces the now-scowling Ashlyn.

"You know her?" she asks. "She your friend?"

"I don't know yet, Ashy," he says, smiling. "She might be. Marlboro Lights? In a box?"

"I almost called the fucking cops, Charlie! You tell her that."

"She's cool. I told you that I would take care of it."

Ashy gets his cigarettes and offers a free book of Kum & Go matches; he thanks her again, apologizes for the ice-machine incident, and makes a vague comment about hanging out sometime.

"You know where to find me," she says.

He takes the cigarettes out to the woman, who's almost finished her beer.

"Well then," she says, as he hands her the box and the matches. "You didn't have to do that. I thought maybe you had a pack of your own."

"My father told me to always carry cigarettes with me, and a lighter, so I'd have a reason to speak to beautiful women at parties and things like that," Charlie says.

"Very smooth," the woman says. "But you forgot his advice?"

"I didn't expect to run into a beautiful woman," he says.

"Well," she says. "Ta-da!"

She flings the bottle over her shoulder into the alley of Dumpsters behind her, and they both hear its loud clink and shatter.

"Whoa," he says. "I just told the cashier not to call the cops. Let's keep it down out here."

"Sorry," she says, laughing. "I haven't slept well in days."

She lights a cigarette and he opens another beer for her.

"We're not supposed to be drinking here, are we?"

"I doubt it," Charlie says. "Is Kleinbourne still the night cop?"

"Who knows? I almost never leave my house anymore," she says. "Don't you want a cigarette?"

It is quite amazing to see her grinning.

Finishing his first beer, Charlie feels the tension of the long interstate haul releasing from his muscles, and he goes and stands beside her, closer. They both lean now, against the side of the minivan, hidden in the darkness at the far end of the parking lot. She exhales a silvery stream of smoke, blowing it away from him, but the breeze brings it back toward their faces.

"Sorry," she says.

"Don't be," he says.

He tells her he doesn't mind the smell of the smoke, not in spring, not late at night, not in this parking lot where he'd spent many nights sitting on the hoods of cars, smoking.

"I've wasted my life," the woman says.

They look at each other for a moment and then she puts out her cigarette in the now-empty bottle. She burps into her fist and goes to toss the bottle in the trash can a few yards away. As she walks back, she shakes out her short ponytail and slides the rubber band onto her wrist. She shakes her head as if she is trying to wake from a dream.

"Thanks for the beer," she says.

She walks toward the college, then breaks into a jog. Charlie watches her for a minute, downs the rest of his beer, and gets into his van.

He finds her soon enough, two blocks away, outside the college chapel. She is no longer running. She walks slowly, backward, looking up, it seems, at the illuminated stained-glass window depicting the agony in the garden, an anguished, pensive Jesus staring at the moon.

Charlie stops the car. He decides that if the woman takes off running, he will, of course, let her run away. But when he stops his car, she stops too. When he rolls down the passenger-side window, she comes over and rests her fingertips just above the door. He admires the muscles of her arm and he leans toward her.

"What do you think he's thinking?" she asks.

"Who?"

"Jesus."

"Well, he's probably wondering how the fuck he got himself into such a mess."

She doesn't laugh at this joke, so he takes a moment to think of something else to say.

"You haven't," he says. "Wasted it. I don't believe that."

The woman takes her hand off the window then, as if it's suddenly electrified.

"Get some sleep," she says. "It's good sleeping weather. Do you have a place to sleep?"

"My parents' house, which will soon be their old house. It's going up for sale."

This seems to give her pause.

"Good," she finally says.

"What if I had said no? Would you invite me home?"

"That'd be impossible."

He sees in her eyes a noticeable weight that cannot be lifted. It is a look he has often strived after as an actor, playing Hamlet or Edmund or Astrov.

"Do something unpredictable," he says in a low, flat voice.

Her eyes widen, but she doesn't smile. She looks like she might faint.

"Pardon?" she says.

But she's heard him, he can tell. And he waits.

She peels off her tank top, so she is wearing only her sports bra.

"Do you want to know my name?" he says.

"Nope," she says.

She throws the tank top at him through the open window of his van and then goes off running, faster this time.

6

She's lived in Grinnell long enough to know that someone in town might have seen her with that guy, in the parking lot, smoking and drinking. Or even tossing her tank top at him in the dim lamplight of Park Street, in front of the college chapel. And if she tried to explain the night to her husband, or to whoever in town might have seen her and might someday soon confront her about it, she did not know how to explain herself: she'd woken up, wanting to run, wanting to smoke. The house she'd found herself in felt suffocating in its familiarity.

Back home now, Claire checks on her kids. Both fine, both asleep. A weight leaves her shoulders. Every time she does anything purely selfish, she worries she'll come home to find one of the children sobbing or maimed. It is not that she doesn't trust her husband to watch the kids—although lately he is often distracted by work, by money, by something, a dreaminess that is not content but disturbed—it is that she's motivated by an unseen force many mothers believe in: guilt. Guilt as not only an internal emotion, but guilt so powerful that it is a force in the world, one that will, when given enough attention, rise up out of the ground and smother your children while you work late, or go for a massage, or spend a weekend in Chicago.

Her husband isn't in the bedroom, though this is not strange. How often, now, especially with the weather getting warm, he sleeps in the basement, the TV blinking at him. In the morning, while making coffee, he often announces—why? for sympathy? as an explanation?—that he hasn't slept at all, but of course he has. She'll rub his back, say she's sorry, and then resent him.

And he'll say, "And I have a shitty day today too. So much to do."

How much she's grown to hate this song and dance.

She leaves the bathroom door unlocked in case her husband comes upstairs and wants to have sex with her. She'd go for such a thing right now, just as a distraction from whatever is keeping her from sleeping, but doesn't have the energy to initiate it—to wake him from his sleep down in the basement, to straddle him with the TV's blue light behind her bare shoulders. It's rare that Claire ever takes a nighttime shower without him slipping in with her, bending her over, and fucking her against the tiled wall. They'd retained a primal attraction to each other over the years, and instead of the sex getting worse or worn or tired as they aged, it was getting better and more frequent. Everything else, well, that's gotten worse. For a long time, a healthy sex life had been her proof that their marriage was stellar. When her friends complained about their husbands—slobs with waning sexual desires and emotional unavailability—Claire always felt smugly superior.

The master bathroom is a ridiculously palatial room with a double walk-in shower, a sunken Jacuzzi tub that fits their whole family, and two separate water closets. Her husband had picked most everything, all of it with a sort of subtext. He'd been born poor, raised poor, and spent much of his twenties poor. This house, as tacky and sprawling as it seems to Claire, and this bathroom in particular, an unnecessarily lavish place to piss, shit, and wash, means to her husband that he had escaped something most people could not escape. She understands. Sometimes she dreams of a farmhouse in Vermont, mice infested, a barn in decay, or a loft in Brooklyn, cramped by her family but in the heart of something bigger. Places to hide. She wonders what it would be like to live elsewhere, without her husband, even, but that night, exhausted, bewildered, sore, she loves the water pressure, a cascade of calming heat washing off the scent of sweat and cigarettes.

Usually, that is enough.

After her shower, overheated now from the long, luxurious length of it, Claire goes out to the back deck in her robe, first shutting off all the lights inside and outside the house. The breeze has picked up considerably—it is nearly three A.M. now—and the mosquitoes are not as abundant as they'd been on her run. Her skin still steaming from the extended shower, she opens her robe a little at first, and then fully, and then, safe behind a privacy fence and giant pines and maples that circle the edges of their half-acre lot, she drops the robe entirely and stands naked under the stars.

When was the last time she had stood naked like that, outside, in the dark? Fifteen years ago, the summer she was twenty-three; she'd been at an art center in Vermont and had gone skinny-dipping in a river with some other artists. Drunk, she had coupled off with a sculptor, a man ten years older, later, in the woods. She'd already been dating her husband—they'd been college sweethearts—though they'd had a huge fight a few nights before, over a shitty pay phone connection, and had agreed to take a break from each other.

Soon, when her residency was over, she came back to her husband; she never told him about it, the skinny-dipping, the sculptor whose hands she still remembered. He would have been jealous. He would have considered it something that was about him, not her. Was he better looking than me? What did he like about you? Did you fuck him?

But what she remembered more than the water, or the slickness of skin in the hot night, the leaves on her back later, was the possibility in the air. She had stopped the sculptor before he entered her—but they were there, naked, him on top of her, and it would have been so easy for her to let him. She wanted to, and when she said, *No, I don't think I can,* he told her he wanted her *for real, forever.* She had laughed at him then, still holding him in her grip when he finished into a mess of leaves and then he quickly dressed and left her in the dark woods alone and she thought for a moment of staying in those woods forever.

Now, lying on this deck, thinking of what might have happened if she'd ended up with the sculptor, or even more tantalizing, maybe, all alone, she doesn't think of the sex, though it would have been mind blowing of course—in one's mind, the sex one didn't have is always mind blowing—but what kind of trajectory her life might have had. Would she have ever returned to Iowa? Had children? Finished a second book?

Her thoughts return to the man who had given her a beer at the Kum & Go: she had known him before, years ago, as a teenager. He was heavier then, a cherubic face and a softer, pudgy build. But she had seen him in something—Chekhov's *Uncle Vanya,* a disastrously ambitious production at the local high school, when they had just moved back to Grinnell. It would have been maybe thirteen years ago. He had played Astrov, and even at sixteen—so he was twenty-nine now—he had perfected the weary weight of middle-age ennui. She remembers him giving a speech in a tight tweed jacket and having been moved by it. So he's back, she thinks, and she wonders why, why do people seem to come back here? And then she dozes out there on the deck, asleep in the nude, outside, almost hoping somebody finds her and is scandalized.

Among the things mothers don't do: they don't leave the house first in the morning, without explanation. Fathers can do this. They can blame work or a need to hit the gym or an early meeting or a doctor's appointment and be gone before the family wakes up; but mothers need to be seen in the morning, present, directing the day's traffic.

But when she wakes up on the back deck, still before dawn, Claire can think of no good reason to stay home. What kind of life is this? When you cannot leave the house if you want to leave the house. She's awake again, alone in the early morning, four thirty, and the kids will sleep almost four more hours. Her husband's still asleep too, it seems, in the basement, in front of the television.

She goes to the kitchen in her robe and flips on the coffeemaker. She hesitates to do this, because she worries the simple smell of coffee might wake her husband, and she wants solitude, but she wants coffee too. Isn't that her life though, now, at thirty-eight? A storm of competing desires, one threatening to ruin the other?

She waits for the coffee to brew, just enough for one large mug of it, and she surveys the kitchen, a disaster. The dishes from last night's supper stacked in the sink, the butter dish left out, rancid and liquid now on the kitchen island. Four empty beer bottles (Don's) and a mostly empty bottle of Tempranillo (hers) near the sink. Fruit flies flit around the remnants of the wine. The trash can in the corner full, brimming over with a dozen gnawed-on ears of corn and bare bones.

She sets her coffee mug in the disgusting sink, goes into the downstairs bathroom, puts on a hint of makeup, brushes her teeth, drops her robe, and slides on a navy blue sundress, which she finds in a pile of clean laundry she dumped, two days ago, on the family room couch. She has no clean underwear. It is all upstairs in the three baskets of laundry she has yet to put away. If she goes upstairs, she might wake one of the kids, and then slipping out would be out of the question.

Fine, she thinks. It's hot.

She walks out the front door and leaves.

Her husband will wake up later and find her gone. He'll look around at the kitchen and then panic. The chaos of his life will seem insurmountable. How to give the children breakfast in such a filthy kitchen? And how will he get them all ready for the day, while he arranges showings of his newest listings? How will he shit, shave, and shower, his morning rituals, if he's alone with the kids?

How many times, Claire thinks, in the past twelve years, has she forgone those three simple dignities of the mornings to care for the children, or how often has she done those things with a child in the bathroom watching her, crying, whining, or asking a million cheerful and relentless questions as she tried to take a shit.

She would come home and find him fuming, though he would say, "No, no, it's okay."

She goes to the house where she expects to see his van and she sees it. She sees the light on in an upstairs window, and she goes into the front yard and stands on the flagstone path, and then when she sees him, the man she had expected to see, the guy she'd talked to outside the Kum & Go, pass by the window in jeans and no shirt, holding a mug of coffee, she goes to the door and knocks.

Charlie Fucking Gulliver.

Behind her, she sees the glowing promise of a sunrise and the trees filling with it too, a spreading flame in the sky, and she remembers how much that once mattered to her, those brief moments of the new morning, when she had first moved back to the Midwest and was still in love with its light.

7

When Don Lowry wakes, just before dawn, he is dry-mouthed and fully erect, and his head buzzes with the strangeness of half sleep, but he knows exactly where he is. He's in a hammock on the Manettis' sleeping porch, hungover, maybe still stoned, hungry, and next to him is ABC. Her hand is under his shirt and on his bare stomach somehow.

How does one exit a hammock without waking a second sleeper, also in the hammock?

This is a question he's never considered before!

ABC shifts her hand as she stirs, moves it off his stomach, grazing it against the front of his pants, unintentionally, yes, but a pleasurable wince seems to rush up to Don's forehead from the bottom of his spine. He rolls from the hammock and stands, straightening his clothes and watching ABC, still sleeping, as the hammock sways slowly back and forth.

She's probably pretending to sleep. She just wants him gone.

He smooths his hands over his body, adjusting himself. Trying to make himself something like presentable in the waxing daylight. Her pants came off at some point in the night. Don Lowry, who considers himself a light sleeper, almost a nonsleeper, has slept the sleep of the dead.

He has to pee, finds the bathroom, and then, holding his shoes, walks down the steps. His mouth is so dry and his head thumps and he makes his way into the spacious kitchen and seeks a glass of water, two Advil if he is lucky. He looks at a gleaming fridge—it's a new kitchen, a significantly sleek set of appliances, butcher-block countertops, and custom-made cabinets that he had not imagined such an old home having: it would push this home over the $300,000 mark. Inside the fridge, he finds a whole shelf of bottled water, juices, beers, and cans of seltzer. He grabs one of these cans, pops the top, and then smells, in the distance, burning leaves.

Shutting the fridge, turning around, he sees the white-haired Mrs. Manetti, Ruth, in her bathrobe, lighting up a joint.

"Don Lowry!" she says. "You wanna burn?"

"Um, sure," Don says.

He sits down at the kitchen table across from her, his sparkling water in hand. She hands him the joint. He takes it, and holds in the smoke, less smooth than what he was smoking upstairs. He thinks he remembers a morning hit is good for a hangover and he is hungover and will be all day.

"Not easy to roll a joint with arthritis," Ruth says.

"I guess, what, it's supposed to help with that?" Don asks.

"At my age," Ruth says, winking, "it helps with every goddamn thing. Do you have any big plans for the summer, Don?"

"Um," Don says, stuttering a bit. He has known Ruth Manetti most of his life, but he's not made small talk with her in years. She had faded into the scenery of the town for him, another old lady he knew and whose house he would someday sell in order to settle an estate. "I guess we'll probably go up to Minnesota again. Lake Superior."

"You still use the Merrick place every August?"

"Good memory!" Don says. He remembers, now that he sees

her face light up, Ruth had grown up along the North Shore of Minnesota. "Have you been back there?"

"Almost a decade since I've seen that lake," she says. "That's a shame, isn't it?"

ABC walks into the kitchen in her underwear and T-shirt, gets a glass pitcher of orange juice from the fridge, and pours two glasses.

"The fireflies came back last night," Ruth says.

"Fireflies?" Don says. "I didn't see them yet."

"I did!" ABC says. "I thought I saw a few just before Don showed up!"

Ruth is silent for a moment, the smoke coming out of her mouth seeming more powerful than the frail lips that exhale it. Don feels as if she herself, in her thin robe, might dissipate into smoke. Her face is blank, as if she is staring toward something beyond the kitchen, beyond the house, beyond Grinnell. ABC is watching her too.

Christ, don't have a stroke, Don thinks. Not now.

But then her thoughts return to the kitchen and she looks at them and says, "The night they return is a night of upheaval. Always. It brings profound change."

ABC takes Ruth an OJ, sits at the vacant chair at the small table, and takes a long drink of her own juice. She reaches over, takes Don's can of sparkling water, and splashes some if it into her own glass.

"A spritzer," she says. "Want one?"

"No, no. I need to go. It's almost dawn."

"Do you turn into a pumpkin at dawn?" ABC asks.

"I never sleep," Don says. "I don't know how I fell asleep so soundly."

"Isn't it obvious?" Ruth says. "That's why I started smoking weed again. Ten years of insomnia, aches and pains, and a spinning sad mind and I had had it. Purely medicinal, of course. A balm for a suffering old lady, nothing more."

"Me too," ABC says.

"I gotta go," Don says to both of the women. "Thanks for everything."

"Tonight," Ruth says, "keep an eye out."

"For what?" ABC and Don both say at once.

"Fireflies," Ruth says. "Upheaval!"

After Don leaves the house, Ruth turns to ABC.

"He's married," Ruth says.

"It's not like that," ABC says.

"It's okay. I'm not judging. Loneliness is a justification for a lot of behavior. Loneliness is a kind of suffering you can alleviate. It's not something you have to endure, like grief."

"I'm not lonely."

"You are," Ruth says. "It's the core of your condition. You practically stink of it."

"Thanks," ABC says.

"What I mean is this, ABC. You, and by that I mean everyone, take comfort sometimes in life where you shouldn't. People get hurt in life—there's no way around that. And people will do anything to find grace."

ABC drinks her juice and feels Ruth looking at her expectantly.

"You're rather philosophical this morning."

"Fireflies," Ruth says.

ABC waits for her to elaborate and when she doesn't, ABC fills the silence, which always feels more meaningful than awkward with Ruth.

"When Philly and I were dating—I mean, when she was still alive—there was this one morning when we were just joking around. You know, in bed," ABC says. "The way couples sometimes do, right? Just talking nonsense, exhausted and satisfied."

"One of the great pleasures in life," Ruth says. "Postcoital contentment."

"Yes," ABC says. "Anyway!"

"Are you blushing?" Ruth says. "I thought you were so modern!"

"Well, one of those mornings, I got this wave of panic in my heart and I asked Philly, 'What'll I do if you die?'"

"You had a feeling?" Ruth asks.

"I had a feeling that such bliss was not sustainable."

"I think every good relationship has that fear. You should feel that happy. So happy, you worry."

"I guess," ABC says.

"And? What did she say?"

"She looked at me and said that she'd send Don Lowry."

"Oh my," Ruth says.

Ruth stands up then, which takes some doing, and goes to the window. ABC thinks she looks worried, or maybe she is making sure Don is not still on the porch, listening.

"Did you tell him this?" Ruth asks.

"No. But that's why, when he showed up yesterday—I'd just been sitting in the park, crying, missing Philly worse than I ever had missed her and who is standing there when I open my eyes? Don Lowry!"

"Oh my," Ruth says again.

"Coincidence, right? A crazy coincidence."

"You get to be my age, ABC, you don't believe in coincidences much."

Ruth closes her eyes and then opens them wide, smiling, a wave of energy coming into her cheeks and flooding them with pink light.

"So what are you saying?"

Ruth thinks a long moment, staring into her almost-empty juice glass. She comes back to the kitchen table and sits down with a great, slow effort. Eyes closed, she exhales.

"I think you should follow him. I think Philly was right. Don Lowry is here for a reason."

"Oh my God, Ruth. I dunno about that, I mean, how crazy . . . "

"Why would she have said it then?"

"Coincidence," ABC says. "We thought he was funny. We thought his billboards and advertisements were very funny."

Ruth asks to be led to her bed. She tells ABC she is suddenly very tired and wants more sleep. When ABC has helped her get into the bed, has covered her in a warm quilt and dimmed the lights of her room, Ruth, closing her eyes, finally speaks again.

"It's not a coincidence," Ruth says.

Ruth begins to fall asleep and ABC shakes her arm, gently.

"Wait! Before you fall asleep! What are you saying?"

"It's no coincidence, ABC. Don Lowry is going to lead you to a magical place, a place where you'll find Philly."

"What? Ruth?"

"That explains the fireflies," Ruth says, and then she's off into Nod, and ABC is left with a racing heart whispering to the walls the word *Philly*.

8

Charlie has opened up all the windows in the musty, vacant house, but the wind is too faint to do much good. The scent that does waft in through the pollen-coated screens is a familiar one—earth, cut lawn, the blossoms of the pear and plum trees in the side yard, the sweetly dank manure that's been spread on the black earth of the cropland fields outside town. It's not yet light, but already he hears the first birds of the morning, the chatter of mating robins and grackles and wrens.

He goes to the front porch and he sees her, standing there.

"You're not asleep," he says.

"I have to go in a second," Claire says.

"I want to show you something," Charlie says. And he walks toward the backyard and she follows, still moving fast, as they make their way to the edge of the yard, through the gate of the tall cedar privacy fence, to the patio in front of the guesthouse, which was his father's study for three decades, and then Charlie disappears around the corner and lights flip on and before them, the pool—now full and clean and glimmering.

The sky seems to lighten along with the pool, as if the flipped switch has triggered the sunrise.

Claire stands on the deck, looking at the water, and even before Charlie reappears, she knows she should go.

"You did this?" Claire says.

"My mom hired a pool service. She wanted me to have an empty house and a clean pool. There's something Zen about it. Or something."

"That's very sweet of her," Claire says.

Charlie laughs, a sort of sad chuckle, and he says, "My parents did things for me, not with me. There's a big difference."

Claire crouches down and dips a hand in the water.

"It's nice," she says. "A perfect temp."

"I thought it'd be too cold."

"It's been a warm spring," Claire says.

"Let's swim."

"Um," she says.

"Come on," he says. "We're all grown-ups here."

He sheds his jeans and, in his boxers, dives into the water.

Claire is on a precipice. Not just the pool's edge. No, Claire's on a cliff, staring down at some abyss, scared but not scared. How easy life seems all of a sudden, though the day before, her husband had asked, "Why is it all so difficult?"

"It just is," she'd said. "I think you like it that way."

Charlie surfaces and treads water in the deep end.

"Come on!"

"Um," she says, "I'm not wearing underwear."

He goes underwater and slips off his boxers and surfaces and tosses them to the side of the pool where they land with a thud, and soon, off come Claire's shoes. Claire feels so hot, feels so in need of something to make this day different from so many others: what would it hurt to swim?

Charlie surfaces, smiles at her, presses himself out of the pool with one fluid stroke of all his muscles and walks to the outer wall of the office. She notices every inch of him, every gesture, as if he is glowing. He flips a switch and all is dark again, except for the growing sliver of dawn beyond the trees to the east.

"Is that better?" he says.

She lifts her dress over her head and she leaps into the water. When she surfaces, Charlie eases himself back in—she watches him enter the water slowly, and he swims up alongside her. They move to the shimmer and swale of the pool.

She feels his body moving the water, and she surfaces. He nears her, and when his hands go to her hips, she says, "We can't."

"No?"

"We just swim," Claire says.

But as they swim there, in the dark, closer than they should be swimming, it is as if she can feel him through the water, she can feel him so much that when she leans on the wall and he comes swimming up behind her, not touching her but almost touching her, she moans.

"You're not happy," he says. "But you should be."

In the water, she feels him, or the waves he's making, against her thighs.

"What?" she says. She can barely speak. She turns to face him and in the sky sees the river of orange light that is flowing just over the tree line now.

"It's beautiful," she says. "And we can't."

She gets out of the pool. He floats on his back, watching her.

"There are towels on that shelf there, do you see?"

But she is already wrapping herself in one when he says this, and she is shivering despite the warmth of the morning that is filling the air. He is getting out of the pool, and she steps into the guest house to dress, suddenly feeling more modest with the dawn.

Though it's been over a decade since she finished a book, her only book, what Claire has always been good at, for better or worse, is the reconstruction of certain narratives so that they contain a fictional element that makes the impractical seem practical. They had just gone swimming, she thinks to herself as she walks, and we are all adults here, and so we swam without suits—I would have swum in my underwear, she thinks, had I been wearing any, and furthermore, she thinks to herself, it was a onetime thing, a whim, and even if it was a bit over the edge of propriety, she had been faithful to her husband for over fifteen fucking years and so, what the hell is wrong with a whim?

This is what she is thinking when she sees Don Lowry walking toward her, and he walks almost with a tremble, as if he is shaking with something like guilt but not quite guilt. What is it, lack of sleep? Hopelessness? The knowledge that his life has irrevocably changed?

Does he know where she's been?

What, exactly, did she just do?

Now the sky is alight with dawn. They meet on the sidewalk.

"I was just—" they both say, at once, and then stop.

"Out walking," Claire says.

"Looking for me?"

This question she doesn't expect.

"Well, I guess. Where were you?"

"I fell asleep."

"Where?" Claire says. "Downstairs?"

"Claire," he says. "It was the strangest thing."

She puts a finger to his lips.

"Shh," she says. "I don't want to know."

Whatever strangeness he is about to confess will only trigger something inside her and she isn't sure what—would she confess? And if she begins to talk, will she ever stop? Will she explode somehow—I don't love you, Don, and I can't explain why—releasing something dormant and pushed down that will spark then turn to flame amid the lush omnipresent green of dawn?

When she'd left Charlie's, after drying off and dressing and peeing and composing herself in the guesthouse/study she'd slipped into, he'd been asleep in a deck chair, covered in a large white towel. Looking at the bookshelves in the guesthouse she'd found, surprisingly, among the books in Gill Gulliver's study an old hardcover copy of her first and only book, *Everybody Wants Everything*, and she had pulled it from the shelves and found a black marker and she had, for some reason, signed it: *To Charlie.* She had almost stopped there but then she added something: *Tell me what you want.* Before putting it back on the shelf, she looked at the jacket photo, now nearly fifteen years old. Claire, in 1999, a black tank top, short hair swept back and slick, big hoop earrings, a wide black belt, faded jeans. Her face serious, not exactly a pout, but a pensive wince. She both hated and loved to see herself like that. Her publicist then, an Ole Miss graduate named Amber who, she was sure, no longer worked in publishing, had said, "You need an author photo that makes you look, pardon my French, like a good lay."

Sometimes she thinks that one comment is why she stopped writing.

Now the light is in the sky, and Don moves Claire's finger from his lips.

"What's going on?" Don says.

"I thought you were downstairs watching Netflix."

"I wasn't. I was just—"

"Shh!"

"Do you not want to know where I've been because you don't want me to know where you've been?"

"The kids will be up any minute, Don. We have to get home."

"Have you been swimming?" Don asks.

She looks up at him, as if she hasn't understood the question at all. As if it were a non sequitur, completely insane.

"Why are we still married?" she says.

Now a police car comes up alongside them and an officer asks them to get in. Don knows the officer. He calls him Steve. Claire is not sure who he is but follows Don's lead.

"You know Steve Halverson," Don says.

"Hello, Steve," she says, though she doesn't know him at all.

Halverson explains that he and another deputy had arrived that morning to serve papers—strictly doing my sworn duty, Don, I wish it could be different. Foreclosure papers, a notice that the sheriff would be auctioning off their home in thirty days, and what Halverson and his partner found, when knocking on the door, were two confused and sleepyheaded kids, neither of them knowing where their parents had gone.

"I thought Don was home," Claire says as they ride the few blocks across town. "Or I thought he was about—foreclosure papers? Don't we get more warning about those? Weren't you in the basement, Don?"

"No," Don says.

"Well, ma'am," Halverson says, "by this point in the process, the home owner has generally had numerous notices from the county. And for months before that, from the bank."

"I don't understand," Claire says.

"Claire," Don says. He reaches for her arm then pulls back. Looking at him, she knows that he knows the whole story, everything, and that there is no misunderstanding here at all, but a secret he has kept from her.

"Anyway, ma'am," Halverson says, "yes, you would have been given, according to the usual process, at least six months of warning. These days, people get longer. The system is backed up. It's the least pleasant part of my job. Next to dead bodies."

Don smells of sleep, morning breath, sweat, beer, smoke. The dank smell of damp vegetation seems to come off him, as if he had stepped out of a leaf pile.

"Not that we get many dead bodies around here," Halverson says, "but when we do, it's awful. It gets to you."

"Don? Where were you?" she asks.

Don puts his hand on her knee and whispers. "We got the notices," he says.

"What?" she says, her voice a high involuntary whistle, like a broken flute. She thinks she might be sick in the back of the car. She wants to roll down the window. She feels as if it is too much to ask. She doesn't deserve to roll down the window.

"We got lots of notice," Don says. "I just thought I could—"

"We see this a lot, Claire. We see this more than you would think," Halverson says as he eases down the cul-de-sac. "One spouse is often in the dark. It's shameful for men. They are breadwinners. All of that. I feel for you, Donny, I really do. I've been there, if it helps. Lori and I went broke about nine years ago, and then I became a cop. You know all of that. My business went belly-up and—"

"Okay, last night, Don," Claire says and interrupts the cop. "Where were you?"

Don turns and looks out his window. "It's hard to explain."

"Because I was . . . ," Claire begins, but stops. Don is right. How does one explain something that seems like a dream, separate from real life?

In the light of morning that narrows the shadows on their front lawn, Claire sees her children outside, gathered near another cop. They are in pajamas, drinking from boxes of juice.

"The kids were a little frightened. My partner knocks loud. He's new. He's from Milwaukee. The kids, I'm afraid, woke to some pretty loud knocking," Halverson says. "You wake up to that kind of knocking, I guess, I mean, if you're a kid, it's just—anyway, they want us to serve these in person, but when you didn't come to the door, we nailed it to the door, which involves hammering and which broke into your door, which is not really good wood. Those doors, from Home Depot, they don't last."

Claire leaves the car to go to the kids before Halverson has the car in park. The children stare at Claire as she comes toward them: like victims of some natural disaster, they have had blankets put over their shoulders. Cop blankets. What kind of mother allows her children to end up wrapped in cop blankets while she skinny dips the night away?

A bad mother.

"We gave them some juice," says the other cop, a younger one who has been waiting with the kids. "The littler one, your girl? She got a sucker. The other kid didn't want one. He demanded a phone call and a lawyer, like he was on a cop drama. He's a cool customer."

Bryan smiles at this, a big grin.

A few neighbors are out on porches, in robes, but none of them come over.

Claire lets out another whistle and waves her arms at the kids as she runs and shrieks again in that flutelike manner, "Oh! Oh! Oh! Hey! Hey!" and then, "Everything's okay! It's all okay!"

She gets to them and begins kissing them, hugging them, trying not to make eye contact with the grim deputy who has been assisting Halverson; she turns and sees finally that Don Lowry has not yet left the squad car.

It is as if he's hoping to be taken away.

PART II

Marriage is a small container.

—*Jane Smiley,* The Age of Grief

1

Three times in the course of a long, mostly happy, but occasionally uncertain marriage, Don and Claire had considered, at least elliptically, the possibility of a divorce. The first time this happened was only six months into the marriage; they were twenty-three and they'd been up late arguing after drinking late into the evening with friends in the Village. This was the only year of their married life in which they had lived somewhere other than Iowa. New York, where they had gone simply because Claire had missed it and had cried on their wedding night because she missed it and all her New York friends so much, seemed like a long part of their shared history, but really, it was now just a sliver of it.

The argument itself had started during sex—Don could not remember exactly what had been said, but it involved the accusation of boredom or dissatisfaction or sleepiness—and he remembered, at some point in what became a long night of endless, edgy bickering, just before dawn, Claire, sitting at the edge of the bed, staring out at the dimmed building across the alley, had said, "Maybe we were too young to get married."

"I think so," Don said, though he didn't think that at all.

"Do you think people will laugh about it? If we get divorced?"

Claire said. "I think a lot of people—even my own mother—thought this was a big mistake."

Don had not known this, though he suspected it. By twenty-three, in rural Iowa, you were plenty old enough to be married, and none of his family or childhood friends would have batted a proverbial eye; but Claire, having been raised in Manhattan among a crowd of academics and artists and activists, understood marriage in an entirely different way. It was what you did when everything else on your life list had been accomplished or was at least under way. What united them in their view of marriage was this: their parents, both sets of them, had been miserable with each other and had ultimately divorced, and so there was not exactly a good road map for them to follow.

This had made the idea of marrying young a little, well, thrillingly rebellious; Don remembered how sometimes Claire's voice would rise with a kind of glee when she would tell her New York friends—*Well, I'm getting married. Yes, to a guy from Iowa!*

But they'd been fighting a lot, already, less than a year into the marriage, and Don knew this was probably normal, but then again so was divorce.

"Would we care if people thought this was a big mistake?" Don said. "I mean, do you care what people think?"

"I suppose not," she said.

"I never do. I never care what anyone thinks."

"How can that be true?" she said, her voice rising almost violently. "Everyone cares what people think. Even people who say, 'I don't care what people think,' want other people to know they don't care. So in a sense, they are caring what other people think just by saying that they don't care what people think."

"What are you talking about?"

"Fuck off."

"I never understand you," he said.

"Because I married a fucking idiot."

He remembered she went to sleep on the armchair then—it was a small studio apartment and so he could still see her from the bed—and in the morning, he woke up with a terrible headache and she was next to him, spooned against his back, her hand on his hip. The apartment was alight with morning, though those windows never got quite enough light to be impressive, but right around nine A.M. they sparkled with it.

He stirred but did not turn toward her.

"Do you want me to call a lawyer?" she whispered, her eyes still closed.

"It's Sunday. Let's talk to a waiter who's serving brunch instead."

They finished the unfinished sex of the previous night then, and never did call a lawyer. Sex had solved many of their fights in the past, and Don supposed this was not uncommon for couples, though it was the kind of thing you could never really be sure about, the sex lives of others. You could wonder about it, as he often did. Claire was the only woman he'd ever slept with and he wondered how it might be different with other women just a few months into their marriage. This too may be normal, but no one would admit it.

Then, that Monday, she received a letter accepting her into graduate school.

"It looks like we're going back to Iowa," she said. She was crying tears of joy and despair all at once.

Iowa! Who knew the pull it would have on them, for better or for worse?

The second time the possibility of a divorce shadowed their marriage was shortly after Bryan was born. Perpetually sleep deprived, sexless, unshowered, and, yes, back in Iowa, they fought an epic fight that began like this: Don had lit a match after using the bathroom in their small apartment, hoping to mask the smell of shit, and he'd left the match on the edge of the sink where he'd already left a week's worth of post-shit matches. Claire had gone into the bathroom after him and called him a horrible wreck of a slob and begun weeping. "I feel so lonely" was one of the only things he could understand through the sobbing.

There is nothing harder to hear in a marriage than one partner saying to the other, "I'm lonely here."

For three or four days, they didn't speak to each other unless it was to communicate something about the baby (*I changed his diaper, he just ate*). Don worked during the day—he'd drive to Grinnell and work construction for an uncle there—and then he'd come home just after five, they'd eat a rushed supper together, and Claire would leave with a large travel mug of cheap coffee and work on campus until one or two in the morning. On one of those nights, after waking with a crying baby, Don Lowry made the decision that he had made a mistake.

Claire walked in, looking exhausted, smelling of beer and cigarettes, and found Don sitting in the armchair, staring out the window at the dark softball diamonds behind their apartment.

"You didn't work?" Don said, after Claire had come up behind him and given him a kiss.

"I stopped off for a drink on the way home."

"With whom?"

"What do you mean 'with whom'? With some folks from the workshop. We were all working late."

"Bryan's been up three times."

"I'll go feed him."

"In your condition?"

"Don, Jesus. I had one beer and one puff of a cigarette."

"Whose cigarette?" Don said.

"This is so dumb," Claire said, and went into the bedroom.

She came out a few minutes later, undressed, wrapped in Don's flannel robe.

"I don't want to wake him," she said. "I'll feed him when he wakes up. I need to pump though. Why don't you get some rest? You look tired."

"Whose cigarette, Claire?"

"A guy named Trent. He's the visiting writer this week. We were talking shop."

"I live in a goddamn Bruce Springsteen song," Don said, and walked out of the apartment a few minutes later. It had taken him a long time to find his wallet and his keys and Claire was sitting on the yellow love seat, slumped and half asleep, her legs spread out, her breasts being suctioned by a small electric pump. "Jesus, Claire," he said. "The blinds are open. Put on some fucking clothes."

He did not stay out long. Only went out for his own one beer and half a cigarette, awkwardly leaning on a bar rail lined with undergrads in black and gold. There was a basketball game that evening and they were celebrating some hard-fought win or mourning some unexpected loss. He could not figure out the mood in the bar. After that, for a while, Don would lie awake in the long, cry-rattled nights, thinking through the logistics of the divorce, but by the weekend, the skies had cleared. Calm waters returned. Don said, "I'm sorry that I am insane," and Claire said, "It's understandable, baby."

"Do you think you are also insane?" Don asked. "About those matches?"

"Yes," Claire said, and that was that, though he never left a match on the sink again. He would wet them and drop them in the trash bin, and he'd always say to himself as he did so, "That's one tidy motherfucker, that Don Lowry."

*

The third time the word *divorce* comes up is right now, when Claire, standing in the kitchen, calmly, eerily calm, actually, says, "Do we need to have a conversation about divorce?"

It's a Saturday, one week from the morning when the sheriff found them out wandering in the weak light of early dawn, their kids home alone, a mortgage nine months in arrears.

"Not really," Don says, "we can't afford a divorce."

He smiles, trying to push the conversation into the realm of shrugged-off humor, but Claire remains stoic.

"I mean, if we're going to have to pack up the house anyway, we should have a sense of what's next," Claire says. "I don't know if we have to stay together as husband and wife."

Don moves around the kitchen. He opens and closes some cabinets.

"Sure we do."

"It's just, you've never answered my question," she says, "and given the circumstances, I think it's an important one."

"'Why are we still married?'" Don says. "That question?"

"Yes. We never have answered it."

"What is happening?" he asks.

"You smother me," she says. "Your sadness, your worry—I mean, the other night, I had a taste of something kind of like freedom from you. In town, when you work, you're Mr. Happy, the joke-teller, the flirt, the good-time guy. You know everyone in this goddamn town. How many people do I know?"

"None of this is true."

"I've lived here over ten years, Don. And how many friends do I have who live in Iowa?"

"You want to separate?" Don says. "Because you have no friends? That's my fault, that you hate everybody? That you still resent me for living in Iowa?"

"*Separate* is a good word," Claire says. "Efficient, workaday:

separate the eggs from the yolk, the sticker from its backing, the wheat from the chaff. Separate the Don from the Claire."

"Jesus," Don says.

"Yes," she says. "I want to separate."

A load of boxes and packing tape and tape guns had arrived via UPS the day before, and they are on the dining room table now.

"I don't think it's as hurtful a topic as you seem to consider it," Claire says. "We've been miserable with each other for weeks, months, years."

"We have kids, Claire."

"I've been lonely."

"You said you felt so free the other night?" Don says.

"I did? Yes, I did say that, I guess."

"You just said it. What night?"

"When I was without you. The night I wasn't here and neither were you."

"Where had you been that night? I was gonna ask you just as Halverson pulled up in the squad car."

"Where had you been?" Claire says back.

"I told you. I'd been smoking pot with this person, this woman I met totally randomly."

Don doesn't tell her that he's gone to see ABC four times in the last week, to drink beer, and smoke pot, and fall asleep on the wide, swaying hammock.

Don takes some scissors and cuts the plastic band from around each stack of boxes—book boxes, small boxes, medium boxes, large.

"Umph," Don says. "And that's all we did." He tries to say something else. "Umph," he says again. "You haven't told me anything!"

"I don't think it's your goddamn business."

There is a sharp edge to the statement. The abrupt force of it is terrifying.

"It's not?"

"We need to talk about the larger issue, whether it is painful or not. Question: why are we still married?"

Don often agreed with Claire's assertion when she would say, "We need to talk." She was usually right. He wanted to help her make the process smoother. But what would he tell her now—that last week, as he was driving to work, he felt an almost unimaginable pull to keep driving, to veer onto West Street and down Highway 146 and continue on a trajectory south until he reached the Gulf of Mexico? Why more people hadn't done this, in fact, is something Don Lowry considered one of the great mysteries of the Midwest. How, in fucking February, for example, did people manage to stay put, to show up for work, to tough out the slog year after year?

"I'm going to sleep down in the basement guest room for a while," Claire says. "Anyway, I need a shower. Before I go out."

"You gonna do your 'nice little Saturday'? Good for you."

What he wants is to veer Claire back on the tracks of routine, of their life, of the rhythms and predictability and, yes, love, that guided their days, which were simple, even if now they were stressful.

"Then I'll take the kids over to the pool, if you want to come."

"Why?" Don says. "You hate the pool."

"Because," she says, her voice coming at him from the staircase she's descending. "I promised. Why else do I do anything?"

2

Charlie Gulliver greets the mornings in a strange house that is, in fact, his house. It's the house in which he spent his first eighteen years, and it's still owned by his parents, and it's his own mother who's asked him to return to the house in order to clean out his father's study, but when he awakens each morning on the air mattress in his parents' old room, it does not feel like it is his house, or like it ever was his house. For starters, almost everything is gone. His mother sold off most of her possessions after the divorce, and the swift subsequent decline of his father while the divorce was becoming finalized allowed her to get rid of many of his things too. What she has left behind, the things she actually wants, she's told Charlie, are in a storage locker at the edge of a hog farm near Montezuma; all of his father's things are out in the guesthouse, the study where his father worked for three decades. There is almost no room to walk in that study, piled high with boxes, papers, books, knickknacks, file cabinets, and furniture.

But the house itself is empty—there's none of that familiarity he'd fantasized about: not the couches he'd once napped on, or the paintings in the hallway he'd once stared at while imagining the stories behind them—horses in a pasture, houses on a hill, a man falling into the sand under a sliver of silver moon. What is here:

on the counter, a coffeemaker, and on the white fridge, a calendar bearing the smiling face and contact information of Don Lowry, his mother's realtor.

It's your home, but it's my business!

Also on the kitchen counter: a note from his mother, who is still in Colorado with her new friend Lyle Canon.

It is a simple message: *Charlie, will you call me when you arrive and get settled in? Let me know how your father is doing. Do you think you can make any sense of his study? Do you need money? Also, are you drinking too much? Please be careful. Also, Lyle and I are experiencing a kind of wonder I once thought impossible. Be happy for me.* LOVE MOM.

The last two sentences of this note, sans commas, sound more like a command than a closing. Maybe he should be happy that in her fifties his mother has suddenly grown a spine and a sense of her own needs and desires. But it is still fucked up: his mother camping with a man a decade her junior while his father lingers, half-senile, in the Mayflower assisted living complex.

He has not yet called his mother, nor has he gone to visit his father. One of the strange dynamics of the Gulliver family, a dynamic Charlie is only now beginning to realize, is that the three of them—father, mother, and son—seemed to exist in a way in which they feel absolutely no sense of obligation to one another. Charlie, though he never felt completely alone or unloved as a child, spent much of his life feeling somewhat unnecessary. It's different from feeling neglected or unloved, this condition. But he always felt, as he still feels, that he was somewhat expendable. That his parents liked him, even loved him, but didn't depend on him for happiness the way he imagined many parents did. A long time ago, he thought this meant his parents were cool. Now, he isn't so sure what it had meant.

And now, although this does not feel like a homecoming at all, after a week of waking there in that house on Elm Street, spending his days drinking beer, swimming, reading random novels from the pile of books nearest the study's front door, his old life in the wider world—the one he'd deliberately made without his parents' help or support—seems thoroughly gone. And for once, he feels needed by his parents: clean out the study, prepare the house for sale, go visit your father. He doesn't feel as if he has a fresh start or a blank slate exactly, but he does feel that by simply changing his physical location to a place like central Iowa, he has erased several years of pursuing all of the wrong things—meaning, beauty, art, even, in his way, wealth—and now he has returned to the Midwest, the world of the practical, the realm of easily achieved and sensible to-do lists.

He makes such a list that morning as he waits for the coffee to brew.

1. Clean out my father's study.
2. Assemble the drafts I find into a potentially publishable manuscript.
3. Assess and curate the letters, notes, and ephemera that might make a useful archive of my father's long career.
4. Take that archive to the college librarian for assessment and possible storage.
5. Await the sale of my parents' home and the small but still meaningful percentage of the profit that my mother has promised me.
6. Fuck Claire.

This last thing he writes to amuse himself, to give himself a jolt of energy, but yes, all week he's thought of her, so close to him in that pool, and he wonders how he will see her again and how he can convince her—husband and kids aside—to fuck him in that pool. It's a goal and he's glad to have a goal. He is glad to have a challenge before him; he wonders what he's capable of achieving. Once, in college, he played Iago. And wasn't that Iago's real motivation? Boredom? Not revenge for a passed-over promotion, but an interest in how far terrible things could go?

Lately, Charlie's done nothing. No auditions, no voice-overs, not even a guest-directing gig with some obscure community theater. Writing this dark and ambitious final task, *Fuck Claire*, puts something in his heart like lust. He never knew why he wanted what he wanted, not ever.

But he wanted.

He puts the list up on the fridge with one of Don Lowry's business card magnets.

Out the back window, he looks at the small guesthouse where his work is, in piles and boxes and mazes of clutter, and he looks at the glimmer of the swimming pool between him and all that work.

He gets the coffee, which is terrible, and goes out to the guesthouse/study and begins to look through the stack for something new to read; maybe he'll go to the coffee shop downtown and have a decent espresso and read. He is in no hurry to do anything—tackle the clutter of the study, see his father, or give his mother a progress report. None of his friends know where he is or why he has left Seattle: they are all actors and writers and artists, their heads stuck so far up their own self-obsessed asses they have not even noticed his dramatic and sudden exit from their world. It would be weeks before they wondered about him. A man exits a pond without a ripple, he thinks.

He writes this on a Post-it note. Maybe he should write a book, but nobody writes a book simply by thinking *maybe* and *should*. His father once said that after a long day of working on his own book. He remembers his father coming in one day at cocktail hour, and taking a gin and tonic from his wife's hand.

They sat in the living room together, Charlie's parents, and his mother asked, "How is the book coming?" and Charlie's father said, "You know what gets me? When people say things like *maybe I should write a book*. Because the truth is, honey, if you're a real writer, you have to write a book. It's as if you don't even want to do it. You have to do it."

There was a long silence then and as Charlie sat playing with Lego on the rug in front of them, his mother exhaled.

"That's insane, Gill. That makes no sense."

Charlie's father, wounded and indignant, took his drink back out to the study. Charlie still remembers going to the window and watching him walk down the path. Maybe Charlie was seven, maybe eight. He turned to his mother. He said, "Is he mad?"

"In one sense of the word," his mother had said.

Out in that same study this morning, that place of constant retreat, he does nothing but scan the spines of his father's bookshelves. There seems to be no order to anything, and he flips through novels he's heard of but has never read—*The Mill on the Floss*, *Vanity Fair*, *Pale Fire*. It is next to this last book that he finds *Everybody Wants Everything* by Claire Lowry. He turns to look at her author photo, over a decade old, and thinks of her ass now, as she shimmied out of his pool, and he thinks, yes, I want to see her again.

3

In the café downtown that morning, Claire sits in the corner, wolfing down a scone and coffee, suddenly aware of how badly she craves the sugar and caffeine. This is her "nice little Saturday," a term Don took from a comedy he'd watched a million times, a movie about frat boys or something, with Will Ferrell. Or Seth Rogen. Or a Wilson brother. He liked to make a big deal of how Claire got Saturday mornings to herself, until ten thirty, sometimes eleven, to do whatever she wanted.

Two hours! All her own!

With this endless vast freedom, she would usually go to the only coffee shop in town and waste two hours on her computer while eating scones and drinking coffee, because she had no idea what else to do. Two hours, she'd always thought, was not enough time to do anything when you lived one hour away from even a decent midsize Midwestern city.

Don always said, "You should work on your novel!" which is something he had been saying for ten years, which really meant, of late—you should try to make some money.

She logs on to Gmail. She finds an e-mail from an old college housemate, Lonnie Wilson, announcing that a one-man show about growing up gay in rural Iowa, *Queer as Corn*, would premier in some hip Chicago venue the next weekend. She clicks on the link.

Claire's been invited, along with sixteen hundred other friends of Lonnie's, whose tiny thumbnail heads smile at her under the banner "Who's Going?"

Back in the inbox, she begins to delete other things: a slew of marketing messages from companies she'd once shopped at online—Lands' End, Audible, Athleta; a credit card account update (Re: URGENT—your account is now closed!); a note from an old college professor who is now at NYU, Tim Holiday (Re: My new book is now out from Milkweed!); something from a former college friend, Annabelle Sanderson-Maynard (Re: Sorry for the mass e-mail! Here's my address in Paris!). Also banished from her inbox: a college pot-smoking pal, Will Molsen (Re: New job in DC!); Bank of America (An Important Notice: Action Required); and Hanna Andersson (60 percent off on select winter styles!).

And like that, all of the exclamation points and all caps and embedded imagery and links to dancing goats and ads for sports bras and Frye boots she cannot afford disappear into some other place, far, far from this outpost in the corn-choked, hog-tied center of Iowa.

"Can I suggest something? Just delete everything."

"Pardon?" Claire says, turning toward the voice to see Charlie Gulliver grinning, wearing fitted khakis and a bright white T-shirt, freshly showered and shiny.

"That is what I did," he says. "When I left Seattle. I deleted my whole online identity and threw my cell phone in the bay. It was liberating."

"Why?"

"So," he says, grabbing a chair and putting it next to her, rather than across from her. "I was playing Hamlet at Seattle Shakespeare last fall, and I was onstage, and I was killing it, we'd sold out every show, the reviews were good, Gwyneth Paltrow came to see me backstage and got tears in her eyes. She touched my elbow while patting her heart with the other hand. And I remember, on closing night, I was getting into the famous speech, I don't even have to tell you which one, I'm sure."

"*To be . . .* ," Claire says.

"Yep. The role every actor wants to land, wants to nail, and I am onstage, and I am nailing it. I'm doing 'To be or not to be' in a way, I think, that's never been done before. It was my thing, my interpretation, almost jaunty and crazed instead of grave and tortured, you know? And I was fucking IN LOVE with Ophelia too, the woman who played her, I should say, and I was thinking to myself as I was onstage—well, she's married, I can't have her, and then I realized so much of my life is wanting things I can't have, like certain women, or a lake house, or whatever, and my whole career has been auditioning for things I usually can't have, but then I get one of those things, like the role of Hamlet, and I start to think all my self-worth is tied up in that role, and it becomes me. I fall in love with Ophelia, for fuck's sake, right? Her husband is the managing director of the theater."

"Did you have an affair? Is that why you left?"

"Does that matter?"

The barista calls out a name—Stanley!—to suggest a mocha is ready.

Claire clears her throat. "I don't know. I think it would matter?"

"I had an affair."

"You thought she'd leave him?"

"No. No, it always starts out that I think I'm going to love somebody. But then I realize what I am really doing is seeing if she loved me."

"Did she?"

"She did."

"That's why you left?"

"No. Not exactly. I'm checking out."

"Of what?" Claire asks.

"Striving. Trying to get what I want?"

"Love."

"Laid," he says.

Claire widens her eyes.

"Kidding," Charlie says. "I mean, I am checking out of anything that prevents me from enjoying each day. And e-mail and all of that shit actually prevents me from living in the moment. I'm done; no more. Expectation, anticipation, fear of change. Good-bye to all that! To desire things one can have or can't have or whatever—all desire leads to the same thing."

"What if you need to communicate with the outside world? E-mail is practically a necessity," Claire says.

"This is what e-mail is: either a cowardly way for people to ask favors of you that they would never ask in person, or a way for people to pretend they are having a friendship with you when they really are not."

She looks at him with a smile, a kind of smile she hasn't smiled in years. It even feels different in her cheeks and lips, a tingling, a buzz.

He seems to notice. "Most of our relationships with people are fleeting. All relationships are, essentially, disposable. When they're done, they're done," he says. "Shit like Facebook keeps everything alive way too long."

He lowers his voice and points to a tab on her screen. "Click there and you're free of all of these fuckers."

"Here?" she says and then she does it.

A warmth begins to flood her body. She's flushed.

"Yep. And then there," he points to another button, his hand grazing hers.

“Type your password and then click okay,” he says. His hand touches the small of her back.

The computer asks her if she’s sure.

“You can never be sure,” Charlie says. “That’s why I played Hamlet. But you have to act.”

He is leaning in as if they are studying, together, something on the screen, and she catches his smell, he’s so close, bourbon, chlorine, coffee, and the scent of overpowering soap, like the little harsh bars you get at cheap motels.

“Ha!” she says and then clicks *I Am Sure* on the screen in front of her. A box of coded letters appears and she has to decipher them and type them into a box. The box disappears, replaced by *You have deleted your Gmail account.*

“You really did it!” he says. “Good for you.”

She’s all heat now, and a dampness at her center feels like it’s spreading out inside her body.

Her calf touches his. He exudes a kind of tangible aura, a palpable heat, as if the air between them is solidifying. If they were in darkness, she imagines that his skin would glow and the air between them would be phosphorescent with a strange solid light.

“You use Facebook?” he asks. “Log in.”

“Yes, I go on it every morning and keep refreshing it, hoping for justification for logging on in the first place.”

She logs on, then turns and looks at him expectantly. “What do I do with this?”

“Oh boy!” he says, reaching over and commandeering the mouse. “Someone took a picture of the brunch they were enjoying in Boston. A couple in golf shirts with blond hair! And look, Claire, that waifish girl who won’t look at the camera just posted a link to an article about her upcoming art installation in Detroit. She is sooooo way talented. Also you can see right down her shirt. No wonder you can't sleep. You've got all of this useless bullshit ruining your brain synapses."

"Well, shit," Claire says.

"Good reaction," he says. "What do we have here? A notification!"

One "friend" has updated his relationship status and Charlie reads it aloud: "*Sam Kukla is in a relationship!*" Then he adds, "Yay!"

"You're really invading my privacy here. You know that?"

"There's no privacy in Grinnell," he says. "You don't need Facebook, Claire! It's all people bragging about their awesome lives, or pretending they have awesome lives, or cluttering up your intellect with the things that should be steeping in their own intellect, you know, ideas that require some time before they are shared with the world. Or pictures from people who are living a fuller life than you."

"You're totally right. I know that."

"Are you living a full life, Claire?"

He still has the mouse. He moves through the Facebook menu with a series of clicks and says, finally, "May I?"

He hovers over a button that says, Deactivate My Account.

"Sure," Claire says. "Why the fuck not?"

He does it. Five friends pop up—Sara will miss you! Tyrone will miss you! Marisol will miss you! Simms will miss you! Okkar will miss you!

"God, that is so sad," Charlie says. "Poor fuckers."

"They won't really miss me."

"What's your password?" he says.

"Um, Ophelia69."

"No way!" He types the password.

"I'm kidding. It's WendyBrybry." She types it instead.

Facebook asks her to type a random phrase to verify her

humanity. She types the words that appear in the box: FAIL HARD.

They bust up laughing over that, she hanging down her head and pressing her forehead into his shoulder. Heat.

"Do you tweet?" he says.

"No," she says.

"Good for you. My work here is done," Charlie says.

"Thanks," Claire says. "I just lost eleven hundred of my closest friends."

"Your friends who love you!" Charlie says, almost shouting. And then he stands up and gives a kind of awkward wave. Oblivious to the ears of all the other café goers, unconcerned with who might see or hear him, Charlie says, "I'm the only friend you need."

4

How do these things happen in a small town? What odd and awkward conversations Claire finds herself in that day. For instance, there she is, under a tree on the lawn at the city pool, next to Ruth Manetti, an old widow whose lawn Don used to cut as a boy. She'd been a faculty wife, Claire knows that much, and must be in her eighties now. She's sitting in a deck chair, her walker beside her, wearing a pair of yellow capri pants, orthopedic white sneakers, and a thin white hoodie, as well as a large sunhat and giant blue blocker shades. She's in a small circle of shade near the fence, shade made by a leafing-out redbud tree. The redbuds had bloomed early that spring, bursting forth in the gloom of mid-March.

Claire, undoing her oxford shirt to reveal her new navy-blue-and-white-striped bikini, just arrived from Lands' End, sets up next to Ruth in one of the only patches of lawn left on that crowded opening weekend.

Claire's in full sun but skips the sunscreen.

Ruth sips from a large bottle of Gatorade, a dazed kind of smile on her face as she watches everyone frolic about the pool. She turns the dazed smile toward Claire; Claire knows she has to say something. Claire smiles back. The woman looks stoned, Claire thinks, and wonders if she too is suffering from dementia, like Charlie's father, as if senility is moving through Grinnell like a plague in the warm miasma of late May.

"Hot day," Claire says.

"It feels excellent!" Ruth says. "I didn't think I'd survive the winter."

Ruth giggles, which, Claire thinks, is an odd thing for an elderly woman to do, though it is certainly a giggle. There is no other way to describe her laughter. She is giggling.

Claire scans the pool, mentally checking off each member of her family, something she does every two minutes at the pool, a kind of mothering habit that is likely the impulse sent out by a gene somewhere deep in her female DNA.

Don has gone off into the water with the kids, joining the other farmer-tanned fathers, all of whom seem to be in a competition as to who could be the most fun. In the pool, on the diving boards, on the waterslides, and the kiddie section, fathers, set free from their desks and factory floors for Memorial Day weekend are shouting, splashing, and hurling their children through the water, as the kids scream with delight and beg their normally sullen dads to "do it again" and "higher" and "catch me if you can!" Later, these fathers will grow distant, drinking beer in a deck chair, but for now, they are omnipotent heroes and joyful, smiling gods.

Claire sees a man she knows vaguely, an administrator from the college, look at her for the third time. Tall and bearded and handsome, he waves at her and she pretends not to see him. Everyone is looking at everybody.

At the start of swimsuit season in the Midwest, it is hard not to inventory your peers and note how they fared over the course of the brutal winter. Claire does her best to ignore the lifeguards in red trunks and sporty bikinis, all impossibly sexy and young, something about their skin suggesting a glow, a pressure, as if they might burst into flame or light at any second. She also does her best not to see the college students, easier in their sexuality than they had been as high-schoolers, flirting with a kind of arrogant abandon. She pretends not to notice a young woman in a gold bikini, full hipped, big breasted, shimmering near the entrance to the pool's shallow end, luxuriously piling up her brown hair on her head, nor does she acknowledge the fact that Don watches this minute-long process with something like a tortured look on his face before he shakes himself away from the siren and returns to the game of sea monster he has been leading with nineteen or twenty children.

Claire focuses on the many middle-aged women, mostly mothers, around her, also wearing bikinis, but none of them, as beautiful as some of them are, suggested that kind of pending eruption she sees in the half-naked young people around her. No, Claire and her almost-forty contemporaries stand about suggesting the virtues of endurance. They've made it to middle age with a remnant of hotness, and despite the attendant sagging and indignities of aging, they've managed to transcend the reality that a tattoo above the ass or behind the shoulder had been a bad idea. Yes, many of the women, Claire included, have approached forty with a verve and vigor, had Pilated and power-walked themselves into a level of fitness that they had not seen since sixteen, and when they went to the city pool, the self-loathing they'd been taught to feel as teenagers had been replaced by a sexy confidence. Many of them love fucking in a way they have never loved fucking before, and when Claire thinks this to herself, she cannot help but think of Charlie Gulliver, whom she knows she could have fucked that morning, last week, in the pool.

"You look lovely," Ruth says suddenly and Claire feels as if she has been caught doing something illicit. "When I grew up in Minnesota, my mother used to swim, every morning, in the frigid waters of Lake Superior, completely naked!"

Again, a giggle and a sparkle in her eye, and Claire wonders if there is any possible way that this seemingly near-delirious old woman might have seen her swimming with Charlie Gulliver, skinny-dipping just before dawn the weekend before, but she knows where Ruth Manetti lives—Don has been waiting for that particular listing for several years, assuming she'd be dead soon—and there is no way to see Elm Street from Broad. It is impossible; even if she had been on her roof with binoculars, the monolithic science building would have blocked her view.

It's a coincidence.

"Swimming naked with a man, alone, in midsummer," Ruth says, her voice lowering, "is perhaps the greatest pleasure of adult life. Seeing each other come out of the water, slick and cool, smelling of salty sweat."

Another coincidence?

She licks her lips and pulls a cookie from her purse and takes a bite.

Claire has brought a book to the pool and begins to read it, while the old woman dozes off in her chair. She cannot concentrate on the book though, because this is not a pool, really, but a goddamn fucking waterpark, complete with the blare of Top 40 music from megaphonelike speakers near the snack bar. Behind her, Claire hears the thump of a song by Taylor Swift that she'd once caught Don singing in the shower: *You belong tooooo meeeeee*. She smiles thinking about him singing with his unsteady crooning, then watches him flinging himself about the pool again, both of his children clinging to his broad shoulders and back. How could she ever stay angry at such a dork? How could she separate herself from him? No matter how dark her thoughts had been the past week, no matter how mad she'd been at him for his secrets, whatever they were, she'd also been mad at herself, how her own head had been in the sand of her own petty miseries, refusing to see that her family was falling apart and that Don was working himself to near death.

Trying to read again—she'd vowed to finally finish *Anna Karenina* that summer—she hears a mother a few chairs down from her say, "Oh my God, I'm totally gonna tweet that!" and another mother, in a red two-piece, screams, "I'll kill you if you do!" The mothers both thumb furiously at their phones, giving their necks a painful-looking curve downward.

She watches as a group of girls near the slide begin to sing along and dance to a second Taylor Swift number. They kick and scream and make a spectacle of themselves, likely for the benefit of some nearby boys. Behind them stands Wendy, apart from them but watching, sullen, with a huge inflatable tube at her side. Claire has a twinge of regret watching this—her own shyness, her inability to join the chorus lines of laughter that more fun women often share has been passed on to her daughter.

"I like watching your daughter," Ruth says, out of nowhere, again, as if she is reading Claire's mind. "She seems to have more sense about her than most of these kids. Would you call her an old soul?"

Claire, snapped from her trance, says, "Oh, yes. Thank you. I thought you were asleep."

"How can I sleep," Ruth says, "with the inane cackle of grown women posting selfies on Instatweet or whatever the fuck it is?"

Claire howls with such force she clasps her hands over her mouth.

"It's like your daughter—what's her name?"

"Um, Wendy."

"It's like she already understands how much of this is bullshit."

"I hope so. She is kind of an old soul."

"It shows she has a good mother. I wish I had helped my daughters understand bullshit more, but I was only then figuring it out. It was a different time."

"I'm sure you were a good mother."

"I was," Ruth says. "I loved them so much. But I was afraid of telling my kids the truth. I was afraid of scaring them. It gets lonely when you're not honest with your kids. When you try to be something you're not; when you pretend the world is better or simpler than it is. And once you get lonely, you start to fall apart."

"You're not in touch with them?"

"I try to be. But I did something they consider unforgivable."

"I won't ask what it was," Claire says. "But I'm sure it was forgivable."

"It doesn't matter," Ruth says. "Nobody forgives mothers."

"Oh?"

"Fathers get forgiven. A million novels and movies about that—but mothers, mothers die and then the forgiveness comes. If they're lucky, there's a deathbed sort of confession. Maybe they weep over your ashes. That's not what I want."

"You know, you look amazing for your age. Very healthy; there's still time to reconcile."

"I feel like I want to be done with all this," Ruth says. "I want to leave."

"The pool?" Claire says.

"Yeah, you could say it that way."

"Well, my husband could take you home, if you'd like."

"I walked here today. The woman who takes care of me was out doing whatever it is she does on Saturdays, her day off, and I was in the mood to see people. So I walked here."

"You walked here? From Broad Street?" Claire says, scanning the pool again. Bryan shivers in line for the diving board, standing in front of Don, who is standing sucking in his gut and flexing just a little bit, in a way Claire can notice but nobody else would. And Wendy: no longer with the gaggle of kids.

Wendy?

"It's about half a mile," Ruth says. "I barely made it. I bought a Gatorade and then collapsed into this chair."

Claire's close enough to the pool to keep an eye on the kids, though in the crushing throng of a hot Saturday she often loses them. Both of her kids are excellent swimmers, and the hormone-addled lifeguards keep a decent kind of watch on the pool, but she still panics if she scans the pool and can't find them with ease. When her kids were very small, she always refused to go swimming unless Don could come. It stressed her out too much to be solely responsible for their survival.

"Just a moment," Claire says and stands. She moves to the edge of the pool, scans the perimeter, a rise in her heart rate making her face feel flushed, her eyes momentarily blurry. She yells for Wendy.

Then she sees on the steep red slide her daughter rushing in a torrent of water to the pool below. She watches her daughter emerge, smiling, and she heads back toward her chair.

"Sorry," Claire says, flopping down again. "I lost one of my kids for a second."

"It's scary when that happens," Ruth says.

"You've lived in Grinnell a long time?" Claire says. "Right?"

"I was married at twenty, moved to Grinnell that year. My husband was twenty-seven and he had a job teaching history," Ruth says. "We thought we'd come here briefly—he was from Boston and wanted to be farther east, in a larger place, but we ended up having our life here. I dropped out of college at St. Olaf after I met him. He'd been there for a job interview, which he bombed, and I was the waitress at the diner he came into to bury his sorrows in a piece of pie. He ordered three slices of pie in a row and then asked for my phone number."

"Do you regret that?" Claire says. "Marrying young, I mean."

"You mean do I think I wasted my life?"

"No," Claire says. "That sounds much harsher than I intended it to sound."

"I was alive and then I was dying," Ruth says. "Who knows

when that transition takes place? It's different for everyone. And that would have happened anywhere. Everything else is insignificant."

"You started to die when? When you got married?"

"I'll sound terrible saying this, but yes. That's when some people, usually women, start dying."

The loud whistles of the *Baywatch* wannabe lifeguards signal, along with a garbled announcement from the loudspeaker, that it is now adult swim. Claire stands up and sees Don and the kids schlepping toward her. She readies their towels, giving one to each kid, then four quarters apiece to hit the snack bar. When she is handing Don his towel, she finds herself leaning into him as she wraps it around him, giving him a hug that turns into a kiss. She is feeling warmth toward him for the first time in days, and wants to let him know. How easy it is, sometimes, to think of life's simple pleasures.

"You look amazing," Don whispers in Claire's ear. "Amazing."

And for some reason this annoys her, the affection bursts and goes cold.

Don, dry now, exchanges pleasantries with Ruth, then finds the phone in his duffel bag, checks his messages, and, after a few silent minutes, hangs up his phone and says to Claire, "I have to go show some houses. This couple, they're just in town for one day and they've still not found the right place. They decided to up their price range, I don't know, I guess they wanted a real deal—anyway, it's gonna be a good commission if I can show them one of the listings I have in the three hundred thousand range."

"You don't have to explain," Claire says, her nose back in her book. "You tend to overexplain things."

"We could really use the money from a sale," Don says.

"Well, I'm not helping matters any in that department, reading *Anna Karenina* in a new bikini that cost ninety-five dollars."

"You deserve it," he says, though she doesn't believe she deserves it.

"Good luck," she says. "Will you be home for dinner?"

"Most likely. I'll text."

Maybe he could make a big sale that day, earn enough in commission to buy the family some time with the bank. If anybody can pull out a ninth-inning surprise, it is Don Lowry.

"Ruth," Claire says. "Don's leaving. Would you like a ride home? Ruth walked here."

"You walked here?" Don says. "Why didn't ABC drive you here?"

"Who's ABC?" Claire says.

"She's a woman who takes care of Ruth."

"We take care of each other, mostly by staying out of each other's way. And, yes, I would very much like a ride home. ABC loses track of me sometime. She does that. She's in a fog. Some fogs you never get out of, do you?"

5

Sometime in that hot afternoon, Charlie ducks into the ice-cold air-conditioned dank of Rabbit's and finds a beautiful woman, younger than him by a few years he estimates, sitting alone. He had expected the usual midday crowd, which his father had always referred to as the formers: former husbands, former farmers, former athletes, former fair queens, former meth heads, former everything.

She, in this case, he guesses, is a former student: she has thick unwashed dark hair, pulled back into a ponytail, wavy with humidity, fighting the rubber band and springing out behind her. She wears a kind of gray cotton sundress that ties in the back and flip-flops. She has dirty feet and a rubber band around one ankle. She has a beautiful, big smile, full lipped, and her skin is deeply tanned, though he can't tell if it is always dark or if it is from a springtime of sun or if it is simply the dim light in the bar that makes everything seem darker. Her eyes are bloodshot.

"Is this seat taken?" he says, pulling out the stool next to him.

"Yes," she says.

"Well, fuck that guy," Charlie says and sits down.

The woman lets out a whoop of laughter.

"I'm ABC," she says.

"ABC?"

"My initials. You are?"

"CG, I guess. Charlie Gulliver."

"Gill's son? I thought I recognized you from the pictures he used to have on his desk! I think you were a senior in high school in that picture—the framed one, on his credenza?"

"I never knew he had a picture of me in his office on campus."

"Well, he did. How is he?"

"Not good, from what I've been told. I just got back. I haven't seen him yet."

The bartender, Rabbit himself, comes over and asks what they're having.

"Whatever he's buying," ABC says.

"Two Mooseheads," Charlie says.

"No Mooseheads," Rabbit says. "I got Molson."

"Two of those then."

"I heard Gill sort of lost his mind," ABC says. "Is that true? He was brilliant."

"It's a rare form of dementia. Apparently, he has great lucidity one moment and then is totally lost the next. Are you one of his students?"

"I was. I graduated a year ago, lost the love of my life in a freak accident, and came back here to be sad."

"You came back here to be sad?"

"I wanted to be as sad as possible."

"I want to know the story," Charlie says.

"Which one?"

"The one in which your heart gets broken," he says.

"Where to begin?" ABC asks.

"At the beginning," Charlie says. "Because I have no plans for the day or for the next year or for the next forever."

He leans in, and Jesus Christ, he thinks, I'd like to fuck her too. The truth is, he knows, this is when he feels most alive: when a woman is about to fall for him. He looks at ABC, a deep kind of gaze he's mastered in the past year. He thinks it says this: I want to make you happy.

"Are you gonna puke?" ABC asks. "You look like you're gonna puke. Let's get some air."

In college, ABC had come to Grinnell a bit overweight, wearing the same baggy T-shirts and jeans every day. She had oversize glasses and acne. She had been teased mercilessly in high school, the Mexican girls making fun of her bookishness, the white girls making fun of the same. She had never even kissed a boy, and was terrible at dancing and sports. When she had a chance to leave Los Angeles, on a scholarship, she cared nothing about how bad the weather would be and how strange the landscape would seem and how drab Iowa might be compared to where she lived in East L.A. She didn't even worry that it'd be too white—she had met at least five students of color from L.A. who'd gotten the same scholarship she had from some foundation she had never heard of until her acceptance letter arrived. They'd all gone to an orientation together after they'd been accepted. And once, someone from the college had flown out to see them to help them prepare for the transition to college.

ABC cared only about leaving, about fleeing her neighborhood, where she never fit in, the girls at her school boy crazy and fashion crazy and money crazy. And she also wanted to, if she was honest about it, leave her exhausted and often drunk mother, a failed artist/waitress/cleaning woman/substitute bus driver, who took care of ABC and took care of ABC's abuela, but did nothing to care for herself and was now entering the diabetic phase of her rum and Coca-Cola and Catholicism-fueled life.

At Grinnell though, with its clear, clear skies, she met others who wanted to be smart. They devoured scholarly articles and philosophical novels like candy, drank coffee under the trees, and pondered the historical forces that still worked against feminism. They got stoned before attending French films at the Harris cinema. They proclaimed themselves atheists and vegans. They dressed in an eclectic blend of hip grunge; *sexy shlubbery*, Philly had called it. They debated the causes of poverty in America, took a break for Frisbee, and then debated the causes of civil strife in Syria. In the cafeteria over large bowls of ice cream, they discussed the reading for the next morning's seminar. They felt everything so intensely, the strange flattening golden hues of the sunsets in September and the rainbows that appeared almost weekly in the post-shower skies above Old Main. They attended office hours in small groups, bringing their questions and thermoses of tea to intense professors who got almost teary over the students' earnest enthusiasm. They baked cakes for each other's birthdays, they babysat for the children of their faculty advisers, and they alternated between the ravages of smoking, poor nutrition, and sleep deprivation and periods of juice fasts, mindfulness meditation, and workouts at the rec center. It was all so heated and perfect and what ABC loved was that it was no longer shameful to be smart and different and to question everything relentlessly. How weird could you be? Simply as weird as you wanted to be, provided the weirdness was the result of resisting social convention rather than conforming to it. This was the heart of Grinnell. And this was the life she had always wanted, and here it was, before her, a gift.

By the end of her four years of college, it was as if her happiness extended into her physical body. She almost effortlessly lost weight that first year—giving up Coke and McDonald's was easy to do—and she got contact lenses through the student health plan, and her skin cleared up and developed a healthy glow. By her second year, ABC had gone from kissless to making out with half a dozen other students. She went on dates. She liked the heat she could feel between bodies. She liked how everyone tasted different. She had a few bouts of strep throat and one of mono. Still, she savored all of the affection. Her professors liked her and treated her with enthusiastic kindness. They invited her to their homes for dinner with their families. Her female friends confided in her, brought her small presents whenever they traveled, and stayed up late in her dorm room drinking tea and sometimes smoking weed and always spilling their guts. She was secretary of the Latino/a Students Association. They would cook together on Sunday nights and listen to *ranchera* music. She even went to the dances at Harris—twice she had made out with women and found it as pleasurable and more thrilling than making out with men—and found she liked dancing and had a reasonably good rhythmic sense about her. She could work her hips and her newly slimmed legs in a manner that made people watch her and often they would try to dance with her. She'd dance with anybody if they could keep up with her. Who knew? ABC was an excellent dancer!

Philly was her best friend though. It was Philly she often danced with at these events. She and Philly ran in the same social circles, but some weekends the closeness of the campus was overwhelming, and, since Philly had a car, she and Philly would drive to Iowa City or Des Moines, or, if they were feeling more ambitious to Madison or Chicago or Minneapolis. They'd rent a cheap motel room if they had the money and crash in a king-size bed in some Red Roof Inn or they'd stay up all night and doze in parks during the day. One night they slept at a lakeside park in Madison, huddled together in a double sleeping bag, shivering, ABC burying her nose in Philly's chest for warmth—or was it for warmth? Was she trying to crawl inside Philly?

She loved the Midwest instantly, in a way that made her feel like she had always loved it. She loved it for its openness and because it was hers alone and because her mother and the bullies from high school and the teeming crowds of California could not follow her there. She had not sat in traffic once in Iowa. People told her it would be too white, and sometimes it was, sometimes her brownish skin and blackish hair and faint accent would cause some clerk or passerby to ask her where she was from, but then again, she wasn't from Iowa, and so why not ask her where she was from?

Philly said the question was racist; ABC wasn't as sure.

In the same way she instantly fell in love with Iowa, she knew now, she had always been in love with Philly. She loved her from the moment, during freshman year, when Philly had sat across from ABC at a two-top table in the dining hall. They were already roommates, but in the whirlwind of that first week, they had not done much socially. ABC was in orientation with the other Posse Foundation scholars; Philly was busy meeting every fucking student on campus. Left and right, people were falling in love with her.

ABC had been reading a book at lunch one day—*The Stranger*—and Philly had sat across from her suddenly and said, "Howdy, Stranger."

ABC looked up at her, startled.

"The book," Philly said. "Get it?"

ABC smiled.

"How's it going?"

"Fine. You?"

"I'm homesick," Philly said. "Aren't you?"

"God no," ABC said. And Philly laughed. Philly was from Philadelphia. Hence the name. It was her given name; her parents had been in graduate school there and had not planned on staying, but they had stayed. Her mother worked at a museum, her father at a radio station. They were divorced. And Philly grew up with the odd experience of having a first name that was the same as the city she lived in.

"I love that. I love that you're not homesick," Philly said.

"Thank you," ABC said and looked over at Philly's plate. It was nothing but a huge heap of chocolate cake drizzled with vanilla soft-serve ice cream from the giant machines near the dessert table.

Philly looked down at her own plate. "I guess I'm sort of depressed," Philly said.

"Who isn't?" ABC had said and then she did something that was completely out of character for her as a freshman. She set down her book, slid over her tasteless salad, and reached across the table, fork in hand, and took an enormous bite of Philly's cake. When she put it in her mouth, a drizzle of vanilla ice cream ran down her chin and Philly reached across the table with a napkin and wiped it clean.

"I'm so happy to be your roommate, ABC," Philly had said. "I'm so glad."

All of that had happened at Grinnell, here in the middle of nothing, where everything important that had ever happened to ABC had happened and she was never going to leave it, she was never going to go away from it again.

6

Don helps Ruth Manetti into the house.

"Do you want the TV on?" Don says.

"No. No, just quiet is fine. I'm exhausted."

"You overdid it," Don says.

He helps her into the bed, helps her remove her shoes, and gets her some water from the kitchen, a cold bottle of it.

She closes her eyes now and she seems so tired. The air-conditioning is on in the house, and he draws the blinds shut for her, then covers her legs with a quilt that is folded on a chair next to the bed.

"Should I try to find ABC?" Don says.

"Why? For me? Or for you?"

"I have to go to a showing, but, well, I don't think you should be alone."

"Why?"

"I'm, well, you're so tired."

"That's true. I'm also old. Tired is normal."

"And I just don't think you should be alone."

"In case I die? I've been alone a long time now. People are scared of dying alone, but . . ."

"I didn't say that. I don't mean you'll die."

"I'm not afraid of death, Don. Would you bring that book from the desk? It'd be nice to die reading."

Don does. It's an old book club edition of *Madame Bovary*, probably fifty years old.

"You're not gonna die, are you?" he says.

"Not intentionally," Ruth says, "though I would if that were possible. This would have been a nice last day."

"You plan to read?" Don asks. "I can open the blinds then."

Ruth says nothing. She opens the book to reveal a hollowed-out chunk of pages, a square cut out with a razor blade. Inside, a few rolled joints and a lighter.

"I used to love this book, Don," she says. "I used to read it every summer. That and *Anna Karenina*."

"I see."

"Your wife was reading that. *Anna Karenina*."

"Was she?"

"People aren't fair to women, Don. They don't want us to have inner lives after a certain age. They don't want us to have time for it."

"Claire has an inner life. She's a writer."

"It's been over a decade since her last book, Don. I've waited for it. Did you know that? I've read her book. My book club did, at the library, because she was local. Everyone found it depressing but me."

"She's a good writer."

"I don't think she is a writer anymore. I think you think she's a writer."

"Is ABC around?" Don asks. "I could use . . ."

Ruth picks up a lighter from the nightstand.

"Burn?" she says.

"Yeah," Don says, though he has a showing and there's no way he should be here, doing this. "I feel like my life just caught fire," he says.

"That can be good," she says.

He lights the joint and Ruth shuts her eyes as Don tells her all of his troubles—the foreclosure, the funds, the fact that he knows in his heart of hearts that his wife no longer loves him and that it is in the shadow of this unspeakable truth that he must conduct the rest of his life.

"Do you know ABC wants to die?" Don says.

"She thinks she does," Ruth says.

"You don't think she'll actually do it, do you?"

"Kill herself? No."

"You sure?"

"You'll save her, Don. That's why you're here."

"I can barely save myself, Mrs. Manetti. My life is in trouble."

"Every life is in trouble, every minute of the day. Sometimes we are keenly aware of this fact, and sometimes we can ignore it."

Don feels his head lighten from the weed; his hands seem to fill with air.

"I'm not sure how to help her."

"You're here to lead her to something. Back to something."

"What are you talking about?"

"Before Philly died, Philly told ABC that she'd send you. She'd send you to lead ABC to a sacred place where she could be with her again."

"Ruth?" Don says.

"Yes."

"Do you know who I am?"

"You're Don Lowry."

"And you think Philly sent me to ABC?"

Ruth doesn't say anything, he is not even sure if she is awake, and soon her breathing slows and he knows she is asleep. Was she dreaming? Is she senile? He wonders if he should wait there, for ABC to return from wherever it is she is, but eventually Don Lowry knows he must wander out into the summer's staggering brightness and meet with clients, in hopes of making a desperately needed sale.

For a moment, Don Lowry feels invincible: he can make Claire love him again.

"I'm going to go now. I'm going to sell a house today, Ruth," he says, though he knows she is sleeping, "I'm going to make enough money to save everything, including my marriage."

Ruth doesn't open her eyes. She barely moves, but she answers him: "Most marriages are never saved, Don Lowry. Most marriages are just kept afloat. That's much different."

7

They leave the bar pleasantly day drunk and with a mission: ABC will take Charlie to see his father. And soon, they stand outside the assisted living complex at the Mayflower, a sprawling compound of housing for senior citizens settling in for the last breath, some of them hoping it would not come for a long time, and some of them waiting for it, ready to be done with all of this living.

ABC leads him through the door, his hand in hers—it was her idea to come—and she goes to the check-in desk and says, "We're here to see Gill Gulliver."

The nurse, or attendant, or whatever title the thick and frowning woman at the desk is given, looks at Charlie.

"We were wondering if you'd come," she says. "You've been back for a while, haven't you?"

The woman looks at a computer screen, clicks and types, clicks and types, clicks and types again. "Your mother called to see if you'd been yet. She says you should call her."

"I lost my phone," Charlie says.

"He's just had his dinner," she says. "He likes to eat early."

"Dinner?" Charlie says. "He never ate dinner early."

"Dinner is what we call the midday meal. At night, there's a light supper."

"Oh," Charlie says.

"You'll smell some wine on his breath, perhaps. The doctor has okayed that—we do it for alcoholics, you know. To prevent withdrawal," the nurse says.

"He's an alcoholic?" Charlie says.

The nurse says nothing.

"Is he, um, recognizing people today?" ABC asks.

"I just heard," the woman says, "that he was talking a lot at lunch."

"You mean dinner," Charlie says. ABC nudges him with her elbow.

"Right," the nurse continues. "I just looked in on him. He's having his coffee and working. He likes to type away on his laptop in there. But don't look at his screen. I think he knows he is typing nonsense but doesn't want anyone to see. He wants everyone to think he's writing a book."

"Well, that makes sense," Charlie says.

"Room 118," says the nurse. "Have a nice time."

Gill Gulliver, Charlie's father, began teaching at Grinnell College in 1982, four years before Charlie was born. The country was rattled by recession and Gill Gulliver, toting a doctorate in English literature from the University of Michigan, arrived in Grinnell driving an old Ford Fairmont wagon that he'd bought used a week before. He was thirty years old and single.

There were so few jobs that year, but Gill had landed a temporary two-year visiting gig out in the prairies of Iowa. He'd known of Grinnell—a reputable and shakily prestigious (in the Midwestern sense of the word) liberal arts college with a lefty bent. The campus, in August, was beautiful enough, as compelling and green as any campus in late summer, but noticeably flat, and his office in an old brick building, tucked away on the third floor between the offices of an ancient Joyce scholar and a maudlin historian, was the kind of place that a young professor might do a great deal of writing. His goal was simple: to spend two quiet years of teaching at Grinnell, working on shaping his Ph.D. thesis—"The Glamorous Tragedy of Unbridled Optimism: The Fall of Jay Gatsby and the Rise of Ronald Reagan"—into a publishable book.

Gill did not buy a house, but lived, instead, in one half of a duplex owned by the college, a short walk from his office. His routine bordered on the monastic. Each morning, he woke at five, exercised—a vigorous run followed by calisthenics and dumbbell work in the duplex's empty second bedroom—then showered, ate a bowl of oatmeal and a piece of fruit, drank black coffee, and left for the office. He always arrived by seven, the first one to show up on the third floor. He would work on his own book, expanding, revising, and annotating it, until ten o'clock, when he would open his office door and shift into teacher mode. Lines outside his door were long. He was a charismatic teacher, with wild eyes and wavy long hair and a sartorial sense that was often missing in academia. Charlie had seen the pictures and saw them again now, on the walls of his father's study: Gill Gulliver with his first tutorial class; Gill Gulliver with his award-winning independent study students; Gill Gulliver accepting the President's Medal; Gill Gulliver speaking at commencement, the wind blowing his hair and his robe and perhaps even his mustache in a way that suggested something epic.

It was Gill Gulliver's desire for stability, for routine, and for stoically Puritanical work habits, that—after one sexually thrilling and ultimately heartbreaking affair—attracted him to the woman who would become Charlie's mother, Kathy Mulligan. Kathy had, on a few occasions, referred to the "woman Gill would never get over," but Charlie had only overheard such talk in late-night, alcohol-fueled arguments, and he didn't know the full story. Gill Gulliver, by all accounts, had been drawn to Kathy instantly: she was raven haired, complicatedly attractive, and desperately bored, a lifelong Iowan who had spent four years commuting to Iowa City because she couldn't afford the college that was literally in her front yard.

When Gill Gulliver's visiting professorship turned into a tenure-track position, he had the brief idea that he might leave Grinnell anyway, head east or west or at least to one of the more prestigious public land-grant schools of the Midwest, but there were still so few jobs available, and besides, he hadn't finished the book yet, and Kathy had her mother to care for (she was an only child), and so, why not, why not accept a position at Grinnell when they offered him one? He did so, thinking that once Kathy's mother had passed away (her health seemed to be fading; she'd had Kathy late and was already seventy, suffering from a bad kidney and heart disease) and once he had finished his book, had secured a contract for its publication, they could leave. Someone would hire him. After all, he'd been on *ABC News* once and National Public Radio twice talking about Ronald Reagan! He was, in academic terms, a rising star.

They did not leave though. Instead, Gill applied for jobs each year, and failed to secure one. Eventually, Charlie's parents took out a home equity loan, using the paid-for house as collateral, and had gradually built, at the rear of the large lot, a building housing Gill's study and a small guest room. A small kitchenette and a full bathroom connected the two rooms, both of which looked out at an inground pool. On weekends and summer evenings, Charlie remembers playing in the yard, or swimming in the pool, constantly aware of his father's omnipresence at that study window, a massive desk piled with books and papers.

Charlie can still picture his father in the study, a wonderfully comfortable place to work, but Charlie knows well that Gill Gulliver had never pictured that room, which he loved, which may have been his favorite place in the world, as the kind of place that would stand, decades later, as a kind of sad storage unit: packed with all his books and papers and notes and letters and research, a labyrinth of unfinished ideas and in-progress projects, while Gill Gulliver rotted away, half mad, prematurely mad, in the local nursing home.

They go into the room.

Gill Gulliver is in a chair. He types away on a small laptop computer.

When ABC walks in, Charlie right behind her, Gill stops typing. He looks bewildered for a moment and then clasps his hands to his face and says, "Oh my God."

Charlie and ABC walk toward the chair; Gill seems to have no idea of how he might slide his rolling tray table away from himself and stand to greet them. It is as if he is in an invisible prison. ABC turns to see Charlie, his eyes drowning.

"Oh God," Gill Gulliver says again.

ABC stands back while Charlie goes closer to his father. She wonders if she should slip out now. She wonders what Charlie wants. Charlie tries to say something, but the only thing that comes out is a phlegm-crippled *hey*.

"Oh, oh," Gill Gulliver says. "ABC! ABC, it is good to see you. So good! Come here."

ABC goes toward Gill. "Charlie's here too, Gill."

Gill says nothing about that, just stares at ABC in a kind of rapture. She moves the tray table and the laptop and coffee out of his way.

He reaches out to her and she leans in and hugs him for a long time, and then, when she finally lets go, Gill Gulliver looks right at his only son, Charlie, and smiles and says, "Well, who's this handsome man?"

And then turning to ABC and winking, he says, "Whoever he is, he likes you. I can tell."

8

In the haze of a dying afternoon, they walk home across the empty campus. In almost every building, from the original chapel to the shiny new fitness center, ABC can locate a memory of Philly, still burning, like the corner library table where she often sat with Philly, where Philly would sleep more than study, her head in ABC's lap.

What do you do when you can still smell her hair?

Charlie and ABC sit at the kitchen island of the Gulliver house on two metal stools, drinking beers, side by side, and ABC finds herself swept up in some inner turmoil of both grief and urgent lust. Her whole body is a moistening sponge, sweating, ripening, and she presses her beer to her forehead and she focuses on this feeling so she will not cry or moan.

"I should turn on the AC," Charlie says, and he leaps up and does that.

"It's the humidity," ABC says. "Blah! It's too early in the summer to be this hot."

Charlie comes back to his stool, nodding, and says, "I tend to run cold so, you know, sometimes I don't notice it. Maybe I'm used to the stage lights."

"So, how long will you stay in Grinnell?" ABC says. She feels the urge to ask Charlie something easy and concrete, in an attempt to ground herself. She feels as if she's floating. She needs to be distracted from this wave of grief.

"I don't know."

"What's your next role?"

The small talk is almost too much. She wants to communicate in a different way.

"I told you. I'm done acting! Are you okay, kiddo?"

She wipes her forehead, her hands almost shaking. "I can't believe how much I'm sweating!"

"Well, it's hot."

"Right? But gross! Look at me?"

He smiles at her. She feels the beads forming on her face. Her stomach sinks. She is feeling the intensity of her grief as if it is brand new.

"You look good."

"Do you really think you're done?"

"How are you not done after Hamlet?"

"Sometimes I feel like I am finished too. Like after Philly there isn't anything left."

They say nothing for a minute and ABC sort of paces around the kitchen, looking out the windows at the view. Charlie just stares at her. She moves slowly, fingering the sills, and then she whips around and does a little jazz hand move and says, almost singing, "This is when you tell me I have so much to live for, I think."

Charlie smiles. "I can't do that. I don't know if it's true."

"I knew I liked you!" ABC says. "You're the first honest person I've met in a long time. Let's play a game. Let's make a list." She finds a scrap of paper and a pen near the fridge. She notices the scrap of paper is a page from a notepad with Don Lowry's picture on the bottom. *It's your home, but it's my business!* She sees on the fridge that Charlie has already made a list, last item: *Fuck Claire.*

She thinks of Philly, tries not to shudder. "So, what do you have to live for, Charlie Gulliver?"

"Um, well. I'm going to clean out my dad's study and finish my dad's book, you know, get it so it can be published."

"Do you care if it gets published?"

"Ha! No!" Charlie says. "I guess not. But you heard him—I think he still does. I mean, he didn't know who the fuck I was, but he talked about his work. And he remembered you!"

"I was one of his favorite students," ABC says. "And that was less than two years ago. You've been away, what? How long?"

"He always preferred his work."

"You know, it's not weird that he didn't recognize you. Dementia, especially this kind, is so unpredictable."

"Please tell me you didn't fuck him," Charlie says.

"God! No! I was with Philly in college."

"He probably wanted to fuck you."

"Well, he probably did. If I am honest about it. Wouldn't you want to fuck me?"

"Why don't you finish his book for him? Weren't you an English major? He was your adviser, I bet."

"He was."

"There you go! You finish the book!" Charlie says.

"Look, of course it's unfair if his life's work goes unpublished," ABC says, "but it's not a rare thing. How many people die with novels in their drawers? You're under no obligation to finish his unfinished work."

"I'm curious to read it," Charlie says. "For my own sake; I barely knew the guy."

"Why? I don't think you should do it unless you feel it gives you meaning and purpose in the world."

"Oh, sex does that for me. This is just a way to kill time between sexual encounters."

"Funny," ABC says. "Very flirty."

"You think I have nothing to live for," Charlie says. "That's what you're saying."

"I want to be dead by the end of the summer so I can find Philly in the spirit world."

"Seriously?" he asks. "Why do you keep saying shit like that?"

"Because I mean it," she says.

ABC likes the wavering edge in Charlie's voice and the way he pushes his beer bottle back and forth across the kitchen table. She always liked Professor Gulliver a great deal, but had often wondered how strange, perhaps bad, it might be to be his child. She had always been attracted to damaged and wounded souls. Sexually, sometimes, but more often she simply enjoyed being near them, talking with them. Eventually, if the soul was wounded enough, if the soul's bearer exposed enough of themselves, she sometimes fell in love. She could perhaps fall in love with Charlie, if she gets bored enough, and she had always been a little in love with his father, a harmless academic crush.

Also, she is about to be sick with grief. She can feel herself shutting down.

They should do something, ABC thinks, because sitting still is going to lead to a maudlin spiral of epic despair. She goes to the fridge and takes down the to-do list. She picks a pen up off the kitchen counter and crosses out the name Claire at item number 6.

She writes *someone else.*

Charlie smiles. "I was sorta drunk when I wrote that."

"Claire Lowry? She's married. I know her husband. He's incredibly sweet. And sort of sad."

"Not my problem if she wants to sleep with me."

"You're sure she does?"

"That's one unhappy woman," Charlie says. "I knew it the moment I met her. I can make her happy."

"Is that how you felt about Ophelia?"

"Is it weird that I like to make sad women happy?"

"Is it weird that nothing else makes you happy?" ABC says.

"I didn't say that."

"You didn't have to say it."

"You're the strangest woman I've ever met."

"That's a good line. How often do you use that?" ABC says.

He smiles. The man is pretty, she thinks. He can get away with anything he wants. She imagines that Ophelia was the first woman he couldn't make fall in love with him and that it nearly destroyed him.

"Can I see the study?" ABC says.

"I haven't looked through anything yet," he says. "I can't make myself."

"I'll do it with you then," she says. "I can help you get started."

He shows her to the back door and then leads her through the yard to the small structure. They open the door, where the AC is running and a cool blast of air comes at them from amid the stacks and the boxes and the books. The mass of printed matter, wobbly and foreboding, heaps of intellectual detritus, a silo of sundry papers which may or may not be of any interest to anyone.

She looks at Charlie, who has been picking at a mosquito bite on his arm. ABC notes a small speck of blood there and she says, "Look, I was one of your dad's best students. I can help. Do you want to get started tonight?"

"My arms feel so heavy," Charlie says. "My hands feel like stone. I can't explain it. Every time I walk in here, I feel so weak."

"You can sit on the desk and watch me read the files," she says. "Drink beer and I'll guide you through it, okay?"

"I feel like my fucking arms are going to fall off," he says.

Without knowing exactly why she is doing it, without knowing why she suddenly so badly wants to do it, she goes up behind

Charlie and leans into his back, puts her arms around his waist. An embrace. She moves her hands down his stomach, then moves her hands to his belt and undoes it.

"Has it been a long time for you?" she says.

"Mmm-hmm."

"Me too," ABC says. She undoes his fly.

"We just need to do something today," she says. "That doesn't involve talking or thinking or crying."

She leads him, by his belt, to the desk, and she knocks all of the stacks of papers and books and even the pencil holder and sharpener to the floor. "We just need to keep busy."

Then she leans back on the desk and reaches behind her neck, almost as if she is posing for a painting, and then, after a long minute, she says, "There's a knot in my strap," and Charlie comes up above her, presses himself against her, puts his arms around her neck, and with a tug, he undoes the stuck string and pulls down her dress.

She's flooded with desire now, the unmistakable aching rush of someone who hasn't been physical for a long time. She's ready to lose herself in this, and, just as she unzips Charlie, she thinks too that maybe she is doing this for Don Lowry.

9

Claire decides, late that lingering afternoon, that whoever had come up with the expression "a day at the beach" to signify relaxation and ease had not been a parent. They had not had to shout at a sulking twelve-year-old boy about the reason he could not walk home by himself, nor had they tended to a panicked ten-year-old girl who shrieked whenever a wasp was spotted in the general vicinity. Don had had a good time, in the one hour he was present: he was the man to call on for things like waterslides, snack bar runs, games of water basketball with twenty neighborhood kids screaming at him and leaping at him as he groaned like a monster. If it has to do with fun, particularly with fun that required some kind of specialized equipment or horseplay, he can do it. He could always rise (briefly—an hour or two at most) to such occasions no matter how stressed out he was, how sullen his mood. Guilt fueled his enthusiasm; like most fathers of a certain age, he forced himself into joy for the sake of his children.

In fact, Claire has always admired Don's ability to have fun, his capacity to be enthusiastic about life, or at least about the pleasures of recreation. In college, he was the guy playing Frisbee during finals week, or the guy renting a bounce castle for the "All-Campus Welcome Back Ice Cream Social."

But Claire is in charge of the logistics of fun these days, the overall management of it: nutritious snacks to prevent sugar meltdowns, plenty of water to prevent dehydration and heat stroke, bathroom breaks. She breaks up the fights, she forces the children into the shade for more sunscreen, she makes them use the sanitizing wipes before they delve into the trail mix she'd made. She isn't a control freak—her checklist of appropriate safety guidelines is small and insignificant compared to most mothers'. But the children simply fight her on each one of her requests and Don is no help. Every time a child would tell her no, or worse, roll their eyes, Don would look out at the pool as if some phantom sea monster, or perhaps the college students in their small bikinis, had captured his attention.

She'd brought Tolstoy to the pool. Ha! Ha! Fucking ha! She'd brought Tolstoy! Again! Every summer for the past five years, she had planned to read *Anna Karenina*, which her old college roommate, Leslie Mendelsohn, had insisted she read. She'd sent her the copy, the new translation Oprah had picked for her book club. Leslie was active on a Website called Goodreads and Claire received weekly updates on Leslie's voracious reading habits. But Leslie was childless; she lived with a man who owned a summer house on the Cape!

The Cape!

Leslie would often text her: *You should totally come to the Cape soon!*

Claire had never been to the Cape and if she ever did go to the Cape, she'd not enjoy it. She'd be managing the logistics of a trip to the Cape the whole time. She'd fall asleep each evening around nine, in the guesthouse with the children, exhausted, missing even the after-dinner drinks on somebody's deck.

The house is a mess again, and the kids are hungry, and all she wants is a drink and a hammock and a massage. She is sunburned. Her feet are dirty; she also wants a shower. Her hair smells of chlorine and there is sunscreen sticky on her back and grit between her toes and a rawness on the skin near the elastic of her new bikini bottoms. But she can still rock a fucking bikini and she knows it; Leslie cannot.

Fuck Leslie.

Why has she suddenly become so petty? Why does she have such pride in her ability to rock a bikini?

Is it because she does not love Don anymore? Does she secretly want to attract someone new?

She has never had the thought before, or at least she has never allowed the thought to rise into her mind before, and now she stands in the kitchen and thinks: I don't love my husband.

Don comes home from his showings and unloads the truck, sullenly, which means he has not sold a house. His way of helping to unload the truck: he has dropped the swimming bags and wet towels and half-filled cooler in the foyer for her to deal with alone. She stands there regarding his handiwork, half mad at the incompetent attempt he's made at putting things away, but even more mad at herself for becoming the kind of woman who looks at her husband and wishes he was better at putting stuff away. Where did this angry woman come from? How did she emerge, so quietly and swiftly, from some deep, disregarded corner of Claire's personality? Her mother, she knows, years ago had gotten this angry and begun to fuck her way across Manhattan starting on her fortieth birthday. Was there a gene in her family, a switch that blew at forty that made you hate your husband? She knows that one of her mother's lovers had been a millionaire, a day trader who kept Claire's mother in gorgeous clothes, designer shoes, and weekend trysts in great hotels just a few blocks from their home.

Don comes up behind her.

"What are you thinking about?" he says, though he always says this and never really wants to know.

"My mother," Claire says.

"Why?" Don asks.

"How did the showings go?"

"Not great," Don says. "But I'm gonna go and show them one more and I think it's perfect. It won't be on the market until next week, but it's vacant."

"Now?" Claire says.

"Yeah, I know, it's late, but they have a flight back east in the morning. They'd love to find a house on this trip. The guy is starting a job here August first, and the wife is due to have a baby a few weeks after that. So they'll have to buy something."

"I suppose."

"Why were you thinking about your mother?"

"I don't remember," Claire says, and gets to work on the mess at her feet. She makes a pile of clean laundry and a pile of dirty laundry as Don laces up his shoes and looks for his wallet.

"Are you mad?" Don asks her. "Because I have to work tonight?"

"One doesn't get to be Grinnell, Iowa's, top-selling real estate agent five years running without putting in some hours," Claire says.

"That sounds sarcastic."

"Well, I didn't mean it to be. If you feel guilty about going to work, that's not my problem."

"I won't be long."

"Just don't go to your office and drink beer and fuck around online. Just come home when you can. We have to talk."

"Pardon me, but I haven't been Grinnell's top agent since 2008 by drinking beer and 'fucking around' online, Claire. Have you seen my wallet?"

She goes to the table near the foyer, picks up the wallet, and hands it to him.

"I have to do this on my clients' schedule, not on mine. Look, when the kids are in bed, we can talk."

"We have some decisions to make."

"And I think they'll be a hell of a lot easier if I can nab us a twenty-thousand-dollar commission this month."

"Of course," Claire says. "I understand. You are the worker bee. You come and go as you please."

And despite the sarcasm, which feels almost inevitable of late, she does understand. Don works a lot. Long hours, weekends and evenings. And now that he is going out of the house and she will be home alone unpacking the day, trying to put back the chaos, even while Bryan creates towers out of Lego—an obsession he's had since was a toddler—about the house as she does so, she has no idea why she has been so cold to Don about the fact that he is working. She is not working, obviously. She is not writing or earning a fucking dime or even working toward the earning of fucking dimes.

Already, scrubbing out her own wineglass, Claire knows what she will do after dinner. She will take a walk and she knows where the walk will lead her.

10

A few minutes after leaving the house, and a few minutes before picking up his clients at the Comfort Inn near the interstate, Don Lowry texts Claire and says, *Do you want me to pick us up some wine on the way home? Or ice cream or anything?* which is his way of seeing if his wife is still angry with him. She texts back, *Fine. Whatever.* And he texts back: *I'll be home ASAP. Promise.* And Claire texts this: *Good. As I said: whatever.* And to be funny, to try his hand at humor, Don texts, *Whatevs. #YOLO*, to which Claire does not respond.

Don isn't sure if texting has helped his marriage. The tone between them has grown more clipped, punctuated by abbreviations and sentence fragments—though his own parents always talked in fragments, even without the aid of technology. Still, they were at a point where their communications were so swift that Don could not interpret their tone. Is Claire mad that he is working so late? Or does she really not care? Is that rage or nonchalance in her *whatever*? Has she found the humor in his *whatevs*?

What else can he do? He has potential buyers and, in this market, any potential buyers have to be coddled. These buyers have no realtor of their own either, so there will be nobody to split a commission with, and that means over $15,000 if he makes the sale—the house he is about to show will be listed at $280,000. There'd be an actual profit to take home, to catch up on his own mortgage, to pay some of his own back taxes, and to buy the kids some new clothes and shoes and backpacks for the fall.

Don Lowry can do this!

Claire texts back: *Take your time. Even when you're here, you're not here.*

He does not respond to that last text.

In 2005, Don Lowry flipped his first house. And then he flipped three more, and soon he was buying up houses across central Iowa, hiring crews of cheap laborers to give them curb appeal, to fix the most necessary fixes, and then selling them for a tidy profit. In the fall of 2008, as the small town in Iowa was awash in the optimism of Obama's seemingly certain victory, Don Lowry was working on flipping seven different homes. And when the market crashed, when the downward spiral of everything, including the once infallible investment of real estate happened, Don Lowry worked harder. He could still make it, cut his losses. He borrowed some more. He used his credit cards to keep his business afloat. The commissions dried up. A restless nation of movers had suddenly become a terrified nation of stayers.

How much do they owe now? If he doesn't count the house, which is heading toward foreclosure and, barring a late-breaking miracle, a flurry of sudden sales, will soon be the bank's and not theirs, the Lowrys are still firmly up shit's creek. Up shit's creek in a leaky boat, with chronic leg cramps. And dumbbells tied to their feet.

Total debt? It is a figure he has added up in his own mind a hundred times: even if, somehow, he can stave off the foreclosure, they still have a battle ahead of them: six thousand dollars left on her student loans, four grand on his. Twenty thousand on the MasterCard (ER visits and car repairs and dental bills and a serious plumbing emergency and a hundred pizzas and one trip to New York so the kids could see it, but why had they done that?), four thousand on the Visa (a balance transfer meant to tide them over until a commission came through but which somehow never got paid off), five grand on American Express (business expenses, a total creeping up each month), and eleven hundred on the Best Buy card he should never have used, since the interest rate is 20 percent, but how can he work without a laptop and a printer? They owe fifteen grand on each car, though neither car is worth that anymore, not with the wear and tear the Suburban has on it, or the hundreds of thousands of miles he has on his pickup. They'll have to file for bankruptcy after the foreclosure and then, he guesses, divorce: could any couple survive such a terrible financial free fall? If he were a bankruptcy lawyer, he'd find a way to double-specialize in divorce law. How often the two go hand in hand, he imagines.

Even Claire, who really doesn't seem to care about money, will be crushed by such a huge setback as foreclosure and bankruptcy. They are almost forty. Shouldn't they have something to show for two decades of work? Somehow they would be lucky to come up with a security deposit and first month's rent to start over. But maybe they could move anywhere, elsewhere, out of Iowa (though the kids would not like that). It could be a real clean slate. They have to think about the kids though. They could stay in Iowa. Lots of people do that. Millions of them, like four million of them, stay in Iowa, year after year.

There is no shame in it. Why has Claire always resented it?

The prospective buyers, coming now through the lobby of the Comfort Inn & Suites, are a young couple moving to Grinnell. The man has gotten a job at the college in some kind of administrative post. The woman is incredibly pregnant. They are moving from Brooklyn—not the small town just down Highway 6, they joked! The real Brooklyn! Brooklyn, New York. Penny and Clark.

"It's a great place to raise kids," Don reminds them as they get into his truck and buckle up.

"The house or the town?" the man says. He is a man incapable of smiling. He generally has the expression of a mole squinting into the light. A mole that has just sucked on a lemon wedge covered in rat shit. He'd scowled at all eleven showings that day, even when his wife seemed to think a house would work for them.

"Both!" Don says. "Just a great place for kids."

"Well, I hope so," the woman says. She is pleasant and attractive—a short woman with a smile that seems warm and genuine. She speaks with a slight accent Don cannot trace, and when he asks her where she'd grown up, she says Vancouver. She has the sort of smile you might encounter on a road trip, Don thinks, and then a few years later you'd be married to it. A smile that, once directed at you, could own you.

Don wonders how this couple—seemingly opposites—has ended up together. His grimace and her smile seem incompatible to Don. But then, he is sure, there have always been people who think such things about Claire: How did she end up with him? How had he gotten so lucky?

"We're in a bit of a hurry to find a place," Penny says. "Can the sellers close immediately?"

Don nods. "Yep. This is a great house. And it's a great college. Congrats on the job. I'm an alum. Class of ninety-five."

"Really?" Clark says. "You never left?"

"I did leave, briefly," Don says, "but Iowa has its charms. I'll probably be here forever."

Clark turns to his wife and says, "Please don't let me die in Iowa."

"How wonderful!" Penny says, doing that thing Don notices that wives sometimes do. She's being extra enthusiastic on account of a dickish husband. Don knows that drill. He is sometimes the dick.

“We couldn’t find a listing of this house online,” Clark says. “We looked.”

“It’s not for sale yet. It belonged to a very famous professor here, Gill Gulliver. Beloved, dedicated man. It’s a great house.”

When they pull up to the house, Don hopes the front door might be unlocked, because he has not yet been given a key. A lot of doors in Grinnell are unlocked. Kathy Gulliver had planned to list the house in early July, after her son had cleaned out the rest of Gill Gulliver’s study and gone away from Iowa, but she has not listed it yet.

But Don Lowry needs a win.

11

Just at that moment, inside the Gulliver guesthouse, Charlie still hovers over ABC, whose back is flat on Professor Gill Gulliver's desk and whose damp, twitching thighs are still wrapped around Charlie's midsection. At Charlie's feet, on the wide-planked wood flooring of the study, there is a mess of papers, pens, knickknacks, books, and files, which they had swept from the desk in their hurry.

"That's one way to clear off a desk," Charlie says.

ABC, her heavy breathing starting to slow, disentangles herself from Charlie and sits up on the desk. Charlie reaches down and picks up a pair of charcoal gray underwear from the floor. They'd been thrown off onto a couple of manila folders and a copy of Fitzgerald's *The Crack-Up*.

"Jesus," ABC says, dabbing at herself with a tissue and then slipping on her underwear and looking around for her bra.

"Jesus," Charlie says.

"You look worried," ABC says.

"No," Charlie says. "I don't."

"Just, well, I don't expect anything else," ABC says.

"Can we get dressed first?" Charlie says. "Before we do the post-game wrap-up?"

"Gotcha," she says. She seems in no hurry to find the rest of her clothes.

"How about a beer?" Charlie says, and goes to his father's mini-fridge, which his mother had stocked with beers when she'd hired a crew to clean the pool. His mother was always giving cold beers to laborers. This is something he remembers from his childhood, his mother offering a house painter or plumber a beer at the end of a job, and it occurs to him, my God, she must have been so lonely. He cracks the bottles open on the built-in metal opener nailed to a support pole on the guesthouse patio, and comes back with two bottles of his father's favorite beer.

"So, you're done acting," she says. "Tell me more about that."

He hands her a beer and she drinks.

"Wow," she says. "It's like college again. A hookup, a beer from the mini-fridge. You wanna burn a joint?"

"Totally," he says, grinning. She goes to her purse, which is by her discarded dress, and he looks at her body as she does this—it's what you might call a slamming body, in fact, and he finds himself already aroused again.

"Can we smoke in here?" she says.

"Yeah," Charlie says.

"Isn't this fucking awkward?" ABC says and laughs again as she walks over to him, joint in mouth, lighter in hand, and then Charlie gives her a swift sucking kiss on the side of her neck.

"I like you," he says. "You taste a little like chives."

"Is that good?" ABC says.

Charlie sucks her neck again. "Mmm-hmm."

"I cook a lot. And I worked in the garden this morning. So maybe it's that."

They both take two long swigs of beer.

"Tell me the story," she says.

"Which one?"

"So, you played Hamlet and . . ."

She starts to light the joint and he starts to talk.

"I was onstage, and I was thinking here I am, playing the role I've always wanted to play, about an indecisive, overbrained twenty-something who can't trust his mother and can't communicate with his father, and I thought, this is me. I am playing myself."

He accepts the joint from ABC and takes a long drag.

"I love being stoned," she says, after a few more silent tokes between them. She extinguishes what's left with her moistened fingers.

He tells her about Ophelia, about his love for something he could never have, and then Charlie's hands go to her breasts, and he fondles them, and her hands go to his boxers and reach inside.

"Back already?" she says. "By the way, for the record, sadness isn't really a turn-on for women. Could you give that memo to all the arty bastards you know? So stop sulking about Ophelia. Fuck Ophelia."

ABC slides off his boxers. "Maybe you'll help me want to stay alive? What's the line? '*Pull'd the poor wretch from her melodious lay*'?"

"Impressive," Charlie says.

"You're a melodious lay."

"But doesn't that line end with the words '*to muddy death*'?"

"We'll see." She pulls on his neck and kisses him as hard as she has ever kissed anyone, gnawing playfully on his lower lip. "Stay away from Claire Lowry," she growls.

"So you're not a lesbian, I guess?" he says.

"I'm a human being. I have only truly loved one person in my life, and that was a woman. But here's something: man or woman, I don't ever want to fall in love like that again."

Now he is on top of her.

"Don't worry about that," he says. "I'm wholly unlovable."

12

Claire, happily without Don, cracks open one of his cans of Miller, and drinks it down—so light, so cold—in less than a minute. She does not like to think about her parents at all, and when she does, she drinks. After the beer is gone, she opens a bottle of wine, a peppery Zinfandel she buys by the case from the grocery downtown, and suddenly it all feels oddly celebratory. It feels like something she wouldn't have done had Don stayed home, slamming a beer and then opening some wine. She'd have done the chores, put away the schlepped bags from the pool outing. She'd have done the dinner prep, and the bedtime baths and showers, before allowing herself a drink. Wine in hand, she goes downstairs to check on the kids in the basement rec room, watching a stupid movie they probably shouldn't be watching. Nothing terrible, she notes, and what harm does it do, really, to let them watch the movie, a high school special on the Disney Channel with smart-ass teasing of teachers and heavily veiled sexual innuendos between students. When she was Wendy's age, she'd watched *Porky's* at a sleepover. Wendy has heard worse things on the playground, and Bryan is, well, twelve. Already, she'd found a *Maxim* magazine stuffed under Bryan's desk in his bedroom; her Victoria's Secret catalog had been pilfered from the recycling bin the week before. A few weeks ago, she had ordered fifteen pairs of panties because there had been a panty sale advertised on the catalog's cover. She had thrown all her old underwear away, some of which she'd had for over a decade. When the package arrived from Victoria's Secret, Bryan had blushed a shade of crimson that made Claire feel his forehead before she realized what was happening.

She feels too guilty to allow the kids to pass out on the couch, filthy and stuffed with junk food like most American children—she does not have a parenting philosophy per se, God help those who do, but she knows that the average American child would grow up to be a brainless idiot and she wants to fight that with all her being; it's her contribution to the larger project of social justice, she figures.

But when she goes to turn off the television, in a fit of parental moral conviction that will ultimately make her night less pleasant, she feels incapable, suddenly, of enduring the protesting whines.

"You guys okay down here?" she says.

They barely nod in response.

"Okay," she says. "You can stay up late. Just don't bother me or ask me for anything."

Her mother used to say that very phrase when Claire would stay up too late at night.

"Whatever," Bryan says.

"I'm just very tired. And my back hurts. I'm going to have a glass of wine and take a walk. You put yourself to bed tonight."

"No!" Wendy protests. "I'm afraid of aliens."

"Fine," Claire says. "Then go to bed now and I will tuck you in."

"Baby," Bryan says.

"Never mind," Wendy says. "I'll stay awake."

Alone, back in the kitchen, Claire pours a glass of wine and walks around the first floor of the house, surveying the evening cleanup ahead of her. She's fuzzy-minded, her cheeks numb. She steps over piles of laundry and through explosions of Lego; she ignores the tower of pool toys she needs to put away in the foyer and she ignores the plates from breakfast, still stacked in the sink, and beneath those, plates from dinner the night before.

She goes outside, wineglass in hand, and begins her walk. The night has exploded in birdsong and the croaking of spring peepers and the chirp of crickets and drone of cicadas. The light is going out—her marriage, her life, suddenly at a precipice, and the effect of it is dizzying, so dizzying she almost falls, but instead, she straightens up, drops her now-empty wineglass on a neighbor's lawn, and heads toward Elm Street.

13

"I like the house," Clark says. "But it's an odd layout. Many small rooms. No big ones."

"It's from a time before big-screen televisions and sectional sofas," Don says.

"I know that," Clark says.

Fuck this guy, Don thinks.

He turns to Penny. "Are you an artist?"

She shakes hear head no. "God, I wish."

"Well, in the back—you guys will love this—there is an office that could make a great guest suite or an art studio. It has a full bath, a small kitchen, and it's right by the pool. A great guest place for your parents or whoever. They could come and help you with the new baby and have their own place."

"Oh, that's perfect! My mother might stay for the fall, to help."

Clark grunts and goes out the back door into the yard again. Don and Penny follow him and that is when they see Claire, walking barefoot through the grass.

"Oh hi," Claire says as Clark goes to the high fence that surrounds the pool deck.

"Pools cost a ton of money to operate!" Clark says. "Is it in here?"

"Yeah!" Don calls and ushers Penny toward Claire, who is going through the gate. "Penny, this is my wife, Claire."

They shake warmly and Don gives Claire a look that says, quite clearly, WTF, but Claire focuses on Penny and they make small talk.

Perhaps Don Lowry feels the walls of his life collapsing, but he is a professional and he carries on, calmly.

"I have estimates on the cost of removal, as well as estimates on average annual expenses," Don says to Clark, calling ahead of him.

Penny whispers to him, "It's not you, or the house. Clark is under a significant amount of pressure."

Don nods. "It's a challenging time," Claire says.

Don looks at her again. WTF? Claire? Why are you here? They've been married so long he can communicate this without words, with simple gestures.

Claire smiles. "My hubby," she says, employing a word she has never ever used, "is the best at steering people through the stress of relocation."

"Still, my hubby's being a dick," Penny says, as the three of them stand there on the pool deck. Clark makes his way to the office and they all follow.

"You don't deserve to be treated this way," Penny says to Don, though she looks at Claire and then Don feels warmth from his heart, from the deep doubt that is inside him. This is where he got his charisma from, he knows, from the energy it takes to mask all of his self-loathing and doubt. He wants to kiss the greatly pregnant Penny on the mouth. He wants to rub her back and her feet and coach her through her coming labor.

"What the fuck?" Clark says, and then there is someone else saying, "Get the fuck out of here," and then the scream of a woman and they all rush to the door, to find ABC on her knees, scrambling for her clothes, Charlie, covering his bare crotch with his hands the best he can, and Clark staring, mouth ajar, as Penny averts her eyes and Claire looks as if she might pass out.

Once things calm down, once towels are secured for both Charlie and ABC, Don Lowry extends his hand to the younger man in front of him, a tanned and lean man with six-pack abs and a mess of dark curls atop his head. He is about Don's height, and wrapped in his white towel, he almost looks like a version of Don's former self, after a football game, freshly showered, smiling with the kind of clueless invincibility and vitality that begins to leave everyone, slowly, after the age of thirty.

"Don Lowry," he says. "Jewel of the Prairie Real Estate."

"Of course," Charlie says, shaking his hand back. "Charlie Gulliver."

"Your mom said you'd be here soon," Don says. "But I am sorry, I had no idea you already were here."

ABC, wrapped too in a white towel, says, "Hello, Don."

Don says nothing.

"Who is this?" Claire says, and both Charlie and Don say, "This is ABC."

ABC adjusts her towel so that it hangs lower on her body, covering more of her upper thighs, but less, Don notices, of her breasts, which he cannot stop looking at, which makes him feel incredibly foolish, and then he looks at Claire who is not looking at him, but at Charlie, maybe with the same kind of lust in her heart, he can't be sure, and he says, "Claire, this is Charlie," and Claire says, "Of course," and reaches out her hand to shake just as Charlie looks at Don with a smirk—could the fucker really be smirking?—and says, "We've met."

"You have?" Don says.

"You have?" ABC says.

"We have," Claire says.

"I'm ABC," ABC says, and extends a hand to Claire.

Claire shakes it, silently, and looks at Don.

"Hi," Don says, to ABC, but looking at Claire, and so they sit, and Don Lowry feels a kind of agony flare within him, and his chest pulses with it.

But Don Lowry is a professional, and Don has just committed a professional faux pas.

"I'm very sorry, Charlie," he says. "I had no idea you were back home. It's just, Penny and Clark here are on a tight schedule, and this house seems perfect, plus your mother said, you know, if I had a buyer, I could let myself in . . ."

She hadn't really said that to Don, of course, but Charlie seems to buy it.

"Well, I'm back," Charlie says. "But looks like my bare ass scared off your buyers."

Don looks behind him, and sees that Penny and Clark have gone. He excuses himself and goes to the front yard, where Clark stands at the end of the driveway on his phone, and Penny looks up at the house from the sidewalk.

"He's trying to call a cab," Penny says.

"It's Grinnell. There are no cabs. I'll take you back to your hotel."

Penny places her hand on her rounded stomach, and Don looks down at her hand, the shimmer of a massive engagement ring and a gold wedding band.

She starts to cry.

Clark is looking at his phone now, yelling at it.

"I'm very sorry," Don says. "That was probably stressful for you, and I didn't have any idea someone would be home, let alone two people screwing by the swimming pool."

Penny begins to cry. "They weren't fucking," she says, with this kind of laugh that crumples into tears. "She was blowing him!"

Penny screams with laughter.

"We'll walk!" Clark bellows at her, and begins storming away down the street. "Fuck off, Don Lowry!"

Most of the neighborhood will have heard that, and for a moment, Don imagines everyone on Elm Street coming out to their porches to echo the sentiment. "Fuck off, Don Lowry!" they would call over their rosebushes and from the edges of their swept driveways and from the balconies off their second-story master bedrooms and from the workshops in the garage. The whole city gradually coming to realize what an asshole Don Lowry, lifelong Grinnellian, truly was! "Fuck off, Don Lowry."

Clark makes it two blocks and then he turns and they lose sight of him. Penny is crying now and Don touches her arm as tentatively as one can touch an arm and says, "I'll drive you back."

"He's very stressed out," Penny says.

"Moving is stressful. New babies are stressful. New jobs are stressful," Don says. "I've done all those things. Sometimes you snap."

"It's not his baby," Penny says, when they are in the truck, and on the short drive to the Comfort Inn, she tells him everything, about a man she worked with, whom she loved but who did not love her, and how she and Clark had been having trouble conceiving, and how she had conceived the baby with the other man, but had only told this to Clark a week before.

In the circle drive of that depressing hotel, she says, "I'm a terrible person," which reminds Don Lowry of something his own father said years ago, to which Don Lowry's mother had said, "Yes. I think you are."

But he says something different to her, because he doesn't think she is any better or worse than anyone else he knows.

"We're all terrible people," he says. "Eventually, we all become terrible, maybe around the middle of our lives, and then, if we're lucky, we have time to find a way to be good again."

"Do you really believe that?" she asks.

"I just thought of it," he says. "But yes. Yes, I think that's true."

He drives around a bit, windows open, the heat of the long day turned to a breezy dusk. He is not sure what to do next. Eventually, Don stops off at the Hy-Vee for beer. He buys a twelve-pack of decent beer, Stella Artois, for Charlie, an apology. He buys a twelve-pack of cheap beer for himself, Miller High Life Light, because he is broke, and a six-pack of root beer for the kids. Next he stops off at the Pizza Hut, and buys two large Hot-N-Ready pizzas. Moving through downtown, he sees Clark, sitting on a park bench, his head in his hands. He pulls over, breaks open the twelve-pack of Miller, and comes out of the truck holding the beer, which he hands to Clark without a word, and then gets back into his truck and drives away toward home.

Home, he finds his kids watching television in the cool basement, a movie about a soccer-playing dog, and sets down one of the two pizzas in front of them, along with the root beer, a development they cheer.

"Thanks, Daddy!" Wendy says, and leaps up with a hug so swiftly it nearly knocks him over. He feels as if his bones are made of melting ice, and he starts to cry, so he heads for the stairs before the children notice it. From the stairs he calls out, "Is your mom home yet?" to which Bryan says, "No!" and to which Don says, "Really? Still gone? Well, Bryan, you're in charge. I have to do one more errand! I'll be home soon."

"What are you doing?" Bryan says. "What's the errand?"

"Just a thing."

"You and Mom are always coming home and then going back out," Wendy says.

"Well, we're busy," Don says.

"It's stressful," Wendy says.

He drives slowly across town, a zigzag pattern around the

campus. It is dark now. The remaining pizza is hot, but not as hot as it should be for an apology pizza, and he laughs at the phrase *apology pizza* and thinks of what a good business that could be, a website that facilitates the ordering of pizza anywhere in the world, to be delivered, paid for, to the address of your choice. Fight with your grown children? Send 'em an apology pizza! Insult a colleague on a different coast? Apology pizza! Awkward Skype session with a former lover? Apology pizza!

He moves through the backyard, coughing loudly as he hauls the pizza and beer. He doesn't want to surprise ABC and Charlie again. He has to set down the beer and pizza to unlock the safety gate of the tall cedar fence, and when he opens the gate awkwardly he sees all three of them, ABC and Charlie and Claire, sitting at the table, drinking beer. There is a bottle of tequila on the table, and a bowl of limes, and a shaker of salt.

Claire is smoking a cigarette with her feet up. You can see right up her dress.

"Why, Don Lowry," ABC says, "you brought us pizza, and just in time. I'm ravenous!"

And then Claire stands up, a feat that requires some effort, it seems, as if the pool deck is spinning and swaying beneath her. She pulls her sundress over her head and hurls herself into the pool.

That night, when they get home and find the kids asleep in their clothes as an R-rated movie flickers on the television—a woman is being chased by a gun-wielding maniac—half-eaten pizza and empty root beer bottles littering the couch around them, Claire says, "We're terrible parents."

"Touché," he says.

Years ago, when the children were small, Wendy barely two, they'd been having a whispered fight—trying to argue without waking the children. Claire had used the word *touché,* and Don had never known what that word had meant: he thought it meant fuck you in French, some misinformation he'd learned in middle school and had never, somehow, corrected. He raged when she said that until, after some painful conversation, she finally explained to him, with the aid of a dictionary, what *touché* actually meant. Their fight, that night, had ended in laughter. Actually, she remembers now how it ended: they had gone into the laundry room, which had a lock on the door to keep the kids away from the chemicals they stored there, and they had fucked against the washing machine as it whirred a load of cloth diapers clean. It had been an almost angry fuck, the two of them violent and loud with each other and she had come harder than she'd ever come in her life, feeling him explode inside her. She made him do it again to her, finding newfound freedom in a room with the white noise of a washer and dryer and a bolted-shut door. For a while, they'd find each other in that room almost nightly. She thinks about it now—and misses him.

Once they have half carried, half nudged the kids up to their beds, she undresses and slides on one of his T-shirts and finds him again on the deck outside. He has cleaned up the pizza and the root beer bottles and has straightened up the pillows on the downstairs couch and is now sitting outside in a deck chair, drinking a beer.

"God," Claire says. "I was pretty drunk. I'm sorry."

"It's okay. It was a fucked-up day."

"Fucked-up summer."

"It's a small world. I didn't know you knew the Gulliver kid."

"Well, I knew Gill. I remember Charlie from some of the plays he did in high school, the year we first moved here. He was in a few things."

"And you remembered him?"

"He was good. Memorable enough, and he was Gill Gulliver's son, you know, so . . ."

"I always thought Professor Gulliver wanted to fuck you. I hated him."

"He wanted to fuck a lot of people," Claire says.

"I fucked him," Don says. "Still got a B."

They both begin to laugh, silent laughs that make them shake and tear up a bit, because it is the kind of laughter one engages in when everything else feels hopeless.

"We're broke and we're smoking pot with twenty-year-olds," Don says.

"Like twenty-nine is more accurate," Claire says. "In Charlie's case."

They laugh some more, but Don gets sullen.

"They are so young and beautiful," Claire says. "Do you remember us like that?"

"Claire, I still see you as young and beautiful. It doesn't change for me."

"You're sweet. But it changes."

"We're so fucked. I totally didn't make that sale."

"The house isn't supposed to be shown yet, Don."

"How did you end up there?"

"I was on a walk, Don. I saw your truck. I thought maybe I could help make a sale."

"Yes, here is my depressed wife who hates living in Grinnell. Would you like her to help you with this major life decision?"

She moves closer to him, sitting on his lap.

"No matter what happens," Claire says, "I can always forgo underwear to save money. As I am doing right now."

"You never have wanted to help me make a sale," Don says. "Why today?"

"We need it."

"And what do you mean 'no matter what happens'?" Don says.

"Don," she says, "stop talking."

She runs her hand along his thigh. He's gritting his teeth and looking away. She knows the look. They have been in love for a long time, and she can tell when he is resisting without resisting. Don Lowry, like all men, wants to be desired. Nothing is sexier to him than a woman coaxing him gently, begging him. She's played the role before. She knows the terrain. In fact, Don Lowry's really the only sexual terrain she knows, a thought which has always comforted her, but, sometimes, if she's honest about it, also terrifies her.

"See," she says, taking his hand and running it up her thigh, under the T-shirt. She leads his fingers to the moistening warmth under the T-shirt, and sighs in his ear. He responds. He begins to touch her. "No underwear, no problem. That's like sixty bucks a year right there."

"The kids," Don says. "They're asleep?"

"Exhausted," Claire says. "They'll sleep forever."

She lets out a low moan in his ear, moves her hand to the front of his pants, feels him hardening there and moans in his ear again. "What I want is for you to fuck me right here," she says, "but someone will call the police when I come, because I will scream."

"Claire," Don says.

She knows he is turned on, can feel and sense that, but she knows he has trouble responding to her dirty talk. She has to keep going forward. It has started, almost, this sex, as an act of pity, of habit, but now she wants him, and maybe it is true that she wants anyone and he's the only one here. Maybe she wants him to be Charlie. She pushes that thought out of her mind, rubs him through his pants again, and thinks of seeing Charlie naked, swimming toward her.

"I'm going to go downstairs," she says. "Join me?"

"Okay," he says, finally smiling. He stands and she follows, pressing herself into him as they make their way inside.

"I know this is all very sudden," she whispers.

"What do you mean?" he says.

She buries her face in his neck. She does not acknowledge, even to herself, that the neck that flashes in her mind is Charlie's and not Don's. "I mean, we just met at that party tonight, but I liked watching you swim. Have I told you my name? It's Claire."

"I liked watching you too," Don says, finally catching on to her game, and having the same flash, too much to acknowledge, of ABC, and her breasts, and how they would have moved when she dropped her towel. "I've noticed you at soccer practice before too, actually."

"You have kids?"

"Home sleeping," he says.

"You left them home alone! What a terrible father!"

Don shrugs. "You should meet their mother. She does it all the time. Total slut."

Claire laughs. In her private thoughts of late, in the fantasies she has entertained on an almost hourly basis so far this summer, she is insatiable, fucking Charlie Gulliver, and other men too, in showers and pools and on the desk in Charlie's father's desolately cluttered office.

"We'll go to my place," she whispers. "So I can be loud. My kids are staying with their father tonight."

They go to the basement, locking the old child-safety lock they had put up high on the door years before, when Bryan was still a toddler and Don and Claire had been remodeling the basement and worried he'd get into the power tools and paints. Now they lock it behind them and know they are safe. On the staircase, she undoes his pants. Don kicks aside a pizza crust someone has dropped there, but they both pretend not to notice.

He takes off her T-shirt. "Sit down, on the steps," he says and she does as she is told. It's been a long time since he's told her what to do. She likes it. He begins to move down her body with his mouth, and she puts her legs up on his shoulders, and when he finally fucks her there on the staircase, silent the whole time, she shudders in a way she has never shuddered before, scratching his back, kicking her legs, and finally biting on his chest so hard she leaves a huge welt.

Afterward, still entangled on the floor, damp with sweat, torsos twined together, Don says, "Did you? With him?"

Claire pushes herself up and Don runs his hands down her back, clutches at her hips.

"No. Did you? With her?"

"No," Don says.

"Isn't it weird?" she says. "I'm not sure I'd even care."

"It might even be hot," Don says.

"We've been married a long time," she says. "You never know."

She takes his hand and leads him down the rest of the stairs, both of them still naked in the easy way of two people who've been together so long it makes no sense to be modest. Everything has already been seen, every circumstance has been played out. Hasn't it?

It's done, Claire thinks as they fall asleep, spooning.

I'm done.

In the morning, they shower in the downstairs bathroom, get clean clothes from the dryer in the laundry room, and come up the stairs to find the kids in the kitchen, eating Rice Krispies.

"Why was the door locked?" Bryan says.

"Was it?" Claire says. "I don't know. I must have done it out of habit."

"You sleep in the basement now?" Wendy asks.

"But you never lock doors," Bryan says. "We almost called 911."

"Gotta go, Team Lowry," Don says, looping around the table once to kiss each kid atop the head. "I'm late."

Only Wendy is delighted by this, only Wendy kisses him back, a wet, milky kiss on the cheek. Bryan rolls his eyes.

Don kisses the side of Claire's neck before he leaves.

Already, Claire wonders if it has been a mistake, the erotic abandon of the previous night. It has confused the issue, of course. Don would come home from work and try to get her to stop talking separation, to, as he would probably say, "stop the shenanigans." He was a big shenanigan stopper. It had become one of his favorite phrases as a father.

He would think that everything was better, that separation, that divorce, was off the table.

Now, with her wet hair slicked back, feeling Don still, somehow, on her neck, inside her body, she makes scrambled eggs to supplement the shitty cereal the kids are eating. The kids, groggy, have gotten their own glasses of orange juice and sit at the table in sleepy silence, having stayed up way too late the night before. Now, as they eat breakfast, they're reading books. Both of them like to read, and Claire does not allow any "screen time" before the sunset during the summer, so they always have books going. They go to the library every week for more books. They can walk there, even, by themselves now, and Claire suddenly, that very morning, is amazed that her domestic life is changing so much, so swiftly. She feels both liberated and adrift.

By the time the kids have devoured the breakfasts she's made for them, the kitchen is a disaster, and the brief infusion of liberation dissipates. She misses Don in a way she hadn't wanted to miss him. How can she even imagine a life without him? She feels guilty for the thoughts she had while falling asleep.

Years ago, when she and Don first started having sex, she would feel the same way after he would slip out of her dorm room in advance of an arriving roommate or an early class. She would feel alone in a different kind of way than she had ever felt before and it terrified her.

We can get through this, she thinks.

No, she thinks. We can't.

What's happened to us? she thinks.

Whenever she thinks of them as *us*, thinks of them as a couple, one image stands out in her mind. It is of them at a wedding, about six months after Wendy was born. They are sleep deprived, both a little out of shape: Claire's still-nursing breasts swelling from a thin-strapped sundress that is too tight across her stomach, and Don is fleshy faced and beer gutted, unused to the slower metabolism of an ex-athlete. They do not look as good as many of their college friends at that wedding—they lack the suntans and new clothes. Broke, they have not been on a summer vacation, nor have they purchased stylish, better-fitting clothes. But they have left the kids with Don's sister for the night, and they are alone in a hotel reception room in downtown Minneapolis, and they are slow dancing. Claire, barefoot, because her heels were killing her, and Don, covered in sweat from the rowdy shaking he'd done on the dance floor earlier. But now she drapes against him, feeling how strong he is, feeling, as they pressed into each other, all of that history, the bond of all of those years they have spent together, growing up. She leans up to him. She kisses him on the mouth—she is not much for public displays like that, but kisses him long and deep, holding him tight, feeling his heat, his strength, those muscles still present under the new flesh. "Wild Horses" is playing. Don, boozily and off-key, begins to whisper-sing the lyrics in her ear, a bad Mick Jagger singing, "'Couldn't drag me a-wa-a-a-a-ay.'"

She remembers it that morning, remembers even how he had one hand on her ass and the other on her hip, and how he squeezed her hip as he whispered to her. When she thinks of them, together, if she admits it, if she is not afraid of any sentimentality and the vulnerability that might imply, she will think of that moment and say, *That's Don and me. That's totally us.*

And then, the answer comes to her, too clear: perhaps we aren't us anymore.

PART III

And at once I knew, I was not magnificent.

—*Bon Iver,* "Holocene"

1

You bring your parents into your marriage. You don't mean to do it, but one day, you amble into what Dante calls the dark wood, midway along the journey of your life, and you find them there, waiting to participate in your miseries. You might say to them, "No, thank you," but they will lurk in the woods anyway, casting shadows, and all that you do will be haunted by them from that moment forward.

This is what Claire believes and this is why, a week later, she says to Don, "We're not going to do this the way our parents did."

"Do what?" Don says. He's washing dishes—having made pancakes and bacon for the third morning in a row, as if the festive breakfasts of summer vacation might help his children not notice the serious cliff the family is about to fall over.

Claire is opening a carton of packing tape and tape guns and Sharpie markers that she has ordered online. She is switching into moving mode, the challenge of it helping to mute that sadness of it all, and she understands what she is doing when she makes a checklist a mile long and pins it to the bulletin board by the fridge. She is letting everyone know that she is in charge; she is the general of this expedition. It feels almost good.

"I called your mother and had a talk with her," Claire says. "I told her everything."

"Everything?"

"Yep."

The kids are out in the backyard with neighbors, running through the sprinkler. It's almost ninety degrees out and not yet ten A.M.

"You told her about how you skinny-dipped with a guy you just met?"

Claire assembles a tape gun.

"Yep. And I told her how you got high with a college girl and slept next to her all night."

Don sets down the dish brush.

"What?" he says.

"And then how we got home from our skinny-dipping party last weekend and fucked each other senseless all night in the basement, stoned and drunk, while our kids slept upstairs."

"Claire, come on."

"And how every chance I get I go and see Charlie and it makes me feel good to talk to him, he calms me down, he gets me, he understands where I am at, that I am sick of striving, of staying afloat, and that you get so jealous you leave the house if I have left before you and you go smoke pot with a girl who likes to smoke pot with a middle-aged realtor for God knows what kind of daddy issues, and I also told your mother that you have gone crazy and you are in love with your own misery more than me and—"

"Claire, Jesus. The kids," Don hisses.

Wendy has just walked into the kitchen.

"So, no, Don, I didn't tell her everything," Claire says, lowering her voice. "What do you want, Wendy?"

"Um, can we have Popsicles now?" Wendy asks.

"No, you just had breakfast!" Claire shouts. "Get out!"

"After lunch," Don says. "After lunch, baby."

"Everyone wants them now. The Hellengas are over and they didn't have breakfast!" Wendy protests.

"They're not cheap Popsicles," Claire says. "They are the good ones. And we can't afford fruit pops for the whole town anymore."

"Here," Don says, going to the freezer and getting out the fruit pops. He hands Wendy the box. "Wendy, here. Go play."

"Are you guys fighting?" Wendy asks.

"Go play," Claire says.

"No, we're not fighting, Wendy," Don says.

Wendy rushes out the back door, but not before stopping, turning around, and shooting them a burning, accusatory glare.

"This is what we're going to avoid. These moments in front of the kids. I told your mother about the foreclosure. I told her we were separating."

"We can't even afford lawyers."

"I told her that we need a few days alone. That is all I told her."

"The kids hate going there," Don says.

"We need a few days to regroup, make a plan, and then when the kids come back, we'll present them with a cool, calm, and optimistic plan for the family."

"What?"

"For moving. Or something bigger. I don't know. I'm confused."

"They're bluffing," Don says. "We won't lose this house. I know everyone involved. I played football with the sheriff. I was a pallbearer at the bank president's brother's funeral. I have ties here, Claire. People aren't going to throw me under the bus. I'm Don Lowry."

"Us under the bus," she says. "Us. It's not just your battle, it's ours. You're not fucked, we're fucked."

"Right. Whatever."

"The letters have been quite clear," Claire says. "As of July first, Don, it's no longer our house."

"Let me come up with something."

"You have twelve days, Don! Even if you sell a house, you won't get the money in twelve days. It's over."

"So why do the kids have to leave tonight? Shouldn't they get to enjoy the last two weeks in our house?"

"Don," Claire says. "We need to spend some time talking. I know you fucking hate talking. I know you'd rather die than talk to me about anything real, Don, but we have to find out what we need to do and do it. We need a place to live, we need to pack, and we need to figure out what each of us is going to do for a job starting next month. I just applied at the dining hall to work summer conferences. It's temporary, but with all the students gone, they need the help."

"You're gonna wash dishes in the dining hall?" Don says. "Claire, you used to teach here. You were a visiting professor! You can't wash dishes."

"Sure I can. Lots of writers and artists take menial jobs when things are slow. I haven't published a book in over a decade, Don. I'd say things are pretty fucking slow."

"And you want me to take a second job too? Because real estate is slow."

"I think so. I think you have to do that, Don."

"I am, of course, willing. I could probably get a job at the hardware store."

"Good! Now we're talking about real life—doesn't it feel sane?"

"It feels sad."

"Admit it, Don. You like to feel sad. For so long, I thought you were sad at home because your life is hard and you work too hard and your childhood was fucked up—but now I see things clearly, after spending time with someone who is actually happy. You like being sad, you sick fuck, you give the world your jokes and your smiles, and you bring home your sadness! And you make me sad!"

"Who makes you happy? Charlie Gulliver? What the fuck is going on, Claire?"

Claire leaves the room and Don goes back to the dishes, washing the electric skillet and drying it with an old kitchen towel, one of the kitchen towels they'd bought at the Ikea outside Chicago after they'd bought their first house. Why Don thinks of this, he doesn't know, but he also remembers walking through the never-ending housewares section at Ikea, following Claire, who was wearing this simple black cotton tank dress and flip-flops, and he remembers wanting to go home, he was so done with the endless shopping and he wanted to head back to Iowa. His mother was watching the kids and she would be getting tired.

He rounded a corner and saw Claire, who looked over her shoulder and then lifted her dress nonchalantly so he could see the thong she was wearing. She did a little curtsy like that, in front of a display of spatulas, and later, they went into the family restroom, and fucked leaning against the sink, him behind her, her panties down around her ankles, his pants falling down his thighs. She was so flushed afterward, her whole chest and neck and face stayed bright red until they checked out, and well after that, and Don's thighs burned with exertion and excitement. They ate two soft-serve ice-cream cones on the way out to the parking lot, both buoyed incredibly, spirits held aloft by the important milestone: it was the first kinky thing they'd done since they'd had babies.

"So, I'll take the kids around four, I guess," Claire says. "I'll probably swing by Trader Joe's, since I'll be in West Des Moines anyway, get us some easy frozen food for the week of packing. We won't feel like cooking, but it'll be cheaper than ordering in."

Don nods.

"Are you listening?" Claire says.

"I was thinking of that trip to Ikea," Don says, "when we bought these dish towels."

"Don."

"Are you in love with him?" Don asks.

"Don. I told you. I haven't fucked him," Claire whispers. "Please stop."

"I didn't ask if you fucked him. I asked if you were in love with him," Don says. "Tell me."

Already, she knows she will soon crush his big, complicated, shadowed heart. She wants out. But he never will want out. He is too Midwestern, too stoic, too hardworking to quit on anything. Wild fucking horses wouldn't drag him away.

So she says yes. "Yes, Don. I'm in love with him."

She watches a shadow come over his face.

2

The son of Russell Lowry, maintenance engineer at the Maytag plant in Newton, and Annie Dobrow, a part-time nurse at Grinnell Regional, Don Lowry had, until he was twelve, a happy childhood. He was good at sports—the boys in Iowa were divided, roughly, into the jocks and the 4-H kids (the ones who won ribbons for pigs at the fair)—and this made things easy for him. He was well liked by his pals before puberty, and also well liked by girls after it. He had a near photographic memory and enjoyed reading, so school was not a problem for him. It was rare that he did poorly on a test or a quiz; he never had to worry about studying.

At first, Russell Lowry was distant in the way all fathers were distant back then: he simply worked and came home. Nobody paid him much attention. You had to be quieter when he was home, but that was about it. The wick of his temper was a short one, and once lit, he could be angry for days, though a young Don associated this with maleness rather than mental instability. He assumed all fathers yelled, the way he assumed all fathers got so drunk on Friday nights that they often fell asleep in the foyer, shoes and coat still on and the door half ajar, letting in the cold.

*

On Saturdays, while Russell's wife, Don's mother, picked up a shift at the hospital, Russell, no doubt hungover, did maintenance work on the house—lawn mowing, snow clearing, roof fixing, lightbulb replacing—all with a cigarette hanging from his mouth and slugging, between chores, scalding coffee from a singed pot. On Sundays, he went to the Catholic church with his family for the ten o'clock mass and joined the family—Don had a sister, Rosie—for a lavish Sunday supper at two (after, he always washed the dishes, "So your mother can rest," he'd say). He attended all of Don's baseball games, all of Rosie's piano recitals, and church. He ate dinner with the family every night (except for the aforementioned Fridays). He hunted birds on occasion and went up to Minnesota for four days every deer season but never seemed to kill a deer. This was all rather standard behavior for that time and that place and Don never wondered about it. It was what dads did. He had no reason to try and understand it and he certainly never asked questions about his father's happiness or stability.

And then the Shadow came. This is how Don's father described it, years later, maybe nine years later, when he had already made up for his mistakes the best he could, which was not all that well. The mistakes were rather straightforward: Don's father had started to drink too much, and not just on Fridays, which heightened his temper, and had begun to spend more and more of his time at the bar. The family fell behind on its bills because Russell began to spend liberally. When he was home, Don's father was misery personified: no longer simply a tired and mildly dissatisfied dad, but a brooding, snarling wreck in front of a blaring television, the floor at his feet littered with crushed beer cans. His kids were older by then—Don was twelve, Rosie was ten—and it seemed as if they were well on their way to being fine human beings. Impressive on some levels, even, which was something Don's father might express in his rare moments of clarity. They'd be fine without him, he used to tell them, somewhere around that time, because he was going over a dark edge and would soon fail them completely. He knew this with a sharpness and fatalism that, in hindsight, was chilling to Don. It was chilling how he spoke about his coming crash with an almost prescient vision.

Don's mother had started to work full-time at the hospital when the Shadow arrived. Though this was no reason for Russell to do what he did. But he did it: he began an affair with a married coworker, a fellow drunk, an assembly-line worker named Dottie Good, fifteen years his junior and married to one of the meanest men who worked at Maytag, Matt Good. Dottie and Russell left at lunch for a quick beer at Porter's Stop, something they'd been doing regularly now that they'd bonded over their addictions. This was a small tavern near the factory, and one afternoon, Russell and Dottie got a little carried away. The Shadow never seemed to follow Russell to the tavern. Soon, Russell and Dottie, laughing, staggering in the dusty heat, found themselves six beers in and entangled in lusty sweat in the back of Dottie's Dodge Omni, parked behind some Dumpsters. When Matt Good came in after his shift, about two in the afternoon, he must have been wondering why his wife had ditched work again and went to look for her car. He found Russell undoing his wife's bra, taking her big breasts into his dirty hands.

Matt Good had a pistol in the glove compartment of his truck, and within sixty seconds that day would become the day that Matt Good killed his wife, and then killed himself, but for some reason he spared Russell Lowry. According to bystanders, including Russell Lowry himself, Matt Good had, before taking his own life, said to Russell, "You got kids. So I can't. But you're a bad man. You're a fool. And this blood is on you."

And then the final shot of the pistol went into Matt Good's own mouth. The sirens were already wailing by then.

Don Lowry was twenty-two when he went to see his father

one afternoon after the final classes of his college career. Russell was living alone then, in a rundown apartment in Gilman that was next to the gas station. Don had just finished his fourth year. He'd driven out to Gilman to invite his father to his graduation. His father was still a drunk, disabled by alcoholism, and he stayed alive on meager disability checks and some handouts from his corn-farming brother and Don's mother. Don almost never went to see him; it just wasn't expected. Russell had never met Claire, for instance, whom Don had been dating since freshman year.

"Aw, Donnie," Russell said. "It's not for a guy like me. I wouldn't know what to do at it."

"It's not that fancy, Dad," Don said.

"I know it," Russell said. "I went one time when your cousin Buster graduated from there."

"See?"

"It's just—I know I couldn't do it," Russell said. He was drinking from a pint of Jim Beam.

"Couldn't stay sober for one morning? It's in the morning. Ten o'clock on a Monday."

"It's important to you?" Russell said.

"Yeah, Dad. You've never even met Claire."

"You ain't ashamed of me?"

"I sure the fuck am," Don said, and Russell and his son wheezed out a congested laugh together, Russell because his lungs were wrecked from cigarettes and Don because he was crying.

"But she's something else, Dad. She's amazing."

"I'll be there."

Don Lowry and his skinny old man walked across the street then, and Don bought a stack of frozen pizzas and a tub of ice cream and a thirty-pack of Busch and a few packs of Winstons for his old man.

"You don't have to do that," Russell said.

"Sure I do," Don said. "I'm staying for supper."

They made a pizza in the filthy apartment's oven and ate outside on a picnic table near the Dumpsters. Mostly, Russell drank and smoked while Don ate. Don told him that he and Claire were moving to New York City in August.

"Who's gonna look after your ma? And your sister?" Russell asked, and Don said it wasn't his responsibility. The underside of that statement was clear even to a drunk. Russell Lowry had no right to make Don feel responsible for his mother and sister. Russell chewed on his lip for a bit before lighting another smoke.

"I should put the extra pizzas and the ice cream bucket in the freezer," Don said.

"Don't work," Russell said. "They let me use the ice machine across the street."

So they walked over to it together and Russell took a key from the ring on his belt and opened the ice machine in front of the Kum & Go. They loaded in the remaining pizzas and the rest of the ice cream.

"You be sure you eat all that," Don said.

"It was like a big shadow, Donnie," he said then. He wouldn't look at Don. He looked off toward the Catholic church, the biggest building in Gilman, and alternated drags of his cigarette with sips of beer. "The Shadow. It just started to creep up on me at forty, you know? And I couldn't get right. I kept feeling like, like—you know, there were layoffs coming then, and we were in debt, big-time, we had made some decisions, your mom and I, which is why she went back to work."

His voice trailed off.

Don spoke: "It's over with, Dad. It's over."

Don stopped short of forgiving him, or saying it was okay. He just said, a few more times, it's over now. It's done.

"I just feel, always have felt, Donnie, that I shoulda gone to prison for it, you know?"

"For what?"

"For how it all went down."

"But you didn't kill anybody."

"But they'd both be alive if it wasn't for me."

Russell Lowry did not show up for graduation, although a number of relatives and neighbors offered him a ride. He was too drunk. But he did drop off a gift for Don, at Don's mother's house, which Don left wrapped in its plain brown package until he and Claire had arrived at their new efficiency apartment in New York. The gun was accompanied by a scraggily and shaky-handed letter from Russell that came with an explanation: somehow, years after the murder-suicide of Dottie and Matt Good, a county sheriff's deputy—Don figured it was Steve Halverson, who had played high school football with Don—had given Russell Lowry the handgun in question. To Don, this seemed like a strange and possibly illegal gesture, but Russell provided no other context, only wrote that it was the only semivaluable possession he had and thought maybe Don might want a gun for the nightstand in a place like New York.

Over Claire's objections, he kept the gun, kept it all of these years. It was in a hidden case, properly stored and cleaned and maintained and locked away. But he had the gun. He thought of the irony of it; in some dark places, he would think, what if he took his own life with that gun?

He wouldn't do that; once you had kids, suicide was off the table, wasn't it? Didn't that make sense? Suddenly, he understood what ABC had been talking about—she wanted to slip out of this world, and hope that maybe there was some threshold to cross, some new world to go into, with a clean slate, with no shadows. But once you had kids, your world was here. If you left it, you left them.

His father had died a few years after that of liver cancer. The gun was all Don had of his father's possessions. Had he not had that visit with his father, had a sit-down those days before his college graduation, the gun would mean nothing to him. But he was glad to have that conversation in his memory, glad his father had had the chance to tell him of the Shadow.

He had had no intention of going to see his father ever again, frankly. His sister, Rosie, never did, and his mother only did so in secret, taking him food and vitamins and money to help him stay alive, though she probably would have been better off if he had died, since Don and his sister would have gotten some Social Security money. But Claire had told him he should do it, that time before graduation. He'd been having dreams about his father, and one day, lying in her narrow dorm bed as the sun came up and blazed onto the window, he was telling her about the dreams, stroking her bare back, and she said, "Go and see him. See him today. Tell him you're going to New York and want him to celebrate your graduation with him."

Claire made it seem easy. She knew how to make, back then, Don feel capable of the impossible feat. She filled his wounded heart with possibility and generous impulses that would not have been there without her. Once, when they'd come back from New York for Christmas, Claire and Don took Russell out to dinner, to a steak house in Malcolm where he'd once loved to eat, and Claire sat next to Russell as he happily cleaned his plate and then Claire ordered him a second dinner, despite his protests, which he ate half of and boxed up the leftovers along with a slice of cake for dessert. And afterward, after Claire had given Russell a hug and a quick peck on the check, he said, "It's been a long time since anybody treated me as if I was a decent human being. Thank you."

And to Don, he said, "You are luckier than lucky, son. You really are. But you deserve to be lucky. You do."

Don was grateful for that night, though he didn't know it would be the last time he saw his father, who must have already been sick. Don had balked at the expense—they'd been scraping by in New York, and a lavish dinner, even one at a rural Iowa steak house, was not something they could really afford. But Don had followed Claire's cheerful lead and picked up the tab as if he had no care in the world when it came to money.

In truth, all of Don's better impulses have been Claire's. Everything in his life that he has done well—anything to do with his job, his marriage, his kids, his friendships—has all come from Claire. Now, he feels as if he has drained all the goodness and happiness from her. The Shadow has come for him too.

3

Oh, Claire! Eau Claire!
I love to see you on campus. I love running into you.
That is all I have to say.
Your new friend, Don Lowry

This was the first note that Don Lowry had ever written to a girl in his life, and he had written it six weeks into his first semester of college and handed it to a girl named Claire Miner, who was in his French class and whom he ran into everywhere: he had served her a slice of pizza in the dining hall, had worked out on a nearby treadmill at the rec center, had seen her at the diner downtown, and, the time when he had finally introduced himself, he had looked up from his book at the library to see her sitting at a desk across from him. He always raised one casual index finger in greeting, as if he were an Iowa farmer passing in a rattling pickup, half-smiled, and turned bright red.

Claire found him adorable.

After French class, she thanked him for the note.

"I just realized, you know, that Oh Claire was the same as Eau Claire, like the city in Wisconsin, and then I realized that, in French class, like, the name of the city in Wisconsin means clear water. And that your name means clear, and it is so fitting because I don't know if this makes sense, but you have the clearest eyes I have ever seen."

"What?" she said.

"You just have a clear face, that's what I mean. Like, I mean, beautiful. And no bullshit. It's there. It's all right there. I love clarity like that in a girl."

And then she, though not a blusher, blushed.

"Woman," she corrected. It was a bad habit of hers, correcting people, editing their sentences. She often did it when nervous, but Don didn't seem to mind.

"Right," he said, grinning, as if suddenly confident. "Woman."

She had always been a force in social situations, never shy, never bashful. It exhausted her, the social effort of gatherings, but in high school, in New York, walking her way to the strange and somehow isolated all girls' prep school where she went with one hundred other girls, she dominated the classrooms and the hallways with her big laugh.

She told jokes of the most raucous nature, belched in the cafeteria, made up raunchy fight songs for the Boswell School Beavers, and, in general, was a card.

She had chosen Grinnell for its strangeness. She had grown up in a small two-bedroom apartment in Manhattan, on the Upper East Side, with summers in Sag Harbor at her grandfather's place. Her father was a philandering poet who did better in Europe than he did in the States and, financially irresponsible and unwilling to work a day job, offered almost nothing to the family's coffers; what he made for giving public readings and lectures he spent on travel and food and drink. Claire's mother was a filmmaker who'd had some early success and then was relegated to freelance work at any place that would have her. She directed and shot toothpaste ads and dog food spots. She began to have affairs out of boredom and revenge, highly visible affairs, messy entanglements that were plain as day and hurt large swaths of people. She often taught five or six classes a semester as an adjunct lecturer. Still, Claire's cultural pedigree had helped her get a scholarship to the Boswell School, and she had loved it. Although acutely aware of how much richer many of the other girls in her school were, she did not mind the disparity. She often spent her vacations in exotic parts of the world, perpetually the friend-who-gets-to-tag-along, and by the time she had come to Grinnell she had been to Greece and Turkey and Costa Rica and London and southern France and Scotland and New Zealand, and never, never in her fucking life had she ever met a guy as cute and with triceps as cut as Don Lowry.

A week later, they borrowed Don's mother's car—he lived at home to save money that semester, which almost nobody at Grinnell ever did—and drove north to see the fall colors, driving up along the Mississippi River and then taking the back roads east to Eau Claire, Wisconsin. They checked into a Super 8 there, Don Lowry charging the room on a brand-new credit card. It was 1995 and credit cards for college students were something new. Don had a $250 credit limit. Don did not have condoms, but Claire did. She was also on the pill, which her mother had insisted she get on before leaving for college. When they checked into the room, Claire, clinically and in a businesslike way, asked Don some questions about his sexual past, as she had been instructed to do in the college's orientation session.

They had three condoms. At six in the morning, Don walked to the PDQ gas station and bought more. It was the era of safe-sex hyperawareness. Even two virgins, with only a handful of blow jobs between them, used condoms religiously, fueled by the fear of AIDS and whatever else might befall practitioners of unprotected sex.

Oh, Claire! he had moaned as he came the second time, sending them into a fit of giggles and pretend moans and orgasmic noises that, although meant to be parodies, turned them on enough to fuck again after a shower.

4

On his way to work that morning, Don swings by the Manetti house with some doughnuts from the bakery and a latte for ABC.

He finds Ruth and ABC on the front porch, enjoying some fresh air before the day swells with humidity and heat, and he is happy to see them, both of them barefoot, swinging in the porch swing. He notices a small pipe next to ABC's thigh. He hands her the latte and sets the box of doughnuts down on the table.

ABC finds a chocolate-cake glazed for Ruth and hands it to her.

"Fuck, this is good," Ruth says after taking a big bite.

This makes ABC laugh and spit some latte out of her mouth.

"Must've been some good shit," Don says.

"It is," ABC says. "You want some?"

"No. No, I have to get some work done today."

"You just came by to bring us coffee and doughnuts?" ABC says. "How sweet!"

"Have you asked him?" Ruth says.

"Asked me what?" Don says.

"About Minnesota."

"Ruth," ABC says. "Not now."

"Not now what?" Don says. "I tend to hate surprises, so you might as well tell me."

"Ruth has this idea."

"I didn't have the idea," Ruth says. "You had it. In your dream."

"What are you guys talking about?" Don says.

"Nothing," ABC says. "We're stoned."

ABC gives Ruth a cold look and Ruth loses her smile and takes another bite of doughnut. She shrugs.

"She has something to tell you," Ruth says.

"No I don't," ABC says. "I really don't."

"You guys are fucking baked," Don says. "And I really have to go."

"It's a portal, Don. You're gonna show ABC the portal to the other side. To find Philly."

ABC makes a small circling motion with her finger, pointing to her temple, as if to say, "She's crazy."

Don uneasily backs down the steps.

"You guys have a good day. Maybe lay off that shit for a few hours," he says. "It seems a little strong."

"You should tell him," Don hears Ruth say, just as he gets to his truck. He shuts the door. Tell him what? he wonders, but part of him doesn't want to know.

5

Don's mother, Annie, comes to the door and tells the children to take off their shoes—easy to do since both of them are wearing Crocs that day—and then she asks Claire if she wants coffee.

Claire politely declines. All she wants is to be alone. She suddenly has a craving for it. It's as if she couldn't possibly bear to talk to anyone any longer.

"Is there anything they need at the mall tomorrow?" Annie says. "I plan to take them. I don't have much money, but I did just get my Social Security check and could buy them some new shoes or slacks or . . ."

"You don't have to do that," Claire says. She knows Annie has enough money.

"I want to," Annie says. "I feel so bad for the kids."

Claire watches as Wendy looks up at her. Claire knows exactly what her younger kid is thinking: Why does she feel bad for us? What's wrong? So Claire smiles and says, too loudly, "What in heaven's name for? The kids are going to have a great summer! Swimming and hiking and then Minnesota in August, just like always."

"You're still going to Minnesota?"

"Yes. It's a free vacation. We love it up there. We haven't ever missed a summer, not since Wendy was born."

"Have you found a place to live yet?"

"What do you mean?" Claire says, gritting her teeth and glowering. She nods her head toward the children and whispers, "Little ears, Annie. Please."

Annie does this thing she sometimes does where she has her eyes fill with tears by making this extended grimace of pain. It is an ugly expression. Claire has seen her do it at funerals and weddings.

Claire ignores the tears; she looks past Annie at the living room, where her kids are flopped, already bored, on the sofa. Bryan leafs through a magazine and Wendy doodles in her journal.

"Grandma," Bryan says. "Can we go swimming tonight?"

"Oh, it's getting late," Annie says. "It's almost five. You'll get chilled without the sun."

The children protest with moans.

"It's light for four more hours," Claire says. "And hotter than hell."

Normally she'd let Annie do her thing, which is to ask the children to sit still and watch television, but she wants to picture her kids leaping into a swimming pool rather than sitting dejectedly in a dim living room of a gated community, eating Sam's Choice lemon cookies from Walmart. "It's at least ninety degrees out."

"Okay, okay," Annie says. "Go get your swimsuits on."

Then Annie hands Claire two hundred-dollar bills from the pocket of her khaki capri pants. "Get some groceries for your family, Claire," she says, without a smile. "I've already bought mine for the month. I don't need much."

Claire takes the money. She's no fool.

6

Is it sad if you admit that, for many mothers, the only moments of solitude come when driving to and from a store, or shopping within one? Claire's at the Trader Joe's twenty minutes after leaving her mother-in-law's condo and it feels like a small vacation to be there alone, away from home, away from Grinnell, walking through the steaming parking lot. It is a new addition to the sprawl of West Des Moines and she hates being there in the traffic and the barren, treeless acres of box stores. She always feels profoundly dumb when she shops at places like Trader Joe's, as if she is confirming her rather pathetic status as an easily led member of a target demographic.

She finds herself, soon enough, cooling off in the overwhelming frozen foods aisle—a visual cacophony of strange wraps and pastries and prepackaged casseroles that promise life will be easier, warmer, more wholesome if only you consume these products. She's trying to remember which frozen whatever it is that Don likes—samosas or the minichimichangas or maybe the pierogis—because she is going to pack up the kitchen soon and they will not be cooking much after that.

The whole store looks garish to her, and all the convenience foods are suddenly some profound judgment of her worth as a wife and a mother, a discounting of her choices and her marriage.

She will have a night alone with Don that evening, and that will help matters. Won't it? They've been spinning their wheels for two weeks, acting on those twin demons panic and impulse, and they've not made any progress, not logistically or emotionally. Maybe she would seduce Don as soon as she got home, fuck him on those basement stairs again. Could she fuck her way back into loving him? Or maybe she could write all night—a night without kids—and go on some manic fifty-thousand-word binge, producing one of those sly, powerful comeback novels in one weekend, a fragmented tour de force about a thirty-nine-year-old woman's emotional free fall, surprising her agent on Monday morning with a phone call and saying, "I have a new book."

She realizes she has paused right there in the frozen food aisle, and gets snapped back to reality when a fat man nudges her aside and opens a freezer door with a chilly blast.

Um: samosas, Don likes the samosas, and there is a pear-mango chutney near the salsas that he also likes. Claire is reaching for the samosas when the phone rings.

"I have a terrible migraine," Annie says. "It's just awful. I am sorry."

"Oh dear, Annie. I'm sorry. What should I do?"

"You have to come back. You have to get the children."

"Really? I mean, if you need to sleep, they can watch a movie."

"They've been fighting since they walked into the house, Claire. They are being monsters."

"Let me talk to Bryan," Claire says.

"Just come and get them. I am going to lie down. I can't do this tonight."

It's clear to Claire that she didn't show Annie a significant enough amount of respect and deference earlier. This is payback.

That is fine, Claire says. She will finish grocery shopping and then she'll come and get the kids.

"You just get some sleep, Annie," Claire says. "Let them watch a movie until I can get there. I just stopped for groceries."

"Are you at the Hy-Vee?" Annie says.

"Trader Joe's," Claire says.

"Oh, well, good for you," Annie says, which means, *You idiot. You're spending too much for someone so broke.*

It is not a big deal. The kids will be happy to see her and Claire will have fulfilled her monthly obligation to take the kids to her mother-in-law's for a visit.

Why isn't she disappointed? Now she could admit it, now that it isn't possible. She had so badly wanted to see Charlie that night, without the pressure of her children waiting for her at home. She had fantasized about calling him from a Motel 6 near Newton and saying, "Come here now."

Would she have done it?

Yes, she could admit this more easily now that it didn't have a chance of happening. She'll be with the kids that night, which is really the only sensible thing she should be doing in such a dark time.

Why is her lip trembling? Why do her hands shake?

In this state, Claire is wandering up and down the aisles of Trader Joe's, randomly placing things into her cart: salsa, granola bars, rice crackers, yeast. She doesn't want the kids to come home because, as she is staring at the frozen foods and busy moms in yoga pants and tight Lycra pullovers are annoyed by her aisle-blocking, she is thinking of Charlie Gulliver.

And now, right there in Trader Joe's, what she really wants to do, right there in front of the sixteen different kinds of vegetarian pizzas, is have a breakdown. She sinks down to her knees in front of the glass coolers. Here it comes: A complete, fucked-up, terrify-the-passersby breakdown. A tear-off-your-clothes and writhe-on-the-floor-weeping breakdown. She wants to crawl out of Trader Joe's with a torn shirt and no shoes, knocking down the displays of two-bite brownies and mango shampoo as she leaves, and get into the car and drive west, perhaps. Men do that shit all the time. Men go out for some eggs and milk and get the fuck out of their lives. Their sad marriages become happy lives. She could do that too. It would not even be permanent. It'd be temporary. A few weeks of being a fucking freaked-out crazy woman. She'd go to some hotel somewhere near some mountains, Aspen or somewhere, and she'd max out her credit card, the emergency American Express that is in her name only, which Don couldn't cancel. She'd do nothing but take baths and sleep and eat. She'd get massages from big ski bums with foul minds. And then she would feel clean and rested and limber, also a bit fuller in the ass and tits from all the room service (who the fuck cares!), and she'd call Charlie Gulliver, she'd tell him to come to the hotel in Aspen and fuck her over and over. She'd be called crazy by then, it'd be widely known, so when Charlie arrived she could do things like pour champagne on his belly and smoke weed and watch porn and yell at him: *Eat my pussy* or *fuck me hard* or *I'm gonna suck your big cock* and she'd yell when she came because who the fuck cared. She'd be the Lindsay Lohan of Midwestern moms for one month. Men could do that. Men could go crazy and then come home and say, "I don't know what happened. I got scared. I lost my mind." Generals and preachers and football coaches tweeting pictures of their junk and snorting cocaine off a stripper's ass. They'd apologize. And the story would be over. Women as brilliant and tough as Hillary Clinton accepted this truth for some reason; they didn't like it, but they accepted it as fairly normal male behavior. But would men ever accept a woman saying the same thing? Would that woman who fucked that famous general get a free pass by pleading temporary insanity?

"Ma'am," a voice snaps at her. "Ma'am! Are you okay?"

Her phone is ringing. A crowd of people has gathered around

her. She's sweating and has twisted the hem of her T-shirt up into a knot that exposes her stomach. She stands with a freezer door open, the pizzas a few inches in front of her face, and she realizes she probably has not moved in at least five minutes.

Someone brings her a bottle of water. A small crowd of other concerned middle-aged women surround her. She drinks some water.

"It takes a village!" she says, trying to joke, but no one even smiles.

She asks for a cigarette, but nobody around her seems to have one, or to have even heard of one. There are three women with her, all of them in an exercising outfit of some kind.

"Do you think that's a good idea?" one of the women says.

"Yes! I'd like a beer and a cigarette pleazzzzze."

"Call 911," says another woman.

"Okay," says the third, the one wearing a sun visor and tennis skirt. She pulls a phone from her small purse.

"I have a brain tumor," Claire says, hoping that would excuse her and get these well-meaning people to let her leave without calling 911. But they all just stare at her.

Here comes the store manager.

"I'm probably going to FUCKING die soon!" Claire yells. "I am so sorry!"

7

What Charlie had been discovering that summer, in his father's incredibly cluttered study, was not a series of brilliant unpublished essays, or the drafts of a secret but genius, genre-bending novel, but several file boxes marked CONFIDENTIAL, in each of which was a neatly kept system of slim manila folders marked with hearts and dated, and in the smallest red-penciled print, a first name: *Jennifer. Hannah. Laura. Li. Suzanna. Belinda. Anjali.* There were dozens of files like that, most of them slim, and containing a letter or two. A few of the files contained multiple letters, thick stacks of correspondence, some of them Xeroxed, some carbon copies of letters sent, some papers printed off of computers on dot matrix, ink jet, and laser printers. Some handwritten.

Charlie and ABC had been going through them in the afternoons, while Ruth napped and before Claire would come and see Charlie or Don would go to smoke with ABC. They killed time reading through the letters, taking breaks for swimming or sometimes sex, or beer and pizza. The letters, buried among so many useless stacks of paper—old syllabi, yellowed department memos, forgotten expense receipts—were the only things of interest in the study at this point. The letters spanned more than twenty years, and they'd all been written to women, the names in the label area of each folder: students, former students, colleagues, women he'd met at conferences, women he'd met on planes. All of them were similar: strangely pathetic and romantic at once, admissions of his unhappiness and his desperation.

"I don't think I should be looking at this," ABC had said at one point. "We should burn them."

"These are not anomalies, ABC. He's written hundreds of these."

That afternoon, ABC stands back as Charlie opens another box of letters.

He reads each one as he goes, as if he is afraid he might miss something.

"It'll take me all summer to read these," Charlie says.

"Don't torture yourself," ABC says. She has opened another file box and is absentmindedly flipping through its folders, reading more first names aloud: "'Cindy, Donna, Emily, Franny, Georgia, Hannah, Ivy, Jen.' Everyone has a secret life, Charlie."

Charlie has even begun to pinpoint the rhetorical strategies Gill Gulliver used in his love letters. He could have written a paper on the topic. He even memorized some passages of prose. Some lines were easy for Charlie to memorize, because his father had used them over and over in so many of his letters. When each written piece is devoted to a private audience of one, some recycling is possible.

Now, he reads some of the passages out loud to ABC. She looks at him with sad eyes.

"These were very well hidden," Charlie says. "If they were real affairs, I wonder if my mother knew of them? Or worse, they weren't really affairs, but pathetic attempts at them? Listen to this: 'In some ways, the only situation that is preventable is love. One must not open up one's self to it. Then one can be free of it. But once the door is opened, as I fear it has been now, there is no turning back. Love must be pursued with an intensity that borders on obsessive, addictive, insane.'"

"There's some truth to that," ABC says.

"But who is this, um, Joanie, he wrote this to and why?"

ABC shrugs.

Charlie reads another letter: "'The weather here has been outstanding, and I find myself taking in each vista as if you were with me, and I can almost hear your reactions, a breathy whisper, a soft moan of approval.'"

"Huh," ABC says. "Don't do this to yourself, Charlie. What's the point?"

"Or how about this?" Charlie says, ignoring her question. There was obviously no point, not really, but how could he not keep reading? His father had been such a mysterious wreck to him. How could one not look at his leavings, the physical evidence of his inner life?

"Listen: 'Your hair with the faint scent of cucumber and lemon when you come to my class fresh from the shower.'"

Or this:

"'If what I was feeling was not so true, so undeniably a wholly new and original feeling for me, I would be ashamed of it. But when something completely new enters the world, what can one do? One can only embrace it with the innocence of a small child reaching for a piece of dandelion fluff.'"

These letters had been saved by Charlie's father for some reason—in that sense it is not as if he had destroyed any evidence of his somewhat lecherous yearnings. It was as if he had meant to chronicle his career as a womanizer, or at least a womanizer on the page, as the legacy of his particular and passionate genius. Why else save copies of such damning notes? Why not just let them remain sent, rotting in a landfill somewhere, or at best, lingering at the bottom of someone's forgotten box of college mementos?

Some of the files contained responses from these women too. Charlie began to look through these as well, and the letters ranged from the mundane *Thanks for your note! I hope you have a great summer too!* to the cautiously interested *Professor Gulliver, I do understand what you are saying, but I am young and such an adventure as you propose—a trip to Rome—would be scandalous if anyone found out. Still, I am flattered. I will think about it.*

Other letters to Gill Gulliver spoke circuitously of past events: *I will always remember Chicago, and I understand why I can't visit you in Iowa, but if you ever make it to Boston, would you please, please call. I will meet you in a second.* Some letters spoke with regret: *If anyone finds out, Gill, oh, God, can you imagine? Burn this letter after reading, please!* One letter recounted, in erotic detail, what had apparently been the woman's first sexual experience: *I remember,* she wrote over and over, *how you did that from behind me, and I couldn't see your face, and I wanted to see it when you finally came.* Other letters were more forceful: *Professor Gulliver, you seem to be crossing a line here that I am uncomfortable with and I ask that you do not write me again or I will have to forward your notes to the dean's office with a formal complaint.*

It is almost midnight when ABC hands Charlie a letter she has found.

And then there is this brief note to a woman named Claire, dated September 1995.

Dear Claire,

If you would please stop by my office tomorrow evening, I'd very much like to personally apologize for my behavior at the student-faculty mixer yesterday. I had intended to walk you home, that is all, since your dorm was on the way, but the stars pulled me along and I felt youthful again, as if being near you had helped me rediscover a feeling I long thought dead. Please forgive me,

Professor Gill Gulliver

"Do you think that's Claire, I mean, Claire Lowry?"

ABC grins.

"I bet it is."

"I mean," Charlie says, "I don't really know where to start. Look at all this shit. I should just burn everything."

"I suppose you could, but is that really what you want to do?" ABC asks. "I mean, if your father spent his whole life writing an epic novel, shouldn't we try to find it and help him publish it?"

"I thought we were just supposed to tidy up," Charlie says.

"Why wouldn't you want to help your father finish his book?"

"I don't care about art anymore," Charlie says. "I told you—that's the way of madness and sadness. Playing Hamlet almost made me insane. Who wants to dwell in that kind of sadness? If my father actually wrote a novel, I guarantee you it is fucking sad."

"So you're avoiding sadness? That can't be done!"

"Look, the only reason I'd finish my old man's book is so that he would turn to me and thank me and tell me what a great job I had done, how much he needed my help. And he's too senile to do that. He could get a contract with some huge publisher, his book could be a best seller, and he'd never know."

"But you'd know!"

"If I write a book, it'll be my own book."

"You want to write a book?"

"Nope," Charlie says.

"I think we're making the wrong kind of list," ABC says. "I think you need a list of things you want to do with your LIFE." She wrote L-I-F-E on the legal pad in huge letters.

"You're the one who wants to die," Charlie says.

"Not exactly. I'm waiting for Philly to find me."

"You really believe this will happen?"

"Let's talk about you: Don Lowry said this house can get maybe four hundred grand, it's just, you know," ABC says, "you have to wait for a person with four hundred grand to spend to move to Grinnell, Iowa. But think about it. You could live off that forever! And, in the meantime, we could use the pool! Skinny-dippin' parties!"

"Could you believe Claire did that?" Charlie says.

"She's on an edge, you know?" ABC says. "I feel bad for her. She's trapped in her life."

"Everybody is," Charlie says. "Even me, Mr. Freedom. There are many aspects of my life that are unchangeable. Does it mean I dwell on them or in them?"

As they speak, Charlie is halfheartedly combing through papers. Throwing old newspapers into a recycling bin, tossing away more of the meticulously archived work done by former students, and starting a box of books that could go to Goodwill. When he first began the work of going through his father's stuff, he still had hoped to find, buried in all of this, a book manuscript. This would, he felt, negate the terribly sad sheaf of letters he'd uncovered. A book! A finished masterwork! With notes and an introduction by Charles Gulliver! Maybe he'd win an award, maybe he'd go back for a graduate degree after all, follow in the old man's footsteps. He would go to his father's room, and he would visit him and say: *I found it. And it will see the light of day. And I plan to be a professor. And aren't you proud of your son?*

But now, even that wouldn't matter.

ABC has gone through his father's CD collection and has put on some music, some Henryck Górecki.

"My father liked to listen to this as he worked."

"It's almost unbearably sad," ABC says. "How could he handle all of that sad music and remain sane? It seems as if it'd be nearly impossible."

Charlie takes down a large hardcover edition of *Jude the Obscure*, which had been one of his father's favorite novels. This is an old edition. Maybe he will take it to his father in the Mayflower. He is not delusional. His father is not dead, but this part of his father's life—the life of professional responsibility and pleasure—is over. Patients who suffer Lewy body dementia tend to have moments of clarity, but a sustained engagement with reality, with a return to the day-to-day life of a scholar Gill Gulliver had loved for so long? Impossible. Still, maybe in some small moments, he might return to Hardy and find something of the familiar in its pages.

"What's that?" ABC asks.

"*Jude the Obscure*," Charlie says. "Have you read it?"

"I have! In your dad's Literary Analysis class. Freshman year. It. Was. So. Depressing."

"My father gave it to me when I started high school. As a gift. I never read it. He was so disappointed by that."

He opens the book.

"Read it now," ABC says.

Inside the book is a small white envelope. In the corner of the envelope, in purple felt-tip pen, is a hand-drawn line of three question marks, thick and ornate, as if penned by a calligrapher. On the other side of the envelope, three hearts drawn in green. Inside, some letters: the first letter was typed on an old typewriter, on green typing paper.

Before Charlie has even unfolded the letter, ABC is standing up and coming toward him. "What is that?" she demands. "Let me see that."

This is what it is:

Grinnell, Iowa
September 16, 2011

G—

I found your note in Ruth's mailbox. At least I'm going to assume that it is from you, that you are the "G" who signed the note. Yes, it is true that I no longer have a cell phone or an e-mail address that works. Sorry. Yes, it is true that I am back in Grinnell and living in the home of Professor Manetti's widow. Yes, that was me you saw walking last night, and yes, I did hear you call to me from your car, and yes, I did sprint away from you, from your voice, at the painful moment of recognition. I'm sorry. I didn't want to explain to you why I came back to Grinnell just four months after graduating, why Los Angeles felt claustrophobic to me, teeming with noise and germs, and why everywhere I looked I felt death. I missed the prairie. I missed the quiet. I missed the big and changing sky, and the feeling that I could see things coming from any direction. I missed Philly, and all my memories of her are here. They live here. It's not something I can explain. I really don't want to explain this, which is why I am not talking to anybody.

And so, here I am, a distinguished alumna of Grinnell College, winner of the Nellie Sifkin Prize, living two blocks away from my first college dorm.

Living the dream, right?

I'm not missing much in L.A., trust me on that. The only jobs available to me are do-gooder jobs in which I labor for slave wages in order to transform somebody else's life while my own life hangs in limbo.

I'm not interested in that, which is not a very Grinnellian thing to admit, is it?

You are right to guess that Philly's death is what drove me back here. Of course, I am not taking it well. One day I will tell you about it. Not what happened, though that is surreal in itself, and it's a story I can tell you if you want to hear it. But I also should tell you why I couldn't stay in L.A. without her, even though I had lived there most of my life: that's a story I need to tell, soon. (I had heard you were on leave, medical leave, and I do hope everything is okay.)

My mother is of no help to me, though of course she has offered me a place to stay, her spare bedroom, since without Philly, it is hard to afford even the small studio apartment that she and I shared. (We had bunk beds and no couch, just one tiny love seat we'd sit on to watch movies on her laptop. We didn't care. We had our own place in West Hollywood and we had no concerns over its tininess. We cared about its our-ness!)

Of course I loved Philly. But also, my God, I think I was in love with her too.

Write back. Or don't.

But if you do, use my new Grinnell post office box, please, number 573.

Mrs. Manetti is nosy. She understands more than she admits.

Yours,

ABC

The next letter was printed on a laser printer and had the words *MY COPY* penciled in blue at the top right-hand corner.

July 6, 2009

Dear ABC,

I trust, or at least hope, this note finds you well. Prague is such a beautiful city and it is vibrant and alive with so much—music, art, sex, rich and heavy food—but it is also, for me at least, a place of profound melancholy, of minor keys. I was there last in 1997, and when I came home, I could barely function. Everything depressed me about Grinnell, the town, the campus, the way my wife never fixed her hair, and my son's constant chatter. It was a dreadful time for me, I felt I was suffocating, and I have always attributed that to a spiritual condition caused by spending a portion of the summer in Prague.

Do be careful.

But you are young! And regret probably doesn't weigh as heavily on your heart as it does on mine. And a city as beautiful as Prague—with its significant architecture and sidewalks teeming with attractive young people—probably does not cause you as much regret as it causes me. To you, Prague must be a city of promise, a city freed from the shackles of oppression and more or less embracing the chaos of Westernization. At least I hope so. I hope too that you are reading some of the Czech authors I recommended to you. Milan Kundera, especially, is most fun to read while sitting in some bar drinking pilsner and eating one of those strange but delicious pizzas they serve everywhere in that city. God, I'd kill for a decent pizza tonight!

Anyway, I did look at your essay regarding Tender Is the Night *and I must say it is accomplished in its scope but still incredibly scattered in terms of its argument. As a sample for graduate school, it is probably not your best work, though I am sending you back a copy of the essay with some comments and notes in the margins. It may, with some revision, turn into your showcase piece. If nothing else, it is deeply gratifying to me to see how much you've connected with Fitzgerald on both an intellectual and emotional level.*

Well, you don't want to waste your days in Prague reading boring missives from a washed-up Fitzgerald scholar, do you? Take care and know that I miss you. I miss seeing you unexpectedly on campus and miss your visits to my office. I miss your laugh, the depth of it, and the sight of you, and even your scent, the shampoo I sometimes could smell when you came to class right from the gym and you sat in the front row and I thought . . . well, never mind what I thought!

Yours,

Gill Gulliver

And then there are two more notes, handwritten, blue pen on yellow lined paper, ripped, untidily, from a legal pad. One reads: *Professor Gulliver, I am so sorry but there is no way, no way at all I am ever going to get this paper done, even with the generous extension you have given me. I really don't know what to say except that I am sorry to disappoint you. With much respect, yours truly, ABC.*

The second note is handwritten as well, but had been copied on a photocopier and is in the strange manic scrawl that Charlie recognizes instantly as his father's handwriting.

Again, in blue ink on the top, the words *MY COPY.*

The note read:

My dear ABC, please do not apologize to me in that way again. I am not disappointed in you. I am proud of you and think the world of you and your intellect. I am only sorry I have to wait a few days longer to read your always brilliant thoughts on this assignment. The connection between Hemingway and Emerson/Thoreau is a notable one, but not an obvious one, so do take your time and get it right. The papers I've read so far, by your esteemed but incredibly inferior classmates, are RUBBISH. I want to speak with you soon. Preferably alone. When I don't see you at some point during the week, I spend the weekend feeling destroyed.

Yours, Gill

"Why didn't you tell me this?" Charlie says. "Why wouldn't this be like the first thing you told a person? Nice to meet you! I was fucking your dad before he went insane!"

"Charlie!" ABC says. "I wasn't fucking him! He had a crush on me, or something, something delusional and strange, and I was kind to him. I liked his attention. But nothing ever happened."

Had Charlie not already read through over a hundred communications like these, he might not believe ABC. But he has seen so many of these notes already. His father couldn't possibly have had legitimate affairs with all of these women.

"Your father was addicted to the feeling of being in love. He told me once—probably inappropriately—that the great love of his life, before he met your mother, was someone he couldn't have."

"He told you that?"

"I think he became addicted to pursuing women he could never have. It was a thing for him, but he never left your mother. He never would."

"He should've."

ABC leans in and gives Charlie a hug. "You are lucky, Chuck. Because I am in the mood to get stoned and then go over to the city pool and ride the waterslide. Maybe my bikini top will come off again! Won't that be fun!"

Charlie flops down on the couch.

"Why the fuck did I agree to do this?"

ABC straddles Charlie. "Hey, hey, slugger. You are way hotter than your old man. That feels good, don't it?"

"I, um . . ."

"He never got a chance to be fucked by me, and you, you will have multiple chances."

"I thought you said this was nothing," Charlie says. "A onetime thing."

"It is nothing. But who counts nothing? Two times zero is still zero."

"Right! Of course! I'm not good with math."

She is grinding herself on him, kissing his mouth, and then the phone in the study begins to ring.

"I don't hear that," she says. She pulls off her shirt, and as she does, he reaches over to the table and picks up the old-fashioned desk phone.

"Hello?" he says. "Gullivers'."

ABC puts her shirt back on when she sees Charlie's face fall. Stands up, smooths out her clothes.

Then Charlie says, "Yes, I'll come. Don't worry, I'll help you."

"What is it?" ABC asks, but Charlie ignores the question, distracted.

He hangs up the phone, finds his keys and wallet, and says, "I'm sorry. I have to go."

"Where?" ABC asks.

"It's really complicated. It's Claire."

"Why is she so fucking complicated? I know two men in this town and they're both very wrapped up in her complexity."

"It's just—right now, she needs me."

"Is that why you like her?"

"I don't know," Charlie says. "I've never been needed before."

8

Perhaps the most profound crack in a shattering marriage is how often one spouse ignores the calls of another spouse. That Saturday, as he works on the stack of neglected paperwork—tax documents, state regulation forms, MLS listings—Don Lowry ignores three calls from his wife as well as two text messages that say *Hello???!!!????*

Why does he do this?

One explanation, which is the one he gives himself, is that he is simply busy—no, not simply busy, but awfully busy, and whatever dramatic thought has popped up in Claire's head, whatever possible misdeed or trespass she is so eager to talk about, would simply distract him from what he's really trying to do: get shit done. Since his friendship with ABC began, along with its attendant recreational weed smoking, he's been about as productive as a pill-popping starlet at the Chateau Marmont, at a time when he needs nothing more than to work and work hard.

It's time to get shit done.

Another possible and perhaps more plausible explanation for his refusal to answer his phone, or even listen to the message she left on her third call, is harder to admit. He is hoping ABC will call. She had mentioned to him something about a day off, and how she usually spent Saturdays getting stoned and wandering around Rock Creek State Park or some other outpost, and she wondered if he wanted to come along.

He is working on an Excel file that is itemizing his expenses for the year, so that he might somehow estimate the quarterly taxes he will certainly not be able to pay, when his phone rings again.

This time, he answers, because it is not Claire. It is exactly whom he wanted it to be.

"Yo," ABC says.

"Yo," Don says back, though he probably hasn't said *yo* in decades.

"I was hanging out with Charlie," ABC says. "But he ditched me. Come by the pool and hang out."

Don Lowry's heart floats up to the drop ceiling and explodes in the fluorescent light. Pieces of his heart fall down on his head when he says, "Sure. Cool."

9

If she's ever been happier in her life to see someone, she can't remember it. Charlie, smiling but bewildered, coming toward her as she leans on the Suburban next to a female police officer.

"Is this your friend?" the cop asks her and she nods, and starts crying, which embarrasses her to no end, as does the hug, more awkward than she expected it to be, and she cries, more and more, as Charlie talks to the officer, explains that he'll drive Claire's car home and leave his own car there.

Eventually, the officer seems satisfied and she even gives Claire a hug, tighter than Charlie's hug, and Claire feels the ridiculous shame of being the kind of woman sobbing in a parking lot, hugged by a cop.

"We have to pick up my kids," Claire says, once they are in the car. She explains that her mother-in-law has a migraine.

"Of course," Charlie says.

"I am sorry to take you away from your work," Claire says. "I couldn't reach Don, or anybody." (This is kind of a lie. She had called Don, had texted him, but was secretly glad when he had not responded.)

"Claire, it's okay. I had nothing to do today."

"You're a savior."

"You're an angel, Claire. You don't deserve this."

"What?"

"This life. This foreclosure. This upheaval."

"What do I deserve?" she says, laughing a snotty, post-cry laugh.

"You deserve to be happy," Charlie says and starts the car.

10

"Don Lowry!" ABC says as she throws open the door. She is wearing nothing but a towel. The skin on her shoulders seems to be steaming and her wet hair drips onto her neck and the tops of her shoulders, beading down her collarbone and her clavicle. Don Lowry looks like he wants to bite her, like he wants to suck her hair dry. It is an evening in which impulse and drama are winning and she feels herself not exactly in control of her own behavior, as if the steady parade of grief that has been her life for the last year is finally unraveling into something more permanent: a breakdown, a crack-up, a collapse, a departure.

So there she is in a towel, greeting a sad and likely horny realtor of thirty-eight.

It's as if she feels Philly watching her cracking up. She feels as if Philly is her audience that night and she is putting on a hell of a show. This is her swan song on earth, before, as her dream perhaps predicted, she will meet Philly in the spirit world and leave all of this insanity behind.

"Are you okay?" Don says. "You look like you might faint."

The night air is humid. It seems to shroud ABC's body in steam. "Is it okay with Charlie that I am here?"

"Yes," she says, leading Don into the foyer. "Sure it's okay with Charlie. Why wouldn't it be?"

"I didn't know you were spending time with Charlie, I mean, not this much time," Don says, his face oddly fallen, as if he'd been slapped by something much larger than himself.

"I'm helping him go through his father's papers," ABC says. "Turns out they are mostly love letters to people other than his wife!"

Don nods. Then says, "Hey, can I borrow your towel? My car just hit a water buffalo."

"The towel?" ABC says. "What? A water buffalo?"

"It's an old joke. Never mind. From a movie called *Fletch*. Have you seen it?"

"Can't say I have," ABC says.

"You haven't seen *Fletch*!"

"Why do older guys always do that? Make some obscure movie reference and then act all shocked because a woman fifteen years younger doesn't get the reference? Is that supposed to be flirting?"

"Never mind. But why are you in a towel?"

"I've been swimming, dipshit."

"Right."

"So," she says. "How's Don?"

"Fine," Don says. "You were Gill Gulliver's student, right?"

"I was."

"Frankly, he was always kind of a dick to me," Don says.

"He preferred female students, I'm pretty sure," ABC says. "Based on the letters we are finding."

"He was always incredibly nice to Claire."

"When we went to see him at the nursing home, he recognized me, but not Charlie."

"Jesus," Don says. "Where is Charlie?"

"He had to go. Some kind of emergency," ABC says. "You wanna go sit outside?"

"It's too hot. Plus it's still daylight. People will see us smoking."

"Wimp."

"Well, the neighbors, you know. They know me. They might see. They've probably already witnessed the skinny-dipping party. I am sure there are rumors."

"I suppose," ABC says. "There'll always be rumors. Let's go upstairs where there's a window air conditioner in the master bedroom. Give it ten minutes to kick in and then it'll be nice and cool and dark."

Don nods.

"Who knew?" she says, smiling at him, and turns with the skip of a dancer toward the steps. "Don Lowry is a total stoner!"

Don feels his mouth go dry already, before he's even had one hit. But he is too terrified to ask for a drink because with ABC in the towel, with her wet hair still dripping, he feels as if he's in a dream and anything he might say or do could break him from that dream.

They go from the foyer straight up the staircase.

Don follows ABC up the stairs, which grow progressively darker, since ABC turned on no lights. Of course, he looks at her legs, bare and damp, as they go up. He feels himself needing to moan but instead he lets out a kind of shivering sigh through his nostrils. He is aroused. He has read articles, while killing the insomniac hours with the inanity of Yahoo news, about ABC's generation. They hook up. They do not date. Sex is physical, not emotional. They have all kinds of sex. Oral sex is just a thing they do; they take pictures of it. They say stuff like, *We hooked up. Whatevs.* It is hard not to feel like a dirty old man imagining all of it, and he feels like one now. Is that what she has in mind? Is she about to hook up with an older man, just for the experience of it?

In the bedroom, ABC keeps the lights off, but there is just enough light coming from the windows and the bathroom down the hall for them to see. She ushers Don Lowry in and directs him to the only chair in the room. It's in a corner, an old futon chair.

ABC goes down the hall, to the bathroom, and comes back wearing clothes, cutoffs and a man's tight white undershirt, through which he can see a dark bra.

"Shut the door," Don says. She shrugs and shuts the door and pushes in the button on the knob.

"Okay," ABC says. "All secret now!"

Don frowns. "No, no," he says. "Whatever."

"You're already paranoid and you haven't even had one toke, Don Lowry."

At that moment, he wants to be nowhere else. Nothing seems real in this small room. There is no urgency in the universe, no failure, no unhappy circumstances one couldn't overcome with joy.

ABC is holding a small purse from which she retrieves a joint that has been hidden with a mess of joints tucked into a small Altoids tin. She cranks up the ancient window AC unit and kneels on the floor in front of it and lets the cold air blow on her face. The machine hums and buzzes and rattles, but it works, and then it stops working for a moment, and then it kicks on again.

"I put on some clothes," ABC says. "It seems more appropriate than a towel. Anyway, it's hot in here but will cool off soon."

After one hit, he feels clarity: he doesn't want to cheat on Claire. He is on the precipice of cheating, maybe, which in itself is a kind of thrill for him, and yet, if he thinks about it too much he knows it is the same thing. On the precipice or over the precipice, once you're there, you're there. But for now, he pretends he is discovering something innocently, has heard some distant music and has simply gone toward it, naive and open to the universe.

"Just relax," ABC says. She sits cross-legged on the floor on some pillows she'd found in another room. She is sitting right in front of him, at his feet, and she has to reach up toward him where he sits in that comfortable chair to hand him the joint.

"Remember, you have to be funny. That's our deal."

When she reaches up to him, he looks down her shirt.

She doesn't acknowledge this in any way, no coy smile or annoyed adjustment of her neckline. Her tits are big. This is the extent of the clarity he is now having. Wow. She has great tits. Claire has small tits, also great. The number of tits that Don has touched in his life is an incredibly low number.

"What are you thinking about?" ABC asks.

"Nothing," he says.

"Good."

Don Lowry is beside himself. He exhales and closes his eyes. ABC takes the joint back, takes one more hit, and then curls up against the sad stranger next to her and hushes him to sleep. She places a pillow behind his head.

"There's something in this pillow," he says, and reaching into the case, he pulls out a small white tank top, like his wife wears over her sports bra when she runs. He holds it up to his face and smells it. It smells like Claire.

"Let's sleep next to each other," ABC says. She stands up and asks Don to stand up and then collapses the futon chair into a large twin bed.

"Lie down, Don Lowry," she says. When he does this, she gets down and cuddles against his side.

"I won't sleep," he says. "I'm not someone who can just fall asleep like that."

"You fall asleep with me all the time. Maybe I'm your sleeping charm," ABC says.

"What were you and Ruth talking about this morning?"

"What do you mean?"

"She kept telling you to tell me something. To stop hiding it from me?"

"Just try," ABC says, "try to sleep."

"That was amazing shit," Don Lowry says. "Or is all stuff this amazing now? Should I be smoking pot every day?"

"Yep" is all ABC could stand to say. She wants him to stop talking now. She wants her dream of Philly to come back. "Please sleep next to me now."

"God, I'm so thirsty. I want to know what Ruth was talking about."

"Charlie has beer in the fridge downstairs. And some juice, I think. I can't move," ABC says.

"I'll go get us two beers," Don says, but doesn't move.

"What do you think she was talking about?" ABC asks. "Ruth."

"I think maybe you're in love with me," Don says. "I think maybe she was telling you to tell me you're in love with me."

"Don," ABC says. She lifts her head and kisses him lightly on the cheek. "Don't be dumb."

Sometime later, in the darkness, ABC is at the shore of the vast lake again, and Philly is walking toward her, emerging naked out of the soft but frigid white surf.

11

What Charlie decided to do, upon picking up Claire's two confused and bored kids, who'd been cheated out of a day of swimming by their passive-aggressive, migraine-faking grandmother, was stop at the Hy-Vee for pizzas and root beer and ice-cream sandwiches, plus gin and tonic fixings.

He would throw these kids, and their mother, his friend, a pool party. He announced this aloud and the kids cheered.

Now Charlie wears orange swim trunks and a blue oxford, half unbuttoned. Next to him, there is a sweating tumbler of gin. A triple, like hers? Claire has a desire to gulp her drink. But the kids are there. She needs to slow down. A lime floats among some ice. She already feels more than just buzzed.

"Jesus, now that was a weird day."

"Do you want another drink?" Charlie says.

"No," she says.

"How are you holding up? Do you want a swim?"

"In this case," Claire says, watching her kids jumping in and out of the pool, Taylor Swift playing from the FM radio, "I think I'd need a suit."

"Probably a good idea. You want me to go to your house and get one?"

"No. I feel better," she says. The gin, piney and strong, flushes her cheeks warm with blood. A strap from her sundress falls then, baring a shoulder, and she lets it ride. "I guess I had my first panic attack today."

"Mazel tov," Charlie says. "I have had so many already. You're a late bloomer. When I was leaving Seattle, my last few weeks there, I had one every day at five o'clock. Like when everybody would start leaving work, and I had no work to leave, I just got terrified. I was convinced I'd die in a terrorist attack or some natural disaster."

They clink glasses. "To panic attacks," Claire says.

Wendy shouts out for them to watch the cannonball. They turn and wait until she launches herself in the pool. When she surfaces, they applaud wildly, Charlie standing up and whistling swift and shrill with his fingers. Claire likes men who can whistle like that.

"Enough about me," she says. "How was your day?"

"Oh, you know, lots of discovering that my father was a fraudulent and deluded man. That kind of thing," he says. "But really, Claire, tell me, how are things? Things must be terrible."

"Ha! Ha! Yes! Yes, they are," she says. "We're gonna be fucking homeless!"

He laughs. "Totally," he says. "Homeless with Kids. Maybe that could be a new reality show? You're a total MILF. You could totally rock that show."

"I hate that word," she says.

"It just means—"

"It just means mothers aren't real women. So they need a special term if they're fuckable? Right?"

"Touché."

They smile these dorky smiles at each other and drink and look at the empty pool and the full trees and the goldfinch and chickadees all about the yard and then Charlie says, "You know, I have a house. Consider it yours."

And though he swears he is serious, and he repeats his seriousness over and over amid the joyful shouts of her children, she laughs it off, she says it is a ridiculously extravagant gesture, ha ha ha, Charlie, you're crazy!

Later, the kids swimming in the twilight, Claire and Charlie clear the table, take the dishes and cups and pizza boxes to the trash before it gets too dark, and as she is stuffing pizza boxes into a trash can inside the garage, Charlie feels a speech emerging from some dark place inside him, an urge to say something, an urge to make something happen, just to see if he can. He feels his father's blood buzz in his veins.

"I want this. I want a full house," he says, making eye contact with Claire. Holding her gaze. "I want to help. I want to be near you, in the same orbit, and I want to know when you wake up and when you go to sleep and I don't expect anything more, Claire, but I want you to come live in this house. I will live out in my father's office. I prefer to sleep there anyway. It has everything I need. Otherwise, this big house will just go to waste."

She does not think about it, she simply says, "That is an insane and generous offer."

And as they are walking back to the pool, Charlie calls, "COWABUNGA!" and breaks into a full sprint, whipping off his shirt, leaping off the pool deck, and finally landing in a colossal cannonball amid her shrieking children. Claire's hands fly to her face as if she is trying to stop the exploding grin from being a reality.

Charlie surfaces and feels invincible.

12

Outside, Don Lowry hears shouting and laughter and music. He looks next to him, to ABC, sleeping. If she does love him, if that's really what she meant when she kissed him and said, *Don't be dumb*, maybe he can get past the idea that his own wife, the woman he's loved for nearly two decades, doesn't love him. It'd be easier to get through all this, just maybe, if he already had his next love lined up.

"ABC?" he says, in a throaty whisper. His mouth is so dry. Outside, the music seems to swell and a wave of laughter, unmistakable laughter, echoes in the yard. His children. His children, laughing.

He gets off the futon, heavy headed, and pulls up the shades of the windows and sees, in the gloaming, his family in a state of raucous and unremitting happiness. Charlie leaping into the pool. His children shouting and splashing.

And Claire, his wife, smiling in a way he has not seen her smile in months. He presses his forehead to the windowpane, though he makes no sound and nobody notices him.

PART IV

How is it possible to want so many things
and still want nothing. The man wants to
sleep and wants to hit his head again and
again against a wall. Why is it all so difficult?

—*Stephen Dobyns,* "How to Like It"

JULY 1,
91 DEGREES

Here is Don Lowry, here is the morning's new light, and here is the U-Haul truck that will take away the only life he ever imagined.

There is Claire on the front lawn, there are the boxes that will be loaded first, there is the Sharpie marker that she uses to write explanations of the contents inside: BOOKS, TOOLS, FRAGILE, HEAVY.

What Don wants more than anything is for his wife—she is still his wife despite the circumstances—to walk toward him and hold him and whisper a word—*sorry*—into his ear.

And maybe he'd see her cry—he's not seen that for a while and it terrifies him. Is it really that easy to fall out of love? Have the last two decades been negated from their memory?

Don imagines that they have hugged, and then cried, and now are wiping their eyes with the palms of their hands as if they could press all the tears back in. But they do not do that. Instead, Claire calls out for the keys. He tells her they are in the truck and goes inside.

What he finds even more unbearable is that soon the kids will wake up, and soon they will see the truck, and they will know that they are moving and they are moving to a place where their father will not come.

Bryan is twelve and that means he's old enough to help, not cry. He is getting stronger. He can lift heavier boxes now, even heavier than the ones his mom can lift. He does not have the aches and pains he hears his father complain about.

When Bryan wakes up, Don greets him in the hallway.

"You wanna help us load up?" Don asks. "We could use the muscle."

But Bryan does not want to help. He doesn't say this, or anything else, just sulks by Don in silence and goes into the bathroom and locks it. Don stands outside the door. The shower begins to run. Don almost knocks on the door, but then doesn't knock on the door.

In her room, down the hall from Bryan's room, Wendy is awake. Don can hear her stirring and he knocks and when she mumbles, "Come in," he pushes the door open and finds her dressed, looking out her window, sitting on a box packed with her books. You cannot see the front yard from her window, so she has not seen what Bryan has seen: her parents in the morning light, in the long shadows of the U-Haul. But her shades are open and to the east you can see the mottled sun of early morning, the sunrise, which you can always see from this window. Some mornings last winter, when the low, thin clouds in the sky striated across the blue expanse, Don would find Wendy there, staring out at the sky.

"I'll miss this view," Wendy whispers and when she says that, Don thinks it sounds like something an adult would say.

Don tightens his face and goes down the hall to the master bathroom to brush his teeth so that he will not cry too. But the toothbrushes have been packed and his weeping attracts Bryan, and then Wendy. Bryan is wrapped in a towel, Wendy is holding a box of tissues. They regard him as if he is someone they don't know well at all, and maybe they really don't.

"I had a dream that you all moved without me," Bryan says. "In my dream, I woke up and found the house empty."

"That's the dream I had!" Wendy says. "Almost the same thing. I came home from the pool on my bike and the house was completely empty."

"We'd never move without you, kids," Don says. "That's impossible."

"But you are, Dad," Bryan says. "That's what you're doing."

"Not exactly," Don says. "I mean, not forever."

His voice somehow doesn't sound like his own. He clears his throat. He says the same thing again. And now his own voice sounds even stranger than it did before, as if he is underwater and shouting up toward the surface.

It is hard for Claire not to admit that what she likes most about the new house—Charlie's house, the Gulliver place—is that it is empty. The clutter of the Lowrys' lives has choked the energy out of the old place, but they have gotten rid of so much, have schlepped boxes and boxes to Goodwill and have managed to make fifteen hundred dollars at their garage sales. So the move will not be so hard. They will not fill the Gulliver place. There are three bedrooms upstairs and each of them will have their own. Charlie will sleep out in the guesthouse, amid a small clearing he's made in the chaos of his father's intellectual clutter, so the children feel comfortable and unconfused.

Charlie and Don move the beds in one at a time. Bryan and Wendy bring in random boxes and odds and ends and ABC is already setting up the kitchen. If you had just driven by and seen the U-Haul, you would have assumed that this was one big extended family helping out on moving day.

At one point, Claire and ABC find themselves out near the

pool, taking a break from unpacking. As the temperature climbs toward 100 degrees, the kids have quit helping unpack and have taken refuge in the water.

"Hey, Ma," Wendy hollers while treading out in the deep end, "I don't like our new house, I LOVE IT!"

"We should totally go for a swim too," ABC says, after walking over to Claire, who is standing outside the guesthouse in a small shaded spot. ABC had been drinking an iced tea in the air-conditioned comfort of Gill Gulliver's study when Claire and the kids came out and the kids jumped, shrieking with pleasure, into the pool. It seemed antisocial not to come out of the room and chat.

"If I can find my swimsuits. They are packed here somewhere."

"Hasn't stopped you before," ABC says.

"Touché."

"Anyway, God. I hate moving."

Claire nods, sips the glass of tea ABC has handed to her. "When you don't have a choice, it sucks."

ABC and Claire watch the antics of the children for a bit.

"Look, Claire," ABC says, "I just want to say, um, I think it's really cool how you and Don are trying to do this in such a drama-free way. My parents made my life a living hell for six years when they separated."

"No kid deserves that. It's strange—nobody I know comes from a family that stayed intact. You, Don, me, Charlie. I mean, what the hell?"

"Do you think it scars us?"

"It makes us incapable of love," Claire says. "I mean real, healthy, focused love."

"No," ABC says. "That's not true. I was in love once."

"Yeah, but she died," Claire says, and it sounds harsher than she intends. "I guess, I mean, maybe she died before you had to deal with the end of love."

ABC can sense the distance coming from Claire, even on the sweltering pool deck. She feels she has to say something.

"I want you to know that Don and I are just friends," she says. "We've never, you know, done anything. I know it must seem like it, it must be hard to believe, that's all."

"I don't think at this point it would make sense to lie. It'd almost be impossible. And anyway, you and Charlie are obviously together?"

"We're just friends."

"With benefits, right? That's what they say? Or was that a one-time thing?" Claire says. "When we walked in on you?"

"Do you care?"

"No," Claire says.

"Here's what matters now," ABC says. "Don and I are just friends. That's all I intend, even with all this upheaval. He loves you. You guys have such a good life. Take your time. You don't need to decide anything."

"It's not that good a life."

"What do you mean?" ABC asks. "I mean, you have such a great family."

"I don't think I've loved him in a long time."

"But he—he really wants to make it work."

"Yes," Claire says, flatly. "But do I?"

JULY 2,
93 DEGREES

Everything that Don Lowry takes to the home of Ruth Manetti fits, conveniently, into his pickup truck, which he and Charlie had unloaded the day before with minimal effort. Don is proud of the way his family behaved during the relentless heat and stress of moving day—the children had been good humored and optimistic (big new bedrooms and a sparkling pool helped a great deal), Claire had been even and efficiently pleasant, and Charlie and ABC had simply done a lot of lifting, using the strength and energy of youth—they both looked radiantly sweaty all day. And now, it is midafternoon and Don is setting up his own room for the first time in his adult life.

There is an empty guest room at the Manetti house: years ago, the attic had been converted into a guest suite—a small bathroom with a shower stall, a double bed, an easy chair, a small desk, a chest of drawers, and an empty closet awaited Don Lowry.

"Whatever you do, keep it away from the children," Claire had said the day before they moved.

"What? Keep what away?" he'd asked.

"You and ABC. Whatever you have going on there," she'd said.

And Don had replied, "I think you're the one who needs that reminder, Claire."

The night before, he'd had a dream, and woke up before dawn in a kind of blistering agony. He had dreamed of Claire making love to Charlie. She'd been flat on her stomach on a bed, Charlie fucking her from behind. Don had been sitting behind a large desk, looking, mainly, at his phone, trying to ignore the sex act taking place in front of him. And then the dream turned into a nightmare when both of his kids walked into the room and started howling with sorrow. It made him sick; he woke up puking into the trash can by his bed.

He knows that Claire will be the first of them to break the bonds of marriage—if any of them are left in any sense other than legal ones. Claire simply had to ask Charlie Gulliver to fuck her and he would. Why wouldn't he?

Don doesn't know what ABC thinks of him, not really. He wonders if she is helping from a truly genuine place or if she simply likes the drama of it—of something so miserably adult in her life. Or maybe she does want him. Maybe she would fuck Don Lowry and afterward laugh about it with a friend. He doesn't really even know her, he just knows she is sad, and that she wants to be dead. Don never understood, not in the past, how someone could fall this low, so low they wanted to leave their life behind.

Maybe now he can.

ABC had helped unpack his things. Everything he needs for work he keeps at his small office downtown, so he has only his clothes, a few books, and a box of things he had wanted to save for sentimental reasons. The Lowrys had rented a storage unit out at the Munger farm—his old pal Ike Munger had built sixteen storage units out there long ago, when corn was not so lucrative for a time—and a lot of the family's stuff that had not been sold or given away was there. Ike had waived the rent.

There is one thing ABC might not have let Don bring into the house, so he hides it from her: the gun his father had given him remains hidden away in his shaving kit.

Back at the Manetti place, it does not take Don and ABC long to bring up Don's remaining things to the attic bedroom. They have not even woken Ruth, who is napping in her usual spot, in the first-floor study. It's a sweltering day, and when ABC appears with two already sweating bottles of Bud Light, Don is happy to see the beers. He drinks most of his in the first minutes of swigging and ABC, who has been sipping hers, hands her own bottle to Don.

"I actually don't feel like a beer," she says. "I feel like a shower and a nap."

"Jesus," Don says. "This is too fucking weird."

ABC goes over and rubs his back the way she might try to calm a scared dog.

"You packed light," ABC says. "That's a good sign."

"Yes. I promise that it's temporary. We have stuff in storage."

"For your family's sake," ABC says, "I hope it is temporary. But Ruth doesn't mind. You can stay as long as you want. She told me that. She likes you."

"And do you mind?" Don says.

"No, I'm glad we could help. I'm glad Ruth could, at least. I'm also a squatter. Anyway, go ahead and get settled in—I'm making tacos for dinner. Will you join us?"

He nods.

"Okay, Don Lowry. Come down around seven thirty and fill your belly."

With that, she turns, almost like a gymnast might turn, sharp and tight, one foot six inches off the ground and pointed forward, the other foot a pivot. Then she stops and faces Don again.

"If something happens to me," she says. "You'll take care of Ruth for a while, right?"

"What's going to happen to you?"

"If I die, Don."

"If you take your own life, you mean?"

Don goes to the shaving kit and takes out the small handgun. He has a box of bullets in there too, and he loads one into the chamber and sets the gun down on the desk.

"Jesus fucking Christ, Don!"

"This is a gun my father gave me."

Without looking up from the gun, he tells ABC the story of his father, of Matt Good, of the murder, of the strange way he became the owner of this accursed weapon.

"Why do you have it here?"

"If you're serious about killing yourself," Don says. "Here. Do it now."

"What are you talking about, Don?"

"You say you want to die. Stop saying that unless you mean it."

"Do you want to die?"

"Right now? Yes."

"Why?" ABC asks.

"Look at me. Look at my life."

"Don, it's not that bad."

"But it is for you. You can go around telling people you want to be dead. Why? Because you're young and beautiful and that makes it all somehow romantic?"

"Don. Stop."

"Do you love me? ABC? Do you love me?"

"Of course."

"I mean, are you in love with me?"

"No."

"It's just, when Ruth was on the porch that day, she wanted you to tell me something. Like a confession. And I want you to know I am open to it."

"To what?"

"To loving you. I know my marriage is still in the process of crumbling, but I can see it. I mean, if that's where you're going with this."

Don fingers the gun on the desk timidly, as if picking it up again would cause it to go off.

"Just don't kill yourself, ABC. Don't say that's what you're doing."

"Don. You're confused. I just—listen, when Philly was alive, we used to joke about you."

Don starts to unpack some more, and doesn't look at ABC. It's been an exhausting day and the thought of another emotional conversation makes him feel nauseous. She tells him the whole story, though, of Philly, in bed, telling her that she'd come back through Don Lowry.

"Why me? Why did you joke about me?"

"I know. It's dumb, but—we used to laugh about your billboard. Your slogan."

"It's my business?"

"Yes. That. When we were stoned we found that unbelievably funny."

"Okay."

"And then one night, after we'd had sex, I felt this overwhelming melancholy—and for some reason I said to Philly, I said, 'What will I do if you die?'"

"That's not funny."

"No, but you know what she said? She said she would send you to get me. She said she'd send you to lead me to the spirit world."

"What?"

"I know. I mean it seemed like some dumb stoned joke you make in college, but, I mean—that evening when you found me under the sycamore, and I realized who you were, well . . . "

"So you're friends with me because you think Philly sent me?"

"Is it not a weird friendship?"

"I thought it was a friendship."

"It is!" ABC says. "I shouldn't have said anything. I know it's fucked up, but I mean, how weird is that? And when I told Ruth about all this, she was convinced. She believes somehow you'll lead me back to Philly. And maybe it's only in dreams. When we get high, and I fall asleep next to you, I always dream of Philly. Isn't that weird?"

"It is pretty random."

"I don't believe in random things anymore," ABC says. "Ruth says I have to follow this, see where this leads me, even if it ends in death. I believe she's out there, in the beyond, waiting for me."

"Why?"

"Because love like that doesn't disappear."

Downstairs, Don hears the voices of his children. They said they would walk over, they wanted to see where he would be living. They wanted to see him in this small rented room, the symbol of his shredded life.

"Yes it does," Don says. "It disappears all the time."

"The gun," ABC says, and just as she says this Don takes the gun, then the box of bullets, and slides them into the desk drawer. There's a key for the drawer, which he locks at just the right moment, just as the kids come running in saying, "Dad! Daddy! Is this where you live?"

JULY 3,
94 DEGREES

Claire has been generous with the children: she's allowed them to bring as much as they wanted to the new house and now they are busy upstairs unloading boxes of clothes, toys, books, and keepsakes. Charlie's been generous too—"Spread out," he says, "hang stuff on the walls, *mi casa es su casa*."

"Are you sure? I mean, this is temporary. I know that."

"I know it's temporary, Claire," he says, "but the kids should still feel like it's home. And I just want you to be happy."

She has to admit, it does feel like home, already, in little ways. The simplicity of it, the clean lines of an uncluttered life: as she unpacks the kitchen, she can see the next few months evolving; she's been promised full-time work at the dining hall in the fall, a prospect she once found pathetic and discouraging, and now feels as if it is a step toward something else, some new unseen life. She'll be a shift supervisor, most likely. She'll take the kids to school in the morning come autumn, after feeding them a healthy breakfast in this really amazing kitchen, and then she'll go to work at the college. She'll chop vegetables and stock the salad bar and put puffs of whipped cream on lemon bars all day, then greet the students—who are a naturally friendly sort at Grinnell, all *please* and *thank you*—and head home before the dinner rush, perhaps, just in time for the kids to be done with soccer practice and after-school art class and piano lessons. On Wednesdays, Don will take them for pizza. On weekends, he'll take them on hikes and adventures they'll remember into adulthood.

It will not be a terrible life. The kids will be okay and so will she, Claire says, hoping she believes it.

And Charlie? Where will he be? Done with his mother's charge, his father's study put into order? Perhaps he will be back on one of the coasts, giving acting one more shot? Or maybe he'll still be out in the guesthouse, editing his father's abandoned book after all? Or maybe even in the house with Claire and the kids, maybe sleeping in the same bed as Claire? One never knows. She will never admit it to anyone else, but she does picture it. Not necessarily with longing, but with a kind of fictional curiosity. What would that life be like? What would that road lead her to later?

She had tried to store most of her family's kitchen stuff, but since the Gulliver place was largely empty, she has packed four or five boxes of things and is unwrapping glasses when she sees movement in the long shadows of the backyard: Charlie, shirtless, cleaning the pool.

Despite the waning light, it is still so hot outside.

It is almost unbearable.

JULY 4,
95 DEGREES

On the Fourth of July, Grinnell, like most small towns in America, has a party that includes almost everyone in town. It begins with a Pioneer Pride 5K at seven in the morning, then a parade down Main Street at ten, and then a BBQ chicken dinner at noon at the American Legion. There are games for the kids at the municipal pool, a Vietnam vet who skydives into Ahrens Park at the afternoon ice cream social, and a rock and roll concert/sock hop heavy on patriotic anthems by Willie Warren & the Wayward Sons. The holiday ends with the town's fireworks display and a series of drunken gatherings to watch said fireworks.

It is not Don Lowry's day with his children—that will be tomorrow—and as he wanders through the gathering crowd in the sweltering downtown, the only thing he notices are other children. The sweet, happy packs of four and five—two adults at each helm. He sees old high school friends married to their old high school sweethearts, leading their children through the growing maze of people, looking for a spot along the curb. He sees a professor of history with one child on his shoulders, holding the hand of his wife, a professor of political science. He even sees the college president, with his partner, two well-dressed men chasing two running boys across the expanse of the downtown park. Don, unsure of what to do with himself, stops for an iced coffee at Saint's Rest, and when he emerges, sucking the bitter brew through a straw, he looks across the street to the front of the post office and sees his own children: Bryan is sitting sullenly in a lawn chair, large noise-protective headphones on (he hates marching bands, fireworks, and gunshots, so he's pretending to listen to music during the parade, his old trick). He sits next to Claire, who has on a white sundress and white sandals, and she is laughing and looking up at the man standing beside her, Charlie Gulliver, and holding Charlie Gulliver's hand is Wendy, Don's younger child, Don's little girl, and she is pointing with one hand at something coming down the street (the parade is starting!) and with her other hand, she pulls on Charlie Gulliver's arm.

Don walks into the street. He turns to his right and sees that yes, the first fire trucks of the parade are maybe twenty-five yards away. He stops in front of them, right in front of Claire, and Charlie, and the kids.

"Daddy!" Wendy yells.

The fire engines inch closer, two firefighters throwing candy from the bucket of the cherry picker.

The band is playing Sousa, behind the fire engines.

Wendy and Bryan wave, squinting into the sunlight.

Claire says, "Don!"

Charlie says, "Dude, come over. The parade's gonna mow you down."

Dude?

Don keeps staring at his family, unable to speak or move. In front of the approaching fire engines, the parade marshall, Olympic speed skater Leslie Hammer, is waving to the crowd. She wears red, white, and blue shorts; sneakers; and a white warm-up top. She is ten yards away. The candy flies from the fire engine. Her smile meets Don's eyes and then her smile fades and Claire says, "Don! Move!"

It is a police officer who finally moves into the road, and escorts Don to the side, away from his family, and when the slow fire trucks pass between them, Don Lowry disappears.

JULY 5,
95 DEGREES

The heat would not break and even the sun at the city pool could grow unbearable after ten minutes, and so, because it is Don's day to take the kids, his first outing as the noncustodial parent, he drives them to an indoor waterpark outside Des Moines; Claire has found him a deal on Groupon, a cost-saving move she's taken to since the separation, and he is grateful for the idea.

Back home, in the sultry late afternoon, Charlie takes an ice bucket of six beers out to the deck by the still-empty pool. On his fourth beer, he reads another cache of his father's letters; these he finds in a manuscript box in a bursting file cabinet in the closet. Letters in front of him, both from the admirers and to the admired—fervent declarations to Melinda and Sidney and Jamaica spilling out in front of him, all of them carefully photocopied and dated and saved in manila folders. His father had been serious about saving these, and he wonders, if early-onset dementia comes for him someday, would there be something shameful like this that he too will leave behind?

Do we all have secrets and do we all leave evidence behind of such secrets when our end comes without notice? What would Charlie want burned if he were to become incapacitated someday?

Maybe that is the sign of a good, ethical life? The idea that there is nothing you need to burn before you die.

He watches Claire walking through the backyard toward the pool. She is wearing a pair of paint-spattered white overalls over a white ribbed tank top. She has been eager to earn her keep around the place, and has taken to painting the mildewed walls of the laundry room and the downstairs bath. She tells Charlie it will help him sell the place quickly when he's ready to do so. She'd said so yesterday as she recaulked the upstairs bathtub where Wendy would soak for almost an hour nearly every night.

"Don called," Claire says to Charlie now. "They're having so much fun that he is using that coupon to stay at the hotel tonight. The kids seem happy about it."

"Oh," Charlie says, barely looking up. He is reading a letter about a woman wanting to go back to a riverfront hotel in Davenport with his father and he reads it aloud to Claire: "'Gill, can't believe you got me to go to a gentlemen's club! That was kind of naughty. I was drunk!'"

"Jesus," Claire says.

"Right?" Charlie says. "Crazy, right?"

"He wrote a lot of letters. But why torture yourself?"

"Some to you? Maybe?" Charlie says. "There were some to ABC and some to a woman named Claire."

"I am sure we wrote notes. I took like four classes with him. And then I was his colleague for two years. All of this before e-mail. So we wrote notes. Not like that one though."

"At any given moment," Charlie says, "it seems like my father was in love with a hundred women."

"I think you shouldn't read these," Claire says. "We could burn everything without reading them and set you free."

"But there's a book somewhere in these piles. His life's work, Claire."

"He won't know the difference. And if there was a book, why would—" she says, and then stops herself, reframing her statement. "Wouldn't he have published it if he had wanted it published?"

"He was a perfectionist," Charlie says. "He would have been afraid to, I think. Afraid of rejection, maybe?"

"I understand that. One bad review in the *Times* is enough."

"Your book got a bad review?"

"The worst!"

Claire stands near him for a long time, not speaking. She is glad to see him. Her whole body sways, as if she might fall on him without meaning to, and she plunges her hands into her pockets and feels the warmth there.

"Why didn't you ever write another book?" Charlie says.

"I didn't want to," she says.

"Is that the truth?"

"Something happened to me," Claire says. "I don't know what. I stopped wanting things."

"And now?" he says.

"Now," she says, "I just want."

JULY 6,
97 DEGREES

The house is filthy, at least by Ruth's standards, and had, in her able-bodied days, been impeccable. ABC knows she has not been as good a live-in aide as she had first set out to be when she arrived in Grinnell. She loves Ruth. She genuinely wants to do a good job, and she knows she has left Ruth home alone for stretches that are too long, spending her time with Charlie, sorting through his father's papers, or with Don, smoking, hoping to take a nap beside him and dream of Philly again. She knows she has not made the meals as nutritious as they should have been—frozen pizzas and grilled burgers. She knows the house is not as clean as it could be. But it is an odd situation, incredibly informal. In exchange for room and board (ABC has a monthly grocery store allowance to spend on Ruth's behalf) and a small monthly stipend, Ruth hasn't asked for much: an eye on her, keep her company, help her with whatever she needs help doing.

Mainly, ABC has helped the old woman stay high.

So that morning, ABC apologizes to Ruth for any recent oversights and inadequacies.

"I'm afraid I am not taking very good care of you," ABC says.

Ruth says, "Oh, phooey, honey. Who cares? I'm dying, and

hopefully soon. You have a life to live. Anyway, there's only one thing I can't do for myself. I can't drive to Newton and buy my grass."

"The house is dirty. I will clean all day. It'll look better," ABC says.

"God, the hours of my life I spent cleaning," Ruth says. "Some of the only hours I regret. I was a housewife. They used to call us that. And I cleaned so much, as if it was the only way to demonstrate my value to the world."

"Well, this is no way to live," ABC says. "You deserve better."

"I'm done living," Ruth says. "And I am not trying to be dramatic here."

"I understand," ABC says. "We went to see my friend's dad at the Mayflower. He's gotten a kind of dementia that comes and goes. He's a lot younger than you. It doesn't seem like a dignified way to go. I wouldn't want to go that way."

"Gill," Ruth says.

"You know him?"

"They don't let people go in a dignified way anymore," Ruth says. "You promise me, if you find me on death's door one morning, you won't call 911? You give me some weed, maybe some painkillers—or whiskey if that's all you have—and don't call a soul until you are sure I am gone."

"I got it."

"This is the one major kindness the young can do for the old, yet they are all afraid to let it happen. They call 911, and you get six months of medical care and a month of hospice instead of an easy way out."

ABC looks at Ruth, whose eyes have taken on a dark sheen, the pupils overwhelming the deeply blue, almost purple, irises.

"Okay," ABC says, although she isn't sure she could do what has just been asked of her.

"You see?" Ruth says. "This is why I like you more than anybody else. When I give you the straight dope, you don't reel off some optimistic bullshit."

"I understand wanting out," ABC says.

Ruth pats ABC's hand.

"I've lived a full life," Ruth says. "A very full life indeed," she says.

Anytime Ruth says "a very full life" in a dreamy whisper, ABC will stop whatever she's doing and sit down and listen to the story at hand. On this particular morning, Ruth talks not of a trip to Europe with her husband, or something she'd studied in college, when she was the first woman from her small town in Minnesota to ever go away to college, but of something that happened later in life.

Often, Ruth begins her story by asking ABC a question. "Your friend Philly. Was she your first lover?"

"It was something new to us. It had just happened. We'd been friends first."

Ruth nods slowly. ABC is afraid Ruth will fall asleep. She wants to talk more, wants desperately for Ruth to remember this conversation, to bring her some insight and meaning, two things she feels are perhaps no longer existent in the world. Certainly none of the events of the last year indicated that insight is a real possibility, or that meaning is something one could discover.

"We grieve for lovers differently than we grieve for friends or parents," Ruth says. "The physical separation—it can be unbearable."

ABC feels as if she can hardly move, or as if something inside her body will turn to water, will liquify and turn to nothing. And she'll cease to exist. She feels—there was no other way to say it—suddenly unsolid.

"The way that you carry your grief," Ruth says, "it's the look of passion, taken away before it had run its course."

"Yes," ABC says. "We'd just begun."

"Do you only like girls?" Ruth says. It is funny, the way she says it, laced with bluntness and naiveté all at once. If some frat boy had phrased it that way, ABC would be offended and angry. But she understands that to Ruth it is a real question, a desire to know her better; *girls* was a generational term. To Ruth, ABC is so young. A girl.

"I don't know," ABC says. "I loved her. I wanted her to be my lover. I have not loved a woman like that before."

"Or anybody?" Ruth says.

"No."

"Do you love Don?" Ruth says.

"When I am near him, if I fall asleep near him, I still have those dreams of Philly, you know, emerging from that body of water. Only if he is here, only after we smoke pot and lie down together, do I dream of Philly. Those are the only times I get her in a dream."

Ruth stares off into the dark corner of the room, as if she can see something there, and then her face lights with recognition. Ruth says, "Oh, I see. He's a vessel."

Ruth has gone pale and her voice is almost inaudibly hoarse. And then, just as swiftly, she perks up and resumes talking in her usual way.

"Ruth, are you okay?"

"Your generation, all of this shame!" Ruth says. "My generation—our parents didn't think about us much. And if they did, they whacked us when we were in trouble. But ever since your generation's parents gave up spanking? They've shamed their children into submission. Even the very good people in your generation, especially the very good people, just have so much shame. Everything you do makes you feel guilty."

"True," ABC says.

"I was over fifty," Ruth says. "Can you believe it?"

ABC smiles, but she doesn't follow.

"When I took my first lover, other than my husband. When I finally had a second lover, I was practically an old lady."

"Wow."

"How many lovers have you had?" Ruth says.

"There was only one who mattered."

"Hmm," Ruth says. "I think that is a good thing, sweetie. I loved my husband, loved him since we met the summer I turned twenty, wanted to have a family with him, wanted to feel him next to me each night. We had a good life, but, well, when the kids left, there was some distance, and I was, I was too old to consider the dangers of it. I'd always wanted a lover, deep down; somehow I knew I would take one if an opportunity arose. I wasn't looking for it though, and assumed it would happen only if something happened to John."

She gets teary for a moment, dabs at her eyes with a tissue. "And he had his. I am sure Mr. Manetti had his. Back then, it was different. In the seventies, professors did that sort of thing. With students. He traveled with one girl and I could see the sadness in his face when the trip was over. A conference in England. He said he had gone alone."

ABC, suddenly exhausted, shrugs. "I'm sorry." What else can she say? She stands up and thinks she might put some soup on the stove for lunch. Ruth is tired. She'll nap soon and probably forget the entire conversation.

"I was slender, still, and walked every morning, and I did my weights and exercises, my hair was still dark, not as black as it had been, but with the exercise, which back then, was not a very common thing to do, and the hair, and my figure—my hips had always attracted men. I was so sad when I broke one a few years ago. I had always considered my hips my best attribute. I used to wear the dresses and blue jeans that flattered them. I was somewhat vain! It's hard to believe, right, with this afghan on my lap, my hair a whitened bird's nest."

ABC finds a brush in the junk drawer. "Should I brush it?"

"Sure," Ruth says and ABC stands behind Ruth, behind her chair, and brushes as gently as she can. The old woman feels as if her neck is easily breakable, as if brushing might take out her remaining hair.

"It was a summer morning, and I was walking, briskly," she says, "dumbbells in hand, out on the path that goes behind the observatory, and I met a young man, a new professor, dashing—that's the only way to describe him.

"I would see him out there every morning and our nods and hellos soon became friendly exchanges. It was summer. He'd just arrived, hadn't taught his first class yet, and one day, I just . . ."

Ruth smiles.

"What?" ABC says, still brushing.

"I blew him," Ruth says.

ABC shrieks with a kind of shock and begins to laugh. Ruth's slender shoulders shake with laughter too, silent laughter. It takes ABC almost five minutes to recover.

"In some ways, it's terrible, but now, it's just, well, it's just a fact."

"Where did you blow him? Right there on the path? Oh my God!"

"That's what they said then. It was 1982. They said 'blow job.' They said, 'She blew him.' Isn't that still what they say?"

"I guess so. Sometimes we say oral sex."

"Oral sex? Sounds clinical."

ABC smiles.

"Did you have oral with Philly?" Ruth says.

ABC says, "That's private."

"I did always wonder about that. I always thought a woman would know just what to do."

ABC smiles. "Yeah, pretty much. So, oh my God, you just blew this guy?"

ABC wants details before Ruth loses her energy and clarity.

"I didn't just blow him. The kids were gone by then. Away. Grown. And John was at a conference in London, was spending most of the summer there. John annoyed me. It was hard to get used to being a couple without kids around. Everything he did annoyed me. And I think it was mutual. I wanted time away from him, just away from his snoring and the slurping of cereal and the general noise of him. It was the first time I'd ever lived alone in my life, that summer.

"And so, one day, on the path, this man, this shirtless beautiful man, was tying his shoe when I passed him. And so we got to talking. He was new to town, to the college, he said, and I invited him for coffee, I said I could tell him about life in Grinnell, and he looked at me, looked at my breasts, my face, my hips, and I felt him looking at me, and he said he'd finish his run and take a shower and come over."

"And you did? Then?"

"All summer, we kept it up, and then John returned and school resumed, and it was different. He found a young woman to marry. He stayed on in the English department, and so I would see him, from time to time, and yet it was actually never that awkward. It was kind of, I don't know, compartmentalized? It didn't feel like my real life. It felt like some self-contained interlude . . . Jesus, I'm tired, ABC. All of a sudden I need to sleep."

ABC helps her to bed.

As Ruth starts to fade, ABC asks, "When did all of this happen?"

Ruth, now smiling, closes her eyes, lets out a sigh. "Oh, years ago. Three decades ago. 1982, it was."

"1982?"

"Yes. He wrote me some letters that fall. He disguised them by using envelopes he had stolen from the Presbyterian church. My husband always thought I was just getting the Presbyterian Women newsletter."

"Clever," ABC says.

Ruth, dozing now, murmurs, "He always wrote wonderful letters. I have some of them still. We should get rid of them, you know. Before I die. Remind me tomorrow."

"Is this why your kids don't talk to you anymore?" ABC says, though she's already figured this out from the tears that flood Ruth's eyes. "Your kids are lucky to have a mom like you," ABC says. "You think they'd be more forgiving, you know?"

"Mothers have secrets," Ruth says. "I mean, all women do. But mothers? Oh, they die full of secrets. There are certain things nobody wants mothers to say, to think, or to feel. There are restrictions, rules. And if those secrets get out? Unforgivable."

JULY 7,
97 DEGREES

It is sweltering and Don and ABC are on the porch when a letter arrives by certified mail. They've taken to sitting in the heat, drinking cold beer, and then going into the house, blasting the AC, and getting stoned. It is a way to pass the day.

Don knows the mailman, Ron, who usually will stop and chat a bit with Don and then continue on his way. ABC has seen it happen a few times, and has always found it pleasant—the small talk of a small community going about simple business. But today Ron delivers a certified letter and as soon as Don signs the letter, Ron brisk-walks back to his truck. He has not even so much as smiled or nodded at ABC.

"What is it?" ABC says and Don already knows as he opens it. The return address is from a family law firm in Iowa City, the envelope marked confidential and urgent.

Don takes the letter from the envelope, a thick sheaf of pages.

"She filed for divorce," Don says. "I've just been served."

ABC breathes deep, puts a hand on Don's shoulder. She feels as if there is the vibration of shattering plates coming from inside his body.

"Don Lowry," she says. "I'm so sorry."

He doesn't want to talk about it until they are inside, in the hazy smoke, and then all he says is this: "I want to kill myself too."

"No, you don't. You have a lot to live for," she says.

"And you don't?"

"It's different for me, Don," she says. "You have kids."

"I'm like my father, ABC. People are better off without me now that I've hit this point."

"That's so not true," ABC says. She knows he's feeling bad about himself, and that he is scared, and she wants to let him vent.

"You don't believe me," Don says. "But I do. I can't do this anymore."

"Do what?"

"Watch Claire leave me for someone else? Watch my kids live with someone else? Watch my kids realize what a loser their father really is?"

"A loser father is better than a dead father, Don Lowry," ABC says. "And you're not a loser."

"I want to be dead. Just like you."

"Don Lowry."

"Let's make a pact. We'll pick a date. We'll find a place. We'll go down together, make it look like an accident. That way the kids will get my life insurance."

ABC doesn't want to tell him yes, but she does. They shake on it. She wants him to wait for her to be ready, and before then, she's sure, she can talk him out of it. Maybe she can save him. Maybe she can save his marriage. Maybe that is how she will find Philly again. Maybe if she saves Don Lowry's life, Philly will come back to hers.

JULY 8,
89 DEGREES

Charlie finds, in a cabinet beneath the bookshelves of his father's study, nine manuscript boxes hidden behind hundreds of back issues of *The New Yorker.*

He'd been browsing through the magazines, thinking he might try to sell them on eBay or maybe just keep them. He had the idea that he might read each one of them, cover to cover, and keep a journal about the experience. It would be one of those self-imposed regimens he'd been longing for and when he finished he imagined he would emerge smarter and less ignorant and better disciplined. But it is after he removes the first stack of magazines that he discovers the boxes, each one labeled with the word BOOK, in all capital letters and black marker. In smaller letters beneath the word BOOK, there are numbers, each box labeled with a digit one through nine. Nine boxes.

He opens the first one.

The top page reads: "Novel, Draft One."

He takes out the manuscript, which has been typed, not printed, and is beginning to yellow somewhat with age. The manuscript is bound with a spiral, obviously a professional job, something his father had deliberately organized and collated and preserved and he opens the book at random and reads this line:

> Instead of being the warm center of the world, the Middle West now seemed like the ragged edge of the universe—

It's a good line. A hell of a good line, and his heart rises a moment, thinking that he has found, perhaps, the manuscript that his father had worked on for decades.

He flips to another page and reads:

> He had passed visibly through two states and was entering upon a third. After his embarrassment and his unreasoning joy he was consumed with wonder at her presence. He had been full of the idea so long, dreamed it right through to the end, waited with his teeth set, so to speak, at an inconceivable pitch of intensity. Now, in the reaction, he was running down like an overwound clock.

He's found the manuscript! His father had, in fact, written a book and Charlie already wonders how he might go about finding a publisher to look at it. It appears to be a novel. Excited, he randomly grabs the fifth box, sees the "Untitled by Gill Gulliver" on the cover page and opens the manuscript randomly again.

> And so with the sunshine and the great bursts of leaves growing on the trees, just as things grow in fast movies, I had that familiar conviction that life was beginning over again with the summer.

And then, as swiftly as his enthusiasm rose, his doubts come rushing into his mind: what does it matter? What if his father had written a decent book, had not wasted those long hours in the study, weekend upon weekend. What does it change? Charlie doesn't know. It will change something, he believes that. Maybe it will even change his financial position in the world. Maybe his father's story will be one of those stories you heard about on public radio, the story of an eccentric man, now dead, or gravely ill, who had been crafting a masterpiece, the Great American Novel he was too afraid to show anyone.

Charlie grabs the ninth box; it must be the final, or at least the latest draft, he thinks, the one he will have to work to get published. He begins to think of the afterword he might pen. He'd recently read the journals of John Cheever and found his son's introduction to be one of the most fascinating things about the book. What if Charlie's father had been a tortured genius like Cheever? What if there are journals? What if he can publish even the letters eventually? He thinks for a moment that he may even make a career of it, of bringing meaning to his father's life, which is not parasitic but clarifying, an endeavor to provide context for a complicated life.

For the first time in a long time, he's excited about something that has nothing to do with sex.

He opens the ninth box. This manuscript is printed on a laser printer, clearly newer than the papers in the first box. This is a more recent draft. It reads on the title page: "Unfinished Project, Ninth Draft, February 2010."

This will be it. This will be the manuscript. He will go and see his father again. He will take a copy to his father and ask him about it. His father might remember something and he might weep with gratitude. His mind will flicker with magnificent recognition and he will thank Charlie for caring, for finding the life's work that Gill Gulliver's mind, at the end, was too cloudy to finish. Gill Gulliver's career had been one of endlessly obsessive revision, but Charlie will put the final punctuation on it. He will bring it clarity. Gill Gulliver will look at Charlie and understand that he has squandered his time with his son, that he has not been present enough, and he will feel unworthy of the gesture that Charlie is about to make: Charlie will finish his father's work, will secure his legacy so that even after Gill Gulliver has forgotten everything, the world will not forget him. What a perfect son. Charlie is fundamentally wonderful; this will be Gill's bittersweet, final moment of clarity, his last grounded thought.

Charlie opens the ninth draft to the first page and reads:

> In my younger and more vulnerable years my father gave me some advice that I've been turning over in my mind ever since.

Charlie begins flipping through the pages frantically, reading more and more, not wanting to believe that the names of the characters in this book, upon further perusal, are undeniably familiar: Nick. Tom. Daisy. Jordan.

Gatsby.

JULY 9,
87 DEGREES

This is the day during which Don Lowry sends Tom Merrick a lengthy pleading e-mail from his office and begs him, really, truly begs him: Could we—Claire and the kids and I—stay there for the whole winter? We need somewhere to be, away from everything, and I have nowhere else to turn.

After Don hits Send, he finds himself almost choking on a sob.

When Don hears from Merrick a simple, *Okay with me. You'll pay utilities?* Don goes over to see Claire. She is poolside typing on her laptop, wearing her tiniest black bikini, a stringed affair she had bought almost seven years ago, when they had gone away to Jamaica for a week, without the kids. Don finds it absurdly sexy. He tells her so, and says, "Is that *the* bikini?"

Claire says, "It's hot, Don. Do you want me to wear a sweater?"

"It's not so bad today. Not even ninety. Where are the kids?" he says.

"At the city pool. Charlie took them over so I could write."

"What a hero."

"If it's unclear to you that Charlie's generosity has saved us a great deal of heartache, it's not unclear to me."

"Can I go swimming?" Don says.

"Go for it," she says.

"God, I remember that," Don says. "By the way, I have good news. Merrick says we can stay all winter. At his lodge. It has heat and I can plow us out with the snowblower; there's one in the garage. All four of us, together round the fireplace."

She blinks at him. He is undressing. Stripping down to his black BVDs. His body is tan and looks good, though he is gaining some weight. She can see it in his sides and his chest.

"Will you spend the winter in Minnesota? Will you do it? Say yes?"

He says it with the earnestness he had years ago. She closes her laptop. She tells him to leave.

"It's a great plan!"

"It's not, Don. For one, school. Our kids are in school."

"We can homeschool."

"Oh, they'd love that."

"They might. We could snowshoe and ice-fish and ski! It's not like they like school all that much here. The school's not even that great, you always say that yourself."

"A valid point," Claire says.

"I'd chop wood all winter. I'd get buff again. I'd grow a beard."

She likes him with a beard but he thinks it's bad for business.

"I want you to start living in reality," Claire says.

"Before I do that," he says. "When I see you in your bikini, I can remember every detail of that trip."

"I was younger then," she says. "Good-bye, Don."

She tries to go back to her writing then, but Don hurls himself into the pool, swimming across it, getting out, jogging back over to her side, and hurling himself in again. He whoops and hollers as he does this, which at first sounds exuberantly joyful, and then quickly sounds painful, like an unwanted compulsion has seized control of his body.

Claire finds herself smiling though—she knows *this* Don, *this* Don she loves—and she resists the impulse to hurl herself into the water alongside him. He is still, on some level, irresistible to her, but resist him she does.

But when Charlie comes home, she finds herself sunning on the pool deck, in that tiniest of tiny bikinis. She's given up writing for the day by then. For him, she almost goes to the small diving platform and dives in the water, a show, a seductive show, but then she sees that Wendy is with him, sobbing.

Charlie shrugs as he comes near Claire. "Sorry," he says.

"She puked!" Bryan says, appearing suddenly in the yard as well. "In the pool, Mama. She puked in the pool! Will I get sick now? I don't want to puke."

"I couldn't help it," Wendy sobs. "I swallowed so much water!"

Claire wraps herself in a towel and says, as soothingly as her shaky voice can say it, "Okay, okay, everyone. Let's all fucking settle down."

This is not the word she means to say, but it is what she says.

"Mom!" Bryan says. "Mom!"

JULY 10,
84 DEGREES

ABC is bereft of dreams—such vivid dreams, all of June, and now they are gone. Now that Don Lowry has moved in, for some reason, lying next to him no longer makes her dream.

She is in the hammock on the sleeping porch—where she spends almost all of her down time now—and hears Don Lowry coming up the steps. It is late afternoon. Maybe he is drunk; his footsteps seem heavy and unsure, the clomping plod of a drunk man trying to walk soberly.

ABC stands up and smooths down her sundress and is surprised to find Ruth standing there.

"How did you get up the stairs?" she says.

"I walked!"

"You did?" ABC says.

"I feel good. It's four twenty, ABC. It's after four twenty. Do you want to smoke?"

"Okay," she says. "Is Don home?"

"No. No, he is going to go tell Claire some idea he has, then take the kids out for tacos."

"I see," ABC says. "Are they getting back together?"

"Would you care?" Ruth says, with a sideways glance and a smile.

Ruth sits in the large armchair next to the hammock. ABC reaches into her pocket, pulls out an Altoids tin, and lights a pre-rolled joint, and they smoke there, together.

"I wouldn't care at all," ABC says.

"Close your eyes," Ruth says, and ABC does.

"Think of her," she says. "Think of Philly."

ABC shuts her eyes and feels the hammock gently swaying as Ruth says, "Do you see anything?"

"What am I supposed to see?"

"My mother's mother, my Finnish grandmother, used to say that if you closed your eyes and saw fireflies, you know you're entering the spirit world."

"Do you see them?" ABC asks. "Because I don't see one firefly!"

"Oh," Ruth says, closing her eyes just as ABC opens her own. "Oh, yes, they are here! Happy to be here, aren't they?"

ABC closes her eyes again. "Seriously?" she says. "You just shut your eyes and boom—just like that? Spirit world?"

Ruth falls asleep marveling at whatever it is she sees, whatever show that's playing out on the back of her eyelids.

Looking out the window, ABC sees real fireflies all over the backyard, just floating around under the canopy of the trees. She goes out to the yard with a mason jar, catches, easily, twenty or thirty fireflies, and then begins walking. She wanders across campus, and strolls into Charlie's backyard.

She finds the study unlocked and goes inside, where she finds Charlie in a robe. He looks as if he's been swimming and has now dozed off on his cot while reading. A copy of *The Stranger* is on the floor next to him. ABC clears her throat. Charlie sits up with a start.

"Jesus, come on in, why don't you?" he says.

She locks the door behind her.

"I've been wanting to tell you something," he says. "I found something weird in my dad's things."

ABC slips her sundress over her head and hangs it on a hook near the door. He takes off his robe. He looks good, his body tan, his shoulders muscled and his waist lean. He is already aroused. She likes how easy it is to tell with a man.

She kneels down on the rug in front of him. She will make him forget all about Don Lowry's wife.

"First this," she says. And then, as Ruth Manetti might say: Reader, she blows him.

JULY 11,
90 DEGREES

"You know what, Charlie," Kathy Gulliver chirps, literally fucking chirps, "I'd forgotten how awfully hot Iowa can be!"

His mother has come back to town with Lyle Canon. They have been to a wedding in St. Louis and are swinging through Grinnell one last time before heading out to northern California for the fall, where Lyle has a friend who is not using a cabin, or something along those lines.

"It's a record-breaking summer, Ma," Charlie says. "It doesn't reflect reality."

"Maybe it's a new reality. No rain, no snow. A dust bowl!"

"Don't be so excited."

"Oh, Charlie, you've inherited your father's relentless gloom. It doesn't suit you though. You have my kind eyes."

Charlie and his mother walk down Broad Street in the heat on their way to see Gill. His mother is wearing a huge sunhat and a kind of hot pink tank top that ties in the back and a white skirt. She seems to skip a bit as she strolls. She's lost fifteen pounds from all the hiking and camping and canoeing and her hair is longer than it has been in years, dyed a saucy auburn. She had not given him advance warning. She had simply shown up that morning, rapping on the front door. Of course, Claire had answered, and had to point Kathy to the study out back, where she had been greeted by ABC, emerging from Charlie's chosen bedroom with wet hair and a sheepish smile.

As she watched ABC walk out of the yard, Kathy had said, "You've got quite the little harem going here, don't you? Like father, like son?"

Charlie had to explain, as best he could, exactly why Claire and her two kids were in the main house, and Charlie was sleeping like some squatter in a cot out by the pool.

"It's cleaner that way," Charlie had said, which wasn't much of an explanation.

"And who was leaving your little love shack when I arrived?"

"Mom. Jesus."

"What. I'm teasing. Life is for the living! God knows I would have fucked around a lot more when I was your age, if I could do it all over again."

"Mom!" Charlie had said.

"She looks familiar though, that one," Kathy had said. "I think she was one of your dad's groupies."

Now, only a few hours later, they are heading to the Mayflower to see Gill, and Charlie is still feeling stung by the whole operation, as if he has been ambushed by his mother's appearance, her newly tanned self, and her snark.

"That's quite a summery outfit," Charlie says. He is in jeans and a white T-shirt and canvas sneakers.

"I don't know how you can wear jeans in the summer," she says. "You know one thing I learned from Lyle: if you dress for the weather, if you have the right equipment, you don't ever want to be indoors!"

It is late afternoon and they find Gill sitting in a wheelchair near his window. The vertical blinds are drawn and he squints into the stripes of fuzzy sunlight that manage to get through to his room.

Gill's able to stand, for they both watch him for a long moment before making themselves known to him, and Charlie sees that his father will stand periodically and look out the slats in the blinds, as if he is waiting for someone to come and get him. Charlie walks over to him and says, "Dad? Mom's here."

His mother's eyes are drowning. Her flush face suddenly goes pale.

Gill looks like he's about to stand again but then he sits back in his chair.

"Oh?" he says. "My mother?"

He doesn't say Charlie's name but Charlie senses something different in his face this time, he senses that this man does recognize him, if not as his son, then as somebody who has some import in his life. As somebody he has known for a long time but whose name he cannot recall.

"How's it going?" Charlie says.

"Are you here with a car for me? To the airport? It's so much effort to get to the airport from this goddamn town, isn't it? That's what makes people go crazy."

"No. No. Sorry. That's not me, Dad."

Charlie motions for his mother to come closer and she does, but she seems hesitant to walk into Gill's field of vision.

"Well, what do you want?" Gill says. "How's ABC?"

"Dad, I have been in your study. I've been looking through your papers."

"My papers! My office on campus?"

"Well, it's all at the house now. All of your things."

"Kathy took them all there? Did she come home?"

"Dad."

"She left me, you know," Gill says. "Don't blame her really."

"Kathy is here, Dad. My mother. Your wife."

The word *dad* seems to surprise him, though he says nothing.

He makes a small *O* with his mouth and whistles vaguely through it. Charlie decides not to use the word *dad* again.

Kathy, meanwhile, is trying to turn her crying face into something resembling a smiling one.

"Do you know me, Gill?"

He shakes his head no.

She bends down and kisses him gently on the mouth.

"It's me," she says.

"Claire?" Gill asks. "Jordanna? Amy? Meredith?"

Kathy walks out into the hallway.

"I'll be right back," Charlie says. Gill says nothing. Charlie finds his mother—this stoic, optimistic, bizarrely carefree lover of Lyle Canon sobbing in a stained orange chair.

"Mom," Charlie says. "It's not personal. It's the disease, he can't help it."

His mother looks up at him and laughs through tears. She blows her nose in a tissue and then sets the tissue down on a copy of *Better Homes and Gardens*.

"I know that," she says.

"Mom," Charlie says. "Come back inside. It might be the last time . . ."

"All I ever wanted, Charlie, was not to be an afterthought in some man's life."

Charlie understands. He was also an afterthought, but he has a task ahead of him and he goes back inside with the word *afterthought* like a staccato beat in his head, a million voices, stomping on bleachers, chanting: af-ter-thought!

Af-ter-thought!

Af-ter-thought!

Af-ter-thought!

Charlie stands near Gill and kneels down so he can be at eye level with him.

"I want to finish your book for you, Professor Gulliver."

"My book?"

"Yes." Then, "Dad, it's me. Your son."

"What book?" Gill says, his voice breaking with sorrow or confused exasperation. It is hard to tell which, though Charlie wants it to be the former.

"The one on Gatsby. And Reagan."

"Oh, that."

"Yes, that one. Only I can't find the manuscript anywhere. Not on your computer, not on your CDs, not in your files."

"You can't?"

"No. Do you have any idea? Is it in a safe or file cabinet or—"

"It's not easy to find," Gill says.

"I know. Tell me, Dad. Where is it?"

"In fact, it's impossible to find it. Tell me who you are again?"

"Charlie. Charlie Gulliver. Your son."

Gill looks back to the window, as if he is now sure that someone is waiting for him on the other side of those blinds.

"There is no book," Gill says.

"What?"

"There is no book," Gill says again. "There never has been."

Charlie watches as his father's chapped lips begin to tremble, and his hands, shaking, begin to clutch his forehead as if he is suddenly in the grip of a blinding headache. Softly now, he says, "Son, there is no book. There never was. Tell your mother. Tell her I am so sorry for all of the things."

JULY 12,
90 DEGREES

A sale! Don Lowry makes a sale, a small fixer-upper ranch on the southwest side of town. After the closing, he has a check and he deposits the check just before the bank closes at five. Not a big commission, but a commission, his first in months. It's a check for four thousand dollars. He deposits three and takes out twenty fifties for his wallet. He drives out to the Hy-Vee and buys a bottle of champagne and some flowers, and he's not sure, even as he is buying the champagne, whom it's for, and the flowers, he has no idea, but he decides, for some reason, that he wants the flowers, and then he drives to the Gulliver place, and he rings the doorbell. Claire answers and invites him inside. He follows her and sees she's been in the kitchen cooking dinner with Charlie. The kids are outside in the pool.

"Are they out there alone?" Don asks. "Is that okay?"

"Yes," Claire says. "What are you implying?"

"They're excellent swimmers," Charlie says.

Don ignores this and gives Claire a stack of bills, counting them out onto the counter where Charlie is chopping an onion.

"Thanks," Claire says. "What did you do, rob a bank?"

"Yep," Don says.

Next, Don goes to the yard and strips down to his BVDs and throws himself into the pool to the delighted cries of his kids and he comes up splashing, roaring like a monster, the volume meant to thrill them like he did when they were toddlers and they run from him, giddily shrieking, and they do not know how real are his roars.

Later, the champagne is warm, but he sticks it in Ruth's freezer and he finds ABC in the yard. His khakis are wet from the rushed way he dressed after swimming, his hair still dripping onto his dress shirt. ABC is watering flowers in her cutoffs and a black swimsuit.

He says, "I have champagne," and she smiles but doesn't smile.

"I have flowers too," he says then. "Do you have grass?"

"I don't," she says. "I'm sorry."

She shuts off the water and goes to her room.

Don takes the flowers to Ruth's room, where she breathes a rattled breath as she dozes. He has arranged the flowers in a vase that he has found under the sink and when he sets them on the shelf across from Ruth's hospital bed, she sneezes in her sleep.

The champagne he drinks in the hammock alone.

JULY 13,
90 DEGREES

Claire gets a call from dining services that afternoon—there is a reunion at the college, a reunion of the school's past athletic teams, and they ask if she could help with dinner. They offer to pay double time, since it's technically the month off for Dining Services employees, and they're desperate for the help. Three people have called in sick; the sub list, in the summer, is thin.

Claire agrees, asks Charlie to keep an eye on her kids, and walks the few blocks west to campus. At the dining hall, in her visor and black T-shirt, she wonders, if she looks down at the register while she swipes dining hall passes, if people might mistake her for a student.

It is not long after she has that thought that a woman says, "Claire, is that you?"

Claire looks up to see Rachel Pettis and Holiday Furness in front of her, two soccer players from the class of '97. "Oh my God," they both say. "Hi!"

Claire says, "Hi."

"Do you still work here?" Holiday says.

"Not still. Again. I work here again."

"Oh my God, that is so crazy," Rachel says. "Are you a professor? Holiday is a professor at Carleton now. Women's history!"

"They let me help with the soccer team too," Holiday says. "My husband is the associate dean. I have connections."

Claire smiles. "I'm not a professor. Professors don't usually work the dining hall."

"Ha!" Rachel says, but she doesn't say much else.

"You should try the vegan bar," Claire says.

"Are you still with Don?"

Claire looks at the line forming behind Rachel and Holiday. "No," she says. "But it's complicated. That's kind of new. But he still lives here. Yes. We have kids." She makes a gesture toward the line behind them. "I can't talk now, I guess."

"No, totally," Holiday says, and takes a business card from her wallet and sets it in front of Claire. "My cell is on there. You should call us tonight. We're having drinks."

"Okay," Claire says.

Rachel takes out her own card. Rachel, apparently, is the theater and drama coordinator for the NEA. She takes a pen from Claire's check-in station and circles a phone number on the card.

"That's my cell. We're thinking around nine," Rachel says. "Will you be done by nine?"

She is speaking in a way that makes Claire feel like Rachel thinks that perhaps she doesn't understand English anymore.

"Later," Claire says, and then apologizes to the women who are next in line. She swipes their dining hall passes, too. "Sorry for the wait," she says. "I used to go here."

Here is a moment from that summer that, later, one might go back to again and again. Does it change anything for Claire? It's hard to say. But when she comes home from work, she sees that Charlie has used the relatively cool afternoon as a chance to mow the brown lawn. Claire sees the lawnmower and goes straight to the pool. The door to the bathroom off the study is unlocked, slightly ajar even, and when Charlie finally comes out of the shower, he sees Claire there in the bathroom with him, wrapped in a white towel, naked beneath it. She had gone swimming for a minute, to wash off the fried food smell of the cafeteria, but is now wringing out a swimsuit in the sink and Charlie is there, and she hands him a towel, a blue one, and says, *I have been standing outside the shower for a few minutes.* The steam in the room is thick, it has nowhere to go. *I have been trying to decide what I would do.*

She goes up to Charlie now and begins to dry off his body for him, running the blue towel down each arm, down his back, and finally, as she moves the towel down his chest, down the small trail of hair on his stomach, down to his hips—

And in the yard, Wendy: "Mama, are you here? Mama! Mama are you here?"

Claire struggles to put her wet swimsuit back on as Wendy's voice comes closer and closer. She slips out of the bathroom just in time, leaving Charlie standing there, and Charlie hears her say, "Yes, baby, yes. I am here."

Later, in the evening, Claire makes a gin and tonic in the kitchen, drinks half of it in one long pull, and says to Charlie: "This has all been a big mistake."

"What has?" he asks.

"All of this," she says. "This pool, this house, your face, my life."

She puts her hands on his chest and buries her head there, her face between her fists.

JULY 20,
84 DEGREES

The heat finally breaks, temporarily. The purple clouds of a sluggish dawn linger in the finally dry air. In the cool morning, the sudden small relief from the oppressive heat has Don Lowry thinking: he has failed to breathe in life deeply enough, but at the first hint of chilled air on the horizon, he vows to change. Come autumn, he will show his children the wonders of the leaves. He will become a different kind of father.

It is not yet seven A.M., but Don Lowry stands outside Mrs. Manetti's gate, getting the morning paper, and he turns and surveys the yard as he thinks these thoughts, just as he did decades ago with his lawn mower, his ancient truck behind him full of yard tools, his young heart then also heavy, but heavy with different woes. Older now, a man who sells homes, he has no tools with him this morning and has not been hired for any task; he is only stepping out into the morning to collect the daily paper, which he will, as has become his custom in the past few days, read aloud to Ruth Manetti over breakfast while ABC sleeps in upstairs. He thinks of how the Manetti house would look with his FOR SALE sign in the yard—even better, with a SOLD sticker slapped across it.

He is concerned, mostly, for his children this morning, who have been stoic, even cheerful through the past few months, but who have seen their parents at their intolerable worst, have probably noticed, at least intuitively, how their parents have been hungover and even sometimes asleep with other people and sobbing for no reason and smoking cigarettes and grass. Have they seen all of this? Understood it? Bryan is twelve, surely he's seen or heard something that has troubled him. And Wendy is so empathetic, she can sniff out stress from a mile away. She knows things were amiss, greatly amiss. She has resumed bed wetting since the move to the Gulliver house. Claire hasn't told him this, which made him angry. He's heard it from Bryan.

Truth be told, damage has been done. The kids will probably remember images from that summer for a long time, will file them away as pathetic memories of a father and mother gone nuts. Years later, Bryan will think of these images every time he drinks too much and quarrels with his wife. Wendy will call up recent episodes on some therapist's couch, where she has gone to get over a breakup with some tattoo artist but will instead spend hours discussing her sad and confused and distant father. "We moved into this guy's house," she will tell her shrink. "I have no idea who that guy even was, but he was way cooler than my dad. My dad was this big depressed loser. I don't talk to him anymore."

Don Lowry has succumbed to the Shadow; he's cast it over his children now, and they'll feel it too for the rest of their lives. It is not something one can undo. He should have seen it coming, but even if he had, he would have felt powerless to stop it.

When he is back on the porch, holding the newspaper, somehow his mood lifts again. He can change all of this. He can reset the course. His father had given up, had seen his mistakes as impossible to recover from—but Don Lowry has not made those mistakes yet. He has gotten a bit lost is all, hidden the wrong things from his wife, said some mean things, and sneaked out into the darkness and lingered in its pleasures. But he can come back.

He kicks the porch railing with his slippered foot. The porch itself needs to be jacked up; three rotten boards need replacing. Some of the steps should be rebuilt entirely. The left-side railing wobbles. The more he looks at the Manetti place, the more he knows it won't sell for as much as he once thought. You can't begin to sell a place with such warning signs greeting potential buyers at the entrance. He will talk to Ruth about it, hire somebody to do it for her before—wait. Before what? Before she is dead? Why will she care about the price her home fetches once she is dead?

At the kitchen table, he's greeted by Ruth. It's as if she is waiting for him. She looks well and alert. Up earlier than usual.

"Ruth," Don says. "Good morning. I hope I didn't wake you."

"Nonsense," she says. "I've been up since dawn. Since before dawn. Last night's fireflies are almost gone. I think the night was too cold for them."

Don doesn't quite know what to make of the last statement, but he smiles. When he is that old, if he lives that long, he hopes he will see fireflies when nobody else does.

"Well," she says. "Maybe you can make us some coffee and toast?"

Don sets about getting breakfast ready, brewing coffee.

"How are the kids?" Ruth asks.

"Hanging in there," Don says, which he knows implies they are not doing well at all.

"They must be excited about the upcoming vacation," she says. "You know how magical it is up there, on Superior. I want to talk to you about something. While the coffee brews."

"What is it?" Don asks, and he can't help but sparkle inside. This is it. She is going to ask him to sell the house. His earlier pessimism gives way to a sudden optimism. The house, he has already figured out, could list at $449,900, even with the work that needs doing: it's one of the most majestic houses on Broad, all of the original character still intact. His commission would be

7 percent of that if he brings in the buyer himself. A new dean has been hired at the college who is moving from Winston-Salem, and Don has already sent him a helpful e-mail. He will need a house in a hurry, and—

"I want to go on that vacation with you," Ruth says.

Don doesn't answer.

"Next month?" he says. "To Lake Superior?"

"That's where you are going, yes?"

"Yes. Tom Merrick's lodge. We go every August."

"I'm from up there, you know."

"I know that," Don says.

"And I want to see it again before I die," Ruth says.

"Ruth, you—"

"Are you going to tell me that I am not going to die soon? Don't do that to someone nearing ninety."

"Is that how old you are?"

"I am making a simple request. You're not paying me any rent."

"It's just . . . I don't know if we—Claire and I—can care for you properly."

"I know about Merrick's place. We went up there, John and I, almost twenty-five years ago. It's huge."

"Yes."

"There're still several cabins, right? And a lodge."

"I know. It's our family vacation though and—"

"I will bring ABC along. You won't need to help me with anything."

"We wouldn't have room in the car," Don says. "It's a long drive. We often take the third row of seats out of the Suburban so we can haul all of our stuff. We have these two inflatable kayaks that take up a ton of room."

"Charlie Gulliver will drive both of us. ABC and me. I've spoken with them about the logistics."

"Why with us? Why don't you go to some other place? Have Charlie and ABC drive you somewhere else? You could go anywhere."

"Because I want to see your family there, enjoying it. Bryan and Wendy, playing on the beach. I know their names, you know. I bet you didn't know that."

"I remember how much you like kids."

"I want to see your family in that cold, clear water. I've been dreaming of it for years and years, Don. That's how long it has been since I've been back. Don, I love Merrick's place. I don't want to be at some hotel or crowded resort. I want a private place, someplace that won't freak out if an old lady wants to be helped into the lake. I want to swim again, one more time."

Don tries to picture the old woman walking across the rocks and wading into the lake. The temperature of the water, he knows, could be as low as forty-five degrees. Even in this hot summer, the water will not be comfortable for swimming. And someone that old, if she fell in, she'd die, wouldn't she? Body shock.

"Ruth," Don says. "I want to help you. It's just very complicated. This trip is kind of a last-ditch effort for me."

"I know. You and Claire are having trouble. Do you think I don't know that couples have trouble? Believe me."

"That's an understatement. You do know I live in your attic? You do remember that, right?"

She smiles. "Do you think I am that senile, Don? I'm almost offended."

"It's not that easy to do this, to take other people."

"If you seek misery, Don, if you seek complexity, those things are easy to find."

"Ruth, please. The thing is, we may stay up there, for the winter."

"Charlie will bring me back here when I've had my visit."

"Ruth, I don't know."

"I know you are in despair, Don. So I have a plan for you. This is a step toward a solution, or part of one. If you take me up there with you for August, then I will transfer ownership of my house over to you in the fall. I already have Mendez working on the papers, so when I die, you get the house. You can sell it or live here, but it'll be yours."

"What? What about your kids?"

"I have some money set aside for them. They do not know this, but when I die Mendez will give them a letter. They'll get all my other assets."

"I'm not sure this is legal, really," Don says.

"Mendez will figure it out. ABC is taking me back to his office today, to work more on the papers. We're updating everything—my medical power of attorney is most concerning to me. ABC gets to pull the plug!"

"Jesus."

"Mendez is a genius. He's been our lawyer for decades—he can make everything easy."

"For taking you up to Lake Superior? For three weeks on the lake you'll pay that much? You'll give me your house?"

"I won't be needing it. I want to travel one last time and I want it to be somewhere I know I like. I miss Lake Superior so much. I want to be with people I trust. And I want to help you, Don," Ruth says. "We can help each other. It's my last wish. Don't you think I see what you and Claire are going through?"

"So that's it. You want to help me? What about ABC? Give her the house."

"ABC has her own plans. She doesn't need a house in Grinnell, Iowa. You can even take out an equity line of credit before I die, Don. You can pay off all your credit card debt like that. It'll be your house."

"It seems too much like charity."

"It's a business deal. You will be taking me on a dreamed-of vacation. I've wanted to go back since I turned seventy. Nobody takes an old lady on vacations."

"I don't know," Don says.

"You're at the hardest time of life, Don. Midlife is when you have to accept what you've created, knowing that the life you have is the only one you will live. And that can be terrifying, until you accept it, and then you're free of terror."

Don says nothing.

"Then it's just day by day. And most days are beautiful, Don. It's regretting yesterday or overthinking tomorrow, that's when ugliness comes in, right?"

"Uh, yeah. I guess."

"We're helping each other, Don," she says. "Like we always have. You used to cut our lawn. And dog-sit that awful dog we had."

"Pepper," Don says.

"The dog that shit five times a day," she says.

Don hears noises upstairs. The toilet flushes, the water runs, the floorboards creak. He pours the coffee, butters the toast.

ABC walks into the kitchen.

"Don Lowry!" she says. "It's your business!"

Then she looks at Ruth and back at Don.

"Did you ask him?" ABC says.

Ruth smiles and nods.

"Did he say yes?" ABC asks.

"I said yes," Don says. "I'll take you. But I don't want to be paid for it. I'll just take you."

"I'll just pay you," Ruth says.

Later that evening ABC sits cross-legged on a yoga pillow on the floor drinking wine from a coffee mug. Fireflies have come inside and are glowing everywhere, even inside the sleeping porch. She wants to go wake up Ruth, but she feels as if her limbs are too heavy to even move. She is stoned out of her mind, having tried out some new product her librarian had secured.

"I can't fucking see them," Don has said. "This is so frustrating. Why can't I see fireflies?"

"Ruth says fireflies gather when something new is about to happen, or when something old is about to end."

"Fuck," Don says. "This stuff must be stronger than usual. I don't see any fireflies."

"Totally," ABC says. "I don't know if those fireflies are even real."

Soon, Don is asleep in the hammock, snoring softly. And the realization ABC had earlier that season, on the night in late May when she met Don Lowry, becomes clear to her. She really does have to die in order to find Philly again, and now the dreams and Don Lowry's presence in her life and even Ruth's fireflies make sense to her.

She needs to enter the spirit world through the lake. She has to follow Don Lowry to Minnesota.

"Yes," Don Lowry says, in his sleep, as if he is dreaming about it right at that moment. "The lake."

"Don?" she says. "Are you awake?"

He snores and sways and does not answer. She trembles with the eeriness of it all. He is creeping her out.

"Don, are you fucking with me?" she whispers.

She gets up and goes downstairs and finds Ruth awake, sitting at the kitchen table.

"Are you watching the fireflies?" ABC says.

"So many!" Ruth says. "Gorgeous."

ABC feels weightless. The magnificent weed makes her feel as if she's floating with the fireflies.

"Ruth," ABC says. "It all makes sense now. I know how to find Philly."

"Lake Superior?" Ruth says.

"Yes!"

"You read my mind," Ruth says.

"How did all these fireflies get inside?" ABC says, then busts out laughing.

"The North Shore is a sacred place," Ruth says. "I thought maybe you were dreaming of it all along, the first time you told me about the dream you had, about Philly, the first night that Don Lowry slept here."

"Right? This can't just be coincidence?"

"It's meant to be," Ruth says.

ABC would find Philly again.

"How do I do it?"

Ruth thinks about it for a long while. ABC dozes off, watching the fireflies, and when she wakes up, Ruth is standing in the center of the room, as if she is making a speech to an assembled crowd.

It has to be early, Ruth says, when ABC does it, hours before dawn—in the time of night when the magic is not afraid of being discovered by the morning sun. ABC will take some of Ruth's painkillers and some of her own old anti-anxiety medicine and also wash down a few sleeping pills, those Driftozines the doctor had given Ruth, with beer, plus a bottle of Scotch just in case she is too wakeful, and a Ziploc bag of more pills, also just in case, and push herself out in a small kayak. ABC will wait until the lake is rough, a storm swell, maybe—Ruth has been reading about Superior online—and she will allow herself to be carried out to Lake Superior, where the spirit world will find a way to take her in.

"Just like that," ABC says. "It's like you've been thinking about this already."

"I'm an old woman," Ruth says. "I think about death a lot."

Would ABC drown or would she freeze or would the pills shut down her body before either of these things happened? She hopes to be unconscious no matter what stops her heart.

"Will it work?" ABC says.

"Are you scared?" Ruth asks her.

"You're like a goddess or something. Or maybe a good witch," ABC says.

"You live long enough," Ruth says, "you find much wisdom, you shed what doesn't matter. You want to die, ABC, so you can find your dead lover before she wanders too far into the spirit world. Most of the world wouldn't understand that, but I get it. I understand it."

When ABC goes back upstairs, she looks at Don, swaying in the hammock, and he mutters, "Drown."

He mutters it, so she cannot be sure, but she hears it as *drown*. Inside her body, a brief terror makes her tremble and sweat and shake with chills, but then a strange honey warmth spreads over her, beginning at her very core, as if coming from her womb. She pictures Philly and now knows with an odd certainty that she will find her. That she will soon see her dead friend, as easily as if Philly is waiting for her to get off a plane.

ABC stands and goes to the window, and the blue night floats with fireflies.

And now she's there and she's ready. My God. She isn't even scared.

PART V

I'm filled with desire
Could it be the devil in me
Or is this the way love's supposed to be?

—*Martha and the Vandellas,* "Heat Wave"

1

On the twenty-third day of July, the temperature, which has been rising through the nineties all week long, finally reaches 100 degrees. Grinnell's wide empty streets bake in the desolate light. Claire has dropped off the kids that morning in West Des Moines, at Don's sister's house, and although Rosie has planned to take all of the kids to Adventureland for the day, the heat makes such an idea unfeasible. Instead, Rosie rents a stack of movies, and allows the kids to do nothing but lie about in the basement rec room all day. How did summer in the Midwest get too hot for kids to go outside and play? How many days would they spend inside basements, watching movies in canned and chilled air?

Claire can tell that her kids are disappointed. But she drops them off with their aunt anyway, craving a day of solitude, and, yes, if she is to admit it, there is actually a party she wants to go to that night.

It's been a long time since Claire wanted to go to a party. Claire is the introvert, that's what everyone says. Don is the social one. But now, having lived three weeks without the cloud of Don Lowry storming up her world, she's feeling freer than she has in so long. So, a party! A stupid, shallow party of middle-aged professors and their ilk milling about in a wine-soaked haze of sexual innuendo and intellectual pretension.

She's looking forward to it.

Since she's moved into the Gulliver house with the kids, she's tried to keep herself from being alone with Charlie somehow; her attraction to him seems sadder and more pathetic with kids in the house: Claire, writing in her bedroom late at night—she's resumed working, at Charlie's suggestion having tossed out the ten-year-old bloated manuscript and begun something wholly new—stays up battling the hormonal surges she thinks belong better to a sixteen-year-old girl, not an almost-forty-year-old woman. So it's not that she doesn't want Charlie anymore—she does—but even the thought of her children suspecting that desire is enough to keep her away from him. She wants them to know that she has left their father for herself, for independence from him and his shadows, for a new start at life, and not for another man.

But then, though she'll never admit this to anyone—she can barely admit it to herself—when she had heard that Charlie was going to this stupid party too, she had called Rosie, made up a story, and found a way that she could come home from that party, that night, just the two of them, maybe drunkenly holding his hand, leaning on him as he walked her up the path and to the empty, childless house.

Her foot on the throat of her marriage.

2

Rosie had texted Don that morning, after she had the kids: *Don. FYI I have the kids for a few days. Did u know??? Maybe u and Claire can have some alone time!!! May b just what u 2 need!!!*

Thanks!!!!! he texted back. His sister would appreciate the exclamation points. *GOOD IDEA!!!!!* He offered her some ALL CAPS for emphasis. She was that kind of person. When he read her texts, he always thought of her voice shouting and shouting.

Don knew that Rosie had been praying for Don and Claire to stay together. In fact, Don knew that an entire two-thousand-member megachurch had prayed for them a few Sundays ago. *Please pray for the brother and sister-in-law who do not know Jesus and who are in a dark time in their holy bond of marriage.* That's how Rosie had asked for prayers in a weepy speech in front of all of those Christians. Rosie's husband had taken the video with his phone and had sent it to Don with the subject line: *Jesus and his followers have lifted you up in prayer!!!!* It was a thing they did at that church. They prayed for you and e-mailed you a video about it.

THANKS!!!! Don had texted back. *God is AWESOME!!!* Rosie's husband was also that kind of person.

Rosie and her husband had not sent the video to Claire because they knew she would be mad; Don had not shown the video to

Claire either, for the same reason. Though, truth be told, he wondered if she might have found it screamingly funny too.

Some days, what breaks his heart most is that he no longer knows if she will find the things he wants to say funny. How he loves to make her laugh. How he once loved making her laugh more than anything else in the world, aside from making love to her after he had made her laugh.

Don waits a few minutes before he calls Claire on her cell. She's driving down I-80 when she answers and Don suggests they meet at Relish for lunch.

"Don," she says.

"What?"

"Lunch?"

"I just want to talk."

"We've talked so much."

"When will we go?" he says. "To counseling? Like I suggested?"

"One, that's expensive," Claire says, "and two, Don, I don't think we should stay married."

"Could we just do one session before Minnesota?"

"I think you should go there. With the kids, just you and them. I'll stay behind."

"I'm not gonna sign the divorce petition."

"Don."

"Relish? Twelve thirty. Please? I just want to talk."

"I'm a sucker for you, Don. And I hate it."

She hangs up.

He is sitting outside on the patio, in a normally lush and beautiful garden that is, this summer, dried out and anemic.

"Do you want to be outside?" he says as she approaches in a yellow sundress he's never seen before. So many clothes he's never known before. Was she saving them? Are they new? Where does she have the money? Does Charlie buy her clothes?

"Is this okay?" he says.

He stands and pulls out her chair; she grimaces a little bit, a slight roll of eyes.

"It's fine," she says and sits.

She shields her eyes from the sun, which has come out from behind a cloud in the hazy white light.

"Sorry about the sun," he says. "Should we go inside?"

"No. This is good."

"Is that a new dress? Are you trying to kill me?"

"Sit down," Claire says, grinning, then grimacing, as if suppressing something buried.

"Sorry," Don says.

"For what?"

"For the lunch invitation. And the comment about your dress."

"You're fine."

"I know I'm fine. How are you?"

The waiter comes with water. When he leaves, they sip in silence for a moment.

"Why do you do that?" she says. "It has nothing to do with you. You shouldn't apologize to me when I say things like that. Don't take the blame."

"Sorry," he says again, not meaning to say it.

He suddenly realizes there—one does have sudden realizations like that, in the bright glare of summer, when one's life is falling apart, and Don Lowry has been having sudden realizations almost hourly since he lost his family—that he has faulted himself for every disappointment that Claire has ever had to face: leaving college, leaving New York, leaving graduate school, buying a house she didn't like, the sun in her eyes at lunch.

"Do you see how that infantilizes me? That it implies all of our life has been your choice and none of it has been me. We did everything together; we fucked up everything together."

"We didn't fuck up."

"We're broke, Don."

He nods.

"I'll get my sunglasses from the car," she says, and gets up.

Men notice her as they drive by, as she walks down the street toward the Suburban.

Don watches as a student on a bike, a retired professor walking a dog, and a contractor in a mud-spattered truck all watch Claire move down Park Street and back. He wonders if she is aware of it.

"What is it?" she says. "You're staring at me."

"You look amazing."

"Don, do you see how offensive that is to me? I just told you how I feel like an accessory to your life, to your world, and you've just complimented my appearance as if to confirm that belief."

"I just meant that—"

"Don't. It's fine. I'm done being mad at you."

"I know that we did everything together. It's just this: you had more potential than I ever had," he says. "That's what's so sad about all of this. You know, when someone contacts me, on Facebook or e-mail or whatever, some old friend from college . . ."

"That's why I don't go near Facebook right now, by the way. You should get off it."

"Anyway," Don goes on, "when I tell them that we're living back in Grinnell, they always assume you are a professor now, or maybe an associate dean. They never assume I'm doing anything like that, because they remember us, and they remember how many people looked at us and said, 'What is she doing with him?' Even back then."

"Whatever, Don."

"No, they used to ask that. To my face! And so when I tell them we live in Grinnell, an underperforming real estate agent and a part-time dining services staffer/novelist—"

"Former novelist," she says.

"—and that we've recently lost our home, they don't believe it. And they always say, 'That's terrible. How is Claire holding up?' because me, they think I expected this life, these mediocre expectations and constant disappointments, but they know you didn't."

"Nobody expects the life they get, Don. That's what makes life so strange. I am ready to accept it. Charlie's taught me something."

"Charlie?"

"He's taught me to stop caring about where I am going, what I could possibly do or get or achieve. You, Don, you can't stop. You're not happy. You know what I am understanding? I am a happy person at my core. I don't care if I never write another book. You care. You do. You care what everyone thinks. You think you're a failure 'cause you went broke. We went broke. I don't care. You know what I want? I want someone who'll swim with me at the end of the day and not talk about the next day coming, or the new week, or the next year."

His heart breaks for her, and he suddenly wants to set her free, wants to let her loose in the world without the burden of him. It is okay to end things, he thinks. Still, he can't.

"Are you in love with Charlie?"

"He makes me happy. He calms me down. Is that love?"

Don excuses himself to use the bathroom. He's drunk five cups of coffee that day and it is suddenly urgent.

When he comes back out, Don is prepared to make an "I love you and I am setting you free" speech, hoping it has the opposite effect of Claire breaking free, hoping it makes her love him and miss him again. But at the table, he is disappointed to see ZeeZee Donovan, the art historian, and her partner Jean-Claude, standing near Claire in spandex outfits. They are on their bikes. Jean-Claude is blatantly looking at Claire's breasts from behind his sunglasses, at her tanned legs. ZeeZee is talking.

Don hides inside the foyer of the restaurant until ZeeZee and Jean-Claude pedal away, their firm, spandexed asses wiggling farewell.

"I've been invited to a heat wave party," Claire says when he returns to the table. "At ZeeZee and Jean-Claude's. I saw you waiting inside for them to leave."

"A heat wave party?" Don scoffs and sits down.

"I forgot to tell you about it. ZeeZee just wanted to confirm that I'd actually be going."

"What's a fucking heat wave party?" Don asks.

"Inappropriate summer attire is encouraged. That's what ZeeZee said. They'll have a slip and slide in the yard, sprinklers, kiddie pools, slushy drinks, and cold beer."

"That sounds awful. No way," Don says. "But why wasn't I invited?"

"Well, the kids are gone for the night. I'm going."

"You are?"

"The new Claire, not like the old Claire."

"Oh, Claire!" Don says. He wants a wince of nostalgia from her, but he gets nothing, as if she doesn't even remember, or want to remember, the note he once gave her.

Claire looks across the street and Don follows her eyes, because she is obviously looking at Charlie and ABC, heading down Park Street toward the Mayflower. Don and Claire, obscured, in part, by the café's garden and leafy trees, do not call out. They watch Charlie and ABC in silence, poking at their summer salads.

It is ABC who notices them. Don watches, from the corner of his eye, as she drags Charlie across the street by the hand.

"Hey, guys!" ABC says. "It's great to see you out and about together."

"The kids are with their aunt in Des Moines," Claire says.

"Seize the day," Don says.

"They're spending the night," Claire says, looking perhaps too directly at Charlie when she says this.

"Well, you guys enjoy your lunch," Charlie says.

"It's not anything special. Do you want to join us?" Claire says.

"We're just reminiscing about our twenty years together," Don says, looking right at Charlie Gulliver.

Don studies Charlie's silent, shifting form. Both he and ABC have wet hair, freshly showered or newly emerged from the pool.

"We're going to see my dad," Charlie says.

"If your kids are gone for the night," ABC says. "You should know that there's a party at Zee—"

"Yes, I'm going," Claire says.

"Me too," Don says.

"Really?" Claire says. "But you weren't even—"

"Sure! Seize the day!" Don says.

"We're going too," ABC says.

"Slip and slide, right?" Charlie says.

"You guys are going together?" Claire says.

"Like a date?" Don says. "Very interesting!"

"Yes!" ABC says. "A hot date. Get it?"

"Not really a date," Charlie says, looking at ABC, laughing. Then looking at Claire. Don sees the look, registers it, banishes the idea of clocking Charlie right there.

A few more pleasantries, some discussion of the heat, the promise of seeing each other later, and then Charlie and ABC walk off toward the retirement home.

"Do you think they've just fucked?" Claire says.

"Claire," he says. "I want you to think about this again: Minnesota this winter, you and me and the kids. I won't sign these goddamn papers until I believe that I, that we've, tried everything to save this marriage."

"Do you know what the winters are like up there, Don?"

"Claire, he's got a plow and a snow blower. Just think, all four of us, together round the woodstove. We can go down to Duluth once a month for supplies."

She blinks at him.

"You're nuts," she says. "This is insane, Don. We just moved into new places. We've just set up our kids in new rooms and you want to play *O Pioneers!* this winter!"

"With central heat and a Jacuzzi," Don says. "It's hardly roughing it. And we haven't settled down again. We're crashing with twenty-something stoners! Is that a way to raise our kids?"

Claire frowns. "We don't have a lot of choices."

"That's why my Minnesota plan is a great plan!"

"It's not, Don," Claire says. "It's not going to work."

"Define *it*," Don says. "*What* isn't going to work? Moving to Minnesota? Our marriage? What? This is good, Claire. I've done it. I've come from behind. I have made a small amount of money, just enough money to fix our short-term problems. We can declare bankruptcy and live on cash up there. And then, I've been working with Mrs. Manetti, with Ruth, on this plan, a long-term one. Problems solved!"

It is this final statement that makes Claire, already exhausted and nerves worn down to a nub, burst into tears. When she regains her composure, she stands up. "I hate that you think this is about money, Don. I hate that you think you've fixed a goddamn thing."

And soon after that, she is gone.

Don pays the bill with the last of the cash in his wallet, leaving a gratuity that is larger than necessary.

Later that afternoon, when Don Lowry goes home, as in home to the Manetti place, he finds ABC on the sleeping porch. She is rolling a joint. She points to an envelope on the counter. "That's for you," she says. When Don opens it, he finds a cashier's check for $25,000, made out to him, and drafted on an account from a business named RM Enterprises LLC.

In the memo line, it reads: "consulting fees, summer 2012."

"What is this?"

"Your paycheck. Ruth is paying you to take us up north. In advance of your getting the house, of course. A bonus."

She lights a joint, takes a long drag, hands it and the lighter to him.

"But I never actually accepted her offer," Don says.

"You want to take a nap before the party?" she asks after she's inhaled a long deep pull of weed.

"Nah," he says. "I'm gonna go back to the office and make some phone calls. I made a small sale this month. Are you sure Ruth wants me to have this money?"

"It was her idea." As he turns to go, she says, "It's been a while, Don, since you've slept next to me. I don't have those dreams of Philly without you."

"I know," he says. "I'm sorry. Maybe tonight?"

"I'm sort of Charlie's date for the party," ABC says. "I'll probably sleep there."

"Of course," he says. "Thank you so much for this. For the money."

"Thank Ruth," she says. "She insisted. I tried to talk her out of it."

She grins at him, a puzzling grin he cannot begin to understand.

After making a deposit at the bank with a teller he thankfully does not recognize, some young college kid working a summer job, Don goes back to the office. The last thing he wants out in town is that he's taking charity from Mrs. Manetti. Because it is a cashier's check, there is no waiting period, and he takes a thousand dollars out right away, putting the cash in his wallet.

He is ready for a winter away—Claire will come around. He

is sure of it. Up in Minnesota, they could make that money last almost two years. They'll sell one of the cars. They'll have to figure out health insurance. They'll have some expenses, but not many. Don has never before gone on unemployment or Medicaid or food stamps, it is not in his nature. But maybe he is dumb about that. Maybe it is time to simply swallow his pride and take whatever he can get. It is survival time now. Bankruptcy. Going off the grid. Don Lowry: going, going, gone!

ABC goes out onto the front porch. Charlie is sitting out there with Ruth, watching the darkness set in, and smoking a joint. Ruth counts the fireflies. Then ABC enters this quiet space, twirls about, and shows off a flouncy black dress, short and strapless, that does nothing to hide anything about her body. She wears no shoes and her legs are shiny and bronzed from a day in the sun.

"You are about the sexiest woman who has ever set foot in Grinnell," Ruth says.

"I'm overdressed, aren't I?" she says. "I found this at Goodwill!"

"It's a heat wave party, ABC. You look great!" Ruth says. "I love the idea. A heat wave party. It sounds sexy."

"It sounds cheesy," Charlie says.

"Cheesy?" Ruth says. "I'd say it sounds more boozy than cheesy. If I remember such parties correctly, people will get powerfully and famously drunk. Just don't talk to any professors and you won't be bored."

She winks at ABC.

"You sure you don't want to come?" Charlie asks Ruth. She is toking up on the last of the joint.

She laughs. "No, no, no," she says, and she stands and lets ABC lead her inside. About ten minutes later, ABC comes back to the porch.

"She's asleep," ABC says. "This is a powerful batch."

"You're really something," Charlie says.

"You too," she says to Charlie, who is dressed in red swim trunks, a sleeveless white undershirt, red canvas sneakers with no socks, and mirrored aviator shades. "You also are really something."

"I wanted to look like Burt Lancaster in *The Swimmer*, but I think I feel more like Slater when he worked as a lifeguard on *Saved by the Bell*."

"There have been many adolescent fantasies about A. C. Slater as a lifeguard. I can say that with authority," ABC says. "Is that show still on?"

"It was already on in reruns when we were kids. I don't know if it translates well into 2012. It already seemed strange to me when I was young. I didn't understand the hair or the clothes. I thought I was missing some joke. And then one day I saw, what's her name, Tiffani-Amber something, and I got it. Like overnight, I thought, whoa. Whoa. Whoa!"

"You lucky duck, you get to have sex with me at the end of the night," she says.

"That beats wanking it to a syndicated high school sitcom star in my father's study," Charlie says.

A little later, when they walk into the party, the sun of early evening still bright, they see that the dominant theme is flesh, that everyone has tried to look sultry and hot, and together, unspoken, ABC and Charlie feel the full power of their youth, in a way young people often fail to recognize. They are the sexiest couple there. They can both feel it. Everyone is staring at them.

Charlie takes off his shirt and hangs it on the fence.

Don is working at his desk, answering e-mails, filling out paperwork, trying to figure out if he should or could pay any quarterly taxes, when Claire walks into his office, in a manner so stunning he involuntarily stands up from his chair.

She wears white sandals with a heel, a white two-piece swimsuit, and over it a sheer white shirtdress that's cinched a bit at the waist, comes down to the middle of her thighs, and buttons down the front. Her hair is slicked back and wet and she wears huge gold hoop earrings.

"Wow," he says.

"Too much?" she says.

"No, it's amazing."

"Come to the party with me. I don't want to walk in alone."

Don doesn't feel like the party anymore, but a chance to be with Claire for the evening seems just the ticket. It's his night to win her back—Charlie will be with ABC, and they'll be drunk, in a crowd, and in the sultry heat of late July. They always had the best sex after parties, boozy and flirty affairs that gradually made them more and more aroused as the night wore on and on. If the kids were gone—as they would be tonight—it was not uncommon for Don and Claire to keep drinking when they got home, and fuck each other as many times as possible before passing out in a naked, sweaty heap. Of course, they no longer have their own house, and as soon as Don thinks this thought, he has a sudden plan for the evening.

"My clothes," Don says. "Are they okay?"

He touches his khaki pants and feels the thick wallet in his pocket, and he feels, momentarily, as if everything is finally returning to normal. There even seems to be a flirtatious hint in Claire's eyes. "They're not very heat wave."

"Don't worry about it," Claire says. "You look sexy. You always do."

He doesn't want to admit how high this makes his heart soar.

ZeeZee comes at Charlie and ABC, laughing uproariously as she does so, touching Charlie's chest and saying, "Oh, good, a lifeguard, just in case."

She is quite drunk already. She had been friends with Charlie's parents and had invited him to the party when she'd run into him at the coffee shop. Now, she wears a loose cotton top, white, in a vaguely Mexican style that falls from each bare shoulder, and her freckled neck is exposed, as is the top third of each breast. She wears impossibly high-heeled white sandals and pink-and-white-striped bikini bottoms. She looks like a half-finished wedding cake that has been left in the sun too long.

"You two are hotter than the weather," she says. "Go get yourself a cool drink."

Around the yard, there are tiki torches of smoking citronella, cans of bug spray, and a large bug zapper in the far corner of the yard, where bats zoom in and feed. There's a large kiddie pool, filled with ice and water, but no kids are anywhere near it, and there is a sprinkler gently misting half the yard, and a slip and slide set up along the fence at the yard's rear, though it isn't on yet, but it is clear already, from the forced laughter that echoes from each small pocket of adult conversation, that it soon will be.

Charlie and ABC help themselves to mojitos, which are being served by a young man in a Speedo. They have no idea who it is, though Jean-Claude himself, a barrel-chested hairy fellow, also wears a Speedo suit and cowboy boots, his own trunks decorated with the American flag. A straw cowboy hat is on his head.

"Do you think he stuffed his suit?" ABC says.

"A great idea," Charlie says. "Next time."

Most of the group is dressed in some variant of the same costume: men wear swim trunks and summer shirts or tank tops and sandals, though there is one man in a seersucker suit, which ABC says is much sexier than a lot of the male flesh she is seeing. Lots of paunches and pale skinny legs. Most of the women are in thin dresses, though a few are in bathing suits—bikini tops with wraps around their bottoms and some of the women follow ZeeZee's lead and drop the sarongs and wraps and wear only their swimsuits after a few drinks make them bold enough to do so. Nobody, thinks ABC, looks as good as she and Charlie look. Everyone is watching them. She knows already that Charlie will go home with her, and maybe, if Don can play it right, Claire will go home with him.

The Beach Boys play from a stereo somewhere, though it isn't quite tonally appropriate. It is the *Pet Sounds* album, probably the only Beach Boys album the hosts have, one that hasn't been listened to in a long time. It's an album on which even the ocean-groove love songs carry an impossibly melancholic subtext: *God only knows what I'd be without you.*

ABC downs her drink and quickly gets another. "Personality drinks," ABC says. "The first two drinks don't count."

It's then that they see Claire and it's as if ABC can feel Charlie drop a bit further away from her as he waves Claire over.

"A lot of flowers in the hair, a lot of body glitter borrowed from the dressers of teenage girls," Claire says to them as she walks up, sipping her drink. "Women over thirty should not sparkle. Don't you think?"

ABC and Charlie laugh, a polite party laugh, a little overzealous appreciativeness in their tone. They are all drinking fast, in order to move the evening from awkward to bearable and maybe, possibly, if they drink enough, to fun.

"Well, you look great," ABC says, although she has a rule against complimenting women on their appearance as a means of opening up a conversation. But Claire does look great. It is clear to ABC that Claire is trying to look great. This worries her.

"You too!" Claire says back.

"Damn," Charlie says. "Holy fucking sexy."

"Jesus," Claire says. "That means I'm trying too hard."

"Which is fine if it works," ABC says. "You look amazing! Where's Don?"

"I don't know," she says. "He's here somewhere. We came together."

"Um, I need a drink," ABC says. "I'll be right back."

ABC wants to get back to Charlie and Claire, but she also wants to find Don Lowry. She also wants a drink and it's taking forever to get one. She finally orders a mojito from the shirtless buff bartender, who's been mobbed all night by the quickly drunken professors, and then hears a voice behind her.

"Make that two," Don says.

She turns around.

"Don Lowry!" she says. "You came."

He is wearing a shirt and tie. She undoes his tie and slides it off, tosses it on a chair. She unbuttons three buttons of his white oxford, then rolls up his sleeves. She touches his chest.

"That's better," she says. "Now go flirt with your wife before someone else does."

They see at that moment, across the crowded yard, Charlie talking up close with Claire, looking very much like two lovers in the gloaming.

"Too late?" Don says.

"Never," ABC says. "Not ever."

"I don't want you talking to him tonight," Charlie says to Claire, pressing in close, ending the small talk they had been making up to that moment.

"Pardon me?" Claire says.

"I don't like it. Don fucks with your head."

"Charlie!" Claire says. "Jesus."

"Don't. Talk. To. Him. Talk. To. Me," Charlie says, slowly, deliberately, and with some extra breath in his voice, leaning in to Claire, pushing air onto the side of her neck.

"What if I do?" Claire says.

"I'll be jealous."

"What if I want to make you jealous?"

"That'd be very naughty. I wouldn't be pleased."

Claire's eyes open wide. It takes her a minute to smile. Gooseflesh, even in the humid evening, manages to rise up and down her arms.

"I'm gonna get some more ice," Claire says.

"Don't forget," Charlie says. "Don't make me punish you."

He presses against her then and she can feel all of him, his flesh, his heat, his strength, his reckless and total availability.

"Do you want anything?" she says, shaking the ice in her glass.

"Yes," he says.

3

Ten o'clock and it still must be in the mid-nineties. The air so still. Most of the partygoers have fled the humidity and the mosquitoes by gathering in the misty spray of the sprinklers, and the laughter escalates as they do so. Some people have gone inside the house, an old house that doesn't have central air-conditioning, though people gather near the window unit in the living room and you can see them through the window, a gaggle of scantily clad academics, pressed together in absurd conversations.

Charlie has been making his way through the crowd, bouncing from one awkward stage of small talk to another. He is drunk though, deeply drunk, and although both ABC and Claire seem to be avoiding him, he also hasn't yet seen Don Lowry. Still, Charlie does know a lot of the people at the party, knows them as his father's former colleagues; he knows who they are, but he knows nothing about them, beyond, in some cases, what they teach at the college. He wonders how many of the women at the party his father has written letters to, or fucked.

Everyone asks after Charlie's father, and Charlie nods soberly and says his father is doing as well as one could expect. Almost nobody asks about his mother, though one woman, an art history professor, says she's been seeing his mother's travels on Facebook and it looks like she is having a great summer.

Charlie nods. He says that this is probably true.

The novelty of near nakedness is wearing off for anybody who is still sober, and some of the crowd has begun trickling out. There are babysitters to pay and quiet, married sex to have back home, fueled by the muted and managed sultriness of the affair. At the party are college professors and local business owners and schoolteachers and even the Lutheran minister, a tall woman wearing cutoffs and a halter top, and all of them eating and drinking and drinking and drinking and talking in the backyard and drinking, wearing as little as they possibly can without feeling mortified, most of them wet from the sprinklers and the kiddie pools, and all of them, it seems to Charlie, have known Gill Gulliver.

One couple, a philosopher and a biologist, two men, are snorting cocaine in the upstairs bathroom, one in tasteful Bermudas and a ribbed white undershirt and one in the seersucker suit, and they begin laughing hysterically when they realize who Charlie is. He's only been trying to pee but when he knocks on the bathroom door, they answer it and usher him in and begin praising the legacy of Gill Gulliver.

"That man could party!" the philosopher says.

"Amen," echoes the biologist. "Women loved your father."

Now Charlie is even more deeply drunk and has decided he needs to pee badly enough that the glass brick half wall that surrounds the toilet in the massive master bathroom is sufficient for privacy. For a moment, as he is peeing, it feels as if the stupidity of drunkenness is leaving him, and he wonders if he should find Claire and apologize for what he said, which he had meant to be hot, but which may have come off as insane. The two men are still sitting on the edge of a huge palatial bathtub, watching him pee.

"Oh, your father!" the philosopher says. "Your father would have been amazed by this party! Amazed!"

"Your father loved sex," says the biologist in seersucker, and then places his hand over his mouth. "Oops!" he says. He breaks into a fit of giggles.

"He was fun at parties," the philosopher says. "He would have loved this! You want some coke?"

"Or a blow job?" the biologist asks.

Charlie snorts a line off the mirror as if it is something he does every day, though he's only tried cocaine once in his life, right after college at a cast party in New York. What the fuck is he thinking? He knows, of course, what he is thinking. He knows, deep down, the one legacy he has inherited from Gill Gulliver, and that is this: He likes to be the center of attention. He likes to feel people fall in love with him. The cocaine blows a hole through his brain that seems to light this truth up in dazzling pink letters.

"Once they love you," he tells the biologist, "it's not very fun."

As Charlie leaves, the giggles intensify. Two junior professors come into the bathroom as Charlie is leaving and there are more shrieks of delight.

Charlie is standing by the cooler of beer now, drinking a bottle of Negra Modelo, when ABC and Don Lowry come over to him. His heart is racing and his head feels as if it's full of helium. Don has a small wooden bowl of lime wedges in his hand and he thrusts it at Charlie. "You should have a lime in that," he says, and shoves one into Charlie's beer aggressively.

ABC gets a beer from the cooler and opens it and takes one of Don's limes too. She is leaning on Don. She is drunk. She keeps finding reasons to run her hand through his chest hair, the considerable mat of it visible under the oxford shirt Don wears, which is damp with sweat under the arms and on the back. Charlie is flying. He can barely think.

Don's eyes are bloodshot and he looks sunburned and stoned, like most of the other adults at the party. There are a lot of joints going around. ABC holds up her bottle to toast Charlie and he offers her his bottle, knocking them together with a clink.

"You guys are quite the pair," Don says.

Charlie and ABC both smile at Don then turn toward each other.

"We hate each other," ABC says.

Charlie raises his beer bottle as if responding to some unspoken toast and has a drink.

He bellows into the night, "Wooooohoooo!"

"Jesus," ABC says. "Come on!"

"What are you guys even doing here?" Don asks in a loud, drunken shout. He looks as if he's gone off the rails somehow. He looks dazed, as if he's survived a plane crash. ABC's never seen him this drunk. Mostly she's seen him stoned. He is angrier drunk, sweatier.

"ZeeZee invited us," Charlie says.

"Not here!" Don shouts. "Why are you in Iowa? Why the fuck aren't you in New York? Both of you. This place, kids, this place is a prison."

"I know!" Charlie bellows. "Why the fuck?"

People are watching them.

"No, no, I'm joking," Don says. "Grinnell is lovely. It is. It's just—I mean, why? You can be ANY-FUCKING-WHERE."

"I happen to like it here," ABC says.

"Total bullshit!" Don barks, and for a moment Charlie worries Don might get violent, but he exhales a bit of drunken laughter. Someone, a guy about Don's age who looks vaguely familiar, brings Don a can of Coke, unbidden, and says, "Drink this, Donny, okay? Let's keep it down. It's getting late."

The guy raises an eyebrow as he walks away, as if he's blaming Charlie for Don's condition.

"Not my fault!" Charlie says. "Fuck you!"

Don obediently cracks open the can of Coke and has a drink, sufficiently chastened by whoever that was. Don lowers his voice. This, to Charlie, has always been the mark of a decent man. Even drunk, he understands when he has crossed a line and can quickly regain his dignity. For a moment, Charlie almost feels affection for Don, a pang of sympathy that, inexplicably, makes the idea of fucking Don's wife even hotter.

"Guys," Don says. "Guys. This is what I mean, kids. Why not, what's stopping you from just going to New York and starting a life that is different, a life that means something?"

Charlie wants to swim.

"Go to New York," Don says.

"Kind of a problem with going to New York," ABC says. "No place to stay."

"Place to stay?" Don says, spitting incredulously. "I hate that phrase. *I need a place to stay*. Right? A place to exist in paralysis, right, a place to stay static. You don't need a place to stay at your age. The world is your place to stay. What? Will you cease to exist if you spend one night wandering around Manhattan because you don't have a bed? Kids, here's something I shouldn't tell you, because I am a real estate agent. But places to stay are overrated. *Places to live*. You want to find places to *live*!"

"So we should move to New York and be homeless?" ABC says. "Sorry. I'm not interested. I happen to like it here. For now."

"You want to leave the whole world behind, right? Huh?" Don says, really slurring now, spitting at them.

"Live in the moment, Don. Tonight, I am here. So are you."

"So is he!" Don says, slapping Charlie on the back with an overzealousness that borders on violent.

"I'm just saying, you know, we're happy to have you kids here," Don says. "But don't remain in Grinnell, Iowa, simply because you *have a place to stay*."

"What do you think, Don?" Charlie says, grinning, loudly hissing the words. "Better to ignore a year's worth of foreclosure notices and not tell your wife?"

A few people near Charlie and Don and ABC stop and stare. Charlie has raised his voice.

Nobody says anything in response.

"Let's use that fucking slip and slide, eh?" Don says, devilishly, and leads ABC by the hand. She turns to Charlie and offers him a middle finger as a farewell.

Charlie is happy to see Claire then, out on the patio. She is in only her swimsuit now. In one hand, she holds her dress, in the other her shoes. She's been swimming in the kiddie pool or using the slip and slide. He goes up to her, downing his beer as he approaches. Maybe she's also snorted a line of coke upstairs. She looks wired, as if she might burst into sparks and flames.

"I'm leaving," Charlie says. "Also, you look amazing."

"I hope no one takes a picture of me, because I am sure my mental image of myself is not what the rest of the world is seeing. I bought this dress for a trip we took, long ago. I bought it for Don. But now we're pretty much three bricks shy of done."

"You mean a load," Charlie says.

"What?"

"The saying. It's 'three bricks shy of a load.' Also, I just did a line of coke upstairs with some professors."

"What?" Claire says. "Seriously? You did?"

"I know," he says. "It was insane."

"Okay, now I want to do something insane," she says.

She steps closer to him.

"You what?"

"Do you want to do something insane with me?" she whispers, in his ear, her hand on his chest.

"What?"

"I didn't do it," she says.

"Do what, Claire?"

"I didn't do it. I did what you said. I didn't talk to Don after you told me not to talk to him."

"What?"

"I haven't talked to Don all night. Earlier, he tried to tell me something, and I walked away. I obeyed you. And now, you are going to obey me."

She walks over to a cooler, pulls out two Coronas, opens them with a church key, and hands one to Charlie. She whispers in his ear, "I'm leaving," she says.

The last thing Charlie sees is the crowd that forms as Don Lowry and ABC careen down the two side-by-side slip and slides, shouting *fuck* at the top of their lungs.

On the walk home, they cut through the park and atop a hill, under a massive oak, they stop and Charlie is behind Claire and she feels his hardness through the thin, slippery trunks. She presses her ass against him. She will let him fuck her there if he tries. She is that drunk; so is he.

She leads him down the hill to her house, to his house, to their house. In the yard, she comes up behind him and reaches into his trunks and he turns and runs his hands down her body, reaching under the fabric of her suit, grabbing her ass and pressing her against him again.

"Put your hands behind your back," she says.

He does.

She grabs his hips, turns around, and pushes her ass up against his groin.

"Wait here."

In a few minutes, she comes to the front door and motions for him to follow. He keeps his hands behind his back.

They go inside without turning on any lights. She goes to the kitchen and he follows her. Somewhere they have dropped their empty beer bottles—at the park, perhaps—and now she gets two more from the fridge. She puts her hand on his hip and hands him another beer. She rubs her hand against the trunks again, feeling how ready he is.

"I love the way you feel," she says in his ear and she goes down his belly, onto her knees, and blows on him, nibbling him playfully through the swim trunks. The gesture of this, of being down in front of him, of giving him a love bite on his hard cock, freezes her slightly. She has flashbacked to the time she and Don had worked as lifeguards in college and she had gone down on him; it had begun in much the same way. It had been at a lifeguard party. She had handed him a beer, had felt his hard-on, had teased him with her mouth in the shadows behind the filter shed. She doesn't want to be thinking of Don, but she is.

"Are you okay?" Charlie says. She has stopped moving and she looks up at him.

"You're not allowed to speak," she says.

And now she is wondering if Don is still sliding across the slip and slide in his underwear, making a drunken spectacle of himself, or if he is somewhere else.

A small part of her hopes he is somewhere else, doing the same things that she thinks perhaps she is about to finally do.

4

He is somewhere else. He is, at that moment, breaking into his foreclosed house, which is three blocks from the heat wave party. Holding on to his hips as he shimmies open the side door is ABC. They are drunk, having done shots for each round on the slip and slide, and then they discovered that Charlie and Claire were nowhere to be found. They'd looked everywhere, finding at least three copulating couples in their exhaustive search. They left when the cops arrived.

They are also pretty fucking stoned, having smoked a joint with Jean-Claude in the iced-down kiddie pool. Their clothes are soaked. ABC's strapless dress is a problem. It keeps coming off under the weight of the water. She holds an arm pressed over her breasts to keep them covered.

Inside, they keep the lights off and she holds his hand as he leads her through the dark and up the stairs.

"I loved this house," he says.

Inside the house, the detritus of a domestic life. Things they left behind. Some old bottles of sauces in the pantry, newspapers and magazines on the floor, bottle caps and rolls of paper towels and cleaning supplies. An old towel on the floor in the hallway.

"We didn't leave the place spotless," Don says as he kicks a shoe box out of the way. Finally, they come to the master bedroom, empty, and then they go to the bathroom. The door is shut and then, since that room has no windows, Don flips on the light and the exhaust fan whirs to life.

"Ha!" Don says. "They haven't cut the power!"

"I have to pee," ABC says, and ducks into the small water closet. There's a half roll of toilet paper and some air freshener on the toilet, a half-burned scented candle on the floor. As she pees, she calls from it, "Isn't this really breaking and entering?"

"I don't care," Don says. "It's my house. If the cops come, tell them I lied to you."

Out of the water closet now, in the yellow bathroom light, ABC sees the two of them in the mirror. They look horrible. She looks away from it. Her makeup is smudged and her hair is wet and frizzed and the dress is a limp raggedy secondhand garment from the eighties. She remembers how Don Lowry had found her under the sycamore and how it is, in the strangest of ways, that Don Lowry has led her to Philly in the spirit world, that Don Lowry will somehow be the one to help her earthly suffering, and set her free in some strange realm. Don Lowry is a good man; he doesn't deserve what is happening to him. He found her when she needed to be found. She wants to tell him this. She feels unhinged, she feels insane. She wants to cry and laugh and scream all at once.

What was in that joint?

Don turns on the water in the massive Jacuzzi. "Ha!" he says. "Ha! They haven't cut the water yet! Ha!"

And then he adds, "I loved this fucking Jacuzzi. I loved this fucking bathroom."

"I bet!" she says.

"I loved fucking in this fucking bathroom," Don says.

As the tub fills, Don begins to undress. ABC lights the scented candle she's found and then finds another on the sink. She finds the discarded bath towel in the hallway. She watches him hang his shirt on a hook, and then watches him slide off his pants and hang those too, as if he still lives here. As if tomorrow morning he will wake up and get ready for work. His boxers, red plaid, he hangs on the empty towel rack, and the shoes and socks he neatly places beneath the rack. He looks good. He looks like a man who has some fight left in him, a lot of fight. ABC thinks that Don Lowry must have done this a million times. He stands there watching the water, thickening, already getting hard. How do you not notice that, no matter what your intentions are?

"We don't really have any more towels," he says. "On account of the foreclosure."

And then he starts to laugh.

"Claire never understood the Jacuzzi," he says. And then, "I tried to talk to her tonight. She gave me the silent treatment. My idea had been to break in here with her. To tell her about the money I have from Ruth, about how we could start over, but . . . How do you just decide you don't want to be married anymore? How do you fall out of love like that? That fast?"

ABC reaches behind her, unzips her soaked dress, and drops it to the floor with a thwack. She puts her hands on her breasts.

Don locks the door of the bathroom.

"Just in case," he says.

She bends down and picks up her dress, knowing he is watching her body, looking at her ass in the thong she is wearing. She hangs the dress on a hook. She turns and faces him. She goes toward him.

Looking in his eyes, she grazes the tip of his penis lightly with her fingertips. It is pointing up now, right toward her breasts. He shudders at her touch. She drops her arm. "Let's get in," she whispers in his ear.

They enter the tub at opposite ends. Don sits down immediately. ABC steps in, wetting her body first with her hands, deliberately, slowly, torturing him like she was some *Maxim* model in a shitty photo shoot, playing all the cheesy slow-motion breast-washing cards. She thinks of Philly laughing, but then forces that out of her brain.

And then she lowers herself fully into the water.

Don Lowry feels like he might be sick or have a small stroke.

He feels her foot move up his leg and touch him under the surface of the water.

When she resurfaces, she says, "Do you want to smoke up some more first?"

"No. No, I'm good," he says.

But Don Lowry is lying. He is not good. He has never once cheated on Claire, not since their first kiss on Mac field when he was a freshman in college. He's come close before: there was a woman at a real estate convention in Baltimore, a woman who leaned into him at the bar, who kissed him in the hotel elevator, followed him back to his room, had even started to undress. And then he had told her no, that he couldn't, and the woman stayed in his room until three in the morning, drinking nine-dollar beers from the honor bar, sitting in her black panties and white bra, and telling him that he should leave his wife.

But he hasn't cheated. Has Claire? He doesn't actually know.

He doesn't want to know. He wants to know. If the marriage was really done, did it even matter?

He is so aroused, it is hard to think about Claire anymore, but yet he does, even now, even after ABC has pressed herself up to the edge of the tub and sits naked across from him. The water is still filling the tub. It is too low to turn on the obscuring foam bubbles of the jets. He leans back in the enormous tub and lets his hips float upward, his erection breaking the surface of the water.

"Thar she blows!" ABC says, and splashes the water at him with her toe. She rubs water on her legs. "You're so serious all of a sudden, Don Lowry! This is supposed to be fun."

She is very drunk and stoned and still feels a ripped kind of sadness at the center of her being that she has to push back down over and over. Seeing Don Lowry naked in front of her makes her miss Philly more than she ever has in her life.

"Has my wife fucked Charlie Gulliver?" Don says.

ABC looks at him.

"What?"

"Has Claire . . . Have she and Charlie . . ."

"Not yet," ABC says. "Not to my knowledge. Don't think about that."

ABC flips her legs, splashing him, and lowers herself down into the water, wetting her hair, her breasts submerged by the bubbles that rise to the surface when Don Lowry finally turns on the jets.

"Don't think about anything," she says as Don Lowry closes his eyes.

5

They go upstairs to the master bedroom, where Claire usually sleeps on a double sleeping bag that rests atop an inflatable bed. It is the first time she's had Charlie up there with her; it is the first time they have been without children inside this house.

She has all the windows open and all the lights in the house are off and they don't turn any of them on. She turns the ceiling fan to high and the air whips around them. They barely speak to each other. The beers are empty again and Charlie gets down on the sleeping bag, puts his hands behind his head, and looks up at Claire and then up at the skylight.

"This should be the perfect view," Charlie says. "My parents' bed used to be right here. I remember they liked to watch summer storms from here and I used to lie between them and my father would smell of beer and my mother of wine and I would feel them falling asleep, and I know now, they were drunk, of course, but I can remember that they also held me; it's as if we all, the three of us, couldn't be close enough no matter what."

Claire gets on the sleeping bag next to Charlie.

They lie in silence for a moment.

"Were we just waiting for this? A night when the children were gone? Is this what we want? Or is this just an impulse?"

"I don't see a difference," Charlie says. "You can want an impulse."

In silence, they look at the skylight. Heat lightning flickers in the distance, but there will be no storm. The rain never comes. It refuses.

"There's something I need to tell you," she says.

"Let me guess. You're married," Charlie says. "I fucking knew it!"

She laughs, but only for a second. "Shut up and listen. Look, I recognize you. I didn't think I did, but I do. You were in *Uncle Vanya*, at the high school, weren't you? Years ago?"

"Yeah," he says. "It was awful. Terrible production. High-schoolers shouldn't do Chekhov."

"I was so impressed by the ambition. We had just moved back to Grinnell, a few months before that. And I remember thinking, 'Wow, what a big stretch for a rural high school play.'"

"I got the role because I was forty pounds overweight, and in the right waistcoat I looked like a middle-aged Russian doctor."

"I remember, Charlie. You did look different. And I remember that Don stayed with the kids—Bryan and Wendy were little then, Wendy only a baby—so I could go see it. I was so curious. I thought I would hate it."

"You liked it?"

"So much. I liked you. I was like, who is this kid? Who is this kid who already knows how to play a role so heavy with bitterness, with regret?"

"I had on that gray wig. It was a terrible wig."

"You were good, Charlie. I was moved by it."

"You know what line I remember? What still stays with me?"

"I can't imagine," she says.

He clears his throat and, shirtless still, springs to his feet, and bellows in the overemphatic manner he'd had as a teenage thespian: "'Man has been endowed with reason, with the power to create, so that he can add to what he's been given. But up to now, he hasn't been a creator, only a destroyer. Forests keep disappearing, rivers dry up, wildlife's become extinct, and the climate's ruined and the land grows poorer and uglier every day.'"

"Bravo!" Claire says. She claps wildly.

"Chekhov had global warming figured out a century before the rest of us," Charlie says. "Jesus. Poor Vanya. You know?"

Claire nods. "I haven't spoken to anybody about Chekhov in a long time," she says. "I loved Chekhov, in college. So did Don. Don and I read all of Chekhov. He'd read the stories aloud to me, in bed. We had a teacher who got us obsessed with Chekhov. Here at Grinnell. Jesus, I can't even remember her name."

It's hard to picture Don and Claire so young, lying in bed, half dressed, reading to each other.

"So you remember me!" Charlie says. "Hallelujah! So I was here? My life isn't some dream. Do you know a lot of people in this town act like they've never seen me before in their life?"

"Like *Newhart*?" she says, laughing. "'It was all a dream!'"

"What?"

"The TV show. In the last episode he wakes up and it was all a dream—oh, Christ, you're too young, aren't you?"

"I guess so. I've never seen it. It's called *Newhart*?"

"Yeah," she says. "I used to watch it. My parents were friends with some of the actors."

"Why are we talking about Bob Newhart?" Charlie says, and goes to touch her hip. "Weren't we about to have sex?"

But Claire stands up and goes over to the window that looks out toward the yard. The room is dark but not so dark. When she turns around she sees that Charlie is standing perfectly still in the middle of the room, staring at her. There is enough light from the moon and the lights of campus that she can make eye contact with him. Then she turns and looks out the window again. If anyone is in the yard, will they see her?

"Come here," she says.

He comes up behind her and she presses against the glass of the window. She pushes back into him, feels him through his trunks again, pressing into the small of her back, and then she takes his hands and puts them on her breasts.

She stops then, turns around. "Slide the straps from my shoulders," she says. "Don't talk."

He does as he is told.

She lifts his hands to her breasts, which feels electrifyingly odd, to feel how another man's hands fit onto her body like that, different, completely different from Don's hands though really so similar somehow. It's all just hands and mouths and hips, in the end. Thickening flesh, hardening, softening. All biology. This she must believe if she is to keep going.

He begins to untie his trunks, but she stops him. "Not yet," she says. "Pull this off," she says. "Pull off my suit first."

He slowly begins to unroll the damp, white fabric.

"Faster. Rip it down."

He does, and he is on his knees then, his face in front of her, she feels his breath on her, and then her own hand slides between her legs and she feels her body opening to him, almost liquefying at her own touch. His mouth on her for a moment.

"Stand up," she says.

Charlie stands and he moves his hands down her sides, down her hips, and when she feels him try to go lower, she says, "No."

She pulls down his trunks, then turns her back to him and puts her hands against the window.

"Like this," she says.

Soon, she is moaning louder than she has moaned in many years, free from children in another room or the unsaid expectations of a longtime lover, free in a way she's never quite been able to imagine, but now she won't stop it, can't, and his hands on her, bigger, more clumsy than she imagined, and it is in this way that she shudders and climaxes while pounding a fist against the drywall and grabbing at him with the other hand.

Charlie collapses to the makeshift bed after this. She wraps herself in a towel, leaves the room, and hears him call her name but ignores it. She goes outside, across the yard, to the study, alone. Sometimes, after sex, she has this terrible need to be alone. It always hurt Don's feelings, but, as she had told him, it wasn't him, it was her, and now she has that feeling again, with a different man.

She drinks a shot of whiskey from the bottle of Maker's Mark Charlie keeps on his desk, and then comes out to the pool deck. She waves up to the bedroom window, and for a brief moment, the light goes on, and she sees Charlie there, naked. He waves her up, motioning for her to come back upstairs. Youth, she thinks. She thought he'd be asleep

He flips the light back off. She drops her towel and walks across the deck. The privacy fence will probably hide her from the neighbors, but in her euphoric drunken postorgasm haze, she doesn't really care. She dives into the pool even though the pool lights are on and swims. Floating on her back, she looks up to the bedroom window. The light is on again, and she sees Charlie, watching her from the upstairs window, working his own hand on himself. Somebody is going to call the cops if they see him, she thinks. He stops and motions for her to come back inside.

Youth, she thinks.

She swims to the bottom of the deep end and she screams.

ABC doesn't really want to have sex with Don Lowry. She wants to make love to Philly, but she is drunk and mad and aching. She trusts Don and she also likes him, likes being near him, likes the physicality of their friendship, the dozing in the hammock, the ease she feels with her body around him, knowing he worships it. Did she really believe he would lead her to Philly? Does she really believe that now? It seems so impossible and yet, well—how random a joke is that? Why would Philly say that Don Lowry would come for her?

And now he is here in the bathtub, a sad man, and empty, and she understands his woundedness. And he's hard too, his dick smooth and straight up in the water. Some people are born that way—constantly wavering between overwhelming lust and deep, inexplicable sorrow. They walk around like that. So beautifully fucked up, Philly would say. Some people, she used to say, are only happy when they're fucking. The rest of their lives they walk around missing it. She would appreciate Don. Maybe she's really there, inside him?

Or maybe Philly would say, "Oh, how can you get turned on by some old guy's pecker?"

ABC thinks of Philly and feels her desire for Don deflating.

"How did this happen to my life?" Don says.

"Nobody ever knows the answer to that kind of question," ABC says.

Don looks surprised.

She goes toward him so that she is sitting next to him.

"I have been faithful to her my whole life. And she is the only woman I've ever—"

"Seriously?" ABC says, suddenly, almost too fast. "The only woman you've had sex with?"

"I met her my freshman year in college," Don says.

She reaches under the water and finds him, already softening, but she grips him and in a moment he is hard again.

"I didn't come to that party tonight for this," he says. "In fact, I had planned to break in here with Claire."

"It's okay. It's all okay."

"I mean I think about you. All the time, some days. But I never expected this. I loved being near you in a way that has never made any sense."

"Stop talking, Don," she says.

"I need to tell you something," he says.

"Shh. No talking. Let's just do something instead of talking, Don."

She takes his hand and pulls it up over the surface of the water, and she reaches over to the abandoned bath caddy and pulls a bottle of almond oil from it, nearly empty, but there's enough. She pours some in his hand, and she tells him to sit on the edge of the bathtub. He does. She leads his oiled hand to his cock. He holds it up, smooth and straight and pulsing a bit. She grazes it with her mouth and he moans. Then she moves across the tub, to the other side. She slowly gets out of the tub. She begins to rub oil on her legs, up over her belly, on her arms and breasts. Don moves his hand up and down and she only watches him from the corner of her eye. She does not look at him directly. But it is not long before she knows he is done, she hears him sputter into the water, nearly choking on a stifled moan. Then Don Lowry sinks back into the tub.

She shuts the light off in the bathroom and opens the door and goes out into the plush carpet of the bedroom and lies down there in the dark, exhausted, her head spinning, her mouth hot and dry. And soon, she hears the tub draining, the substantial gurgle of it, and before she knows where Don is or what he is doing, she is in a dream, and then she sees in the distance what she has long wanted to see: Philly, emerging from a lake again, and the lake was . . .

PART VI

I have loved this life so much.
I was prepared to wait out there forever.

—*Charles Baxter,* "The Cousins"

Superior!

It appears on the drive north suddenly, the landscape shifting from scrub pine and dead grass along the interstate to a vast expanse of water as they round a corner outside Duluth. Both ABC and Charlie gasp, in unison, and when Charlie glances in the rearview he sees Ruth Manetti's face in a kind of rapture, a broad grin squinting into the brilliant blue lake ahead of them.

"It's been too long," she whispers behind them. "Why do we do that to ourselves? Why do we stay away so long from the places that make us whole?"

North of Duluth, each time they see the lake, ABC rolls down her window more and pushes her face into the clear, crisp air. Charlie yells back to Ruth: "Too much wind?"

To which Ruth replies, "No such thing!"

This, Charlie thinks, is the closest thing to joy that I've felt in years.

About a hundred yards down the highway, Don and Claire sit in the front seats of the Suburban: Claire's at the wheel and Don's in the passenger seat, with a migraine. His sunglasses on, he drinks from a bottle of Smartwater. "Buying this water always makes me feel dumb," he jokes after the final gas station stop. The kids find this to be hilarious. They begin to call it Dumbwater. Claire chews fiercely on a wad of gum, which she rarely does, but she's been craving a cigarette, a new secret habit that the children don't know about yet.

The children would probably not notice anyway; they're both zoned out on personal DVD players that Don's mother had bought them at Walmart the week before, and now, the carefully selected library books that Claire had checked out two days earlier sit untouched in a heap on the backseat. Both of the kids wear headphones.

"Why don't you guys look out of the window?" Claire suggests. "Look how beautiful the lake looks."

"How beautiful the lake IS!" Don says.

The kids say nothing in response.

"I've deliberately resisted those machines since the kids were infants," Claire says.

"Everything's changing," Don says. "We'll have to lower our standards. Divorce ain't for sissies."

"Why am I doing this?" Claire says.

"Doesn't matter now," Don says. "You're here. We're here. So, one more time: Charlie will be in the cabin. And ABC and Ruth will take the guesthouse. We'll stay in the lodge with the kids. Don't you think?"

"Sure," Claire says. "That is what we already decided, right?"

"The lodge is big enough for us to have separate bedrooms, if you prefer."

"Since we're separated in Iowa, let's not confuse the issue in Minnesota."

"Yes," Don says. "That's sound."

"For the kids," she says. "They need some consistency in their lives."

"Have you thought any more about my idea?" Don says.

"You mean staying there for the year?"

"Yes. That's my best idea," Don says.

"I said I'd think about it once we were up there. It's hard to picture that place in the winter."

"I know you like the cabin," Don says. "I don't want you to be disappointed, but with the kids"—he glances into the rearview to make sure they still have on their headphones—"it just makes the most sense if we all stay in the same place."

"Don't worry about my disappointment."

"Give us a year, Claire," Don says.

"I can't."

"I'm sure they've figured some things out on their own. But," Don says, "you know. We can spare them this upheaval."

"It's a family vacation. And it's the last one, Don. Do you want me to lie to you? Pretend there's hope?"

"There's always hope."

"No there's not, Don. Things die every day."

She hasn't meant for this to sound hurtful, but, instead, pragmatic, tough minded. Still, she sees Don Lowry throw his head back as if he's been punched.

"Look, if we're here the whole winter, we could, I mean, you could stay in the cabin if you'd like. What we could do is, I could go down and get more of our things, what we'll need for the winter. Or you could. We'll order up some firewood, lots of it. We could have some time alone, all of us, in whatever way we need to have it."

"Let's just get there and then talk about your plan."

"You could stay up there alone too, Claire. For the fall? I could handle everything at home. Maybe you could finish a book?"

"And you'd live where?"

"Whatever you need, Claire. That's what I am saying. I can make it happen, whatever it is."

"I'd love some time alone, to think. Maybe to write. But I'd miss the kids. I don't think I could do that. And I am not sure that's what I need."

"Well, for now, are you sure you're okay with these arrangements?" Don says. "With the lodge. All of us sleeping there, all the Lowrys?"

"The lodge is fine. It's great. It's huge."

"But the carpets. I think Merrick said that he had new ones put in in the spring. They might give you a headache," Don says.

"You're the one with the migraines," Claire says.

"If I smoke some weed," he whispers, "I don't get headaches."

She glances in her rearview for Charlie's van, but does not see it.

"You don't have any in this car, do you?" she says. "I don't want to get arrested."

"They have it," Don says. "Ruth has it, actually. Person cops are least likely to frisk if they get pulled over for some reason."

"Are they ahead of us?" Claire asks.

"I just know you have preferences. If you want, we can put Ruth and ABC in the lodge, with Charlie, and you and Wendy can stay in the cabin. It has wood floors, of course, and the best view. And Bryan and I can be in the guesthouse."

"Are you ever gonna stop talking about this? I thought we made a decision about where everyone is gonna sleep."

"Well, if you want the cabin," Don says, "I just want you to have what you want."

"Give the cabin to Charlie. He should have some space to himself. We've been surrounding him for a month in his house."

"He didn't have to come, of course," Don says. "If he wanted space. Anyway, if you want me to, I can sleep in the boathouse instead of the lodge. There is the sleeping porch there."

"It'll be too cold," Claire says. "It'll be in the forties at night."

"It depends on the wind."

"Jesus, Don. Stop thinking. Stop trying to make everybody

happy," Claire says, and tight lipped, she accelerates them forward with a sudden jerk, easing to the left then gunning the gas in order to pass a logging truck.

ABC told herself, many months ago, that she had seen enough of the world—in college, she traveled every break—had spent time on the African continent (Namibia, Ghana, South Africa), had been across Europe, had been to China and Thailand, had been through the Rockies and up and down the coasts of North America, from Vancouver to San Diego, from Maine to Key West. She told herself that being resigned to a mourner's life in Iowa was okay.

But when they arrive at the house—the houses—near Little Marais, she knows she's been wrong about that. She has not seen everything. Here is something she never has seen before—it's almost like Maine, but not quite: there is something clearer about it, and, compared to the moody and fierce North Atlantic, the vista of the icy blue lake seems to make your heart swell rather than tremble. And it swells inside her now, brings about moodiness and longing, but something more than that too. Ruth was right. This is the landscape of her dreams, the dreams she has about Philly. This is where Philly's spirit has gone, and this is where it is waiting for her, and she has come to the right place, she feels, and Ruth, and the whole summer, her whole friendship with Don Lowry begins to make sense. It has all led to this. Now she wonders if she has the courage to do what Ruth has told her to do. Just as she wonders this, they are pulling down a long wooded dirt road to the Merrick estate, and they find the lake again after driving maybe half a mile or so, and when they see the lake, they see an eagle take off from the tallest pine and glide out over the water, as if, ABC thinks, it is a confirmation from the spirit world.

She turns around to look at Ruth, who has grown silent, entranced, a smile on her glowing face. She does not squint into the sunlight, but instead seems to reflect it off her face through the whole car.

"Look at her face," ABC says in a whisper to Charlie, and he looks at Ruth in his rearview.

"What?" he says.

"Her face is glowing."

"God, what were we thinking, coming here?" Charlie says. "Do you know how awkward this is going to be?"

"We're here," ABC says, softly, so as not to startle Ruth.

"Home again, home again," Ruth says, "jiggity jig."

As soon as they park, ABC walks off ahead of the group and down to the rocky beach, hoping nobody has noticed all the tears coming down her finally happy face.

To the water, to the waves that crash and roll in as foamy and loud as any ocean, she says, "I'm coming."

Ruth goes up the three steps to the guesthouse's deck with ease. ABC barely holds her arm.

"Ruth," ABC says. "You're doing so well."

"The water is magic," Ruth says. "The air is magic. You'll see! You'll see! We'll sleep so soundly. So soundly! We used to call it the Merrick effect, when we all came up here. We'd all sleep so well, even the kids, and in the morning you wake feeling so rested."

"I can feel that magic," ABC says.

"This place has always been sacred. I grew up seven miles west. We'll drive out and see it, if you want. Though the house is no longer there. They tore it down and built a palace. But, I told you—this is a sacred place. There's so few of them left."

Out in the water, some black rocks, dusted with orange in the dusky light, are descended upon by a flock of squawking gulls.

"Those rocks," Ruth says, "they know more than we can imagine."

Later, ABC finds Ruth wrapped in a blanket, sitting on the

beach with Claire. ABC, still uneasy around Claire, goes to them tentatively.

"Just checking in," she says.

"We're fine," Claire says, smiling.

It is, or it at least seems to be, a genuine expression of contentment and ABC feels the nerves at the base of her spine untangle and relax. She sits down on the other side of Ruth.

"Ruth," she says. "Are you cold?"

And Ruth holds up a translucent shard of stone and says, "Look, ABC, it's an agate!"

ABC takes it and examines the rings in the glassy stone.

"Put it in your pocket," Ruth says.

There is a natural tendency in couples, Claire knows, to attempt to restore order, solve problems, and rekindle passion while traveling. Claire has never understood this. She is not sure how breaking one's routine is conducive to an action as complicated as repairing a relationship. That should be done in a grueling way, day after day of hard conversation at the kitchen table. Sober, focused, dedicated. She and Don have not done that work. They have, she has finally realized, not *wanted* to do it. She had not wanted to do it. A window opened and she went through it so fast she hasn't even thought the details through; she just went.

And she knows that you can't restore anything after you give it up entirely. After complete destruction, it's only rebuilding that's left to do, and sometimes it is easier to do the work of rebuilding alone. Two small kingdoms separated, built from scratch, rather than one complicated castle rising from ruins.

She doesn't agree with Don's idea that being away from home might give them perspective they might not have at home. She does not think a year spent splitting wood and homeschooling in northern Minnesota is the thing they need. Better to solve problems at the breakfast table in one's own home, if one has such a place, where the pale, clear light of morning shines over everything, where nothing is hidden. If you solve your problems in some idyllic place—and looking around she has to admit, it is pretty amazingly idyllic—you have an artificial crutch. You have help. And when you return home, you will not have really solved anything. In the dim light of the place you left, you will come home in the first hours of the evening, and you will look around at the unpaid bills and the laundry and the crooked molding along the kitchen floor and smell the faintly mildewed wall behind the shower surround and you will say to each other, *We weren't gone long enough.*

She thinks not of Don but of Charlie as she unpacks the children's clothes in the lodge. He's been cool to her of late, but perhaps he's trying his best to be discreet around the kids. They've not had any moments alone since the night of the heat wave party. One night, she saw him sitting out alone by the pool, drinking beer, but she was afraid to sit with him that night, the kids were still awake in the house, and the look on Charlie's face was pensive, sad, far away, not there but elsewhere.

The next day, the car unloaded, the lodge and cabins opened up, the fridges stocked with groceries and supplies from Zup's in Silver Bay, everything feels as if it is secure, safely and happily set up in the place they almost had decided not to come, and Claire and Don go out to the lodge's deck overlooking the lake.

"I'm glad we all came," Claire says.

Don nods.

The children are building a series of castles with the endless rocks on the beach. Charlie is sitting on the porch of his cabin, reading. Ruth and ABC sit on the porch of the guesthouse, drinking tea. And the sight of all this contentment moves Don and Claire to sit down together, side by side on a wooden Leopold bench that is on the deck. Don puts his arm around his wife and she takes it from her shoulders.

"I'm sorry," Claire says.

"Me too," Don says, but he doesn't know if she is apologizing for wanting his arm off her body, or if she is apologizing for something bigger, harsher, irreversible.

The surf of the lake rushes in roaring and retreats in a whisper. They have looked at this shore so many times now; this is their ninth summer here and they had done just this so much—sit on this bench and stare at this water, and Don now knows, they will not tell each other the long, long thoughts they were thinking.

"What are we going to do?" Claire asks. "We need to be less crazy. We need to be happier. Whatever happens next."

"I know."

"But the kids seem good. They seem okay," Claire says.

"I think they are. I think we've handled things well enough. I wonder how they'll make sense of this summer, years from now."

"In therapy?"

"Right. Well, of course. They'll need that. We should set some money aside now. I think parents should have to pay for college, and, after that, therapy."

She smiles at him and it makes her eyes tear up and his too.

"I suppose it depends on how things end," Don says.

"What things?"

"The summer. Us. Me. You."

"I hope it'll end as well as it can end."

"If we end it."

"Don," Claire says. "Doesn't it feel like we already have? That's why I didn't want to confuse the issue, with this trip."

"A last hurrah."

"Your words, not mine."

*

"We shouldn't take it," Claire says, when Don tells her just how much money Ruth has given him and tells her about the house.

"I mean," Don says, "it won't fix everything. But it will help."

"It feels wrong," Claire says. "Twenty-five thousand dollars is a lot of money."

"It buys us a year, up here, to fix things."

Claire looks over to the guesthouse, where ABC is taking an afghan to Ruth. Claire watches ABC moving in the wind, a thin wraparound skirt and white linen blouse, the wind blowing her clothing tight against her body, so different from Claire's own. Claire is lean, muscled, and slender and ABC is all hips and breasts and ass. Ruth appears to have dozed off. Claire doesn't like how the trip has become linked to their floundering financial situation, the mountain of debt. Ruth is there to help them, not vice versa, and it should be vice versa. They should be doing this out of kindness, not need.

Claire also wants to say this but doesn't: *I don't want to fix anything, Don. I'm done.*

Claire wants to say something like this, but when she looks at Don, she sees that he is gazing in the opposite direction, at Charlie, who has stood up now and is walking along the beach away from the compound, holding a bottle of beer. He peels off his shirt and finds himself a sunny rock at the far end of their beach where he stretches out. It is not warm for Iowa, not compared to the July they have just been through, but the sun is high and it is warm for northern Minnesota. Very warm for this part of the world. The lake is the warmest it's been in history, sometimes getting into the sixties off the shore, though easily plummeting back into the forties overnight. It is a moody lake. Don keeps his eyes on Charlie. Claire watches Don's clenching jaw work a piece of gum. She touches Don's shoulder.

"I think I'll brew some coffee," Claire says. She stands.

"Okay. I'd like some too. Can I come with you?"

"Of course," she says.

"What were you thinking about?" Don asks.

Why do couples ask each other such a question? Don used to ask this of Claire often. This was back when they were young, and newly together, and Don seemed convinced that she was always thinking about something sad, about leaving him. But she is not sure he has asked it once since the children were born. It is odd to hear it after it had been a forgotten part of their conversational repertoire.

Claire surveys the scene. She shrugs. On the deck of the guest-house, Ruth sleeps in the sun and ABC now walks barefoot over the rocks (how effortlessly she does that, Claire thinks, my feet always kill me when I do that) and she is heading toward Charlie. ABC stops and waves at the children, who are now splashing about in the shallow creek that almost leads to the lake but today, in that dry month, the creek stops about ten feet short of it. When it rains, the lake's swell will wash up over that ten feet and the creek will rush into the lake and the lake into it.

The children wave back to ABC, who is now walking in the surf and holding her flowing skirt up high, exposing the meat of her thighs. Claire sees Don watching ABC as ABC walks toward Charlie, who stands and walks toward ABC. The surf is significant and loud and when Charlie and ABC come together and sit down next to each other at the water's edge, one can't tell if they are speaking or if they are simply staring at the water.

Claire notices that Don is staring at the two young guests as intently as she has been.

"They're beautiful," she says. "That's what I am thinking."

"Yes," Don says. "Not so much younger than we are, not really, but . . . So. Much. Younger."

ABC stretches into the wind as if she is trying to embrace the horizon. She reaches up as high as she can, steps up on her tiptoes, stretches toward the sun. She wags her hands in the air, as if beckoning something out of the cold deep.

"Have you slept with Charlie?" Don asks.

"No," Claire says, instinctively. She had not meant to lie, but that is the reflex, buried within her. "Have you? Slept with ABC?"

"I've come close," Don says. "I'm sorry."

"I've come close too," Claire says.

"When?"

"The heat wave party. That hot night."

"Me too. That was the night."

"Really?" Claire says.

"Yes. Must have been the heat."

"Did we get married too young?" Claire asks.

"I don't know. I think about that."

"It's only natural," Claire says. "You wonder."

"You have been the love of my life," Don says. "You are the love of my life."

Claire shifts, pulls her knees up to her chest, making herself smaller, more compact. "It's a long life," Claire says. "Maybe you should have more."

"More what?" Don says.

"More life," Claire says. "More love. More joy than I can give you."

"That's fucking ridiculous," Don says.

"It isn't," Claire says.

"No," Don says. "It is."

"Maybe it's just nearing forty—I feel like fifteen years of my life went by without, without, I don't know, without me doing anything."

"We had kids," Don says.

She nods. "Right. And I love them so much."

"But you don't want to be with me anymore? Is that it?"

"Don, you take all my energy. I guess that's it. You take all my energy. Living with you exhausts me. I don't like being around you some days. All of the day. I didn't like the way you changed when things got hard. I think that's it. You're only able to do easy. That's why you hid the foreclosure notices from me. How could I have been so dumb?"

Don says nothing, and Claire, who's been trying to sound comforting, realizes she may have come off as cruel.

"But you have been the love of my life too," she says. "No matter where we go from here."

"No matter what happens," Don says.

"You're funny, Don Lowry," Claire says. "You always have been."

"So, is this it?" Don says.

Claire knows then that she will go to Charlie's cabin one of these nights, and she will sleep with him again. It is the only way to move ahead in her life, she thinks. It is a portal out of this life and into a new one. And, she tells herself, it is the only way Don will understand that they have reached the end of something. One time with Charlie, drunk, and after a long, steamy party, might be forgivable, a mistake. But if she does it now, here, in the cool and limpid light of Lake Superior, it will not be a mistake.

She stares out at the water. Sometimes, a trick of clouds and the light will make you believe you see a ship on the horizon, or one of the Apostle Islands off the coast of Wisconsin. But other times the sky above Superior is perfectly clear, a blank white slate. This has become one of those afternoons. How fitting, she thinks. Blank slates.

"You came more than close," Don says. "Didn't you?"

She turns to him, wraps herself in her own arms, suddenly chilled.

"Don," she says. "I'm so sorry."

*

And now Don knows that one night soon, he will find himself alone in the world, a new person, and he will go off and look for a new life, and the world, and everybody he loves in the world, will be free to move forward, away from his ugliness, the Shadow of him, and they will be free, all of his pretty chickens, to move into the next phase of their lives, which will be beautiful or, as he looks at his kids playing, destined for beauty. He will work harder than ever. If he has to leave town to find work, he will do it. He will send them money. He will work shit jobs. He will allow them, and their mother, to move into a happier life without him. He will do it without bitterness. It will be his purpose. Every day as he ties on an apron at some Home Depot outside Waterloo or loads trucks in a warehouse off the Mississippi in Moline, he will think of his children, the reasons he is doing the work, and he will be okay with it. He'll work happily, intently, his goals as noble as goals can get.

On weekends, he'll drive to Grinnell, or wherever they are then living with their mother. He'll arrive bearing gifts and he will not allow his misery, any sadness he feels, to infect them. If he lives alone, he can keep all of that, he can keep the Shadow to himself. He will show up smiling and the children will take comfort from his newfound stoicism, his warm optimism. He will change what he has felt powerless to change. He wonders though, why not change now, right at this moment? Can't he just wake up tomorrow and understand that life, in fact, is fundamentally wonderful? That he is fundamentally wonderful? That he is not his father? That Claire is fundamentally wonderful? The kids, their lives, Iowa. Being alive should be enough. He wants to say this aloud.

Why couldn't he just say that to Claire and reverse the course of everything?

"I want you to be free of me," Don says. "I want you and the kids to have a different life. A happy one."

The kids shriek in the cold water and sprint back onto the shore, howling.

"The kids are happy," Claire says. "They love you. And I love you. And I, I really have—until very recently—been happy."

"This life though," Don Lowry says. "I feel like it's killing you."

She doesn't say anything to that.

Just beyond where the two children are playing, ABC and Charlie sit side by side, throwing rocks into the water. She begins to cry and Charlie puts his arm around her, the waves swell even higher, a wind blows from the woods behind them, and a cloud passes in front of the sun, turning the warm yellow light momentarily to a metallic, golden hue.

"Are you okay?" Charlie says.

"I have deliberately been trying to avoid anything beautiful," ABC says. "Ever since Philly died, I've been afraid to experience beauty without her."

"Why?" Charlie says. "I don't get that."

ABC lets out a snotty laugh and buries her face in the wrist cuffs of her wool sweater. "Because you're a monster!" she says, the words choked out in a kind of sobbing guffaw.

"Probably," he says.

"Do you think you will end up with Claire?" ABC says. "Eventually."

"You mean, like, forever? Or tonight?"

"Don't do it, Charlie. Leave them alone."

"I didn't do it," Charlie says. "She did it. She doesn't love him anymore."

This life, the one at the lake: it is not killing Claire. She begins to think of what has come to be known in proper terms as the Merrick option, and she is considering it. A year at Superior—how would it feel in the winter? She was certain a lake like this would never freeze, but maybe it would—maybe you'd look out and see a vast expanse of ice, a bridge you could walk across out into nothing. This is what she likes about being so far north—you feel like you could, if you wanted to, get out into nothing. Enter a state of it, escape.

How strange it was to see them, this foursome, Don and Claire and Charlie and ABC, plus the ancient Ruth and two happy children, sharing the same space that week. The space was vast, of course, and this helped. And around the space, around their lodgings and their private beach, only woods and sky and water. It was possible that the clean air and open vistas had transformed all of them, had brought them out from their grief and burdens. They were all like the children that first week, free to roam the beach and the woods that separated the compound from the distant highway, free to sit for hours and stare at the waves, and the changing color of the water, gray, green, blue. They gathered rocks, hunted for agates, watched the eagle, which Charlie had named Lyle Canon, patrol the shoreline, and on still days they heard the haunted call of the loon. Once, at night, a yearning wolf echoed his howls off the stoic cliffs. The gulls gathered away from them, on a massive stand of charcoal-colored rocks at the far end of the beach, and they walked out to the rocks and studied the intricacies of the orange lichen.

The clouds above them changed often, coming in low and swollen in the morning, dissipating into the blue by noon, then returning at sunset, gray and thin, a flattened fog separating them from the moon and stars as Don Lowry built the evening's fire. At night, Ruth would join them until she got too cold, at which point ABC would retreat with Ruth to the guesthouse for sleep. Charlie, who had lied and told everyone he had decided to write a novel, would leave the lodge soon after that. He spent much of his evenings in and near his cabin, reading, drinking coffee or beer, and pretending to write a novel on a stack of yellow legal pads he'd bought at the co-op down the road in Finland. And while his stated intention had been to write a novel, a plan he blurted out over coffee the first morning there, each night he wrote letters to old friends, letters that said almost nothing of substance, but made him feel as if, when he returned from his time on the lake, he would be part of a wider world again. Each morning, he'd drive into Finland, buy envelopes and stamps at the post office, and send the letters out into the world. Some of the addresses he had scrawled into the back pages of his Moleskine journal, some he guessed at, relying on memory. In one instance, he sent a letter to an old professor at Oberlin simply by writing down his name, the words *Oberlin College,* and the city, state, and zip. Some letters would reach their intended recipients and others would not. That was certain. Also certain: He would leave Grinnell. He would leave his mother with what she wanted, a tidy, organized archive of his father's insignificant work, a most unimpressive intellectual legacy. He would attempt no interpretation or insight. The work, what his father had spent decades on, was, when one was forced to be realistic, largely meaningless. He had done very little that would last. Charlie would burn all the letters. They meant nothing. He would burn the typed and retyped drafts of *Gatsby* himself and be done with it.

On the sixth morning, just before the break of day, Don packs a picnic lunch and canteens of water in his backpack, along with a pocketknife, a small first-aid kit, some bug spray, some sunscreen, and a whistle. Once the children wake up and have breakfast, he helps them dress for a hike. Long pants, long sleeves, socks, well-laced shoes, and hats: despite the protests that they are overbundled for summertime, Don dresses them so no skin shows at all. The deer flies and ticks are thick that time of year, and you cannot hike through the woods with bare skin, especially not at the end of a summer that has been so warm. Often, by August, the bugs are dying off, but not this year. This year, they swarm at you once you are out of the wide expanse of windy shoreline. The mosquitoes in the thickets are as big as bats.

There is, across the highway from the Merrick place, a large parcel of land, maybe two hundred acres, all of that also owned by the Merricks, through which a series of hiking trails moves along the ledge of the Little Marais River. This is where they will hike today.

In the woods, on the uphill, Wendy and Bryan trudge behind Don after the first hour and soon they are tired and thirsty, and although it is not yet ten, Don leads them to a spot on the ridge he had found the summer before, while hiking alone, and they take shade under the birches and pines.

"Look," Don says, pointing down the trail toward the waterfall, the white rush of it still intense from the rains of early summer. "We can swim near those falls later. There is a trail down to it."

The image of Claire swimming in the falls with Charlie, nude, flares up in his brain in a way he cannot shake.

"Are there sharks?" Wendy asks. She has an obsession with sharks ever since Don had let her watch some of Shark Week on cable months ago.

"No! Freshwater, dummy," Bryan says.

"And blueberries," Don says, squatting down to show the children the blueberry plants in fully ripened splendor. He picks three berries and pops them into his mouth.

"I want one," Wendy says. "Wait!"

"Plenty for everyone," Don says, and he savors the berries, the tart sweetness of them, makes a point of looking at the falls and listening to the rustle of pine needles as he eats them, the full sensory experience of the north woods. You give your children something like this, you feel like a hero. How many kids would grow up and never experience anything so beautiful and pristine and real? The air seems to be even clearer up on the ridge, and like a drowning man suddenly saved, he begins to take in great gulps of it, filling his lungs.

But it does not change anything. He wants it to, so badly, but it doesn't.

Lunch is served. The children's collective mood, bolstered by food and rest and the sheer beauty of their perch, rises. Would they remember their father this way? The way he is on a small handful of days of the year, the leader of an expedition to a place still and beautiful? Or, more likely, will they remember him in a state of half misery, a sad, shambling man with a clipboard and boxes of real estate flyers, a man muttering out of anger as he pays the bills in his study or muttering out of boredom as he washes what feels like an endless, infinite stack of dishes.

Now, a dull roar comes from behind him, a snort of some kind, a harrumph. Before he turns to look, already Don Lowry knows he will see a bear. How many bears, he wonders, as the musky smell, a dank mix of dead fish and damp earth, hits him. He looks. Three bears: a mother and two cubs. The children begin to whimper behind him. Don watches as the two cubs step ahead of their mother, and despite her throaty moan, ignore her and make for the berries.

The bear, the mother, stands, sniffs the air, and then goes back on four paws. Don stands less than six feet from the cubs. "Bryan," Don says calmly. "Take Wendy and begin to back away. Go the way we came, go back away. I will stay here."

Don has the idea that he can protect his kids if he stands his ground.

"Go on," Don says. "You kids start going back. You go first."

"Come on," Bryan hisses at his sister. "Come on!" The bear, agitated, begins to pace. Don readies himself to act as a human shield should the bear charge. It will kill him, of course, that bear, but his children might be spared.

He waits for a long time like that, standing still enough to be the wall between the bear and his children. The cubs continue to fall on the berries. *On the berries they fell. Fell they did, on the berries.* This is how Don's mind works in those tense moments. He simply runs that sentence in his head as long as he can and hopes to keep the fear from his heart, his lungs, his scent.

A sharp wail echoes off the cliffs above the river and Don tenses his muscles. Wendy . . . Oh shit, Wendy. He has no choice but to go to her. So Don turns and walks away from the bear and feels the bear trotting toward him—he cannot run or he will lead the angry, frightened, or whatever the fuck it is bear right back to the kids.

"Is Wendy okay?" Don yells.

Silence.

"Bee sting," Bryan says.

"Is her face swollen?" Don calls. The bear inches toward him, now three feet from him, maybe less. The bear stands again.

"No," Wendy says. "Daddy, where is the bear?"

"Bryan, you guys calmly begin walking home."

The bear's rotten breath blows in Don's face. He winces.

"The way we came," Don says. And then, once he thinks the kids are safely away, Don begins to inch his way toward the cubs.

"You can kill me," he whispers to the bear.

The bear seems to be calmed by the whispering.

"Yeah," Don says, "please kill me."

The bear sniffs at the air again.

"Me. Not them. Me. You can kill me, but not them."

The bear weighs the offer, goes at the blueberries alongside her cubs. Don begins to back away. If he wanted to be killed, right there, in a way that could only be described as accidental, he could do it. He could harass the cubs. He could charge them, now that the kids were safely away, out of sight. Bryan could lead them home. He could run to the road and call 911 and by then it would be too late.

And what a blameless way to go: *Many years ago, in the dizzyingly hot summer of 2012, on a blueberry-covered ridge above a waterfall in northern Minnesota, our father died while saving us from a bear.*

"Kill me, you fucking bears," Don whispers. "Go ahead."

The bears continue to eat the berries. Every so often, the mother bear looks over her shoulder at Don, but then she goes back to eating.

"Go ahead, I want to die," Don whispers, and the mother bear turns to him and grunts and snorts in a way that seems to say, "No. You don't." But Don has no time to process that, because he hears another scream.

"Daddy!" He hears Wendy's scream echoing up the rocks of the river. "Daddy! Help!"

It is earlier on this day, back in Grinnell, where the weather is not as clear or as crisp and the meteor showers of the North Shore are never visible, that Gill Gulliver awakes from sad dreams two hours before dawn. He has pissed the bed, goddamnit, and stands shivering beside it and suddenly thinks of how ashamed he will be if anyone ever sees him like that, ever sees him in such a state, half naked, pissed on by his own self. Instead of pressing his Help button and turning on the lights, he dresses, which he still can sometimes do, and wears his khakis and his sweatshirt and socks and the slip-on loafers that do not need lacing. He knows his own name and he says it to himself.

He goes to the window. In what is mostly a misty, humid darkness, he sees lights, a small band of dying fireflies that he has never seen before, not from that window, and he opens the window because something in his brain, some stray synapse, fires and says he should try and touch one of the fireflies, and he slides open the window farther than it could ever open in the past when he has tried to open it. The alarms that are supposed to sound do not sound.

He reaches out and catches in his loose fist a firefly and feels it dissolve in his fist and his hand feels strong when he does it. He reaches up and catches another one and again it seems to dissolve in his hand, this time the other hand, and now he is feeling drawn to the warmth of the night, and the noninstitutional air and he boosts himself out into it, that air. He goes out the window and begins to walk to the simultaneously familiar and foreign lights of downtown.

As he walks, he lectures. Why does he lecture? Because his students are flanking him—not just his recent students, but decades' worth of them, all of them young and beautiful, the women and the men, all of them hanging on his every word as he turns and says to them: "And it is not fair to give *Gatsby* the label of a novel of socioeconomic or political or cultural conditions. It is not fair to call it a novel that serves to both mythicize and criticize the American dream as it stood in the raging days of early American capitalism, of Wall Street and wealth run amok. This is not the novel Fitzgerald wrote! Fitzgerald wrote a novel of a young man finding his literary calling, and finding too that the world was not a safe place for a sensitive young person, an easily wounded, easily influenced young person! Not without writing. Not without language and the power of observation and the power to remain outside all of the ugliness. Yes? Are you following me?"

And when he asks this, he looks about himself and sees that they are gone. All the students have left him, except for one, except for—no, she was no student. She is John Manetti's wife, Ruth, his first lover at Grinnell. Fifty, maybe older, she never would tell him exactly, but she is a generation his senior, and she is there, brushing her dark hair in the window of the house on Broad Street where he used to sneak in to see her, back in the days when he used to love her. He has aged, but she has not, has she? He looks up at the window on the third floor and she waves down to him. This is her husband's study. He knows it well. They have made love on his desk, knocking a stack of papers to the floor. She had never loved her husband; she moaned this confession into his ear one day, on that desk. She loved to fuck on that desk, as if somehow she was sabotaging something, taking some power back that wasn't hers to take. She worried that she had wasted her life, she told him that too. Afterward, picking up the papers and the books, she had cried.

"Tell him," Gill had said.

And she did. Gill believed that she had told her husband, told him that she loved another man, a younger man, and that she was leaving him. And Gill had promised her they'd leave Grinnell, just as soon as he could get another job, but then Gill fell in love with someone else, Kathy, someone his own age who could give him a child, only one it turned out, but a child nonetheless, a son, and Ruth rarely spoke to him again. He never loved Kathy the way he loved Ruth, with that sucking, aching need one must love with if it is to last.

He looks up at Ruth, brushing her hair in the window. He will have to tell her he was wrong. He has made mistakes.

He moves through the dark to Ruth Manetti.

The key, as it has been for many years, is under the flowerpot on the porch. He finds the house dark. He grapples for the lights, labors up the three flights of stairs, and finds the study dark. "Ruth?" he says, entering the attic room. It has been so long. His tongue grows thick with the anticipation of pleasure. When the lights switch on, he finds the room empty. He has come from somewhere else. His confusion is a thick honey in his mind.

He wanders through the room, and browses the shelves, fingers the volumes, disorganized and chaotically shelved, until he finds *Gatsby,* and he pulls the slim novel down, a hardcover edition, an anniversary edition from Scribner's, and a key falls from the book. Its pages have been hollowed out to make a place to hide things and hidden here there is a key.

Who would destroy such sacred pages so they might hide a key inside a book?

A small skeleton key: he sees the locked drawer of the handsome desk and he unlocks it and there he finds a gun. Does Ruth's husband have a gun? He might kill Gill with it; he must be considering it, if he knows about them.

Gill pockets the gun.

He repeats his name to himself. He doesn't know so many things. How old is he now? When did he see Ruth last? Is her husband even alive? He wants to stay in this space where he knows who he is and what he is doing and he puts the gun in his hand and walks back to the streets and then across the campus to his home, the home he had made for himself, for his wife and child, when everything with Ruth was over.

In the backyard, there is his study. He goes out to it. He reaches for the door and finds it locked just as the motion lights come on near the pool. He knows then the spare key is always in the small shed that houses the pool's filtering system and pump and he goes there and finds his ring of spares under a five-gallon bucket.

He lets himself inside his beloved study—a *think shack* his old friend Merrick had called it. Where is Merrick? Where has he been? France again, maybe? Gill shivers a bit with confusion and some guilt, because he knows his wife is inside asleep with their young son, Charlie, and that he should go upstairs to the bed and find Kathy and make love to her. His attention on her has waned. He works too much. He feels worthless when he is not working. Does he have to teach tomorrow? He has no idea. He needs to check his calendar.

This does not feel like his study. It is too empty—the shelves thin with books, the file cabinets free of unruly stacks, the large desk bare, the floor free of the boxes and papers.

Where has all his work gone? Has someone done away with it?

There is, on the desk, a stack of yellow legal pads and an Iowa Hawkeyes coffee mug full of sharpened pencils. While he still has clarity—he is oddly cognizant of his current state of awareness—he writes a note: It begins, "Charlie, there is no—" He stops writing. Puts an X through those words. Then writes, in larger script now: "There are only the pursued, the pursuing, the busy, and the tired. —GG."

But the pool. So inviting. So calm. How many hours of his life has he stared at it, thinking, unable to write, his mind awash in a kind of aimless longing for anything different. How often has he wondered about his life and thought, *Really, this is it, this is what comes next forever?*

He puts the gun in his mouth and the trigger gets pulled.

Gill staggers to the pool and falls in. Later, almost three days later, they will find the body when the stench reaches the neighbors: so many of the professors on that leafy street have gone off to summer homes that August that nobody will even report a gunshot. Later, a neighbor will say he thinks maybe he'd heard fireworks, but he thought then that it might be the engine of the train, misfiring somehow, because nobody expects gunshots in Grinnell. Don Lowry's father's gun has sunk to the bottom, but the body of Gill Gulliver, Henry Frederick Watkins '52 Professor of Letters, still floats among the first signs of the inevitable autumn, and, just as Gill Gulliver has so many times imagined, there is *a cluster of leaves revolving slowly around him and a red slick of blood in the water.*

Don finds his children at the trailhead very near the highway. The adrenaline begins to leave his body and seems to vibrate in his joints and skull as it does.

"We thought you were dead," Wendy says. She is holding her knees in a kind of upright fetal position as she sits in the grass and rocks.

"And how did that make you feel?" Don says, one of the questions he had learned to ask her years ago in family therapy, after Wendy's first brush with anxiety attacks. It is a way of letting her talk about her worries without first dismissing them.

"What do you mean?" Wendy says. "How did it make me feel? Horrible, Daddy. HORRIBLE!"

She screams that word and then bursts into tears.

"Hungry," Bryan says, grinning. "We left our lunch up there, half eaten, and we are still hungry."

"It was almost unbearable," Wendy says, and Don smiles, sad and not sad that his ten-year-old daughter knows and uses the word *unbearable.*

Then she says, "Daddy, it's a joke. Get it? Unbearable?"

He hadn't gotten it and now he laughs, almost too loudly, for the kids step back wide eyed when his big sonorous guffaw echoes off the river's stones.

"Let's go back to the lodge," Don says. "Let's just go home."

That afternoon is warm, cloudless, and still, and Claire wakes from a nap, rising in her bed in the lodge's master bedroom to see that the water outside her window has gone flat, a shimmering blue. The wind's gone still. She sits up higher and can see more of the water, sees the rocky beach, and she sees her children, splashing. She hopes the hike has gone well; part of her had wanted to go, but part of her thought that Don should begin to grow used to being alone, more and more, with his kids. She flips off the covers and stands, finding a pair of yoga pants on the ground and sliding them on. She stands at the window and sees the kids are playing with ABC, and she sees Don sitting on the rocks and watching ABC. And then when she looks back into the water, she sees Charlie coming out of it. He is standing waist deep and looking up to the lodge as if he can see her. There is no way he can, is there? Claire feels as if she is making eye contact with him though, as if he is staring right at her. She waves. He does not raise his hand in return.

And then she looks in the water and sees Ruth Manetti, in an ancient black-skirted swimsuit that comes almost to her knees, inching her tiny, pale body into the waves. Charlie goes over and holds her as she goes deeper, almost to her waist. She seems as if she will wash away, so tiny is she, and as she enters the water, ABC and the kids go to the water's edge and cheer her on and Ruth waves and looks up at the sky and Claire can see on Charlie's face a huge and unprecedented grin.

On the beach to the left, Claire sees Don is not just sitting on the beach, but he is building a roaring fire in the fire pit, and once he has significant flame, he begins to arrange a sleeping bag in a camp chair. Charlie is then helping Ruth out of the water and ABC holds open a robe for her and Claire can see the old lady's dazed but real smile. She knows exactly where she is and she, excited, is led to the fire.

Claire puts on a kettle of hot water, and later, as she goes out with a mug of hot tea for Ruth, who is huddled and bundled by the warm fire, Wendy yells to Claire, "Mom! They let Mrs. Manetti go swimming!"

And Claire says, "I know! I saw!"

"Mom! We saw a bear!" Bryan yells.

When Claire hands Ruth the mug of tea, Ruth winks at her. "Don said I'd catch my death out here, Claire. And I said, what better place to finally catch it!"

That night, all seven of them gather in the lodge for a chili supper, and the kids and Don recount the tale of the bear. How Don had been brave and stood between the kids and the bear, how the bear had cubs with her, how Wendy had gotten a bee sting, and Bryan had gotten scared but still acted bravely. Don lets the kids talk. He is exhausted, says nothing about it other than giving a few smiling, affirming nods, as if he is approving of the way the children are telling the story.

After supper, Claire and Charlie take the kids to the beach to build a fire, Ruth goes back to the cabin to turn in early, and ABC and Don wash the dishes.

As he scrubs a cast-iron pot, and ABC dries the large soup bowls, Don says, "Did you see them?"

"Who?" ABC asks.

"Claire. And Charlie. She's choosing him. She can barely stop herself."

"I didn't notice, really."

Don drops his sponge and looks at her, his eyes big.

"I mean, yes. Yes, I saw it," ABC says.

"I want to thank you for what you did for me, ABC. Whatever happens, that means the world to me. You've been a good friend, maybe the best one I've had in a long, long time."

"And I feel like I have to tell you something, Don. I've been looking for a moment alone with you."

"If it's about what happened in the Jacuzzi that night, please, I understand. You don't have to explain. We were very drunk. I'm not dumb enough to think you're in love with me, ABC."

"I do love you, Don, in a strange, strange way—viscerally—and I need you to know that before I go away. And I need you to know you're going to be okay. You've got this, Don Lowry. You can get through it."

"Where are you going?" he asks.

She doesn't answer.

"We had a deal," he says.

Ruth Manetti wakes in the guesthouse and realizes she is alone. She gets up and dresses and feels the wakefulness that tells her it must be one A.M. She goes to make her tea. ABC has not come home.

ABC and Charlie are walking the gravel roads, drinking bourbon, and watching the meteor shower in the sky. They are drunk.

"Another one!" Charlie says. "Another one!"

"Shhhhh . . . ," ABC says, laughing so hard she almost pees herself.

"Another one!"

"How do you keep seeing these?" ABC says.

"I look up at the sky when I walk. You look down on the ground."

"Let's stop and drink some more," ABC says. "I don't want to move until I see one."

They sit on a damp rock at a small cleared space at the edge of the driveway. They both look up at the sky. They are far enough from the lodge and the cabins to not know if anyone is awake or if everyone is asleep.

"Just keep watching," Charlie says. "You'll see one."

ABC stretches her neck and looks up and Charlie pretends to but actually is looking at her neck, which he has never seen her elongate before, has never seen her hold her head so high. He kisses her neck and she sits still as a statue for what seems like a long time. They see what must be thousands of fireflies twinkling amazingly across the vast darkness. Above them, the stars are almost as abundant. It looks as if a million yellow and orange and green glowing embers are falling on the earth, blown about by a soft wind.

"I've never seen anything like it."

He keeps kissing her neck and she makes no move to stop him, nor does she try and kiss him back or touch him in any way. She stays there, looking up, at the light. And when she has an idea, an idea that her last act on earth, before she journeys off the earth, will be for Don Lowry, she just says, "Come on, Charlie," and she says, "hurry," as they walk down the dark path and they get back to his cabin, walking fast, and they undress there in the doorway, and they flop onto his unmade bed naked and already sweating and moaning before they even become part of each other, which they had done before, and which feels so easy right now, so easy, in fact, that when ABC whispers in his ear, "I want you," she thinks that she might almost mean it.

Not much later, but later: Claire goes to Charlie's cabin and stands in the yard behind it, not on the beach, but on the gravel drive where his car is parked. It's well after midnight. She stands in the shadows of the birch trees next to which he has parked his car. She has just showered some minutes before and her hair is damp and this heightens the feeling of cold. Charlie has some of the lights in his cabin on and the small fireplace is going because the night has turned cold. Claire has shaved her legs and under her arms in the shower, has applied skin lotion to her body and makeup to her eyes, and then she put on the black lace camisole and slutty underwear she has packed, if she admits it, for the purpose of this evening. Over all that silk and lace, she wears a simple sweater and jeans, and Ugg boots on her feet. Not sexy. She looks as if she might be coming by to borrow a novel or some wine or tea. He will be surprised when she begins shedding her clothes. She tries to decide on a next step. They could not start talking. She wants him not to talk. If they began talking, they might never have sex. She knows her patterns. She knows they have all talked enough this summer. Someone must make a final gesture, must cross an unseen line, go through the one-way gate.

She will go in and go to his bed and if he speaks, she will kiss him and tell him, "No talking." She will undo his pants as he sits and make him slick and hard with her mouth. Then she will undress for him, slowly, in the light of the fire. She will relish his eyes on her, all of his surprised desire—and then, well, then it will be inevitable.

She hopes he will stand up and grab her hips and take over from that point. It will be fast and it will be far from tender.

Thinking of this, already ready for him, she does not move. She stays near the birches. The stars have shifted. She looks at the sky. A meteor streaks across it, and then another. Two shooting stars with shimmering tails, straight from a Disney film. It is August and the night is clear. A meteor shower. She has seen them up north, on this shore, before. Another meteor pulls across the sky and then down, as if it has landed with a splash in the endless lake. She thinks, for a split second, about Don: that she should go and tell Don, that she should go and wake her children, so that they all could see the meteor shower together. It is something Don loves. It is something Don always wants to see on these trips north. But she does not go and wake them.

Because she does not go out to the beach, because she walks on the gravel road between the lodge and the cabin, she does not know that Don is watching the meteor shower too. She does not know that Don has woken up and has seen those same three shooters, has seen the surprise of their shimmering tails and has seen that last one plummet into the lake, or at least appear as if it has done that, and has gone into the woods across the road, wrapped in a wool blanket, a hat over his ears, so he can watch from the hill near the waterfall where he had encountered the bear.

Claire lets herself inside the cabin. She stands for a long time listening, wondering if she should leave. Her eyes grow accustomed to the dark. Her heartbeat escalates to an all-out drumming, the blood in her neck pulses and her eye twitches as if a migraine might come on without warning. In the small kitchen, she can see enough to make out a half-drunk, open bottle of red wine. She picks it up and drinks from it. She tries to breathe more slowly.

She hears a faint snore coming from Charlie's bedroom, the hum and *woosh* of a sound sleep. In her fantasy, she'd pictured him awake. She drinks from the bottle of wine again. She will wake him. She will wake him and she will not let him talk. She sits down in the dark at the kitchen table. The notebooks Charlie has been writing in are arranged in a neat stack, two sharpened pencils in an X atop them. There is a small candle set on a small metal plate and next to that a book of matches. Claire lights a match. It takes her three tries to get one that lights, that stays lit long enough for her to light the candle.

If anyone is on the beach, well, maybe they will see the candle, but they will not know anything else. She hopes the kids aren't going to wake up from bad dreams, or an earache, or a need to pee. Don is a heavy sleeper only up here in the north woods. He might not hear the sound of children crying, not with the dull roar of the lake and the constant wind outside his window and the utter exhaustion that came after his eventful hike.

She drinks more wine. The cabin's woodstove, still lit, full of enough fire to give off some heat, warms her and she slides off her Ugg boots and rubs her feet together. She is softening, warming, melting everywhere, and she cannot resist much longer. Their first time, after the heat wave party, could be considered a mistake, an error in judgment. Tonight, Claire knows, is a deliberate act. A step into a new life.

Eventually, it will be dawn. She looks at the clock on the microwave in the kitchenette of Charlie's cabin and sees it is 2:22. The time seems a lucky time though she does not know if this is true. She drinks more wine and stands and undoes the button on her jeans, undoes the zipper. She folds the jeans on the back of a kitchen chair, tucks her boots neatly under the chair. She is straying, slightly, from the seduction script. Next she slips off the sweater, and now in her underwear she is shivering again. She's suddenly lost all that heat from the fire. She drinks more wine, and walks, bottle in hand, to the woodstove and tries to warm herself again, but it is cooling. She needs to add a log. It doesn't matter. Charlie will be warm. In his bed, he'll be buried in his covers, trapped in his own heat. She wonders how he will be sleeping. Has he passed out in his clothes, drunk? She hopes not. She hopes to keep the logistics minimal. Boxers will be fine. Naked might be best. She will surprise him, waking him like she has planned. Tasting the first burst of flesh and breathing on him, then breathing him in, the moist sleepiness of him.

She shivers some more, wishes she could climb inside the stove and find heat. Now she needs to pee—for fuck's sake—and she walks in the almost pitch darkness to the small bathroom, sits down on the freezing toilet and shivers some more and pisses. She doesn't flush. Her underwear is already wet, and now feels cold as she pulls it back onto herself. Enough, she thinks, goes back and has the last of the wine, spinning now, a bit; a kind of throbbing heartburn beneath her breasts, she goes into his room. There had been a lot of peppers in the chili. Too many?

It is even darker in the bedroom. She can see vaguely the edge of the bed, but the curtains on the bedroom window are drawn and so what can she do? She cannot even imagine what she should do now. She goes back to the table, picks up the plate with the candle, and stands there in the kitchen for a moment. Breathing deeply, she inhales some of the candle's heat, its vaguely buttery wax, and she goes back to the bedroom.

Inching closer to the bed, she sees his bare feet, his bare legs, and sees that they are intertwined with another pair of feet, another pair of legs. She doesn't have to see their hips or their chests pressed together or ABC's wild hair next to Charlie's sleeping face. She has seen enough to know she is a fool.

*

In Charlie's cabin, ABC wakes from a dream of Philly, a dream of Philly coming from the lake, dressed not in white this time, but in black. She has a dream in which she watches Philly undress, in which Philly stands at the edge of the bed in candlelight and stares at her naked body next to Charlie's. She, in a half-sleep state, almost feels as if she has seen her there, and when she finally wakes and sits up in bed, it sounds for all the world as if someone has slipped out the cabin door.

Philly.

This is the night.

"Philly?" ABC says in a whisper that seems to break her from her sleep.

This will be her last night on earth, and she is glad that she has spent it with Charlie and that he will remember her that way, making love with him in the dark of the cabin. She hopes his grief over her death may even make him avoid falling in love with Claire. Claire will go back to Don. ABC is also glad that she had, before this, told Don that she loved him, because in a way, she does. She loves all of these people for what they have led her to and now it is time to go to it.

Claire does not see him there on the dark beach, but Don sees her, hears her first, hears a strange whimper and the slap of the cabin's screen door, sees her in the darkness, pulling on her boots and her jeans and a sweater over her head, dressing herself as she leaves Charlie's cabin.

Now he watches her nearly trip down the steps, watches her stumble back behind the cabin and into the shadows, into which he cannot see from the beach. He watches that darkness, hears, or thinks he hears, faintly, the smack of her Ugg boots on the crunchy gravel beneath her feet. He watches for a while longer, until he sees one of the lights come on in the lodge, sees her walking through the living room and sees her finally in the kitchen of the lodge, drinking a glass of water. And then the lights go off, and he wonders where she is sitting, there in the dark, drinking, staring off at the water, or is she looking out at the woods, the hill behind the cabin, at him?

Don bundles himself in his blanket and walks along the rocky path in the dark, the one along the Little Marais River, where he saw the bear. He is going back to face it. He wants to see it again, alone. He will charge at the cubs, and let the bear take him.

Claire sits in the darkness of the lodge drinking wine. She is still aroused from her planned but failed seduction of Charlie, and she wonders, really, why she had felt compelled to go to him. She had convinced herself, after the night of the heat wave party, up in the bedroom, up against the window, that she had gone over a precipice. That she could never right her old life—she had erased it. But there comes to her in that brisk northern air a feeling of smallness, of foolishness. Staring out at the big waters, the sky of meteors, the moon, the shimmering shadows of trees, the glimmer of each wave, she understands how insignificant her actions really are, how all of it, all of this seemingly urgently significant summer is small. Life is big. What she and Charlie do or don't do matters to nobody but Don. He would think all of this is important, all of this is an irreversible course of events—the frailty of marriage, the foreclosed home, the regret—that he could never let go. She knows that this is what Don will be thinking. She knows he will believe that his life has shifted into some other life. And that perhaps he has wasted some of his life too.

But one can't waste a life! One can only live it a day at a time. Claire knows that now.

She goes to the room where Don sleeps and finds the bed empty. She pictures Don, suddenly, crying at the top of the ridge, where the waterfall begins. She feels as if she can almost hear it. And then, in her mind, she hears Don saying something he had said to her so many years ago, one night, their last spring in college, after they'd sneaked into one of the academic buildings and fucked in a book-lined alcove across from Gill Gulliver's office—she hears Don saying, as he did that night, sweaty and crumpled on top of her: *If you ever love another man, I think I'd kill myself.*

Now, she knows that he knows. In her mind's eye, she pictures Don hurling himself off the cliff and into the waterfall and she gets up from her chair, spilling some wine on Merrick's sheepskin cushion, and she walks, in her boots, in the dark, toward the slick, rocky ledges that lead to the falls where Don Lowry has gone hoping to find that bear.

Just as ABC is going back up to the guesthouse, walking from Charlie's cabin across the beach, a meteor streaks across the sky and she swears she sees it splashing into the lake. It's so startlingly bright that she says, "Fuck. Fuck!"

She's glad to finally see the meteor because she can take it as a sign. A confirmation of the dream she just had. Anybody would take it that way, she's sure of it.

It is Philly. Philly has come for her and Philly is going to lead her out of this world. ABC enters the guesthouse as quietly as she can, but finds Ruth awake in a chair, staring out the window.

"Fireflies," Ruth says, though ABC sees none of them.

"A meteor shower," ABC says, and then covers Ruth with a blanket and kisses her on the forehead. "Good night, Ruth," she says. "You need your sleep."

"You feel it too?" Ruth says.

"I feel what?"

"Tonight. It's tonight," Ruth says.

"Yes," ABC says. "Good-bye. Get some sleep."

They embrace for what feels like a long time and they feel the tears in their eyes are not enough, and they say something like this to each other. At the same time, they say, "These tears are only half of what you mean to me."

ABC startles, jumps back. How had that happened?

"The spirit world," Ruth says, "gives us the words we need to leave this world."

ABC rolls a joint for Ruth, lights it for her, then gets her things and goes back outside to the porch of the guesthouse. A pleasant night, but turning colder. And so many stars, and meteors every few minutes in front of those stars, and the wind picking up enough so she feels that the lake will be rough in the early morning, which is what she wants.

She believes in the morning, once Ruth tells them what has happened, that everyone will understand. How easy it would be right now to go back to bed with Charlie—to crawl beside his naked body, to make love again in the dark cold air. Or to go and find Don, taking comfort in his warmth, feeling his desire, which was a desire, yes, for her flesh, but also for something more, something he seemed to want but that he and she could not name.

She is dressed in her layers. She has, per Ruth's calculations, taken two sleeping pills and two Advil PMs. She begins to drink a beer. Stars spread out over the sky like scattered bits of glass and the glowing cloud of the Milky Way seems to hover just above the canoe.

It is time for ABC to go into the big water and find Philly.

In her pocket, she has a small baggie of Ruth's heaviest painkillers, morphine, essentially, which she will take in the boat. Twenty of the pills, just in case. She has the Xanax too, twenty of those. She has a six-pack of beer and a pint of bourbon that she puts into the canoe with the folded-up blankets, and she sips on these to keep her calm while she waits. It's not the best way to go, Ruth has said, maybe, but as long as you can fall asleep on that water, by dawn you will be waking up in another realm. The lake will take you. By wind or by water, your soul will enter the lake.

The idea, of course, seems suddenly absurd; though rather than discouraging her, this realization strengthens her resolve. She has no other choice but to do this. She trusts Ruth. Ruth has grown up here, and if ABC looks back on the last year, did it not all seem like fate, like it was all meant to be: coming back to Grinnell, being hired to take care of Ruth, meeting Don, watching Don lose his home, having Ruth offer money to be taken to the lake, the fireflies abundant as ever that summer, and even the comfort she had taken from loving Charlie.

And now, understanding how things are meant to be, she has given herself over to the idea that life will be better elsewhere. She worries that she won't be able to find Philly right away. She worries she'll have to journey through the spirit realm alone. At least Philly is out there, somewhere, she thinks. She can search for her if she needs to search for her. Love is worth it. Love is worth all things. To live a life without love is foolish. If Philly could not come back to the world, ABC would never love again.

If one could choose a last evening on earth, she would choose this very one. A meteor in the sky above her seems to confirm her resolve to push herself out into the frigid waters, to get lost there and pass out and eventually fall out and drown. Or maybe she will just have to throw herself into the deep. She will take the painkillers first if that is the case. It will not be a pleasant way to go. She understands all of that. But it is a way to go.

The doubts begin to grow, pushing back the whole idea of it, but then she notices that Ruth has come onto the beach, and suddenly over the lake, in the cold wind, there's an ecological impossibility: hundreds and hundreds of fireflies come hatching up out of the waves, floating and blinking up to the moon and the stars and all of that meaningless, feckless heaven.

*

Don Lowry has seen a meteor brighter than any he has ever seen before, brighter than any of the previous August meteors he has seen in his life. He feels as if he has changed somehow, and as he finds a place among the rocks near the waterfall, he nestles in and waits for the bear. Why he wants to see it again, he cannot say, he can only say that he has not felt so alive in years and if he can see the bear, if only he could see the bear once more—he waits in the dark there, watching the stars. Does he really want to die? Is that it? The thought stays with him for a moment—it is possible, it is possible that he wants to die. He is struck by the oddness of the thought and he shivers with cold and huddles against the rocks and pulls the watch cap lower, so it covers his ears. This dulls the rushing of the waterfall, the sound, perhaps, of oblivion, which is why it is a sound that calls to Don Lowry right then, and calls to all of us, at some time, in our twisted lives, in a dark wood. Oblivion, Don thinks. If you say it's never called to you, you're lying.

But even with the rush of the falls, and the watch cap over his ears, he can hear the snapping twigs and the breathing of something not human. The air smells of dead fish and a heavy musk, which comes and goes with the breezes off the distant lake.

ABC drags the canoe to the water's edge. It is not heavy but its metal is cold and her hands sting. She wrenches her back somewhat, but she's already taken two of the painkillers and if she has hurt herself at all, in any significant way, she will probably never know.

She has dragged the canoe near the shore, near the fire pit where Don Lowry likes to sit. He is not out there staring at the fire, which she takes to be a good sign. Of course, he would try and stop her if he knew what she was doing. The fire is all set for lighting—Don has already made the wood stack he needs to light a fire, has stuffed paper and birch bark and scraps of driftwood beneath it, but must have fallen asleep before he'd gone through with it. She takes a lighter from her pocket and lights the kindling. It seems the thing to do. It seems there should be flames. Earth, wind, fire, water.

A signal she will leave behind, a way to summon Philly perhaps, though she can feel Philly as soon as she lights the fire. Philly is already here.

She begins to think of Philly, and she calls to her softly, a singing whisper: *Phillllllly!*

ABC stands alongside the canoe and looks out toward the water. She has no life jacket. If she had one, she might decide to wear it and change her mind. She wonders if she will die of hypothermia while swimming or if she will simply drown. They will probably find the boat before they find her. She doesn't want any of the Lowry children to find her so she tells herself that such a thing is unlikely. Didn't she hear once that Superior never gives up its dead? Where did she hear that? She may never be found.

It is hard to picture her earthly body gone, and she wonders how it will work. Will she be dressed in white too, like Philly? Where had Philly found the white clothes, since ABC remembers very clearly that when Philly died, when she'd been thrown from her bike by that recklessly careening delivery truck, she was wearing cargo pants and a blue tank top that said VIRGINIA IS FOR LOVERS.

It is a bear, of course, Don knows that much, though he cannot be sure if it is the same bear. He doesn't know what to do. Move, or stay still, as if asleep.

The air fills with the scent of musk, of dead fish. He might die here, near the river, and his body, by morning, would float into Superior, would it not? He wonders. His stomach sinks and he tries to swallow hard to keep himself from shaking. The bear is on the bank above him, maybe ten feet away. He can see the bear snuffling the ground, coming toward him.

It is this thought that gives him another thought: he thinks of the old Gordon Lightfoot song, the line "Superior, they say, never gives up her dead," and he begins to hum it softly to himself, and then he has another thought, not one about death, or the pain he is about to endure but about his son, Bryan. When Bryan had been four, they had all gone to Lake Superior, and Don and Claire's old college friend Ryan Dawson, a forgettable person to Don now, had come to the cabin, and he had brought his guitar and he had played a song for Bryan, "The Wreck of the Edmund Fitzgerald."

Bryan had been transfixed by the tune. He had asked to hear it four times that night, and in the weeks and months afterward, after Don and Claire and the kids were back in Iowa, his son would sing in his soft small-boy voice as he played with Lego that song, that ballad, over and over. He would sing the lines he knew and he would hum the lines he didn't and Don Lowry remembered one morning as he made breakfast, his son had sung the song, the almost so-maudlin-it-was-silly song, and loudest of all he had sung the line, "'And all that remains is the faces and the names of the wives and the sons and the daughters.'"

Don remembers all of it now. How his boy had been playing with Lego as he sang it, how his boy had been wearing a long-sleeved shirt, with yellow stripes against a blue background, how the family room had been a mess that morning, the children having destroyed it the day before—they were then four and two—and Don thinks back to that, to that time, and he looks back down the river path but he cannot even see the lodge where his family is now sleeping. He's wandered too far into the timber. It is too dark and there are no lights on back at Merrick's. Or perhaps trees obscure the light.

He begins to sing the song aloud. "'And all that remains is the faces and the names of the wives and the sons and the daughters.'"

It will either anger the bear or scare it.
It is coming closer.
Don just waits.

Ruth Manetti is still awake, as she has been all night. She has found in the darkness an incredible resolve, an ability to stay awake that she has not had in years. She has smoked the joint ABC rolled for her, but she does not fall asleep. She has a will and her will is iron, even in old age, and she knows that about herself and she takes comfort in that. Everything has gone well. ABC is on the beach, prepping for her journey, which is how Ruth has planned it. She has known, she has felt it in her bones, as they say, that this night will be the night that ABC will want to leave for the spirit world. She will, Ruth knows, see one of the Leonid meteors—they are abundant every August in the second week; Ruth knows this from childhood. But ABC will see these meteors and believe they are telling her something. ABC will think everything about the North Shore is a sign for her escape, for her transition into the next world. For months Ruth has had to pretend to hear voices and see fireflies and to have visions and answers to ABC's persistently weird dreams, but really she has no answers, because nobody is allowed to have answers, you only get the answers after you die, and nobody has ever come back from death and told the answers to anyone.

Ruth takes her lawyer's business card from the ancient purse she has carried with her to this shore and she leaves it on the table with a note for Don. "It's your house," she says. She has told Mendez of her change in plan but not about what she is going to do, for that might get him in trouble. But somehow she knows tonight that he loves her still. Thirty years ago, Mendez wanted to marry Ruth. Briefly, she loved him too; when the ache of losing Gill and the shame of her children's scorn was great, he was tender with her. He was her second lover, her second affair. He would handle everything the way she wanted him to.

Ruth pictures Don asleep in the lodge. Maybe he is sleeping with Claire. She pictures him sleeping with Claire. It is not a lost cause. She has been around long enough to know that; maybe they simply needed to breathe awhile, and not feel the shame of breathing, the way so many people do.

Nothing but darkness on that beach, a million fireflies up on the lake. These she doesn't need to pretend to see; these are real and she always knows she will see them when the time comes to leave. She does believe in slipping out of the world, does believe in the portals that open up for us when we need them, does believe, has believed for years, that Lake Superior would be her portal—but she has lied, sometimes, to ABC. It is part of what she wanted to teach her. Pay attention. See the things nobody else sees. Ruth has lived to be an old, old woman. She has learned to do just that, those things.

On the beach, there is almost no light at all except for the moon and ABC's small fire, and the stars, and the swell and rising up of fireflies from the lake, and on occasion, overhead, a meteor. She has grown up with the stars and the sound and smell and feel of this lake and she will leave the world surrounded by them. She feels suddenly warm and attentive, as if someone is whispering in her ear an ancient, ancient story where none of the contemporary concerns of the day matter at all. Now, there is almost nothing between her and the canoe but ABC. Ruth has been shuffling along in the dark a long time, wearing her blue jeans and boots and silk thermal underwear and two sweaters and now she has on a knit cap. She has her medicines with her, all of the painkillers she's been given and told not to abuse over the last five years. She has taken five now and the five sleeping pills already and she is sipping from a coffee mug of ABC's bourbon, too harsh for her, though she has had a lifetime of sweet wine, and she doesn't mind that her last drink will be one that burns a little going down. She has missed the North Shore. She has thought about it so much in the last few weeks, knowing she would see it again.

It is Claire, not a bear, who appears on the ledge of the cliff and who grabs Don Lowry's hand, while she clings to the trunk of a tree with her other hand, and who hoists him up from the abyss, even though maybe he doesn't actually need the help, and then they embrace like that, their hearts mad with thundering beats, their faces drenched in adrenaline's acrid sweat, and Claire holds Don and they go to a safer place, to the footpath away from the edge of the ridge and she holds on to Don, and in his ear, she says, "It's not as terrible as you think."

"It's not?" he says, breathless himself.

"Wild horses," she says. And then again, "Wild fucking horses."

Above them, on the path, near the berry patch, huffs a startled black bear.

In the middle of the night, Charlie's cell phone rings.

"It's about your father." Someone whom he doesn't know tells him this. "He's dead."

Outside, something like the green embers of fireflies glow and fade, glow and fade, and Ruth begins to walk up to the canoe, sans flashlight, with a cup of whiskey and with the pills in her pocket, and she walks over the rocks, afraid of falling but knowing, somehow, that there is no reason to save her strength anymore, that this will be the last thing she will need to do in a lifetime of doing things that require strength. She has not said good-bye to anyone but ABC, but how many good-byes does one need? She has been at the age, for years, where people always say good-bye as if there may not ever be another farewell. And she has letters, in her desk drawer, that she has written in her moments alone, painstakingly clutching the pen with her arthritic fingers and trying, somehow, to make conversation with a few distant friends who also write letters.

Ruth finds ABC asleep on the rocks, near the boat and the fire, just as she had hoped. Ruth had told her to take four pills, plus a Xanax—not a lethal dose for someone so healthy, but enough to maybe make you pass out in the middle of an elaborate plan.

In her drugged hesitation, ABC has not gotten into the boat. She's fallen asleep next to the boat. Ruth covers her with one of the blankets from the canoe. Her plan has worked, but now she has work to do, so that she too doesn't fall asleep beside ABC.

She tries to push the large metal canoe into the water. But it will not budge. She is too weak. The pot and the wine and the pills and the nearly nine decades of exhausting life have worn her out. She needs to get the canoe into the water. She does not want to go back to Iowa and wait to die in front of a television in a house she never really liked, in a town, if she admits it, she never would have lived in if not for her husband's work. She has not done much on her own terms in her life but she will die on her own terms. She crawls into the canoe.

Then Ruth nudges ABC with an oar.

"Wake up," she says.

ABC wakes slowly, pushing herself up in a kind of slow-motion stretch. Her face is damp. She begins to shiver.

"ABC, push me out to sea."

ABC groggily stands up. "Ruth!" she says. "What are you doing?"

ABC sits back down. Her eyes are closing.

"I am doing what you were going to do," Ruth says.

ABC opens her eyes, stands again. She tries to get Ruth out of the boat. "You are gonna freeze to death."

She is too groggy and weak from the pills.

"Exactly," Ruth says. "Or maybe drown."

"Ruth," ABC says.

"I've been seeing fireflies all summer and they've given me a way out of life. They were not meant to give you a way out."

She looks out to the lake and there are dozens of fireflies just over the water. ABC knows enough about Lake Superior to know that one doesn't usually see that. The fireflies do not hover in blinking clusters above the open water—it is too cold and windy here. But hundreds of them blink in a weird straight line, like they are lining a path into the open water, like they are reproducing and multiplying in midair.

"See?" Ruth says. "That's for me."

ABC looks around the beach to see if anyone is awake, but there is no stirring anywhere. For a moment, it is as if she has heard the sound of a man singing, but she has not.

"ABC," Ruth says. "You had the right idea, but your timing is off. It's my time to go."

"Jesus, Ruth."

"Look, I've already taken sleeping pills. I won't be awake for any of it. And look, I brought whiskey and morphine. Hurry. Don't keep me here. I'll be in worse shape than I am in now. The lake, that's where I want to end my days, nowhere else."

She laughs then and smiles up at ABC in a way that radiates the now obscured beauty of her youth.

"ABC," she says, "you have to live your fucking life. It's not over."

ABC puts her sneaker on the edge of the canoe, standing behind Ruth, and pushes the canoe down the rocky beach a foot or two, closer to the water.

"That's right," Ruth says.

"Ruth," ABC says, but she pushes the canoe farther with her foot. Her hands are in her pockets because it is cold, and she feels nauseated from the pills and the alcohol. She also keeps her hands in her pockets because it feels less real if she does not touch the boat with her hands. It might be considered a dream that way.

The wind has picked up out of the west and so the relatively still lake is blowing in ripples away from the shore.

"No," ABC says. She starts to try to get Ruth out of the canoe.

"ABC," Ruth says, "you know the right thing to do."

ABC shakes her head no. "It doesn't feel right."

"Don't be a coward. You get this. You understand this. It's what you wanted, but you know now you did not want it at all."

ABC nudges Ruth toward the lake once more, the metal canoe making a gritty sliding sound on the rocks that hurts her teeth.

"Good," Ruth says. "Quickly now, before you wake everybody up. Before you think too much more."

ABC is shivering now. It seems suddenly to plunge from chilly to frigid, the wind, the mist off the waves. Ruth doesn't tremble at all, and ABC leans in and kisses her on the cheek.

Then ABC gives her one hearty push, this time with her hands, and soon the boat is drifting out into the lake. "Just live your fucking lives," Ruth says, and then ABC smiles because she knows she will remember that, the unexpected parting words she can share with everyone, if she is able to tell them what happened. Maybe she'll play dumb. Maybe she'll pretend to be as shocked as everyone else.

And Ruth?

She is almost surprised but not surprised, not really, when ABC, a loyal, helpful friend in the truest sense of true, does shove her out on the lake. Ruth lies down in the canoe then so ABC cannot see her and says her last words, lacking in profundity but certainly memorable. She hopes ABC can only see the canoe from the shore. It will be easier if she says she saw nothing but a canoe. Just a boat on the water in the dark, drifting down a path lit by firefly light.

Another meteor streaks across the sky when Ruth looks up, and then another. She hopes ABC has seen it. And then some fireflies light up the grim darkness just above the canoe and then go dark and do not blink again. Now all Ruth can see is the stars, all she can feel is the cold and the swell of the undulating waves.

She knows that ABC will stay out by the fire, watching the canoe until it disappears.

How could she not? And Ruth seems to see everything then, what will happen in the moments and hours and days and years ahead on the shore behind her. Don and Claire will come running down from the river path, screaming their way toward the beach, though the bear will have long since lost interest and, as it turns out, is not behind them. Charlie, already woken up by the phone call about his father, will hear this screaming and be shaken from his weeping and he'll come out onto the beach to find a shouting, sweating Don and a hysterically laughing Claire, this long-married couple buzzing with adrenaline, half-insane with it. Charlie will ask them what is the matter, what is happening, and when they finally stop laughing and swearing, they will all finally notice ABC, crying by the fire, and they will go to her, and sit on either side of her, and ask what is wrong.

And ABC will pull out her flashlight and shine it onto the water, where a swarm of fireflies will be moving again, in a long, speckled beam of light pointed due north, and Charlie will say, "Jesus, look at that, what do you suppose that is?" and Claire will say, "Fireflies?" and Don will say the reflection of a meteor, and ABC will say, "Yes, it's all of those things; also, that's Ruth."

Ruth begins to shiver with cold or happiness and she is not sure which it is, but it feels like the latter. She is not sure what any of them will say. Maybe they'll finally be quiet. That will be a good start. How much of the story will ABC tell and how much of it will she keep to herself? And if she tells the story exactly as it happened, they'll have to come up with next steps. Whom will they call? How will they tell the story of the summer? And will they call for help right away, or wait until morning? Will they call 911? The Coast Guard? Would they call Ruth's estranged kids or her nieces and nephews in Davenport who want her money, or will they call Mendez, her lawyer back in Grinnell, who will be trying to reach Charlie about the estate of Gill Gulliver, whom Ruth, at that moment, somehow, suddenly, knows is dead.

A cloud drifts up past the moon and the stars grow dimmer. She's long since stopped seeing the meteors above her, and the fireflies have also gone dim, have blown off into the wind like small clouds of ash. On her knees now, she prepares to collapse into the lap of the waves, the unseeable, unsayable truths beneath them.

There will be logistics. Ruth knows this. She thinks of the foursome gathered on the shore. She can almost feel them looking out at the water, paralyzed by what has just occurred. What will they do next?

She doesn't know, but she does know, with some certainty, one simple truth: they'll find some way through. They'll figure it out.

This is, more or less, true of everybody.

ACKNOWLEDGMENTS

My thanks to the Guggenheim Foundation for a fellowship that facilitated the early drafting of this novel, as well as the Mark Gates Memorial Foundation for Wayward Writers. I'm grateful to the incredibly supportive administration, bright colleagues, and wonderful students I have at Grinnell College as well as the inspiring, warm community I find each winter teaching in the MFA Program for Writers at Warren Wilson, especially Ellen Bryant Voigt, Charles Baxter, Maurice Manning, Alix Ohlin, Megan Staffel, James Longenbach, and Stacey D'Erasmo, whose lectures and readings directly influenced this novel.

Big love to my family, especially my kids, Lydia and Amos, artists and storytellers both, for the sustaining joy, patience, humor, and beauty that help me through each day.

Many individuals contributed to the writing of this book with their friendship, creative influence, or both: Christina Campbell, Ralph Savarese, Kim Steele, Coleman, William Jasper,

Lee Boudreaux, Ryan Willard, Tina and Caleb Elfenbien, Tim and Jennifer Dobe, Lee Running, Jeremy Chen, Amy Martin, Michael Perry, Natalie Bakopoulos, Justin Vernon, Mere Martinez, Benjamin Percy, Brian Bartels, Marta Rose, Daleth Hall, Patrick Somerville, Emma Borges-Scott, Steve Myck, Steve Pett, David Wells (and the Terry Family Foundation), and Bridget McCarthy. And extra big thanks to Becky Saletan.

Thanks to the Parkington Sisters—Ariel, Sarah, and Rose—whose music, beauty, and wit lit up a dark night of the soul in Iowa City when I needed it most.

The line "Why is it all so difficult?" on page 42 is inspired by Stephen Dobyns' poem "How To Like It."

The conversation between Don and Claire on pages 306–7 is influenced by a line in Charles Bukowksi's *Post Office*: "This kind of life like everybody else's kind of life: it's killing us."

I'd especially like to thank everyone at Ecco Books, including Daniel Halpern, Sonya Cheuse, and Eleanor Kriseman, and, especially my editor, Megan Lynch, as clear-eyed, patient, and bright as they come. When she showed up, so did the light. And finally, deepest gratitude to my agent Amy Williams, an unflappable, hard-nosed, full-hearted, deal-making, and life-changing pal.